SIR WALTER RALEGH
Gold Was His Star

SIR WALTER RALEGH

Gold Was His Star

Reginald Wood

The Book Guild Ltd.
Sussex, England

This book is sold subject to the condition that it shall not, by way of trade or otherwise, be lent, re-sold, hired out, photocopied or held in any retrieval system, or otherwise circulated without the publisher's prior consent in any form of binding or cover other than that in which this is published and without a similar condition including this condition being imposed on the subsequent purchaser.

The Book Guild Ltd.
25 High Street,
Lewes, Sussex.

First published 1991
© Reginald Wood 1991
Set in Baskerville
Typesetting by APS,
Salisbury, Wiltshire.
Printed in Great Britain by
Antony Rowe Ltd.,
Chippenham, Wiltshire.

British Library Cataloguing in Publication Data
Wood, R.L.C. (Reginald Laurence Charles)
   Sir Walter Ralegh: Gold was his star
   1. England. Social life. History
   I. Title
   942.055092
        ISBN 0 86332 657 9

CONTENTS

Illustration by Jean Wood		8
Chapter 1	*London Bound*	9
Chapter 2	*Baptism of Fire*	23
Chapter 3	*The Queen Trod Gently Over*	32
Chapter 4	*The Queen's Man*	46
Chapter 5	*Her Majesty's Maid*	65
Chapter 6	*'I Have The Heart And Stomach Of A King'*	80
Chapter 7	*'All This For A Song'*	89
Chapter 8	*'Otherwise My Heart Will Break'*	105
Chapter 9	*'I Am Still The Queen Of England's Poor Captive'*	128
Chapter 10	*Fortune's Fold*	138
Chapter 11	*Search For Gold*	154
Chapter 12	*Winning Through*	163
Chapter 13	*Ups and Downs*	176
Chapter 14	*Rogue's Writs*	194
Chapter 15	*Setting Sun*	203
Chapter 16	*Trap Sprung*	215
Chapter 17	*'Justice Never So Depraved'*	229
Chapter 18	*Wolves Pounce*	254
Chapter 19	*Royal Friend*	266
Chapter 20	*Gold To Dust*	278
Chapter 21	*Judas Traps*	300
Chapter 22	*'Stars Must Fall'*	312
Chapter 23	*'If The Heart Be Right'*	318
Chapter 24	*Restored In Blood*	328
Bibliography		332

*TO
JEAN, JULIA
and
ROGER*

Even such is tyme which takes in trust
Our yowth, our Joyes, and all we have,
And payes us butt with age and dust:
Who in the darke and silent grave
When we have wandred all our wayes
Shutts up the storye of our dayes.
And from which earth and grave and dust
The Lord shall rayse me up I trust.
      Sir Walter Ralegh, in his Bible,
       the night before he died.

Hayes Barton, Devon. Aug 1989.

Illustration by Jean Wood

1

London Bound

It was late afternoon in the autumn when the square tower of Sherborne Abbey came into view. A party of six on horseback cantered down the hill into this Dorset town. They were on their way from their native Devon on the Great West Road to London, two young gentlemen and their escorts. They had had a hard ride that day through Somerset on a road dusty and pitted with potholes. It was a route in heavy use by waggons, pack-horses, flocks of sheep, herded cattle, horse-riders and walkers with no more comfortable means of transport. The inhabitants of the parishes through which it ran had the unenviable duty of keeping it in repair. Some fell far short of the ideal. An escort was a necessary precaution, particularly after dark.

The two were half-brothers. The elder was Adrian Gilbert. His companion, some six years younger, was Walter Ralegh. He was the leader: tall, handsome, with a trim figure, dark hair, high wide forehead and piercing eyes. He was quick in speech and repartee, at times long-winded.

His companion was also dark-haired, but stocky and corpulent. He was deeply attached to his young brother and happy to let him take charge.

They both had moustache and beard, as was the fashion, and spoke with a broad Devon burr. The 'Ralegh' was pronounced 'Rawly'.

They paused for a moment outside a smithy at the entrance to the town. It having passed his critical inspection, Ralegh instructed the men: 'As soon as we're settled in the inn, bring the horses here for shoeing.'

They were staying the night at the New Inn, at the top of the town's Green Hill from where the shopping street, Cheap

Street, branched off to the south. They had arranged their accommodation ahead. This was as well. Sherborne was buzzing with activity: masses of people, stalls, horses, cattle and sheep and general bustle.

'What's going on?' Ralegh asked the inn-keeper.

'It's the Michaelmas Fair, Sir. The Pack Monday. Not the best night you've chosen to stay. I ought to have warned you, gentlemen.'

'Not at all. We couldn't have picked a better. We'll have a bit of fun tonight, Adrian.'

Adrian laughed. He was always game for a spot of amusement.

'And thick heads tomorrow,' he replied. 'We'd better warn the chaps to keep out of mischief.'

'That goes for you, too. Come on, let's get something to eat and we'll be off.'

The inn was of grey stone, with lead and stone tiled roof. Their room had leaded-light windows overlooking the busy scene. Their horses when shod had been led through to stables at the rear – with orders to keep them carefully locked up. They might otherwise have found their way into the horse fair still in progress on the Green.

After their meal they set off to explore the town. They strolled through the booths and cheap-jacks' stalls, pausing to enjoy the badinage and persuasive sales talk to gullible audiences. They watched the gypsies parading their wares and selling lucky charms.

In the adjoining market place, in pens, were horses, cows, oxen, sheep and pigs, and crates of chickens, replaced as those sold were led or taken away, or loaded up into jostling waggons or carts. Earthy farmers and men who had clearly emerged from the depths of the country were sizing up the beasts on show, leg-pulling and laughing and enjoying their day at market.

Back among the stalls, the hoarse invitations of the hucksters were hard to resist – stoneware, petty finery, cheap jewellery, anything that could be named at a price which might attract or delude. The milling crowd came from far and wide; parts of Dorset, Somerset and even beyond. This was an important day in their year. Many had set off before dawn to get in a full day's festivities before returning exhausted late that night.

The delicious smell of cooked meats, pies, puddings, cakes, sweets and the like was irresistible. The great numbers of ale-houses with their local breweries were likewise doing a roaring trade.

'What's going on here?' Adrian asked a business-like man inspecting a line of men and girls attired in the dress of various rural occupations – ploughman, shepherd, woodman, dairymaid.

'This is the hiring. When the farm servants are taken on. There's not much choice left. The best have all been picked.' He went on, 'There was a rare to-do last night, I hear.'

'Why, what was that?'

'They say that Teddy Roe's band got out of hand.'

'Who's he, may I ask?'

'You must be strangers here. Every year, at midnight before the Fair, a mock-up band parades round the town, banging instruments in the shape of old pails, metal pots and pans – making rough music, as they call it. Some lads came over from Bristol and went on a frolic. There'll be trouble from the Justices for the ones they caught. The jail wasn't big enough to hold them, there were so many.'

'I trust they get their deserts,' said Ralegh. 'Anyway, what was the idea of this band? When did it all start?'

'They say it was when the workmen finished the Abbey, and packed up their tools, and that was why they called it "Pack Monday". I doubt it myself. I think it's because it was the "pact" day, the hiring like we have here. Or because the packmen came in with their wares. Who cares? It's as good an excuse as any for a holiday. The band is a demon-chaser.'

'I'm sorry. We're interrupting your selection. But did you say "Abbey"?' asked Ralegh. 'We must go and have a look at it.' Then, to Adrian: 'After that, we'll see what's doing.'

The church-yard presented a conglomeration of activity even surpassing what they had already seen. This was evidently the fair proper: cloth, earthenware, apples, hazel nuts, onions, hats, bonnets, caps and ribbons; ginger-bread, sweets, toys for children, to list just a selection of goods on offer for which the throng were clamouring. There was entertainment: clowns, puppet-makers, tight-rope walkers and jugglers. A competition was taking place to see who could toss a hay bale highest with a pitch-fork. Several brawny youths were showing off their skill.

There was also a gypsy woman's fortune-telling booth. Adrian, keenly interested in astrology, necromancy and the like, spotted it and said: 'Just a minute. I'm going in here.'

'All right, if you must. Waste of time and money. I'll wait for you. Tell her to be quick about it.'

He emerged five minutes later, his face beaming.

'Just what I wanted to hear,' he informed his companion. 'There's a big surprise coming. It's my lucky day.'

Unimpressed, Ralegh grunted and led the way up to the Abbey.

They entered through a distinctive Norman porch, rounded, with chevron moulding. To do so, they had to pass the rubble remains of what had evidently been a curiously attached building not long since demolished. As they went in, they were met by an elderly cassocked figure.

'I am afraid you are too late for Evensong. It finished half an hour ago,' he told them.

'We were only hoping to have a look round,' replied Ralegh, 'as we're passing through.'

'I will be delighted to be your guide in that case. May I introduce myself. I am the Vicar of this Church, George Holman, at your service.'

'My name is Ralegh – Walter Ralegh. This is my brother – or, rather, half-brother, Adrian Gilbert.'

He led them round the Abbey, pointing out various features.

'I could go on for a couple of hours and still not do it justice. It is a unique tribute to the goodness of the Almighty. You can see that it combines size with intimacy. Each is part of the whole. There is, for example, no unduly obstructive rood screen as in many cathedrals. Chancel and nave are all one, so to speak. What screen there is will, I hope, be one day removed.'

They moved further inside. He went on: 'Look up and you will see what is perhaps the finest fan vaulting in Europe. The light is sadly fading. You've left your visit a little late in the day. But if you come in daylight you can see the most exquisitely coloured bosses in the fan-tracery – heraldic devices, Tudor roses – there's a modern touch for you – even a mermaid combing her hair.'

'I'll be along first thing in the morning to see it, Vicar,' said

Adrian.

'Yes. The monks used to have a good laugh over that. I did even hear of various rude comments. Now, you're Devonshire gentlemen, are you not? I can always recognize the accent. Slightly, but only slightly, more broad than Dorset. You may be interested to know that the Bishop of Sherborne and the Cathedral here used to cover not only Dorset, but the whole of your county, Devon, plus Cornwall, and chunks of Somersetshire and Wiltshire. Two Saxon Kings are buried here.'

'And they are?' asked Ralegh.

'Ethelbald and Ethelbert – Alfred's elder brothers. He came here more than once. May even have had some schooling here. Bless his memory.'

'Amen to that,' said Ralegh. 'And what are those dreadful red stains on the stone-work – when all the other walls are properly white-washed? Can't you afford a cleaner?'

'You may well ask. That was the result of fire. There was a squabble, believe it or not, between the monks and the townsfolk. The people hereabouts are very determined. A priest of the Church that was then tacked on to the West end of this Abbey – you may have noticed the ruins as you came in – was a little too clever. He lit an arrow and shot it into the roof thatch – to frighten them. He succeeded better than he had bargained for. The whole roof caught alight and set fire to the Abbey. It shows that you can carry principles – or lack of them– too far.'

'Make a note of that, Walter,' said Adrian.

'But you see we have our Table of Commandments – standing out over the scorching!'

' "The Writing on the Wall",' said Ralegh, with a laugh.

'Over here is the tomb of Sir John Horsey. He it was who bought the Abbey from King Henry and sold it to the Town. The townspeople showed great initiative, in my view. So many of these beautiful buildings were demolished for their stone.'

'Ah! Yes,' interjected Ralegh. 'Horsey. Our father knows them. The grandson, Sir John, still lives near here at Clifton Maybank. We did think of staying there tonight.'

'Tell me,' asked the Vicar, 'weren't you up at Oxford a few years back? I seem to remember seeing you on one of my return visits. I was staying with a young friend of mine, Charles Champernoun.'

'Yes. I was at Oriel. On and off. He is a cousin of ours.'

'My brother here was a great talker, Sir,' remarked Adrian. 'And thought to be something of a philosopher. Also rather careless with property. Borrowed a fellow's gown and never returned it, or paid for it – a Worcestershire lad, I believe.'

'It was Tom Child. He gave it me,' explained Ralegh. 'Anyway, it was pretty ragged.'

'I remember being told a story by your cousin,' the Vicar mused. 'It must have been about you. One of the students in your group was being bullied, and was too scared to retaliate. He asked you what he could do about it. The only activity at which he was competent was archery; your advice was: "Challenge him to a shooting match".'

'Yes, that is so. He was a bit of a creeper. But it did the trick.'

'We could no doubt go on with anecdotes for the rest of the evening. There is nothing I would like better. But I have things to see to, as I expect you have. I hope you will both come again.'

'Thank you for giving us your time. We will certainly make a point of it next time we're passing and look at your fascinating building in more detail.'

'And come to a service here. Maybe.' Holman commented drily. 'I trust so. A safe journey to you both.'

'Now for the real business of the day,' said Ralegh as they threaded their way through the jostling masses.

At the bottom of the Church path they passed an attractive old building topped by four unusually tall angled chimneys and having mullioned windows with diamond-shaped leaded lights – the almshouse of St John the Baptist and St John the Evangelist, a notice read.

'One lost his head and the other finished up writing in a cave on a Greek island,' quipped Ralegh.

It had been founded a century and a half before, under licence from Henry VI, in succession to earlier Sherborne almshouses. The Town had long been noted for its charity and its benefactors. Outside it, enjoying the fun were sitting some half a dozen or so old people. The men were dressed in caped gowns and broad-brimmed hats, the women in scarlet cloaks and bonnets.

'I'll bet they could tell a tale or two about the fairs in olden days,' said Adrian. 'Pity there's no time to ask them.'

A great deal of shouting and laughing came from a nearby field.

'Let's investigate,' said Ralegh.

An excited crowd, of all ages and both sexes, was gathered round a long platform serving as a skittle alley. The contestants, mostly male but some female, were taking their turn to bowl three heavy wooden balls at ninepins. A stick-up at the far end was hard put to it to replace the skittles after each go. He was in some jeopardy from over-enthusiastic bowlers who could not wait for him to hop off before their next shot. The charge was a penny a time, the prize a squealing pig tied up nearby. The competitors and spectators had more than adequately imbibed of ale or scrumpy – the rough cider which Ralegh and Gilbert as Devonians knew well.

They watched for a while. They were on the point of leaving when Adrian spotted two girls in their late teens eyeing them – but pretending not to. He nudged his brother.

'This could be promising,' he said.

Ralegh looked over at two bright-faced girls with dark hair and brown eyes, gaily dressed for their day out.

'Yes, they'll do. Let's go over.'

They pushed through to where the girls were standing. In the light of the flares the young men were conspicuous in this gathering by their clothes – and indeed their bearing – but concentration of the onlookers was on the game. They raised their hats.

'Fascinating sport this,' Adrian offered. 'Are you having a go?'

They both giggled. One of them retorted: 'A go at what?'

This was in broad Dorset, akin to their own inflection. From speech alone, it would have been impossible to detect the social disparity.

'What do you think? The skittles, of course. Are you by yourselves, or with somebody?'

'We're with our boyfriends.'

'Oh, where?'

They pointed to a pair of powerful-looking contestants, intent on the rivalry and waiting their turn to play. This seemed a good moment.

'Come on,' said Ralegh to the taller of the girls who was nearer to him. 'Let's go and get a drink. You're wasting your time here.'

A trifle apprehensively, but sensing a bit of unexpected fun, she made as if to comply. Her friend was more cautious.

'Jane, don't be an idiot. They'll be furious.'

She was not to be deterred.

'So what! They haven't taken any notice of us all evening. They won't even know we've gone. They'll be playing till that pig goes. They could be here till midnight. Come on, Katie. I am, if you're not.'

The attraction of competitive companionship and, it must be said, grander company than had hitherto come their way, proved decisive. With a guarded glance across to their engrossed erstwhile escorts, they sidled cautiously away from the scene and with their newly-found admirers went briskly up the road.

'You know our names now,' said Jane. 'What are yours? And where do you come from? Not near here, I know.'

'Oh! We move around here and there,' replied Adrian. 'I'm Humphrey and this is John.'

Ralegh with difficulty suppressed a laugh. Adrian, pulling his leg no doubt, had given the names of his own elder brothers. Humphrey Gilbert he knew might have appreciated the joke. John never. He would have been much aggrieved.

'You ladies must know the place. Where shall we go?'

' "Ladies" – I like that,' said Jane.

'Have you got any money?' asked Katie.

The directness took them aback. It matched Ralegh's customary over-bearing manner.

'That's an odd question. Yes, a little. But why do you ask?'

'Because we're not paying for you. We've been caught out before. That's why.'

'Fair enough. That wasn't our idea at all,' Ralegh assured them. 'So lead on.'

They passed back up Cheap Street through a press now thicker than ever, men, women and children and babes in arms, till they came to an inn at the top, its sign announcing it to be the George Inn.

Adrian grinned.

'Here is where hangs the badge of England's Saint.'

'What's that?' asked Kate suspiciously.

'Never mind him,' said Ralegh. 'Let's get inside.'

'As they were about to enter, a girl passing by called out: 'What have you found there, Katie? Can I come too?'

'No you can't, Mary. Mind your own business. And keep your mouth shut!' she told her. And to the men: 'Take your hats off. They'll be looking at you for sure if you don't.'

They complied, and went in, Jane now the more hesitant. The sawdust and straw strewn on the floor had been scuffled that day by hundreds of feet. They pressed through to the bar, where Ralegh ordered four pints of ale.

'Only a small one for me, please,' said Jane.

'Go on. A pint will do you good. Half a pint goes nowhere.'

The air in the tavern was heavy and hot. An advantage of the thick crowd was that they escaped undue attention. The brothers were thirsty after their journey. They finished their drinks quickly and ordered two more. The girls were less hasty. They found a vacated bench and sat down.

They were both dairy-maids, they said, from a village to the south by the name of Long Burton.

'We could see from your lovely fresh cheeks that you are dairy-maids,' Adrian told them. 'The loveliest girls work in the dairy.'

'Go on,' said Jane. 'You're teasing. Just flattering us.'

'No. That's a known fact,' Ralegh assured her. 'Where we come from, we always pick a dairy-maid for choice.'

'Off the line?' asked Jane.

He laughed. 'No, of course not. You know what I mean. To take out.'

Their drinks being finished, Ralegh said: 'That was good. Let's move on somewhere else. Not too far.' He never was, nor would be, a keen walker.

They went a few, not quite so steady, steps to a solid-looking building nearby where there were sounds of merriment. Adrian looked up at its sign.

'La Julia,' he exclaimed. 'That's an excellent name.'

'Actually, it says, "La Julian",' Ralegh corrected him. 'This will be fine.'

Any lack of normal balance in their steps passed unnoticed in the general hub-bub, and gave them the excuse, if such were needed, to give the girls close support – which was not resisted.

'I see it's a hospice,' said Adrian.

Ralegh, always interested in architecture and detail, observed its unusual shape. It had light, tall, narrow windows and an attic room beneath a sharp, inverted -V- shaped roof. Two centuries old, he estimated to himself. But this was not the occasion to study finer points of design.

Inside, he asked: 'What is it to be? You see, there's no question of you having to pay. Ale or cider?'

The girls had a quiet laugh to one another. Katie said: 'Don't you know? You can't be Dorset, that's for sure.

'Beer on cider makes a good rider,
Cider on beer makes you feel queer.'

They all laughed at that. 'That's very funny. It must be right. It's the first I've heard it,' said Adrian.

'Anyway,' Ralegh responded, 'four pints it shall be – of ale.'

He told the landlord quietly as he ordered it: 'Make it your best March ale.' This was an extra strong beer, so called because it was brewed in March. A man at the bar beside him said: 'You couldn't do better than that, Zirr. It's an old beer that will make a cat speak and a wise man dumb.'

Ralegh roared with laughter at this – as did Adrian when he repeated it to him. He bought the man a pint on the strength of it.

He enquired of the landlord while he was drawing the drinks: 'What does it mean – hospice?'

'It's where the pilgrims stay on their way to Canterbury to St Thomas à Becket's tomb. Or some to Glastonbury: that's where King Arthur's buried and where St Dunstan caught the Devil by his nose. They also go to see St Joseph of Arimathea's thorn bush. It blooms every year at the Feast of the Nativity.'

'You're a fruitful source of information, my man. Let's hope your ale's as good as your wit.'

It was. The quips and merry responses and hilarity attracted no untoward attention because it was at least equalled by that of other parties in the room, and the constant coming and going of customers celebrating this signal day in the calendar.

'Time to move on,' announced Ralegh. 'Where now?'

As they left the Julian, the girls needed rather more support. Somehow, in the general surge of the crowd, still milling round the hucksters or moving on to the next focus of interest, Ralegh, with Jane, contrived to be separated from the others. She expressed some alarm at this, but Ralegh reassured her.

'They'll be all right. They can look after themselves.'

'What do you mean? I'm thinking of myself!'

'Nothing to worry about, my dear. I feel I've known you for years. This mustn't stop here, you know. We must keep in touch. Now, what do you say to a little rest and something to eat?' He held his arm more closely round her waist.

'Where have you in mind?' she asked, rather uncertainly.

'Quite near here. I'll show you.'

He escorted her over the road, avoiding the traffic of horsemen, carts and the like from both directions mingling with and weaving among the pedestrians. He led her under the archway of the New Inn and up the stairs, into his room.

'There, that's better, isn't it? You can have a nice sit down. In fact, we can both have one, can't we?'

He drew her gently onto the bed. She resisted, and protested, but without much conviction.

'I've grown so fond of you since we met,' he said. 'This is the happiest night of my life. You are the most adorable girl, Jane, I have ever met.'

'You've only known me a couple of hours,' she replied drowsily. 'How can you say that?'

'I can, and I mean it. I believe you're fond of me too,' he insisted.

He pressed her down gently and kissed her. She responded, at first shyly, then eagerly. His soft touch was something she had not known before. His hands were strong and firm, but smooth and unlike the horny grasp of the boys in the village. She felt herself slipping away.

To him, too, it was an experience he had not known before. In this brief encounter he had become very attached. He felt tender towards this simple, pretty, country girl.

But there was a rude interruption. Adrian burst into the room. 'Quick. There's trouble on the way. Those two chaps with their mates are scouring the ale-houses looking for us.'

Katie was close behind him. She chipped in: 'Mary must have told them where we were, the rotten bitch.'

Fast thinking was called for. All thoughts of dalliance had vanished.

'God,' said Jane. 'What are we going to do? If they find us here, they'll murder us. I know what they're like when they've had scrumpy.'

'Hurry,' Ralegh ordered. 'Down to the back.'

They tore down the stairs and into the inn yard where the horses were stabled. He told the ostler on guard: 'Saddle up two horses – fast.'

While he did so, Ralegh explained his plan.

'How far is your village from here?'

'Three miles,' said Jane.

'Right,' he told his brother, 'you and I will take them. We can't leave them to themselves.'

'That's all right. But it will be pitch black,' he pointed out. 'The road'll be streaming with people.'

'We must risk it. Are you girls willing to chance it too?'

They agreed without hesitation.

The men mounted and heaved the girls up in front of them. They had never ridden before. Ralegh gave the ostler some coins and warned him: 'If anyone asks any questions, you know nothing and have seen nothing.'

To ride down the street was out of the question. Kate told Jane: 'We must go by Ottery Lane.' The girls directed them to a roundabout route. They skirted the town and rode up a steep track and over a hill. They followed a winding lane past a little church tucked away, it seemed, in the middle of fields, as was the old Manor House opposite, whose gaunt outline they could just discern. The former, Folke Church, was in obvious need of repair. They were taken past another house of similar graceful proportions where Jane murmured: 'That's West Hall and there's the dairy where we work. I hope Mr and Mrs Moleyns aren't looking out. They would get a shock.'

A short ride through a large meadow dotted with cattle brought them to yet another church and into the yard opposite, behind an ale-house in the middle of their village. Unobserved, they lifted the girls down, none the worse for wear.

They kissed before parting.

'Well, Jane,' Ralegh said. 'It was a good evening. I'm sorry it had to finish like that. We'll meet again, I promise you.'

They did – in very different circumstances.

The girls fled swiftly into the dark. Ralegh said to Adrian: 'That's that. I think we've earnt another pint before we head back.'

They tethered their horses near a well and walked round to the front. As they were going through the door Ralegh stopped and exclaimed: 'Here's something odd. Notice anything unusual about the house sign?'

Adrian scrutinized it. It looked like any other display board to him. 'It has roses on it. And a crown.'

'Now look at the other side.'

'More roses and crown, I see. They're red one side and white the other.'

'They obviously sat on the fence in the Wars of the Roses. Very wise of them. Clever of me to spot it.'

They went inside into a stone-flagged room. The bar was empty, the straw-strewn floor barely disturbed. Everyone was either in Sherborne, the Landlord told them, still enjoying their Pack Monday, or home in bed having worn themselves out.

Riding back Adrian, keen astrologist, scanned the night sky. The stars shone, clear and bright. Directly overhead, it seemed, was the one he had been looking for. He had noted it the previous two nights. On the second, it had shone more brightly than when he had first spotted it. Now it was larger and shone with even more striking brilliance. He drew his brother's attention to it, saying: 'Just look. What a marvellous sight. It's not an ordinary star, you know. It's a comet. Very unusual. This one looks ready-made for you, Walter.'

When he was navigating at sea, Ralegh was intensely interested in the heavens. Now he was concentrating on picking his way through the dark and avoiding obstacles.

'Keep your feet on the ground, not your head in the clouds, Adrian.'

Back at the inn, Ralegh said: 'We'll make an early start tomorrow – just in case.' Calling up the ostler, he told him: 'I don't know where our four men are, and I don't want to know. But tell them they must be ready to move saddled up by seven. We'll see you then.'

At seven o'clock precisely they set off, only half awake. All was quiet and deserted. They had to pick their way through the litter and mess that remained of the previous day's jaunting. The stalls had already been taken away. There was no sign of life in The Julian or the George. Their route took them along what they were told was 'Newland'.

'I wonder where "Old Land" is,' Adrian commented.

The road to Shaftesbury ran to the west and south of the Castle, close to the walls which loomed above it. As they hurried along Ralegh pointed out its attractive features: dominating site, impregnability, entrancing setting. 'What a place to own,' he sighed. 'I know who does own it – the Bishop of Salisbury. One of those greedy churchmen.' After a pause, he added: 'It might not be all that difficult to get hold of it, if I went about it the right way.'

Ralegh was so spell-bound by the sight, so wrapped up in his covetous contemplation, that he failed to notice a larger than usual pothole. His escort's warning came too late. His horse stumbled and threw him into the adjacent mire. He swore, picked himself up, unhurt but covered in slime.

Adrian was alarmed – until he saw him on his feet, uninjured but camouflaged with the muddy mess. He laughed: 'That is what comes of Ahab coveting Naboth's vineyard. I can see what's happened: you're so keen to have it, you've already taken physical possession.'

They rode on in silence. Ralegh was wrapped in his dream. Adrian wondered: 'Was it an omen?'

That night, over Salisbury Plain, he examined the stars again. The comet was less bright. It grew fainter each night. By the fourth night it had disappeared.

2

Baptism of Fire

The brothers came of lesser gentry stock. Ralegh's pedigree went back to the Norman Conquest. A forbear had been Sheriff of Devon under Henry II, another a Judge of the King's Bench, yet another Bishop of Winchester. His grandfather, Wimund Ralegh, married to the daughter of Sir Richard Edgecombe, had suffered impositions which severely reduced his fortunes.

Wimund's son, Walter (Walter's father), married three times. The third was to Katherine, daughter of Sir Philip Champernoun and widow of Otho Gilbert, by whom she had three sons, Sir Humphrey, Sir John and (the youngest) Adrian. Her second marriage, to Walter's father, produced two sons, Carew and then Walter.

Her brother was Sir Arthur Champernoun, Vice-Admiral of the West – indicating their sea-faring interests. The Champernouns had likewise held distinctive offices from the Conquest onwards.

Walter Ralegh senior had moved – probably had to move – from their manor-house on the edge of Dartmoor to a more modest house a mile from East Budleigh called Poerhayes (Hayes Barton). It was of Tudor design and built of red-grey stone with thatched roof and mullioned windows. It nestled in a valley in the East Devon countryside, near a stream running down to village and church. It was sheltered to its north by a low hill. To the front on the south side the land sloped down to a lane and then up a long slope to a ridge surmounted by a wood. Beyond were the red cliffs of Devon and the sea.

The childhood of both Adrian and Walter knew the religious turbulence following the Reformation. This influenced their religious beliefs and theological discussions in later years.

Walter Ralegh senior, a firm Protestant, had been caught in the Rising of the West of the Roman Catholics in 1549. He had tried to influence an old woman who was telling her beads: 'What is the good of your beads? These superstitious practices have been done away with'. He explained the new doctrine. Incensed she burst into Clyst St Mary Church and cried out to the congregation: 'The poor are being told unless they give up their beads and holy bread and water, the gentlemen will burn our houses over our heads'. As a chronicler put it, this and similar fiery words made people 'fling out of the church like wasps'. Ralegh senior managed to take refuge until he was rescued by some mariners. He was, however, caught and clapped into custody in St Sidwell's Tower, Exeter, by the rebels besieging the City. He was only freed when the rebellion was put down by Lord Russell and William Lord Grey of Wilton in the battle of Clyst Heath.

In Mary Tudor's reign, the Burnings (of Protestants) took place. Sturdy Romanist priests of Devon came into their own. Adrian's and Walter's mother, Katherine, was of the Catholic persuasion, but a moderate. She visited, in Exeter gaol, a Protestant woman of no education named Agnes Prest who, at the tail-end of Mary's reign, had been condemned to the stake for her beliefs. Katherine did what she could to comfort her and listened to her saying her Creed. When she came to the words 'He ascended' the woman paused and then entreated her visitor 'to seek His blessed body in Heaven, not on Earth' and insisted that the Sacrament re-imposed by the current regime was 'nothing more than an idol'. Katherine was so taken aback that she, despite her education, could find no answer to this simple woman's exhortation.

The year following Elizabeth's accession in 1558, the Reformation was restored by the Act of Supremacy and Act of Uniformity. This was on the insistence of the House of Commons, i.e. the country's elected representatives, and despite divisions on the issue in the Lords.

These were events that helped to mould their childhood. In Ralegh's case, his recollection of the violence before 1558 would have been faint. But this atmosphere and general chat at home on religious themes had its inevitable effect and shaped his future outlook.

Another influence arose from proximity to the sea. The West

of England was a thriving area, second only to London. There was brisk commerce with the Continent, with seafarers and merchants plying their trade with Northern Europe, the Mediterranean and further afield. The Devon, Cornwall and Dorset towns were the homes of sailors who had roamed far and wide over the world. They brought home stirring tales of exploration and fighting, of deeds of daring and barbarity, setting alight Ralegh's vivid imagination. They painted a glowing picture of the wonders to be found in the Americas and the Indies, newly discovered. Accounts, often at first hand, of persecution in the name of religion at the hands of the Spanish Inquisition, of vicious treatment of captured or shipwrecked sailors by the Spaniards, were spell-binding. They stimulated an eager thirst for adventure with stories of Spain's dazzling success in conquering a vast empire and sending back countless riches. The Devon ports were the launching points for officially commissioned expeditions, for adventurers and for piratical sorties – sometimes all three combined. The boys' playgrounds were the harbours and beaches of their native county, with its boundless horizon over the sea.

The imagination readily conjures up a picture of Ralegh sitting on the beach, enthralled by the anecdotes of a roving seaman; of strange adventures, fabulous lands awaiting discovery; and of his determination to follow in their wake and enlist in England's, and his own, glory.

He was essentially self-educated throughout life. But he also had the formal trappings of education. He entered Oriel College, Oxford at the age of fourteen. A cousin of his, Charles Champernoun, was already there as an undergraduate. His attendance was irregular and interspersed with military activity in France and the Low Countries. He had an excellent tutor at Oriel and was reported upon as proficient in oratory and philosophy. These were to serve him in good stead in life. He became an eloquent speaker, accomplished writer and deep thinker. But he never bothered to graduate – he was still an undergraduate in 1572 when he was in his late teens.

Early in 1568 Charles's father, Henry Champernoun, his mother's cousin, called at Hayes Barton. Ralegh was alone at the time. 'Come in, Sir. To what do we owe this pleasure?' he asked.

'What are you doing about your military service, Walter?

Have you been overseas yet?'

'Not yet, Sir. As you know, I'm up at Oriel with Charles. I haven't given it all that thought, to tell you the truth.'

'Every young chap should be blooded before he's sixteen. I was.'

'Can I get you a glass of sack, Sir? There's no-one else here at the moment, as you can see.'

'Thank you. That would be most acceptable.' Then, after a pause while his drink was being poured out: 'The fact is, I've come to have a word with you. I'm recruiting a company of one hundred cavalry to take across to France. There's no end to the religious squabbles over there. Even worse than here, and that's saying something. The wretched Huguenots are being treated abominably by the Catholics. So we're going to help them out. I'm taking Charles with me. Oxford can survive without you both for a while, I'm sure. Are you game? It won't be a party, I can promise you.'

Every young gentleman aimed to have a period of service for martial experience in France or the Low Countries, or both. Ralegh had no hesitation. This was an opportunity not to be missed.

'By all means, Sir. Thank you. When are you aiming to sail?'

'A small contingent, the vanguard, will set off on the first of February, weather permitting, from Plymouth. I'll send you all the details. Bring your own horse, of course. I will be coming with the embodied company later.'

By 13 March Ralegh, dressed as a Huguenot trooper, was fighting at the Battle of Jarnac, halfway between Poitiers and Bordeaux (the region of earlier battles where the English had successfully fought the French). On their side, in addition to the French Huguenots, were a number of Scotsmen similarly supporting the Protestant cause. Their cavalry were led by Louis de Bourbon, Prince of Condé. Ralegh later recounted what happened.

'The Prince's horse was killed under him. He was taken prisoner with a broken leg, having shown the utmost bravery. I assumed that the enemy's General, the Duc d'Anjou, would accept his surrender and treat him honourably, as we would have done. Far from it. He had him put to death, without mercy, and paraded his body on a donkey before the troops – the ultimate insult. We naturally had no alternative but to retreat – dreadful word – at full speed.'

Training and re-grouping followed. The Champernouns had still not arrived with the main body.

By 3 October, the Huguenot forces had moved up north into Brittany, almost to the Channel coast. The combatants were once again in the field, near Moncontour, with the German Prince, Louis de Nassau, commanding the Huguenots.

Ralegh again related events: 'The day started with a mutiny on our side. The men refused to fight unless they first had their pay. This was only an hour and a half before the battle. They were given various assurances and jollied on by the officers. But it was obviously too late – particularly as the enemy had massive and deadly artillery. So there was another retreat. It would have been a massacre had not the Prince broken through the enemy lines with a thousand horse, which saved half our army.' This was his baptism of fire.

Henry Champernoun arrived with his company of cavalry two days later.

The next incident of particular note recorded in which he was involved took place at Languedoc. Interspersed with intervals back in England, he had been attached as an officer to guerilla troops roaming wide areas of the French countryside in a series of skirmishes of no strategic significance. They were now crossing the Cevennes mountain range in the Province of Languedoc, in southern France. They stumbled upon the hiding place of Catholics who had hidden themselves, their plate and jewels, in a deep cave at the foot of a glen. Ralegh described what took place.

'Our commander decided to smoke them out. The men lit a fire of straw and brushwood on an iron chain and let it down the cave. They were soon pouring out and begging for mercy. They were allowed to go free minus their plate and jewels, which they were only too thankful to give up and save their skins.'

Even the massacre of the Huguenots on the eve of the Feast of St Bartholomew, 23 August 1572, in Paris, and similar orgies in other towns had not succeeded in putting an end to encounters such as that at Languedoc. It was Ralegh's apprenticeship in the art of war. On its termination, he took up a more cultured activity. Part of the education of a gentleman about town was membership of an Inn of Court. This was particularly useful for one who aspired to acceptance at the Queen's Court, for which his military experience had already given him a part qualification. It was not necessary to read law, let alone take it up as a career. It was a top people's club. He himself always denied any knowledge of the law. He might have avoided lawsuits later on had he acquired more than a smattering.

He entered Lyon's Inn, an Inn of Chancery, and moved on to the Middle Temple. With others in like circumstances he could give full rein to his roistering activities for which London provided an ideal setting.

He was no mean poet, among his astonishing range of ability. A friend of his in the Temple was George Gascoigne, a lively swashbuckler who, like Ralegh, had served on the Continent and was a poet of talent. He wrote and issued a satire, in blank verse, entitled *The Steel Glass*. Ralegh encouraged him. 'This is magnificent. It breaks new ground. If you like, I'll scribble a few verses to help it along.' He thereupon wrote a complimentary prefix of eighteen verses, which included a sentence which in retrospect could be thought prophetic:

    For who so reaps renown above the rest
    With heaps of hate shall surely be oppressed.

A fellow student (if Ralegh could be called a student) in the Temple was John Meere, whose three elder brothers had also been there. They were a family with long-standing and deep roots and position in Sherborne. They were all there to take their law seriously. They were descendants of Sir John Meere of Maiden Bradley in Wiltshire. A probable relation had been the last Abbot but one of the Abbey, before and during the Reformation. He it was who had built the fascinating hexagonal conduit in which the monks could wash, in water that flowed down from the New Well below Greenhill on which the New Inn stood. He sited it in the monastery quarters. It was moved shortly after the dissolution of the monastery to the bottom of Cheap Street.

John Meere was the opposite in character and temperament to Ralegh. He was small in stature, litigious and penny-pinching, tenacious to a degree, very much the pettifogging lawyer. Ralegh did not hesitate to show his contempt when some difference had brought them into conflict.

'You're a lily-livered little swine,' Ralegh told him. 'Why

don't you get out and about sometimes instead of sneaking round Chambers burrowing like a woodworm and poking your dirty little nose in everybody else's business?'

'You would be very well advised to do a bit more work and a spot less drinking and philandering. It's people like you who give us lawyers a bad name.'

'Whoever liked a lawyer in any case? They're a grasping, snivelling, cheating bunch of crooks, who fiddle the law to suit their own ends. Who wins if you get stuck in the Court for no fault of your own? Why, the legal rogues every time. I've better fish to fry than waste my time on such rubbish.'

They were to meet again in different circumstances.

At this time, Ralegh was living in the village of Islington, north of London, from which the Temple and the life and temptation of the City were readily accessible. He had at least two servants. On 16 December 1577, a band of revellers committed a breach of the peace at Hornsey. Brought before the Middlesex Magistrates, their ringleaders were found to be two of his men, Richard Paunsford and his brother. They were fined and bound over to keep the peace. Ralegh was surety for their good behaviour and described himself as 'of the Court' – a slight – hopefully anticipated – exaggeration.

The second eldest of his three half-brothers, Sir Humphrey Gilbert, was living in Limehouse, east of London. He was unemployed, but fully committed in preparing plans for an expedition. He explained them to Ralegh, whom he invited over for the purpose.

'The idea, Walter, is to assemble enough ships to waylay the Newfoundland fishing fleet. At least half their crews are Spanish Catholics. They do their trawling in the cod fishing grounds, with little or no protection. We could easily take their ships, sell them in the Low Countries, and build warships. With them we could send a strong force over the Atlantic and wipe Spain off the map.'

'Spain?' commented Ralegh. This ambitious scheme sounded promising.

'Well, Spain in the Americas.'

'It seems all right. Count me in, Humphrey. How are you going to set about it?'

'I'll apply to the Privy Council for a patent.'

He put up this grandiose proposition to the authorities. He

had no reaction either to that or to an even more adventurous plan, to search for a North-West passage to the East by sailing through the ice-packed seas to the north of America.

However in June 1578 he had good news. He called on Ralegh to tell him.

'I didn't get quite what I wanted. But they've given me the next best thing, a patent to discover and annex any – I quote: "remote, barbarous and heathen lands not possessed by any Christian prince or people". I like their wording. I suppose one of you lawyer fellows drafted it.'

'I see they don't define the word "possessed".'

'No. It's subject to quite a wide interpretation.'

By the end of the summer the fleet was assembled, comprising eleven sail with its complement of sailors and soldiers. They were a rough collection whose insubordination was equalled only by the behaviour of one of their captains, Henry Knollys, the second in command. He was a kinsman of the Queen and took advantage of this relationship. Plymouth was the scene of brawl and riot which he encouraged.

Sir Humphrey Gilbert, as Admiral, invited him to dinner, with Ralegh's support, to smooth things over. His insolent reply to his commander: 'I have money to pay for my own dinner. You can keep it for such beggars as need your hospitality.' One captain, Denny, a cousin of Gilbert, threw in his lot with Knollys and went so far as to challenge the Admiral to a duel.

On one occasion Knollys was seizing the opportunity in Gilbert's absence on business, of stringing up on the yard-arm one of the captains to whom he had taken exception, Miles Morgan. Gilbert returned just in time to save him. The situation, as so often in those times, was getting out of hand. So Gilbert called in the mayor of Plymouth as Chief Magistrate, who ruled in his favour and signed a certificate to that effect. Knollys's rejoinder was to sail off with four ships on a pirating exploit of his own.

As a prelude to the voyage, Gilbert's men seized a Seville merchant's ship and its cargo of oranges and lemons. This was a necessary commodity for any length of time at sea, to stave off scurvy. Before they sailed, the Privy Council issued a direction to Sir Humphrey's more staid elder brother, Sir John, to prohibit their leaving until answers had been filed to charges for this offence and the Spaniard's ship returned, together with the goods stolen or compensation. An order was also sent to the Sheriffs, Vice-Admiral and Justices of Devon to hold up the expedition.

Ralegh, who always kept his ear close to the ground, got wind of this and shot over to tell Gilbert. 'They've put a stop from London on this trip.'

'Right. We'll beat them to it. He's welcome to his ship back and we'll keep the fruit. We need it. We'll pay for it. Get the men mustered. We sail at high tide.'

The fleet, less Knollys's contingent, sailed on 19 November. They kept the precise details of their voyage to themselves. They must have included the West Indies. In no other way could Ralegh have acquainted himself with details of the islands in that region and of harbourages on the mainland, which he found invaluable for future Guiana expeditions. In the Spring of 1579 they were in action against a Spanish fleet and were defeated, with the loss of one of their largest ships. A redoubtable captain who had been narrowly saved earlier by Gilbert was slain.

Ralegh, in command of *The Falcon*, lost many men in the encounter and was himself nearly killed. He held on till storms and lack of food forced him back to England. Once in Plymouth they charged Knollys before the Mayor for desertion. But they themselves had to pay fines for disobeying the order not to sail.

A few months later intelligence was received that Spain intended to invade Ireland. This gave Gilbert the pretext for another sally forth, ostensibly to protect the Irish coast. He failed to prevent a landing, as will be seen. But he did succeed in sacking a monastery in Galicia, which made his voyage worthwhile – a change from the ill-luck that, despite determination, dogged most of his projects.

3

'The Queen Trod Gently Over'

In the spring of 1580 Ralegh was posted to Ireland to command a company of infantry. Devon men had for years been a recruiting source for service over there. Sir William Gilbert, noted Puritan, had received his knighthood eight years before for a ruthless campaign as President of Munster, in the steps of another kinsman, Sir Peter Carew. Ralegh's military experience in France and his privateering with Sir Humphrey might have recommended him for this assignment. His imprisonment in the Fleet with Sir Thomas Perrot for seven days in February for an affray might also have been an inducement – or his committal to the Marshalsea Prison for an affray with one of the Wingfields next to the Whitehall tennis court could have suggested him as an ideal candidate for service in that country.

The occasion for reinforcement was the permission given by the King of Spain for an incursion into Ireland. This was England's soft under-belly. Its purpose was to link up with the Anglo-Irish Earl of Desmond. It comprised mostly Italian officers, with the scrapings of jails and brigands of various nationalities liberated from prison by papal order and sailing under the papal flag.

They landed on the West coast at Smerwick, at the head of the Dingle Peninsula. They took over a ruined fort there and restored it to serve as their headquarters, Fort del Oro. Their contingent numbered a thousand and had sufficient weapons to arm four thousand. Three hundred of them were sent inland to link up with the Earl. All Europe watched to see what would happen. Assault on and occupation of territory of the British Isles was something new. Sir Nicholas Malby, President of Connaught, wrote to Sir Francis Walsingham, the Privy

Council Secretary: 'It is now a quarrel of religion.'

Ralegh was posted to Cork as captain in command of a hundred foot. His pay was four shillings a day. His first step when he arrived was to report to the Government in Dublin and request reimbursement of his men's pay. This he had advanced out of his own pocket from when they left England. He was told he must seek this from London and that Dublin responsibility did not arise till arrival at Cork. Officialdom is nothing new.

The prime mover pushing the Earl into rebellion had been his younger brother, Sir James FitzGerald, who decided unwisely to ravage the land of his personal enemy, the Sheriff of Cork. He was captured. Instructions were issued by the Lord Chief Justice of Ireland, Sir William Pelham, to arraign and condemn him for treason. Ralegh and a fellow officer, Sir Warham St Leger (who had had his estate laid waste in an earlier rebellion, as had Ralegh's cousin, Sir Richard Grenville), were appointed commissioners to see to his trial and execution at Cork. This they did.

Almost simultaneously, the FitzGeralds ambushed Sir Peter Carew and his brother, George. The former was killed, the latter narrowly escaped. Strict measures were called for. Lord Arthur Grey de Wilton, a stern Puritan, was appointed Lord Deputy of Ireland, i.e. Governor-General. His first task was to destroy the invasion force at Smerwick. He took troops from Dublin to link up with the Earl of Ormond, Thomas Butler, Governor of Munster (a cousin of the Queen), at Rakele, not far from Limerick, before proceeding up the peninsula. Ralegh was ordered to join them at Rakele. They were harassed continually on the way by Desmond's guerilla followers making tactical use of the Munster mountains and passes.

In the hamlets through which they marched was the the sweet smell and sight of blue peat smoke rising into the air from cottage and hovel, their fires fuelled by smouldering hate towards the invaders or, depending on the point of view, protectors of their land. The native Irish only stopped fighting one another when they had to unite to repel a common enemy.

At a stop on the way to join Grey, Ralegh called his men together and said: 'I've noticed that whenever we strike camp, these villains sneak in behind us to see what they can find. As you know, they slaughter any loiterers. This time we'll give them a surprise they won't forget in a hurry. We'll make a great show of leaving, then I and a dozen of you will drop off and creep back into the camp. The rest of you stand by over the hill.'

Sure enough, a number of kerns, armed with skenes, wicked-looking daggers, swooped onto the site for the scavenging activity. They were forthwith captured by Ralegh's small group, reinforced on the summons by the rest of the company. One of the men caught was carrying a large bundle of withies. Ralegh asked him: 'What are they for?' The defiant reply was: 'To hang up any English churls we can get hold of.'

'Well, is this so?' said Ralegh. 'They will now do very well for an Irish kern.' And to his men: 'Tuck him up in one of his own neck-bands.' The remainder of the prisoners were taken to Grey's headquarters.

The weather was atrocious, with gales and heavy rain. The streams on Dingle overflowed their banks, the fields and bogs were saturated, the tracks were running with water. Progress was slow, through thick mud and slime. There was no sign of the age-old donkey races on the Strand – more serious matters were afoot. The natives were hiding, in either their bothies or the woods.

Ralegh's route lay round the coast. Opposite the Blasket Islands they came across some strangely shaped beehive structures, the like of which they had never seen before. They stopped and peered inside one of them. Its occupant was dishevelled and emaciated. They hauled him out to question him but could not make him understand. 'Rattle up the other hives and we'll find out what they're doing here. Spies very likely.' They ejected and questioned them. They only spoke Gaelic, except for one. He was clearly an educated man who was able to explain their presence.

'We are anchorites – hermits,' he assured his interrogators. 'We have sought refuge from all the troubles and we pray to the Heavenly Father for peace.'

Ralegh was too taken aback to say more than: 'I can't see Him being much help here.' But he accepted his statement. They were evidently not in the category of bandits or priests inciting violence. His men indicated a superstitious reluctance to meddle with them. So they were left to pursue their peaceful contemplation.

The English forces established their base on 2 November some eight miles from Fort del Oro. Much could hang on the outcome of this operation. If the Spanish foothold were allowed to develop into a full-scale invasion, and Ireland were to come under the domination of the world's then most powerful nation, Spain, it would augur ill for England. The constant fear was the threat of Ireland becoming a concentration area for attack, in conjunction with assault from the mainland of Europe.

Despite the slowness of their overland progress, they were nevertheless ahead of their fleet reinforcement for essential supplies, including guns. However, the following day the ships arrived. Having unloaded them, Grey invested the fort and carried out two days of heavy bombardment. Twice he called on them to yield, on merciful terms, but they refused. They had been sent by the Pope and must obey his authority.

But when it was clear to the defenders that their cause was lost, they put out white flags with cries of: '*Misericordia, misericordia.*' 'Mercy.' It was too late. Grey told them, 'The choice is yours. Yield and submit, or don't. Just as you will. It must be unconditional surrender.' He gave them no assurances of clemency.

They gave in. Grey sent in Captains Ralegh (whose overbearing attitude and arrogance had already incensed him) and Mackworth. The fort's officers were taken prisoner and held to ransom. All the rest of them, including their hangers-on, were executed and their bodies stripped and laid out on Smerwick sands.

In the course of questioning, the officers admitted that they were really adventurers with no formal commission and no official support other than that of the Pope. They also conceded that on their way over they had seized a Bristol trading vessel and flung its crew into the sea. They were therefore deemed to be no better than pirates who had incited the Irish natives to rebel.

In January 1581, Ralegh, stationed at Cork, risked the perilous journey to Grey's headquarters in Dublin. He sought authority to neutralize the instigators of a current insurrection, the Barry family. Lord Barry himself was in Dublin Castle, locked up. His son, David, was actively supporting the Geraldine rebels and allowing them the use of the family stronghold,

Barry Court.

'My Lord, I won't beat about the bush. The Barrys are completely out of hand. Their court is a base for rebel sorties. You've been far too soft with them. They're cunning. They don't get involved themselves but behind the scenes they furnish the weapons and encouragement. We mustn't let them get away with it, my Lord.'

'It's time you learnt to keep a civil tongue in your head, Ralegh. You'll go too far one of these days. Just remember who you are. You're speaking to your Commanding Officer.'

'Pardon, my Lord, but I must speak out. I don't believe in mincing words. Barry Court is a vital strongpoint of theirs in a particularly vulnerable area for which I am responsible. It must be dealt with. It's only a year or so since they and the Geraldines set Youghal on fire and massacred everyone in the town. The Barrys are aiding, abetting and comforting the rebels – that's treason in anyone's language.'

'What do you expect me to do about it? It'll stir up a hornet's nest if we try and go in. They've a large following.'

'What I suggest is this. I'll move my men from Cork overnight and take over the court and castle – and make an end to it once and for all.'

'I'll put it to the Council and see what they say. Mind you, even if they agree, I won't have any harm done to the family. That must be clearly understood.'

'Very well, my Lord. I'll make sure of that. But we will need absolute secrecy. They're a wily, foxy pack with eyes and ears everywhere.'

The Irish, with their primitive weapons, were facing well-armed troops but whose morale was often found wanting. They moved by stealth and had the advantage of unlimited cover in sparsely populated countryside.

Ralegh duly launched an attack on Barry Court. But by the time he arrived, his intentions had been discovered and it had been evacuated and burnt down.

Riding back late one evening from Youghal to Cork took Ralegh and his small escort through the county of one of their ruthless opponents, John FitzEdmund FitzGerald, Seneschal of Imokelly. Darkness was falling as they rode down a steep ravine, thickly wooded on either side of the river crossing of Corabby in the Ballinacurra. Nothing could be heard above their horses' hooves save a hooting owl calling to its mate and the hoarse rattle of a corncrake from a field on the far side of the river. Watchful as they were, they saw no sign of danger.

Suddenly they received a shower of missiles from the far bank, followed by the onslaught of a score or more who had been lying in wait. The horse of one of his men, Henry Moyle (a fellow Devonian), plunged and stuck in marshy ground at the water's edge. Ralegh jumped off his horse and, armed only with pistol and quarter-staff, beat off the assailants. He saw his escort safely across the river and heaved Moyle and his horse free. Unfortunately, it was barely on firm soil, when it reared, turned and was again stuck. Ralegh went in for a second time and pulled Moyle out of the saddle. But the horse was too deeply sucked in and had to be shot. It was the only casualty. The ambushers vanished and the party continued their journey with no further molestation.

This was typical courage and leadership for which his men, particularly those from the West Country, idolized him. Their attitude contrasted with the prickly and often vicious reaction of his competitive contemporaries. He reciprocated in kind to each extreme.

The difficulty of the terrain was illustrated by another incident. They were transporting arms and equipment by waggon along a narrow track four or so feet up with deep bog below on either side. It was a deceptively beautiful scene. Purple heather mixed with the soft green of sphagnum moss, interlaced with still, dark pools studded with bog asphodel and butterwort. Manhandling it over a small hump-backed, makeshift bridge, it collapsed under the weight; waggon and contents, including occupants, slithered over the edge and landed upside down. The men inside were pulled out but the waggon was visibly sinking.

Luckily they were in friendly territory. Although it was in the middle of nowhere and the day far advanced, a peasant appeared, curious to see what was afoot. They sent him off to get help before it was sucked down altogether. In no time at all, despite its remoteness, upwards of fifty helpers arrived with ropes and with a strong haul the waggon was righted and pulled up, and their helpers rewarded. As they resumed their journey, night fell and will o' the wisps were flying their bog domain.

Ralegh wrote to Walsingham telling him of the ambush, but not of the near loss of equipage. He also told him about the Barry Court disaster.

'The attack was delayed too long. And why? Because of the procrastination and prevarication of my Lord General of Munster. He either wanted the castle for himself, or would go to any lengths to stop an Englishman having it. May I from now on have charge of Barry Castle?' He also reiterated his criticisms of Lord Grey who, he said, was handling Irish affairs badly.

What might have been a bond in Ralegh's friend the poet (by then deceased) George Gascoigne, of whom Grey had been patron, had no effect on their mutual dislike. He repeated to Grey his request for custody of Barry Castle in one of his blunt reports. 'The state of the army in Munster is appalling. Sitting in Dublin, you have no idea of what life is like beyond the pale. There aren't enough troops left even to defend Limerick, Dingle or Kilkenny. I treated the Barrys with care, as you commanded, and had parleys with them and with the Countess of Desmond (Katherine FitzGerald, Dowager Countess). The only upshot was the commission of treacherous villainies. The Countess, to avoid the penalties of attainder of her husband, sent all their possessions secretly, by her younger son, Barrie Roe, somewhere up country. He it was who only five days earlier attacked our garrison at Youghal.' He went on: 'We can do with Barry Castle as a base for ourselves. I would be prepared to repair it at my own expense.'

He renewed his strictures of the feeble way he considered Grey and Ormond were conducting operations against the rebels. He wrote formally to both the Privy Council Secretary, Sir Francis Walsingham, and William, Lord Burghley, Principal Secretary of State, to let them know what he thought. He referred with scorn to the bands sent over. 'The soldiers ran away. They were such poor creatures that their captains dare not take them into action.' And, referring to Ormond, 'considering that this man has been Lord General of Munster for about two years, there are now one thousand more traitors than on the day he came. Would Sir Humphrey Gilbert were still here – with one third of the men he would have put paid to the rebellion in two months. They would have given in to him.'

This typical presumption could not fail to inflame the

Establishment against him. But it had some beneficial effect. He was granted a band of horsemen to supplement his foot soldiers. Walsingham notified Grey of Ralegh's appointment to the cavalry command with an appropriate increase in pay.

More than once in his tour of duty in Ireland he was warned by well-wishers: 'Watch your step, Captain. There are dangerous men after you.' This was in the main from colleens, irrespective of religious persuasion. They were, with exceptions, more responsive – on their own – than their male compatriots, whose reaction varied from fawning subservience to downright surliness. Inherited hatred ran deep. Even the female welcome or, sometimes, overture had to be treated with caution. They could be a bait.

A sentimental attachment arose by chance in a sudden hailstorm. He took refuge in a church porch at the same time as a girl in her late teens. She had a pretty face, blue eyes and fair hair and was of slightly under-average height.

'We were here just in time,' he said, to break an embarrassed silence.

'Yes, it nearly caught us out,' she replied, giggling nervously.

This was an opportunity he felt should not be neglected. 'Do you live near here?' he asked. 'And may I ask you your name?'

'Ena O'Rourke, Sir. I live half a mile along the road.'

As the worst of the storm passed, he offered to see her home.

'No, you mustn't do that. My family wouldn't like it. You are a soldier.'

'Well, can I see you again? We could meet here.'

She hesitated. Was this her dream of glamour come true? An English officer, a handsome gentleman, Prince for *Cailín* – country girl?

'Here, Sir, tomorrow, when it gets dark.'

He saw her several times. She was naive and transparently sincere, of which one conversation was an example.

Their talk had turned on the question of birth. 'I know where babies come from,' she said. 'But how do they get there?'

He was taken aback. 'Has your mother never told you?' he asked.

'No. She says we mustn't ask about such things. The priest wouldn't approve. She says I must have faith: I will know when I get married.'

'That's leaving it rather late I should have thought. Everyone should know.'

After a while, when she had pressed him to tell her, he complied. She was amazed and horrified. 'I would never have believed that in all the world. That surely is the original sin, I mustn't tell mother. Why, it's just like animals.'

'We are animals, aren't we?' he replied. 'Often worse than animals.'

'No. We are special. We follow the Virgin Mary. She is very special.'

He did not pursue this religious theme.

They met by stealth. Ireland has some of the loveliest country to be found anywhere, with its woods, streams and small hedged meadows studded with wild flowers, and purple hills beyond. For him, it was a relaxation from military pressures and a genuine attachment; for her, the realization of a dream which she felt deep down must have its awakening.

At the last but one of these clandestine meetings, she suddenly stopped with alarm. 'Did you hear something?' she asked. 'Over there. We're being followed.' He always kept a wary eye about him. He could see nothing untoward and tried to reassure her. It was a wolf or fox, maybe. But she would not be convinced.

Their final meeting was brief. She was in great distress. 'I mustn't see you any more,' she told him. 'My father and brothers say so. Someone must have seen us. My family say I mustn't have anything to do with an Englishman. They've told me who the man is I must marry. If we meet again they will kill us both. When they've the potheen taken they're capable of anything.'

'It would take more than a few kerns to scare me. If they do try anything they will regret it. Have you told anybody about us?'

'No, only the priest in confession.'

'What was there to confess? You haven't done anything wrong. Perhaps he passed it on.'

'They would never do that. You can tell them anything. They owe it to God to keep it to themselves.'

It was impossible to put her mind at rest. 'I heard the banshee last night. Sure it was the Devil's sign from Hell.' She crossed herself and touched the beads and cross she was wearing, and muttered a prayer.

They parted with a quick kiss. She hurried off, sobbing. He did not see her again.

A source of other light relief was a former fellow undergraduate at Oriel, Edward Unton, also serving in Ireland. When they could, they would foregather for a drink and dinner. They could discuss the Irish problem, army tactics, shortcomings of the High Command (favourite topic for junior ranks), and theology, or reminisce over Oxford exploits.

Another diversion was his friend, the poet Herbert Spenser, in Ireland as Grey's secretary. He, however, being in Dublin, frequent meetings were not possible.

In the summer of 1581 the Earl of Ormond ceased to be Lord General of Munster. Three commissioners were appointed to govern the province, one of whom, Ralegh, was the effective leader.

Reports came in of subversive activities on the part of another well-known source of trouble, Maurice, Lord Roche, Viscount Roche and Fermoy. Ralegh was ordered to arrest him and his family and bring them to Cork. Roche was a popular Anglo-Irish chief – more Irish than the Irish, as many were. They resented interference from England. He was another who, while assisting rebellion, was careful to avoid an overt rôle or personal risk. His seat was at Bally-in-Harsh Castle.

Ralegh detailed a force of some ninety, including ten cavalry, well-armed. They set off under cover of dark. His old enemy, FitzEdmonds, Seneschal of Imokelly, got wind of the operation and deployed eight hundred of his men to waylay them. Ralegh's scouts warned him of the dispositions confronting them. He accordingly made a successful detour to the town.

When they arrived, five hundred townsmen and tenantry were drawn up in a body to block their path. Deploying his men to keep them in check, he made a quick appreciation of the situation and explained his plan.

'Six of you come with me to the Castle. Six more be ready to follow when you get the signal. The rest hold this mob back till we're inside. Then join us.'

He and the first six proceeded up to the Castle. Arriving at the gate, they asked to see his lordship. The gate guards went inside to ask their chief. On their return, they told Ralegh: 'His Lordship says you may come in, but only two of you.'

As the gate was opened, all six pushed their way in and

signalled to those standing by to move up. In the general confusion, they all forced their way in. The courtyard was swiftly taken over by the rest.

Roche at once accepted the position.

'I don't know what all the fuss is about,' he said. 'Let's sit down and have something to eat and we'll talk it over.'

The table was laid, food and wine brought in, and Roche himself proposed a toast, 'Her Majesty Queen Elizabeth, God bless her, of whom I am a loyal supporter.'

They all drank to that. Ralegh then said: 'So, my Lord, you will come quietly with me to Cork, I take it.'

'By no means. Why should I? I've done nothing to warrant it. And you've no authority for this.'

'Yes. I have a commission for your arrest, my Lord. If you care to read it, here it is – to accompany you and your family to Cork. I have no alternative, as I know you will be aware, but to carry out my orders.'

Roche examined it carefully and said: 'It's much too late to travel tonight. The roads are in a dreadful state and the weather's appalling. We'll come with you tomorrow, and make as early a start as you like.'

Ralegh realized that he was playing for time. Also, although travelling in darkness through hostile country would be difficult, it would be far more dangerous in the daytime, when they would be fully exposed. So he explained, 'My orders are to execute it forthwith, my Lord.'

'Very well. Give us half an hour to pack.'

When they left, it was blowing a gale and the rain was teeming down. The road, little more than a rough track, ran through mountainous terrain, with ample cover for the several ambushes laid for them on the way. They could naturally claim no fault on Roche's part for these rescue attempts. With the loss of a few men, they reached Cork with their arrested complement intact. (There was never any more trouble from Lord Roche. Three of his sons fell fighting for the Queen.)

On another occasion, Ralegh was proceeding from Lismore to Cork with a band of eight cavalry and eighty foot. This was in defiance of a warning that a large body of rebels, led by Barry, would be lying in wait. He ran into them, armed with their skenes and pikes, near a wood. He rode at them at the head of his horsemen, without waiting for infantry support.

They made for the wood. He followed. His horse was skewered with a pike. It reared and plunged, mortally wounded. He could not kick loose from the stirrups and was an easy target for a pike thrust himself. He owed his life to one of his men, a Yorkshireman, Nicholas Wright, who galloped in to rescue him. In the hand-to-hand fighting which followed, a number of their assailants were slain and others taken prisoner. The rest fled.

It transpired that this was to be his last engagement in the field. On 25 August 1581 he wrote to his patron, Robert Dudley, the Earl of Leicester, voicing his dissatisfaction with service in Ireland. He had known him since their meeting at a royal pageant in Antwerp ten years earlier. He worded his letter without any consideration for delicacy:

'I have spent some time under Deputy Lord Grey in such poor place and charge that, had I not known him to be one of yours, (i.e. one of his protégés) I would have hated it as much as keeping sheep.' He reminded Leicester of his affection for him, but asserted that it was clear 'you have no use for such a poor follower as myself, who has been utterly forgotten'. Yet he would be 'ready to dare as much for you as any you could command'.

This letter, or others like it, and his general comments on matters in Ireland, may have been instrumental in achieving the end of his tour of duty. For in December his company was disbanded and he returned to London.

He was given the opportunity to express his views to Privy Councillors, sitting informally – but with the Queen present for some of the time. His reputation for bravery, military skill, ruthlessness when need be and plain speaking had preceded his return – as also had his reputation for arrogance.

Lord Grey, as a Privy Councillor as well as Lord Deputy of Ireland, was also asked for his advice on operations in this territory of perpetual troubles. It was known to be a land where attempts to solve one set of difficulties invariably gave rise to others; where quarrelling was endemic; where skilful leadership went hand in hand with vicious cruelty, and charm with treachery; behind a defensive screen of ambiguity.

Ralegh was blunt as ever in his comments: 'As I see it, an English Lord Deputy favours complete subjugation and Anglicization. I believe this to be both impractical and too expensive. The Home Government would like the existing system to continue, with the native princes ("kings" as they used to be called) ruling in their domains.' He believed this to be the Queen's view also. 'This arrangement has however broken down in Munster as the rebellion testified. It will be the same with the O'Neills in Ulster. The princes aim for autonomy – and freedom to fight one another as they have in the past.' He pointed to the shortcomings of the Earl of Ormond, until recently Lord General of Munster, and explained his inability to suppress the natives. They were his own countrymen. He had been too lenient. Irishmen hated coercion by other Irishmen.

'The compromise I put forward would be far less expensive. It is to win over the lesser tribes and their chieftains. Many of them have long groaned under the exactions and domination of their princes. Many have served under, and respect, English commanders. But they resent the acts of English soldiers. There is a distinction between military severity and wanton cruelty. They also fear that a Royal pardon would restore the Earl of Desmond to his estates and his satellites to their positions of power. Their plight would then be that much more dangerous. They fear his enmity more than they do England.'

He also suggested that it would save the Queen expense if the cost of troops defending Munster were met by tax on residents.

Grey emphatically rejected these views 'which are not, have not been and could not be those of the Government. They are fanciful and indicate the difference between the judgement of those with experience and proved reason, which look into the actual state of things in Ireland, and well-meaning dabblers. They contrast with fanciful and impulsive expressions of opinion, grounded on an insubstantial basis, conceived out of the air and impossible for others to carry out'.

Privy Council Secretary, Sir Francis Walsingham, for his part thought it 'no treason to wish Ireland buried under the sea', considering the expense it entailed.

When Lord Burghley as Lord Treasurer later took up Ralegh's ideas for a more economical administration, Grey turned them down flat: 'They are no more than a plausible show of thrift which would merely put in the Queen's head the idea that I have not safeguarded her financial interests.'

But the Queen was more impressed – by the man and his eloquence, if not his arguments. She knew of his reputation. He embodied the vicarious champion on the field of battle she would have longed to be.

Was it soon after that, when wearing his customary finery, he spread his cloak 'in a plashy place', whereon the Queen trod gently over, rewarding him afterwards with many suits for his so free and seasonable tender of so fair a foot cloth? However that may be, it is a gem of the nation's folklore, in company with King Alfred and the burnt cakes. His rapid ascent stemmed from that time.

In April 1582 the Queen, through Walsingham, wrote Grey a letter which enraged him. It appointed Ralegh to a company in Ireland, whose captain had recently died, 'for his further experience in military matters', and expressed her interest in him.

Grey's reply was terse: 'I like neither his carriage nor his company. He will get no help from me, beyond what I am directed or his appointment requires.'

She recalled Ralegh shortly after for his safety – the threats had not been empty – and he was authorized to send a deputy. Thus ended his military adventures in the 'commonwoe', as he phrased it, of Ireland. Some three months later, Grey was replaced as Lord Deputy. The official policy by then was to ease up on Ireland. The death of the Earl of Desmond, at the hand not of the English but of an Irish kern, terminated the rebellion.

The love-hate relationship between the two races continued, with never-ending hopes of reconciliation and close friendships between individuals. Meanwhile English was becoming more and more the vehicle for the rare literary talent of the Irish. It had the versatility to portray their wide range of emotion, experience and imagination.

4

The Queen's Man

Queen Elizabeth said farewell, with a convincing affectation of sorrow, to her unsuccessful suitor, Alençon the Duc d'Anjou. He was an ugly specimen, but marriage would have helped persuade the French to join England in a defensive alliance against Spain. The House of Commons had begged her, their Virgin Queen, to marry and produce an heir. But there were limits.

In the privacy of her rooms she did a little dance of joy at her escape from her 'poor frog'.

'Robyn,' she said to the Earl of Leicester. (She might have said 'Eyes', her love-name for him.) 'I know you'll be delighted. I want you to see him on his way. Take Sir Philip Sidney with you. I gather they're going to do the honours for him at Antwerp by putting on another pageant. You've my full permission to return as soon as he has been delivered and is having his fun. I want your young friend included in the party. Send him in, would you.'

Ralegh entered with a bow and a flourish and knelt before her. 'He really is a well-made fellow,' she thought to herself. 'You can get up, young man,' she told him. 'I've been giving some more thought about what you said on Ireland. It's quite impractical. But I must say you put it across well. And put it across my Lord Grey as well,' she added with a laugh. 'Don't overdo it. Are you settled in with us?'

He was impressed by her graceful figure, comely face, red-gold hair and clear grey eyes. 'Ma'am, I can think of no more agreeable occupation in this life than to serve at your noble feet.'

'They tell me an ancestor of yours was Justiciary to Henry III. Is that so? I know that your family have at one time or another been Devon landowners.' She would never take on a 'new' man, but loved helping penniless men of long-standing family connection down on their luck.

'That is so, Ma'am. Little left now, I fear.'

'Too bad. Now, I've a somewhat delicate job for you to do for me. I have a highly secret letter for the Prince of Orange which I want you to deliver personally. So you won't come back with my Lord Leicester but go on to the Prince. Tell no one whatever. Give his reply to me here. Is that understood?'

'Perfectly, Ma'am.'

When Leicester and the others left Antwerp, wasting no time getting back to Flushing and home, Ralegh stayed behind to contact the Prince. He received him kindly and wrote his reply with a personal message which Ralegh duly passed on to the Queen.

'He asked me to tell you, Ma'am, that they rely wholly on you as their Protector and that, had it not been for your Majesty's help, they would have been overrun.'

Shortly after his new appointment to the command in Ireland, she called him in. 'You're not to take up that post. You can send someone in your place, Mr Ralegh.'

He hid his relief. 'If that is your wish, Ma'am. Could I please know why?'

'I want you here,' she replied. 'So far as the others are concerned, my reason is because your aunt, Mrs Catherine Ashley, has served me so well at Court.'

So, not for him another spell of the tedious, dangerous and ill-rewarded service far from the centre of power.

She for her part liked his eloquence and logical reasoning, unsophisticated as it was at times – and his Devon accent. He was increasingly consulted as one of her confidants. This aroused the jealousy of fellow courtiers. It was said of him: 'He flits like the Adonis of Venus around the Queen'; that she looked on him as a 'kind of oracle'. He did not hesitate to let them all see it. She even dubbed him with a nickname 'Water'.

His protector, Leicester, her favoured Robyn, did not object. It diverted attention from dalliance with his other mistresses at Court or elsewhere. A former favourite, Sir Christopher Hatton (her 'Mutton' or 'Bell-wether'), did not take kindly to it. Hatton, by then out of favour, in his time had feathered his nest well. He had had valuable perquisites by illegal charges on

London and other merchants. He had been adept at filching church lands as, for example, Hatton Garden mansion, which he had persuaded the Queen to pressurize from the Bishop of Ely.

To warn her against Ralegh's influence, he arranged for a fellow courtier, Sir Thomas Heneage (also a former 'lover' – the word to be construed constrictively), to waylay her one morning when riding in Windsor Great Park. Symbolism played a major role in Elizabethan court life. She reined in her horse and stopped. Heneage handed her a pail of water (intended to represent danger from her new favourite); a bodkin (to protect herself or, alternatively, dispose of her erstwhile lover, Hatton); and a letter and poem – they were constant verse-writers.

She simpered girlishly as she read it and told him to reassure her 'Mutton': 'No water or flood will get between us – there will be no fear of your drowning.'

Ralegh meanwhile attired himself with more and more exotic splendour. He might wear such dress as a white satin pinked vest with brown doublet finely flowered and embroidered with pearls, and a decorated sword-belt, a jewelled dagger on his right hip; a hat with a black feather with a ruby and pearl drop; trunk hose and fringed garters of white satin; cape of rich velvet with seed pearls; a pearl in his ear and costly rings on his fingers; his shoes tied with white ribbon and decorated with precious stones.

It was perhaps about then that he wrote on a pane of glass with a diamond ring: 'Fain would I climb, but that I fear to fall'.

The Queen replied by adding: 'If thy heart fail thee, then climb not at all'.

One of the courtiers particularly upset at his success was the young reprobate Earl of Oxford, Lord Burghley's son-in-law. He took exception the moment Ralegh entered Court and treated him with contempt. He called him 'a scurvy knave, the most hated man in the country, Jack the Upstart'. He regarded him, as did others, as an interloper in their exclusive set.

Even so, when his son-in-law was in trouble, Burghley sought Ralegh's help. Oxford had been involved in a scuffle with another gentleman of the Privy Chamber and both had been injured. The Queen banished them from court, with the threat of more severe penalties. Burghley asked Ralegh if he would intercede with her. He replied: 'I will do my best to revive the serpent with the fire' (the Queen) 'but if it recovers, I will be the one in danger of its sting and poison'.

He succeeded in placating her and was able to tell Burghley, 'The Queen said she only wanted to give him a warning.' As he anticipated, he received no gratitude for this good turn. Succour can provoke resentment at being under an obligation.

She was particularly careful to receive his counsel in private. She warned him: 'You're too outspoken, you'll get the backs up of all my Council.' He was no politician. He did not heed the warning.

A mark of her favour was to compel All Souls, Oxford, to lease him two estates, Stolney and Newland. The following month, May, he was given the lucrative wine patent, termed the 'farm in wines'. This required every vintner to pay twenty shillings a year as licence duty for the sale of wine. With it went a share of fines for infringing the wine statutes. This brought in some £2,000 a year (less expenses of collection).

She also gave him the tenancy of Durham House, the freehold owner of which was the Bishop of Durham. It was a large house on the north side of the Thames between the Strand and the river, once the home of Anne Boleyn. It was suitably located for a man of the Court and affairs, but not in the best state of repair. Here he kept forty men and forty horses.

It fell to him to persuade her to allow Sir Humphrey Gilbert to sail on his next voyage of exploration.

'What he wants to do, Ma'am, is set up a colony that will look like England – with parishes, churches, gentry, yeomanry and common folk and plots of land for cultivation. He also aims to find a North-West passage round the top of America. What an achievement that would be. It would be a short cut to the East.'

'He's your brother, so you would think it a good idea. But Gilbert has no luck at sea.'

'Just imagine though: another great land under your Majesty's sceptre. A little England over the seas. A chance for England to spread her wings.'

'It sounds all very well. You're always an over-optimist. Your enthusiasm gets the better of you. You're impetuous, as in everything you do.'

'It won't cost you a button, Ma'am. And it will bring in a good return. I'll give him a ship, and I'll see its a good one. He wants me to be his Vice-Admiral.'

'You'll be no such thing. I won't hear of it. If I agree to his going, it will be on condition that you do not.'

The fleet was ready in March, but the wind did not permit it to sail till June. Ralegh's solidly built ship, *The Bark Royal*, comprised half the tonnage and personnel. Before it left, the Queen gave Ralegh a small token – an anchor led by a lady. 'Give Gilbert this from me. I wish him, tell him, as good fortune and as safe a voyage as though I were there myself.'

But two days later *The Bark Royal* was back in Plymouth, fever rampant among the crew. Gilbert sailed on with the rest of his fleet. He reached a land 'not in the actual possession of any Christian prince' – as his warrant demanded – and annexed it in the Queen's name – Newfoundland. He made generous allocations of land to those of his complement who settled there. The sick were sent back to England. This left him three ships. One of these was driven ashore in fog and broke up.

The two remaining, *The Golden Hind* and the tiny ten-ton *Squirrel*, which Gilbert made his flagship, cruised up and down the coast in wild weather until the crews were famished and in rags. On their urging, he agreed to return and set course for the Azores. He refused to leave *The Squirrel*, vulnerable not only for its small size but because of its weight of cargo and guns. Gilbert was last seen on the bridge, holding a book and shouting out over tempestuous seas: 'We are as near to heaven by sea as by land.' At about midnight their lights suddenly vanished. *The Golden Hind* struggled back alone.

So success had been achieved up to a point and at a price. His brothers, Sir John and Adrian, were authorized the following year to continue the search for the North-West passage. The efforts were in vain.

Ralegh was not to be deterred from the plans for colonization which he had shared with Gilbert. If Humphrey could do it, he thought, so can I. We'll build a great empire, like the Persians, Greeks and Romans. He re-opened the matter towards the end of winter when he joined the Queen and Lord Burghley in conference.

'Ma'am, I've the most stupendous scheme of exploration for

you. It's a sure winner.'

'What – like Gilbert's? I told you how that would end, Water.'

'But he did find Newfoundland. People can't wait to get over there. It could be the start of an empire under your Crown.'

'Let's hear the worst, Ralegh,' said Burghley. 'What have you in mind?'

'It's this. There's vast unexplored land between Newfoundland and the West Indies. It's inhabited by pagans, a gentle race from reports I receive, ready-made for occupation. The Spaniards haven't found it yet. Their hands are full enough further south. But if we don't move in, they will. Or if not them, the French. I can see good pickings – and some more territory under your rule, Ma'am. There's Gilbert's North-West passage also to be discovered. It would be shorter and safer than having to go round Africa as we do now.'

His plans for colonization were beginning to be obsessive, Burghley thought. But she was impressed. It was put to the Council. The upshot was the grant of a charter for an expedition 'to discover such remote heathen and barbarous lands, not possessed by any Christian prince nor inhabited by Christian people' – carefully phrased with legal precision to avoid any diplomatic incident with potential competitors. Ralegh, Adrian Gilbert and a co-adventurer, John Davys, were constituted 'The College of the Fellowship for the Discovery of the North-West Passage'. No foreign state could take exception to that.

Informing Ralegh of the success of his application, the Queen tackled him on a vital point. 'What is in it for me, Water?'

'Ma'am, a great Empire, without a doubt.'

'Yes, I know that – perhaps. But what else? Something more tangible.'

'We thought, Ma'am, say, a tenth of all the gold and silver we bring back.'

'That's rather mean, isn't it, after all my support? I wouldn't settle for less than a third.'

'It's going to cost a great deal to fit it out. Would you be happy with a fifth share?'

'No. But I'll accept it. Let my Lord Burghley have it in writing. I hear you're planning to go yourself.'

'That's right, Ma'am.'

'Well, you're not. I'm not risking it. Send someone else.'

As another mark of her favour, she granted him the right to licence the export of woollen cloth. This would be a useful supplement to the proceeds, already extensive, of the various privateering voyages for which he provided ships – a share of which had to be handed over to the Crown. (Burghley later calculated the profits from this licence and pronounced them excessive).

That month at Westminster, a gentleman by the name of Hugh Pew stole Ralegh's pearl hat-band together with another jewelled article of attire, valued at £113. He recovered them and, highly indignant, had the offender committed to Newgate jail.

Two ships set sail on the voyage in April 1584. They landed on the isle of Wokoken in July and took possession in the Queen's name. They then cruised in the archipelago along the mainland coast and returned to England. Ralegh passed on his captain's report to the Queen.

'Three days after they landed, Ma'am, some natives came up to them. They said their land was called 'Wingandacao', and their ruler, Prince Wingina. They were friendly and delighted with some trinkets given them. A couple of natives came back with them. Your Majesty might like to see them.'

'Is that all they brought back?'

'No, Ma'am. They brought chamois, buffalo and deer-skins – and a cabinet of pearls as big as peas. I have them here. They're all for you.'

They examined them together. She was visibly impressed. 'If this land is all you say it is, we must give it a Christian name. I'll get Lord Burghley in and we'll decide it now.'

They discussed it at some length. Finally, Ralegh suggested: 'What about Virginia? In honour of our cherished Queen and something like the natives' name.'

'That might do. Burghley, my spirit, do you go along with that?'

'Yes, Ma'am, why not, if you like it? It has a good ring to it and seems to fit. But what about the North-West passage, so-called? Wasn't that to have been the main purpose of the expedition?'

Ralegh was not so convincing. 'They hadn't time to look any

further. The weather was bad and supplies ran out. We'll try again. But this is a good start.' He was given permission to have a seal struck as Governor of Virginia, showing helmet and visor. Virginia would comprise not only the islands of Wokoken and Roanoke but a huge area of mainland also.

While the voyage was proceeding, he had run into difficulties over his wine licences. He had leased out the wine patent to a Richard Browne. He in his turn had licensed one John Keymer in Cambridge. The other vintners in the town were enraged. They had had theirs from the University, who claimed sole licensing rights. The quarrel degenerated into a brawl, in which the licensee's wife nearly lost her life. Ralegh initiated legal proceedings to punish the attackers, but it was Keymer who was committed to prison for the affair, being deemed an illegal licensee.

Ralegh pursued the case with the University, who ignored his letters. They believed themselves in the right by virtue of their statutes. In due course Lord Burghley, to whom he had made a formal complaint, received legal advice to the effect that Ralegh's rights did not extend to Cambridge and that those of the University were exclusive.

These and other squabbles over the 'farm in wines' reduced the profit appreciably. He retracted his lease to Browne. That cost him a considerable sum in compensation.

With fond memories of the old home at Hayes Barton he tried to persuade the then owner to sell it, unsuccessfully.

But his rise continued. He was appointed Lord Warden of the Stannaries in succession to Francis Russell, Earl of Bedford. This gave him overall responsibility for the Cornish tin mines and the problems arising therefrom. He had a seal cut for this office, with the insignia of a galloping armoured knight. He was also elected Member of Parliament for Devon.

The next expedition to Virginia set sail in April. It comprised ten ships and carried one hundred and ten householders, largely at his expense. His friend Hariot, the mathematician, was one of them. The Queen still refused to let him go, so Sir Richard Grenville was made its commander. In the course of the voyage which saw the capture of two Spanish frigates and a mixture of entertainment and villainy at ports of call, Grenville established a colony of the householders on Wokoken. On the return he seized another Spanish ship, with a cargo of gold, silver, cochineal, sugar, ivory and hides. Ralegh took care to take charge of it as soon as it docked before the sailors could get their hands on the spoil.

He sent out a ship with stores for the settlers, but on arrival it found the island settlement deserted. Grenville himself likewise called in there a fortnight later, expecting to find them as he had left them. He was astonished to find they had gone.

They had in fact left for England with Sir Francis Drake a short while before. Their settlement had started to show promise. They had planted corn and discovered mines and pearl fisheries. Hariot had tried smoking tobacco like the natives. Unfortunately they had fallen out with them. That and dreadful weather persuaded them to return to England with Drake.

Drake himself had had a successful voyage. He had looted Cartagena and Santo Domingo. He had only dropped in on the settlement to see how his fellow Devonians were getting on. They could not get back quickly enough.

As Ralegh had instructed, Hariot brought back with him some specimens of tobacco leaf and of a vegetable likewise new to this country, the potato.

Grenville meanwhile tried again. He landed fifteen men on Roanoke with two years' stores. On return to England, he called in at the Azores to supplement his takings from the voyage. These islands, isolated in the Atlantic, were similarly placed to Malta and Majorca in the Mediterranean. They were a cross-roads for pirates and traders, for plunder and commerce at all times of the year. Their cowed inhabitants had to be on constant alert. They tried to keep all comers appeased, perforce allowing landing for re-watering and victualling and a haven in storms. At the sign of likely danger they moved themselves and their goods to alternative positions inland. The pleasant environment and equable climate were compensatory attractions.

A product of the Virginian expeditions which was to leave its permanent mark on civilization was tobacco, which Ralegh rapidly popularized, himself becoming an avid smoker. Hariot himself in later life unknowingly succumbed to its effects. Ralegh played a joke on the Queen. He had filled his long silver pipe from his gold tobacco case and was about to light it when she walked in. Although he was not averse to aggravating other ladies with the fumes, he would not have dared affront the Queen. Instead, when she expressed her disapproval, he replied, 'Ma'am, I know so much about this weed that I can even tell you what its smoke weighs.'

'That's impossible,' she retorted. 'I will take you on a bet, Water.'

They agreed the stake. He fetched his scales and weighed out half a pipeful. Having smoked it, he weighed the ashes and subtracted. She enjoyed the joke and paid up.

'I have heard,' she said, 'of men turning gold into smoke, but never one before who could turn smoke into gold.'

His star was in the ascendant – always a time to take special care. When the principal Ministers were allotted counties for defence preparations, he was appointed Lord Lieutenant of Cornwall; and two months later, in November, Vice-Admiral of that county and Devon. He made his eldest half-brother, Sir John Gilbert, his Deputy in Devon – strange reversal of the family rôles which would have astounded his father and their mother.

In March 1586 Leicester asked Ralegh, in view of his close contacts with the Cornish tin-miners from his Stannaries responsibilities, to send, if the Queen so permitted, a band of mining pioneers to the Netherlands. Leicester had long had an interest in their mining activities. From being her cherished favourite, he had been in bad odour with the Queen ever since she heard the rumour of a proposition to make him successor to William the Silent (of Orange), following his assassination. She was furious at what she suspected to be high-handed collusion behind her back. His supporters put it in his head that Ralegh, whose protector he had long been, had disloyally instigated her reaction. On her instructions, Walsingham had disabused Leicester of this notion and assured him that it was none of his doing but entirely her own response.

Her anger having subsided, Ralegh duly sought authority from the Queen to comply with Leicester's request. He wrote from the Court telling him of her permission to the despatch of miners and the likely date of their arrival and added a postscript: 'The Queen is on very good terms with you and, thanks be to God, well pacified; you are again her "Sweet Robyn".'

One man's fall was another man's rise. Anthony Babington was a young Catholic supporter of Mary, Queen of Scots, in her bid for the English throne. He was recruited by priests to take part in an invasion aimed at deposing and putting to death Elizabeth and installing Mary. Their plans, despite careful coding, were discovered by the nation's watchdog, Walsingham, acting with Elizabeth's full knowledge. Babington was caught and secret instructions, including Mary's own confidential papers, were damning evidence in his and his co-conspirators' trial for treason and the ultimate penalty – to be hanged, drawn and quartered in public. Mary's trial followed, with a finding of guilty and, eventually, execution.

Babington's huge estates, in five counties, were automatically forfeited. The Queen granted them to her favourite Ralegh, with the bonus of a conveyance without having to pay any customary fee. He was now a large landowner.

He nevertheless expressed his disapproval of some of the methods of interrogation in criminal matters.

'You are too ready to use the rack,' he admonished some of the Councillors. But it was to continue for some years.

In Ireland, although the Desmond rebellion had been crushed, terrible famine had been the aftermath of civil war. It was reported: 'Travelling from one end of Munster to the other, even from Waterford to Smerwick, which is one hundred and twenty miles, you will not meet any man, woman or child except in the towns, nor see any beast save foxes, wolves or other ravening beasts'. There was no blue peat smoke from the deserted cottages. The occupants had fled, or died.

Six hundred thousand acres were confiscated from the Earl for his treason, to be parcelled out to 'gentlemen undertakers – especially those who served with distinction in the Irish wars'. Sir Christopher Hatton wormed onto this band-waggon even though he had not served in Ireland. The Earl of Ormond was also rewarded, as was Ralegh, who was allocated a seignory of twelve thousand acres in Cork, Waterford and Tipperary. This was supplemented by a further two and a half seignories of equivalent size, nominally in partnership with two associates who were, in effect, sleeping partners. The condition attached was that they should be settled with 'well-affected Englishmen'.

The Queen tackled him about this. 'What are your plans for this land?'

'I'm very grateful, Ma'am. It's most generous. I'm sending

in good Devon and Somerset men. The soil is fertile but it's now overgrown with thick grass, heather, brambles and gorse. It will take hard work to put it back into shape.'

The sparkling lights of the gorse were reminiscent of the New Forest, ablaze in springtime.

'I'm making Lismore Castle my country seat. I've leased it from Miler Magrath, who as you know, is Bishop of Lismore and Waterford.'

'And Archbishop of Cashel,' she added.

'Yes. He wasn't all that keen to let me have it but gave in after persuasion.' He had long desired a castle for its prestige. 'I'm taking over a manor house at Youghal to live in. There's a great quantity of trees in the region, so I have plans for the timber. I'm sending over a hundred and fifty men to fell the trees and make casks. There's a big demand from vineyards in France and Spain.'

'I'm not sure the Council would approve. They might regard them as military supplies. We'll see what they say.'

He requested his kinsman, Sir George Carew, then Lord President of Munster, to supply anything the builders needed for repairing Lismore Castle. He was also involved in various law-suits – a favourite hobby of Elizabethan nobility and gentry.

In 1586 two of his pinnaces covering the Spanish coast and the Azores seized Spanish ships and captured a large amount of loot and a number of prisoners. One was the Governor of Magellan, Don Pedro Sarmiento de Gamboa. Ralegh hurried down to meet them at Plymouth, his normal precaution to prevent pilfering. He rewarded his sailors generously, as usual, and treated Sarmiento as an honoured guest. They had discussions in private. Ralegh's notoriety was widespread. They also knew that he was ambitious. His guest approached him in this knowledge. 'Why don't you enlist your services for my King?' he asked. 'You could fall from grace any minute. Help King Philip by looking after his interests in England. He would not only reward you, but back you up if and when trouble came.'

'You're wanting me to be a kind of spy, is that it? What precisely would it entail?'

'Well,' he explained. 'One thing you could do is help us against the Portuguese, a small nation but troublesome. You might join us in blocking their Pretender's expeditions against our country. You could also sell us one of your excellent warships.'

'That might be arranged. My price would be 5,000 crowns. You could have two ships maybe.'

'If, furthermore, you could do your best to dissuade her Majesty from her naval preparations, King Philip would regard it as a friendly act.'

'I'll see what can be done.'

This conversation was passed on to Madrid for the King who confirmed, through his Ambassador, the overtures by Sarmiento. Neither were aware, however, that Ralegh had passed its details to the Queen, Burghley and the Lord High Admiral, Lord Howard of Effingham. But Philip soon tumbled to the conclusion that the offer to help was probably a trick and that the sale of ships would have landed a load of suspicion on Ralegh's head, making him useless as a mole in any case.

Sarmiento's nephew was to cross his path years later in a more sinister capacity.

Ralegh's next promotion was to be made Captain of the Queen's Guard in succession to Hatton who, to the lawyers' disgust and despite having no legal qualifications, became Lord Chancellor. Ralegh thus became responsible for her safety. The duties included regular attendance, guarding her door during meals and ensuring that her food was not poisoned – always a dread of sovereigns. She liked having 'real' men around her. Ralegh recruited accordingly. One day a gentleman called and offered his son as a guard. Ralegh rebuffed him. 'I won't have boys. Sorry.'

The father replied: 'I'll show him to you,' and called out to his son who was waiting outside. 'Come in – boy.' He did: and showed himself, although no more than eighteen, to be taller than any of the guards and very handsome. Ralegh accepted him at once and arranged for him to carry up the first course at dinner. He watched to see the effect on the Queen as he served her. She was astonished. He heard her say to her dinner companions: 'See – a beautiful giant has brought in our food.'

Ralegh had another seal made, displaying a shield with supporters. He also had a set-back. An arrogant young rival appeared in court – the nineteen year old Robert Devereux, Earl of Essex. As a boy of eleven, he had rejected the Queen's proffered kiss, but by now had learnt the wisdom of compliance. Taking advantage of his rank, he quickly established himself and started throwing his weight about. Ralegh did not conceal his views on this new arrival. 'Young pup. He fawns around the Queen like a little dog. They even play cards and other games together all night long till the birds start singing their dawn chorus.'

Essex likewise could not stand Ralegh. He complained to his friends: 'He's an ill-bred West Country upstart. But he does what he likes with her. He can't do a thing wrong and she won't hear a word against him. She tells me there's no reason why I shouldn't like him too – the rascal.'

Matters came to a head when the Queen and Court were on a progress to Theobalds, Lord Burghley's palace in Hertfordshire. Ralegh was in attendance as Captain of the Guard. On their way they were stopping at North Hall, also in Hertfordshire. Essex arranged for his sister, Lady Dorothy Perrot, to meet the Queen. Lady Dorothy was the wife of one of Ralegh's brawling opponents of earlier years, Sir Thomas Perrot. She was ready to be received and the Queen was told. She refused to see her. She did not like her.

'She can stay in her room,' she commanded.

Essex was furious and told the Queen so.

'Somebody should have told me,' she offered, rather unconvincingly. 'I didn't know she was coming.'

'Ma'am, you have disgraced me. It's all that knave Ralegh's doing.' He knew that Ralegh, as Captain of the Guard, was standing at the door and could overhear them. As he told a friend later: 'He was outside the door, like a dressed-up dummy. I pretended I didn't know he was there and told her what I thought of him.'

'You have disgraced me and my sister, Ma'am, just to please him. For his sake, you reject my love.'

'You mustn't say such things about him. I see no reason why you should disdain him so.'

'He's a jumped-up fellow who has come up from nothing. He's conceited and over-bearing and nobody can stand him. It's time you saw through him. Don't I have every right to reject his love for you? How can I give myself to someone who is scared of such a man as he.'

'He is a loyal supporter and I have every trust in him. As

I've said before, why don't you make friends with him?'

'It's no joy for me to be with you,' he said rudely, 'when you reject my affection in this way, and I am flabbergasted that you esteem this wretch as you do.'

She turned to Lady Warwick who was in attendance on her and said angrily: 'That's enough. What disgraceful impertinence. I won't hear another word.'

Essex later tried another tack. While she and Ralegh were playing cards, he got the Court Jester, Tarleton, to shout out loudly enough for all to hear: 'Look how the Knave rules the Queen.' The Queen gave a suitable rebuke, but it left her with the uneasy feeling that she might be giving the impression of undue subservience to her erstwhile favourite. The next the Court knew was that Ralegh had had a somewhat acrimonious conversation with the Queen and had left for Ireland. It was rumoured that he had been driven there by Essex. He strongly denied it. He divided his time between activities over there and even more demanding duties back at home.

In April 1587, he sent another one hundred and fifty householders to Virginia. The Queen again refused him leave to sail with them. The excuse she made this time was: 'I don't want you getting knocked on the head like that careless fellow Sidney.' His friend and poet, Sir Philip, had died the previous year on 17 October from wounds sustained in battle. He forbore to remind her that his injuries were from a bullet to the thigh, not a knock on the head. In Ralegh's stead one Captain John White was given the command. They were incorporated as the 'Governor and Assistants to the City of Ralegh in Virginia'. They landed on Roanoke, where Grenville had left his small settlement. The houses were still standing but the fort had been razed to the ground and there was no sign of the fifteen men who had been left. There were again tussles with the natives. On the insistence of the colonists who feared starvation, White came home for more supplies, leaving his daughter and grand-daughter behind. Fear for the future impelled half of them to return with him. Ralegh made every effort to send out more supplies, but owing to the threat of invasion from Spain, the Council prohibited shipping from leaving these shores. The embargo included White and his ship. It was to be two years before they were allowed to send out again. White failed to find the settlers. They had moved to another island. Ralegh could not be censured. He had spent £40,000 on colonization. It was no fault of his that further assistance had to be suspended.

He looked up his brother Adrian whom he had not seen for some while. 'A little bird tells me that your silver mine in North Devon – Combe Martin, is it not? – is doing well,' he said. 'You might do something about that money I lent you. Adrian laughed. 'I'll have a lump sent over next week.' It never arrived.

Attack sooner or later from Spain on the nation challenging its supremacy by assaults at and from the sea was inevitable. The execution of Mary Queen of Scots had made it imminent. As the Spanish fleet was assembling, Drake stormed into Cadiz Harbour, their main maritime base, blazed away and sank their ships, without loss of ship or man. He had 'singed the King of Spain's beard' – Cadiz at the bottom end of Spain – for which he was widely praised. It staved off the invasion for a year. In the latter part of 1587, the Armada was known to be in an advanced state of preparation. Strategy was discussed. The young bloods were all for having a go – taking on the galleons and boarding them. Ralegh advised against that. He gave examples of sea battles lost by over-enthusiasm. Sheer size of ship and numbers would have given the Spaniards the advantage. Sir Francis Drake, Sir Richard Grenville and Sir John Hawkins thought the wisest course would be to attack the Armada in Spanish waters before it came anywhere near the Channel. The Privy Councillors considered that would leave England naked. It would be more prudent to keep the Fleet in home waters in defence of the Channel ports. The eventual decision by the Lord High Admiral, Lord Howard of Effingham, was to concentrate in the Plymouth area, so as to intercept them at the western entrance to the English Channel. The bulk of the land forces were to be concentrated in the South-East, considered to be the most likely place for an attempted landing, particularly as Spain already had an army assembled in the Netherlands.

In November, Ralegh hurried back from Ireland. His main function, as Lord Lieutenant of Devon and Cornwall, two potentially vulnerable counties, was to organize their coast defences. He had to raise levies from the tin-miners and, from Devon alone, muster two thousand foot soldiers and eight hundred horsemen. He secured the agreement of his deputies, Sir John Gilbert, the Earl of Bath and Sir Richard Grenville, and general support. The exception was the City of Exeter who, asserting its ancient rights, would not muster with the County but insisted on raising its own contingent. As Governor of the Isle of Portland, Dorset, also he had to see to the strengthening of its defences. This completed, he was ordered to report to the Queen's Command Headquarters in London.

On the evening of 19 July the Armada was sighted. The beacons all round England were lit one by one. Drake on Plymouth Hoe finished his game of bowls (the state of the tide allowed for that).

Advancing in a crescent formation visible from the Cornwall coast, it comprised one hundred and thirty ships, including twenty galleons, carrying 2,500 guns and over 30,000 men, two thirds of them soldiers. Their aim was to sail up the Channel, embark the troops waiting for them in the Netherlands and land on the south coast. The Queen gave her naval commanders an urgent warning: 'Keep an eye on Parma' – Alexander, Prince of Parma, who was General in command of Spain's Netherland force.

Despite preparations, only thirty-four of the Queen's ships were fit for service. Ralegh had presented the Queen with his *Bark Ralegh*. It was renamed *The Ark Royal* and was the Lord Admiral's flagship. Many smaller vessels had helped to swell the English Fleet, including Dorset ships from Lyme, Bridport, Weymouth and Poole.

That night, under a gibbous moon, the fleet glided behind and to the windward of the Armada. As day broke, they raked it with gunfire.

On 23 July, Sir John and Adrian Gilbert joined the Fleet. Both fleets lay becalmed off Portland Bill. The tall, heavy, hard-to-manage galleons were no match for the deft manoeuvring and rapid fire of the English ships. Drake, followed by Howard, swooped in and easily repelled counter-attacks from galleys rowed by slaves.

As they moved up the Channel, a threat of landing on the Isle of Wight was thwarted. The Armada, under constant harassment, sailed over to and anchored in Calais Roads. The Spanish soldiers had played no part in the battle because their opponents had neither tried to board nor been close enough for them to board. After dark, the English launched fire ships loaded with explosives among the Armada. Its captains in disarray scattered and made for the open sea. Many collided or ran aground. They set off eastwards the ten miles for Gravelines to link up with their Netherland troops.

So far, Ralegh had been ordered to remain in London, impatient though he was to get to sea and into the battle. His ship *The Roebuck* had been usefully employed replenishing other ships with ammunition. The Queen now sent him and Richard Blake to join the Fleet and exhort the Lord Admiral Howard 'to attack the Armada in some way, or to engage it, if he could not burn it'.

At Gravelines the Spaniards discovered that, because of the neap tide, there was not sufficient depth of water for the Netherlands force to embark from Dunkirk and join them. A fierce naval engagement took place at close quarters in which they were routed.

To guard against a Spanish landing, 20,000 men had been mustered and assembled at Tilbury, Essex. Even after the defeat at Gravelines, it was thought they might regroup near Denmark and still link up with the Netherlands army and attempt to land. But the Armada was fleeing northwards up the East coast. The Fleet (including Ralegh in his ship) pursued it until it ceased to be a menace. It continued in mountainous seas and gales round the North of Scotland. Two of its ships were wrecked on the coast of Norway. Along the West coast of Ireland some landed for water or were driven ashore. Their occupants were dealt with mercilessly by the natives. The lucky few who survived did so by making their way in conditions of severe hardship across Ireland, at times with the help of local sympathizers, to ports and ships that would see them home.

Only half the Armada made Spanish ports. The English losses were one hundred men and no ships. 'England must always fight for freedom,' Ralegh mused. 'And win.'

With the invasion threat removed, at least for the time being, he resumed his attempts to send supplies to the colonial settlers. It was however to be nineteen years before a permanent settlement was established, his nephew Ralph Gilbert being his representative. But it was Ralegh who was Virginia's founder.

He and his compatriots also resumed their privateering. The Queen received her customary share of the spoil.

Later that year, the Lady Arabella Stuart, then aged twelve, was brought to Court and dined at Lord Burghley's in the presence of the Queen. As the daughter of Charles Stuart, fifth Earl of Lennox (who was Lord Darnley's elder brother and, thus, Mary Queen of Scots' brother-in-law), she was first cousin to James VI of Scotland (later to become James I of England). Guests at the table included Burghley, Ralegh and Sir Charles Cavendish. Burghley was greatly taken by the looks and accomplishments of this pert little girl.

'She speaks French and Italian,' he remarked. 'Plays musical instruments, dances and writes with a very fair hand.' Then he whispered behind his hand to Ralegh: 'She's all right, isn't she? If only she were fifteen.' Ralegh replied: 'That would be convenient.'

But his stock in Court was at a low ebb. With the rise of Essex he was losing the competition and knew it. He was pitched in a lower key and had less to say for himself.

5

Her Majesty's Maid

Elizabeth Throckmorton was born and baptized in April 1565 at Beddington, their home in Surrey. It was her mother Anne's family home. Her mother had been heiress of an uncle, Sir Francis Carew. Her father, Sir Nicholas, had good family roots back to the thirteenth century. He it was whom Queen Elizabeth sent up north (unsuccessfully) to stop the marriage of Mary Queen of Scots to her feeble cousin, Henry Stuart, Lord Darnley. Mary later married his murderer, the Earl of Bothwell. A plan, in which the Pope connived, to divorce him and marry the Duke of Norfolk came to nothing. For his support of this scheme, which in his case was aimed at unseating the Cecils, Sir Nicholas was sent to prison for a spell. He died in 1571 at the age of fifty-six, leaving children all under-age. The eldest, William, was of slow intellect. The next, Arthur, was made his heir. Robert was the third son and Nicholas the youngest. The two younger brothers and Elizabeth were each left £500. Her mother lent Elizabeth's £500 to the Earl of Huntingdon. Despite repeated requests it was never recovered.

Although Elizabeth was brought up by her mother, she looked on Arthur as her brother protector. They were devoted to one another. He was alert and intelligent. He entered Magdalen College, Oxford at fourteen. He observed the customary stint at the Inns of Court, essential for a gentleman about town, particularly if he aspired to the Queen's Court. He followed convention (in common with Ralegh) in gaining military experience fighting for the Huguenots in France. He was a confirmed Protestant who, like all of them, felt the St Bartholomew Massacre deeply. He was duly received at Court.

By 1576 Elizabeth was a bright, attractive eleven year old, with quite a temper – as had Arthur. Her mother took no great pains with her education but Arthur did what he could to fill the gap in his brief intervals at home. He was hard put to it to secure her attention. She was more interested in domestic matters and the things around her, flowers in particular and sketching.

Having no portion or potential dowry meant that her marriage prospects were minimal. This did not concern her at all, at least in her childhood, but her mother and Arthur gave it careful thought. It was realized that the only opening for a girl in her financial straits would be acceptance in Court as a maid of honour.

Marriage for a widow was an economic and social necessity. Her mother by then had become Mrs Stokes, having married the Duchess of Suffolk's widower, Adrian Stokes, a handsome Welshman – the Duchess had married him, although sixteen years his senior, on the Duke's execution. She had left him a fine estate in Leicestershire, so Elizabeth's mother had no financial problems from then on. (He was generous to her and her children in his will, but those benefits lay in the future.)

It was decided that Elizabeth must take an interest in Court as soon as possible. On 3 March Arthur took her for the first time to Whitehall to explain the general set-up. The Queen and retinue were away so he was able to show her round and familiarize her with the surroundings. They stayed the night.

'What did you think of it, Bess?' he asked on the way home.

'It's very big, isn't it?' she replied, 'and rather sombre.'

'It'll look better when everybody's around. They have lots of fun.'

The following month, over Easter, Bess came up to stay with her cousins in Chelsea. She was introduced into the Queen's presence by Arthur and greeted graciously, before returning to their cousins' house.

'Any comments?' inquired Arthur.

'She's a grand lady, but I was rather frightened till she patted me on the cheek. So many fine lords and ladies were there.'

'I believe you made a good impression,' he assured her.

They observed their Church duty on Easter Saturday by taking Holy Communion in accordance with the statute.

Arthur had to regularize his succession to his father's estate, entailed to the elder William, in whose hands it would not have been prudent to leave it. The entail was broken and the estate re-settled following advice from their uncle, Sir John Throckmorton.

The Elizabethans were always getting tangled up with lawsuits and quarrels. Sir John himself was charged shortly afterwards with unlawfully enclosing part of Feckenham Forest, Worcestershire. The penalty imposed by the Privy Council was to deprive him of the offices which Queen Mary had bestowed on him as a loyal Catholic, including Presidency of the Council of Wales, and commit him to the Fleet prison. Prisons in those days had an excellent social mix.

Arthur was now all set for his tour of the Continent, another essential step for prospective society gallants. He took to heart Sidney's advice to his young brother, Robert. 'As you are a gentleman born, you must record all the information that may be of use to your country' – such as fortifications and ships in the countries visited and the state of military training. He kept a diary meticulously thereafter.

He left in July 1580 and was away till January 1582. He wrote regularly to his mother and Bess. They managed to get a Christmas present to him just before his return.

Arthur, now a country gentleman of substance, enjoyed a tour of country houses of various cousins. When he rejoined the Court at Greenwich, the Queen's *bête noir* – her 'pet frog' the Duc d'Anjou – was there. Arthur left to go to the Earl of Leicester's great house at Wanstead, Essex (Leicester had an even larger house at Kenilworth, Warwickshire). There was still the possibility of the Queen's marriage to Anjou. The Privy Council and country as a whole opposed it (much as they wished her to marry and produce an heir) and she was reprieved.

She was surreptitiously informed by the French Ambassador of the marriage of her lover, Leicester, to her cousin, Lettice Knollys. If the motive in disclosure was to induce her to go ahead with the French marriage, it failed. But her fury can be imagined.

Arthur was confined to his room at Court for siding with the troublesome Earl of Oxford against Sir Philip Sidney. This could have prejudiced his Court career, although the characteristically rumbustious Elizabethans were always getting into trouble of one sort or another.

Fans of feathers in the Italian style were all the rage. The Queen had one. Bess stayed in London with Arthur in the autumn and he bought her one to be in the fashion.

By the following year, Bess's mother had resigned herself to the conclusion that her daughter, with her limited resources, had no marriage prospects, and told her so.

'Bess, you've idled around here long enough. We can't get you married off properly unless the Queen can lend a hand. I'll have a word with Arthur and see about getting you to Court.'

She had grown into an attractive, striking-looking girl, with slender figure, large blue eyes and fair hair. She was straightforward and thoroughly trustworthy. She was by no means enthusiastic at the prospect of having to leave home.

'Must I, mother?' she queried. 'I'm perfectly happy here.'

'I've no doubt you are. But the time has come, in your own interests. You'll do what you're told, young woman.'

Her brother pulled all the strings he knew to get Bess a place. It was by no means a cheap operation, and he even borrowed his young brother Robert's £500 legacy, a little hard on him, it could be said. He also pawned his own silver. This was nothing unusual. Before banks were established, the pawn-brokers were in effect the bankers. Also, courtiers 'carried their estates on their backs' – hence Ralegh with his jewelled finery. The cost to courtiers of their exotic Court attire was heavy – velvet suits, elaborate accoutrements and gold-buttoned cloaks.

It did not help his efforts when a cousin of theirs, Francis Throckmorton, and Lord Henry Howard, a devious character and a fervent, but surreptitious, supporter of Mary Queen of Scots with Spanish affinities, were committed to the Tower on Walsingham's orders. Also committed was the Earl of Northumberland. Under the rack Francis Throckmorton confessed his part in a conspiracy to launch a Catholic attack on England, and was executed.

Arthur had to redouble his attempts to polish up his sister's literary achievements. She was determined and eloquent in argument and could stand up for herself, but her book-learning left much to be desired. He tried to improve her spelling.

'It's not enough, Bess,' he explained, 'to speak correctly. You must be able to write and do so intelligibly. That entails proper spelling.'

'I do find it difficult. Why aren't words spelt as they are spoken? I find Latin easier. It's spelt as it's said. Much more sensible. Not that there's much point in wasting time learning it. English is enough for me.'

'It's up to you what you do about Latin. I don't suppose you know more than a dozen words in any case. I found it useful in Chambers with its legal quotations. When any clever chap tried to spring a Latin tag on me, I could usually cap it. Anyway, let's try some spelling. Spell "know" – meaning you are aware of something.'

'KNOO', she offered. He corrected her and told her. 'Try "Queen". That's a useful word to learn. And "cousin".'

'QUINE. COSSIN,' she suggested. He again corrected her and said: 'At least you know your letters. That's something. You must work at it. If the worst comes to the worst, I suppose they'll get your meaning.'

His overtures for entry into Court, unlike the spelling lessons, bore fruit. On 8 November 1584 they were invited to dinner at Hampton Court, where the Court was in residence. After dinner Bess took her oath of allegiance and confidentiality before the Privy Council. As soon as the Council had finished its business, the Queen received her graciously in her Privy Chamber. She curtseyed as she had been carefully coached.

'So, my dear,' the Queen said to her, smiling, 'you would like to join us, would you? You'll find it hard work. We're always on the move.'

'I am most honoured to attend on you, Ma'am,' she replied. 'I won't mind the work. I'm looking forward to it.'

'No doubt your brother has put you in the picture. He reminds me of your father, Sir Nicholas. We have exacting standards here, as I expect he has told you.'

'Yes, Ma'am. I promise I will do my best.'

'I am sure you will. Learn the rules carefully. One I must emphasize. Our conduct has to be beyond reproach. There must be no involvement with any of the gentlemen. And I need to know the names of your friends outside. We can't be too careful. Is that understood?'

'Perfectly, Ma'am. I am not interested in men.'

'That is excellent. All our gentlemen here are well-behaved, and I wouldn't want any deviations. You can go now and wait on me later this evening.'

The atmosphere was friendly, she thought, and exciting. She no longer regretted leaving her former free and easy life, and prepared for her duties with confidence and pleasure.

A friend who took her under her wing was a cousin with whom she had not hitherto had close contact, Lady Mary Darcy. She introduced her to the ins and outs of the Queen's Privy Chamber and bedchamber. Together they examined with awe her wardrobe, with its vast array of dress for all occasions.

She warned her: 'They will all want to call you Bess. They may pull your leg when she's not around and call you "Queen". There are some very handsome gentlemen in the Court, but be careful of them. They gamble at dice and cards and drink far too much. They're only after one thing, especially when they've drink taken, so watch out.'

'What thing is that, may I ask?'

'Do you mean to say that you don't know? Didn't your father and mother tell you?'

'Father's dead, you will remember. Mother did say I had to be careful. But I always am careful.'

Mary laughed. 'What do you mean, always careful?'

'Nothing out of the ordinary, I suppose. I fold up my clothes properly, wash every day, comb my hair, try and not waste my money – not that I have much to waste.'

'I see. I can also see I must take you in hand. These young men, like all men, are only interested in dalliance and a bit of fun. They'll ply you with wine, lead you on, turn your head and, if they can, make a regular fool of you.'

'But the Queen said have nothing to do with them – that they're very – well – gentlemanly.'

'She would say that. She doesn't know the half of it. As for keeping away from them, that's more easily said than done. They're around all the time, like bees round a honey-pot. Or dogs round a bone. If there are two or more dogs and only one bone, then you see the fur fly. I find it rather amusing. But it scared me when I first came here. Anyway, let's go back to your room and settle you in.'

Bess saw that Court life was not going to be merely one of attendance on the Queen or carefree ease. That night she undressed thoughtfully as she prepared for bed and said her prayers with more than usual urgency.

A few days later, the Queen summoned her and stated: 'I want you to wait on me tomorrow morning at seven o'clock sharp.'

She was already awake when Bess entered the bedroom and made her curtsey.

'I will have breakfast in the next room. I sometimes have it here, but today we'll have a change.'

Bess laid the table neatly with linen cloth and napkins, cutlery and glass.

'What would you like me to order, Ma'am?'

'What is today? Wednesday. This, Friday and Saturdays are our fish days. It would be sacrilegious to eat meat, always remember that, my dear. I expect your family observed this rule, too.'

'Whenever they could, Ma'am.'

'That's good. I feel like some salmon, I think, and make sure I have the finest white bread, from Heston wheat. Also, some currant cake. I have a soft tooth for it, Bess. I will call you "Bess" when we are amongst ourselves. I hear you're friendly with Mary Darcy. Why did nobody tell me that you are cousins?'

'We haven't seen much of her family. But I like her very much. And what would you like to drink, Ma'am?'

'I usually have beer with my breakfast. None of your heady March ale. Just some light beer. Make sure it has been freshly brewed. I don't want the dregs of some old barrel. I have wine with dinner, but remember that it has to be three parts water.'

Breakfast over, they proceeded with her toilet preparations, which took over two hours.

'I'm not riding this morning. I have various important meetings. So I shan't require my riding habit. Wash my hair first, girl. In one of the pots on my dressing-table you will find some lye.'

'Lye, Ma'am? Whatever's that?'

'It's only ash. Mixed with water. Very good for the hair. I wear my wig over it in any case. When it's dry we'll put a little dye in it. I might put on my red wig today, to cheer things up. Pass my tooth-pick and a piece of clean cloth, and the marjoram pot to rinse with.'

These basic preparations completed to her satisfaction, she

proceeded to make up her face, with a mixture which included poppy-seeds, powdered egg-shell and white of egg, suitably moistened with soft water. As she did so, Bess was struck with the singular beauty of her hands and long, fine fingers. Bess too had elegant hands.

'Now my silk stockings. And my dress. What shall I wear? Let's have a look and see what there is.'

Bess expressed her astonishment at the enormous selection of dresses, most of which could hardly, if ever, have been worn at all. The Queen laughed and exclaimed: 'It gives one the awful problem of choosing.' She chose a pure white costume. 'Appropriate for both of us on your first attendance in my room.' The ensemble was completed with a string of pearls and an ostrich feather fan.

She left to join Walsingham who was waiting with the day's business of State.

Mary looked in on Bess to see how she had fared.

'I believe she was pleased with me. I like her. She's rather abrupt sometimes, but kind. She must be a very good person.'

'Oh! She has her moments, don't you make any mistake about that.'

'How do you mean?'

'I mean she has her men friends. She's not so pure as you imagine. Wait and see.'

In the New Year the Court moved down river to Greenwich, which Bess saw for the first time. An attractive palace, she decided, in wooded Kent parkland with a spectacular view of the Thames and its shipping and the Essex countryside beyond.

An event took place there which had a sharp impact on her. The Court was assembled, as for a formal occasion, and summoned before them was the most handsome man she had ever seen, dressed in full regalia. He strode in and knelt before the Queen. Bess asked Mary if she knew who he was.

'Why, of course. That's Ralegh,' she whispered. 'Walter Ralegh. He could be one of those men I was telling you about. Her great favourite. She's very keen on him. But the others don't like him one little bit. They say he's arrogant and conceited – a real terror, always throwing his weight about. He doesn't care a damn for anybody. Mind you, I think they're jealous.'

She had heard of Ralegh. Who hadn't? A larger than life figure in day-to-day gossip in England and abroad, this was the first time she had seen him.

A short ceremony took place. The Queen, sword in hand, dubbed him 'Sir Walter Ralegh'.

Bess was transfixed by his magnificence in jewelled array, tall, majestic she thought, with a commanding presence which overshone all the company, save Queen Elizabeth herself.

She murmured her thoughts to Mary, who dismissed any lingering fantasy with a laugh. 'You wouldn't stand a chance there, Bess my dear. He's after far bigger fish, you can be sure. They all say he only wants money and power. Why, you haven't even the prospect of a single-figure dowry.'

'I wasn't dreaming of anything like that,' Bess protested. 'I was only thinking what a fine man he looks and what a great soldier he must be.'

If she had any further ideas, she kept them to herself. In her teens she had known the pangs of unexpressed, unrequited love. But this was deeper – at first sight.

Had she known it, Ralegh likewise had known, as had Arthur and most youths emerging from childhood, the heartache of undeclared worship from afar. He had outgrown both it and more mature emotional surrender.

In the following months, Arthur was in trouble again. First he made an indiscreet remark to Mary, whom he regarded as his girl-friend with hopes of a more permanent liaison. He recounted to her a story about the Earl of Leicester which he had no doubt was true: that the death of his first wife Amy had been due either to a fall downstairs, which he had precipitated, or to poison, or both. Mary and he then fell out and she, or more likely her mother, quietly informed the authorities of this slanderous – if such it was – statement. He was committed to the Marshalsea Prison to cool his heels – and his tongue.

While in prison, by no means discouraged, he wrote some verses for Mary and sent them to her at Court. Mary was horrified and had a word with Bess. 'This is beyond a joke. First of all he misbehaves himself telling awful tales and gets put in jail. Then he has the cheek to write me poetry. From his cell, if you please. If he does it again I'll have to tell the Queen. You know what she'll do if she gets to hear about it. She's made that clear enough.'

'Don't worry, Mary, I'll write to him and tell him he mustn't write to you again – at least, not while he's there. I can't vouch for him afterwards – or even before, I suppose.'

She wrote him a short letter, to the point (but spelt in her quaint phonetic style):

> My Dear Arthur,
> You know how fond I am of you. But you are making a nuisance of yourself and being very silly. Fancy writing to Mary as you did, from prison of all places. Wait till they let you out. She's scared stiff what would happen if the Queen got to hear about it.
> Hurry up and get away from that dreadful place. Mother and I long to see you safe and sound – and sensible.
> I remain your Loving Bess.

Nothing daunted, he tried his charms on Mary's sister, Katherine. They were firmly resisted by her and her mother, who had bigger ideas. Arthur's mother had to plead on his behalf to get his release from prison. This was two days after the Earl of Northumberland, in the Tower for the Mary Queen of Scots' conspiracy, shot himself.

Arthur replied to Bess thanking her for the good advice and help, saying: 'I've finished with Mary and Katherine. I can't understand why I ever bothered. Anne Lucas is the one I am really fond of. I'm inviting her and her mother, Lady Lucas, to Court.'

Mothers could be formidable creatures when protecting their young, Arthur had discovered. 'Please make them welcome. I have high hopes here.' He followed up the invitation with a gift to his new love of a gold pendant set with diamonds. She gave him a bracelet.

Bess was adjusting herself well to Court life. She let its constant gossip and scandal fly over her head. The Queen liked and trusted her. She had quickly learnt the pitfalls. Arthur was keeping out of trouble. One morning Mary burst into her room.

'We're going on a Progress,' she told her.

'Oh! What does that involve?'

'It's great fun. Anything up to two hundred of us go into the country with the Queen. All the gentlemen of the Court and the servants come with us. The trail of horses and waggons stretches for miles.'

'What about the food and drink? Bess enquired.

'No problem. Wherever we stay, the host provides everything,' she explained.

'That must worry them a bit.'

'Yes. They don't look forward to it. They try and make themselves scarce before she catches them. But they can't say "no".'

'Where are we off to?'

'To my Lord Burghley's vast palace, Theobalds, near Waltham Cross. "Tibbuls" she calls it. Isn't that funny?'

This would be one of many Progresses to 'Tibbuls'. Burghley had built it at great expense for this express purpose – an expense readily born for longer-term benefits. Situated in Hertfordshire near the Essex border, it was not too long a journey from her London palaces.

The procession set off headed by the Queen on horseback. With her were attendant nobles and courtiers, Privy Councillors and Government officers. Her immediate staff included gentlemen ushers, maids in waiting, grooms of the Privy Chamber, squires of the body, chief chef, cooks and staff of the pantry and cellary. Cheering crowds greeted them on the way. When they arrived the company took over virtually the entire building. Burghley had made other temporary arrangements for himself and his staff.

Bess recounted some of the details of their stay to her mother and step-father.

'It was a real holiday. I did so enjoy the journey down. To get out into the countryside again was a treat, away from the London fogs and smells. We skirted Epping Forest – a massive forest indeed, with an abundance of trees and wild deer.'

'Did they feed you properly?' her mother asked anxiously.

'The food was ample and delicious,' she assured her. 'We had games in the park by day and dancing in the evening. The Queen herself joined in once or twice. Every morning she went riding and strolled round the gardens. We had a great time. The gentlemen drank too much, of course. They always do: two in particular. But I mustn't tell you who they were.'

Her mother's comments were: 'I hope you behaved yourself.'

'Of course I did,' she replied indignantly.

'Did you meet anyone – interesting? You know what I mean.' Matrimony was never far from her mind – the everlasting problem for doting mothers.

'No, mother. Nobody I fancy.'

In November her step-father, Adrian Stokes, died. His estate followed the settlement of her mother's first husband. That succession having been changed already by the deed of re-settlement, Arthur inherited, not his elder brother, William. There were now added therefore a manor in Devon and other property, including the lease of their house Beaumanor and its plate and furniture.

Bess was left a gilt cup and a bed in the Duchess's chamber in the house. This was to be her own room for as long as she had need of it, together with the furniture which was to become hers entirely in the event of her marriage.

On 7 February 1587 Mary Queen of Scots was beheaded at Fotheringay Castle. The bells rang and bonfires were lit in London, expressing the national relief.

The warrant for her execution had been with an experienced diplomat named Davidson, who had been deputed for that purpose, but who was not used to the Queen's ways. She had signed the warrant on the advice of her head of government, Sir Francis Walsingham, Lord Burghley and Sir Christopher Hatton. Theirs was a heavy responsibility. They were now anxious that it should be carried out before she changed her mind. Having sought their counsel, Davidson had sent the necessary papers up to Fotheringay for the deed to be done.

Queen Elizabeth was filled with remorse. She raged and sobbed. At Court, in Richmond Palace, no other sound broke the brooding silence. This went on for some days.

'Whatever's the matter?' Bess enquired.

'You may well ask,' replied Mary. 'Just listen and you will find out.'

Walsingham, Hatton and Burghley all tried to get an audience and reason with her. She refused to see them. She held Burghley primarily responsible. Instead, in her distress and anger she summoned Mr Justice Anderson to advise her.

'I would never willingly have consented to this,' she cried. 'Tell me. Does not my Royal Prerogative give me absolute power?'

'I would venture to say "Yes", Ma'am,' replied Anderson, overborne by her insistence.

'That is all I want to know. Send me in Lord Buckhurst.' (Thomas Sackville of Knole, Kent.) He entered in some trepidation. 'You, my Lord, are a Privy Councillor and High Steward, my adviser as such and a protector of my interests. Is that not so?' she demanded.

'Ma'am, that is my privilege.'

'And I am this Nation's Queen?'

'No one would dispute that, Ma'am.'

'Right. Then Davidson must hang.'

'On what grounds, may I ask?'

'He executed the Warrant on the Scottish Queen against my orders.'

Buckhurst was taken aback. 'If that were so, Ma'am,' he demurred, 'it would indeed be a grave matter. But did you not sign the warrant? And was it not at the express request of Parliament, and did not both Houses petition for it?'

'That is neither here nor there. If I did, what of it? I told him to hold it up. Burghley and Walsingham only convened Parliament because they knew they could press them and wanted to force my hand. I would never willingly have spilt the blood of a Queen, my own kinswoman at that.'

'One thing is certain, Ma'am, if I might respectfully urge it,' he cautioned. 'You cannot condemn anyone without due process of law. Magna Carta saw to that – to which your noble predecessor, King John, subscribed.'

'My prerogative overrides it. Judge Anderson told me so.'

'Well, opinions may vary. But you must take it from me that it would be a question for a Court of law.'

'You're a useless ninny like the rest of them. Get out.'

He hurriedly complied.

Burghley, Walsingham and Hatton stood firm. For their self-preservation, they had no alternative. Once one head went, others could follow. Burghley, shattered after years of devoted service, was frightened out of his life and did offer his resignation. All three knew, as did the country, that the likely alternative to execution of this conspiratorial Queen would have been another civil war. They also knew that they might be the sacrifice of propitiation to exonerate Elizabeth from any moral and legal responsibility for this final act in Mary's life.

She sat in her room nursing her wrath, or moved restlessly between Richmond and Greenwich. All her female attendants tried to calm her down.

'Ma'am,' they warned her, 'you're not sleeping a wink and you're eating nothing. You will make yourself ill.' It was to no avail.

Her Privy Council likewise urged her to take care of her health. They also decided that the only way to convince her that Anderson's advice had been wrong was to consult all the other leading lawyers. The Establishment was at bay. They knew the choice was to swim together or sink one by one. The judges unanimously advised that they would resign sooner than carry out what would undoubtedly be an illegal judgement.

But there had to be a scapegoat to save face. Her original violent intention was no longer pursued. But Davidson was committed to prison and the Court of Star Chamber imposed a fine. However, after serving a year and a half, the fine was remitted and he was released. Still later, he was given a grant of land – compensation for a faultless fall-guy – but never re-employed. The Establishment (fortunately for the nation) had survived, but hardly triumphed.

Life resumed its former jollity, sycophancy and intrigue.

One evening there was a stir in the Court and all the tongues were wagging – more so than usual. Bess overheard some of what they were saying.

'Fancy giving that terrible fellow the job. He's no more than a pusher and self-seeker: the country's best-hated man.'

'I don't agree,' she heard another retort. 'He's one of our bravest men. You should hear what they say about him in Ireland. His men loved him. He would do anything for them; risked his own neck time and time again and thought nothing of it. The Irish would agree with you. They saw him as the Devil himself. His Westcountrymen worship him.'

Bess asked what all the excitement was about.

'Sir Christopher Hatton – her darling "Bell-wether" or "Mutton" – has another job,' she was told. 'And who do you imagine is taking over Captain of the Guard? None other than her Water! He must be back in favour.'

Her heart missed a beat. Her hero to be Captain of the

Guard. He would be personally responsible for the Queen's safety and for serving her meals, and so close to herself. Perhaps he would notice her. He'd never even seen her, let alone said anything. But she must not let anyone know how she felt. This was her secret. And would probably remain so always.

Hatton, Captain of the Guard, had been promoted to Lord Chancellor, despite his not being a lawyer – other than having, in his youth, observed his conventional attendance at the Temple, where he may have assimilated a smattering of law. His astute property dealings may also have instilled in him some of its craftier aspects. The objections from professional lawyers were ignored.

Ralegh swept into Court, gorgeously attired as ever, his swash-buckling self in gem-studded suit and jewelled shoes, magnificent in all his finery, polished accoutrements and sword pommel gleaming, feathered hat on the tilt. Even for an assembly who were used to grandeur of uniform and ceremony, this extravagance of dress was startling. Congratulations sincere or otherwise, were proffered on all sides. These he acknowledged imperiously, dominating the room as ever. He would have exclusive use of the ante-chamber as the base for his guard duties whenever he was in attendance.

Bess watched in silence from the background. Were there no heights to which this giant, this national hero, would not aspire? She felt that in some way she shared in his success. She was proud of it. But her pleasure was tinged with the sad realization that she would never be likely to share more tangibly in his achievements.

6

'I Have The Heart And Stomach Of A King'

A storm-cloud appeared on Ralegh's horizon and soon filled the whole sky. The young Earl of Essex, Robert Devereux, nineteen years old, automatically joined the Court without the usual preliminaries, by virtue of his rank. He became the Queen's darling.

He was an accomplished rider. The Queen and he rode together in the mornings. At Windsor Park they would be away for upwards of two hours.

Bess, in common with the others, could see what was happening and felt for her idol. She was also an optimist. She knew he was devoted to his Queen. But if Her Majesty did put him on one side, might not she herself step in? It was far-fetched, a day-dream almost too daring to contemplate. But he gave no sign of even noticing her.

She was waiting at table on the occasion Essex referred contemptuously to his rival, loudly enough for him to hear at the door as he stood guard. Essex neglected no opportunity to score knowing there was little he could do, whatever his eloquence, to re-divert the Queen's attentions.

Bess and Mary had instructions not to go to bed until the Queen herself had retired. One particular night this proved most exacting. She and Essex were playing cards alone in her room. The girls could hear the sound of their laughter and an occasional curse. The night wore on. They had to jog one another to keep awake. Day was breaking and the birds singing before the card party broke up and Essex left. Not till then could the Queen be seen into bed.

Bess heard Ralegh's violent reaction to these discouraging developments.

'Ma'am, I must have word with you.'

'Oh, Water! What about?' she enquired innocently.

'My Lord Essex is poisoning your mind against me. He is an arrogant and cunning young man and I am surprised you are so taken in by him.'

Ladies are seldom averse to competition for their favours. It is a diversion, amusing so long as it does not get out of hand. She was no exception.

'You mustn't be hard on him. He is so young – a little headstrong, but he means well.'

'He doesn't mean anything well towards me. I've had enough of his offensive taunts.'

'There's nothing more I can do about it. I've told him how fond I am of you and that he must be your friend. You can be very high-handed and pig-headed, you know. What would the Court think of me if I gave the impression of being under your thumb?'

'Ma'am, that would be a preposterous suggestion. So far as he is concerned, you may as well save your breath. He's after my blood, as you well know.'

'I suggest we discuss this when you're a little calmer. Meanwhile, find some quiet place for reflection till you've recovered,' she offered soothingly. He was not impressed.

'Very well, Ma'am. I'll take myself to Ireland,' he retorted.

She made no rejoinder to this ultimatum. He stalked out, looking neither to right nor to left. Two days later he was sailing to Munster to see to his Irish estates.

Bess heard by chance something of his activities from her brother: 'I imagine you've seen something of the new Captain of the Guard,' he said. 'He's an extraordinary chap, always up to something or other. He owns these vast estates in a God-forsaken part of Ireland. Somehow he's persuaded great numbers of Cornish and Devon men to join him with their families and settle over there. The bait was no doubt the promise of land to farm.'

'Are you thinking of going over there, Arthur?' she enquired.

'I can imagine nothing worse. It's always raining and you stand a good chance of getting a knife in your back.'

'I wouldn't mind seeing what it was like.' This was a long shot on her part which was unlikely to succeed. Nor did it.

'It's no place for a girl like you, that's for sure. I can't think how Ralegh gets round people. He must bewitch them or something. He's certainly not everyone's favourite here – except the Queen's. And that seems to have fallen by the wayside. Londoners hate his guts.'

'That's my Lord Essex's doing,' Bess retorted angrily.

'Why, what do you know about it?'

'I do know this. The Earl has a large house on the Thames and a huge number of followers. He hates the very mention of Sir Walter's name. It makes him see red. I mustn't tell you any details. But Essex treats him like dirt. Like the mat under his feet.'

'You amaze me. I didn't think anyone could better Ralegh. It could teach him a useful lesson. Not that I've any time for Essex, the whipper-snapper. Nor for Leicester either.'

'Arthur, you must be careful,' she urged. 'Your tongue will get you into trouble.' She then resumed the object of her interrogation. 'Have you heard any more of that dreadful man, as you call him?'

'Yes. He had no sooner moved in than they made him Mayor of Youghal – where his manor house is, with its castle guarding the mouth of the Blackwater. They will have cause to regret it, I shouldn't wonder. He's already burnt down a friary. I don't hold with monks having it, but I should have thought a use could have been found for it.'

'Perhaps he had his reasons,' she commented.

That was so. The decision to destroy the friary had not been taken lightly nor was it an act of revenge. It had been the subject of careful appraisal. Ralegh had taken the other Youghal councillors to view it and discuss what should best be done. The town's leading burgesses had accompanied them. 'It's silent and deserted now. I remember it a year or two ago seething with black robes,' he reminded them. 'It's a fine building. So what's to be done?'

One of the townsfolk told him: 'It was only built twenty years back. The Spaniards, or the Pope, I'm not sure which, put up the money.'

'If we leave it standing, it will become a nest of vipers again. The only safe course with vipers and wasps is to smoke them out,' he commented.

As soon as Ralegh had acquired his Irish estates and taken over the manor house at Youghal, he had become entitled to vote for the Borough Council. The English system of local government had been introduced many years before. Local affairs were run by a council comprising mayor, aldermen and councillors. The right to vote for election to the council was limited to those of substance in the borough. The elected councillors chose the aldermen and the resultant council elected the mayor, who did not have to be one of their members. They unanimously invited Ralegh to be mayor – their new Squire and a man of prestige.

The issue of the friary was debated. He told them: 'I'm going to remind the Privy Council of the danger from the priests. The Irish princes have been put down – in Munster, at least. The smaller chieftains have either gone away or gone to ground. Only the priests are left. They will be the leaders of the common folk, of the tribes. They are no friends of ours. So I am for knocking it down.'

They accepted his advice that, if it were left standing, it would be a constant source of friction and danger. So it was destroyed.

He had several meetings with the settlers. They had been allotted their farms – or, rather, considerable areas of former farm, now overgrown with weeds and bracken. With financial help from him they had begun stocking them with cattle, sheep and chicken. Ploughing was proceeding and they had been given seed. He had another idea which he explained to them. 'There are two crops we might try and cultivate. My men brought them back from Virginia. One is tobacco – this stuff I'm smoking. The warm, damp conditions here may suit it. You don't have the snow and ice that we have in England. The other I will tell you about when I bring samples over.'

He kept a watch on his castle and manor at Lismore, which he looked upon as his main Irish seat. Castles had always appealed to him as symbols of status and power. It needed much restoration but this was in hand. He planned to exploit its potential, particularly the timber from the dense woods around it, but more immediate matters had to be sorted out first.

Bess next saw him shortly before Christmas. It was Mary who broke the news. 'Everyone's busy scurrying around, getting ready for the Spaniards,' she said. 'The Captain of the Guard is over from Ireland mustering troops in Cornwall and

Devon. They are the nearest counties to Spain.'

'Yes,' she replied. 'I do know my geography.'

'What a shame you haven't learnt to spell too, Bess. You really ought to do something about it. He's also fortifying the Isle of Portland. He's its Governor. Do you know where that is?'

'Of course. In Dorset. And it's hardly an island. You can almost jump over to it.'

'The Portlanders wouldn't agree with you,' Mary told her. 'They keep intruders at bay with rocks and clubs. Like the Scots and the Irish. By the way, he's coming to Court in a day or two.'

This was wonderful news. But she must hide her delight. 'It won't make any difference to us,' Bess replied. 'But it might to the Queen.'

'He's a fine-looking man, Bess. I've decided that he'd be my first choice for a husband. Not that I didn't quite like Arthur,' she added hastily. 'But Sir Walter's so tall and imposing in his uniform. And rich. I thought I might do something about it. Mother approves too. You will help me, won't you, Bess?'

This was an unexpected and unwelcome development. Bess was certainly not prepared to comply with the request. But how was she to deal with it? She must take care not to give away any hint of her own feelings. It would be neither convincing nor prudent, and it might even encourage rivalry. She had learnt an elementary lesson in feminine psychology.

'I don't even know the man and he doesn't know me. I've never spoken to him. There's nothing I could do.'

Nor was there. His was only a fleeting visit, a courtesy call on the Queen, to whom he reported the steps he had taken to guard the western approaches to her Realm. Immediately afterwards he went straight back to Ireland, only returning when the Armada was reported to be ready to leave its home bases.

The Court was in a state of apprehension and excitement when it was sighted in the Channel. News came in several times a day on its progress. The Queen was constantly in conference with her chief officers of state, their earlier differences long since forgotten. Ralegh was in and out of Court. Bess heard him express his exasperation at being held back instead of being allowed to put out to sea. To her alarm she saw that

Mary was doing all she could to attract his attention. She need not have worried – then at least. He was absorbed with the business in hand. Suddenly he had gone.

A cheer went up when news of the Spaniards' heavy losses at Calais came through. There was now the threat from Gravelines and Dunkirk where a large army was known to be assembled, under the command of the Prince of Parma, ready to embark for England.

The most collected person in Court throughout this anxious period was the Queen herself. The palace was seething like a disturbed bee-hive with the comings and goings but she remained calm throughout.

At Tilbury, the 20,000 men mustered and assembled for the land forces were under the command of the Earl of Leicester, with Essex as one of his officers. They came from London, Essex and adjoining counties. Of them, the City of London alone furnished 10,000 'for the defence of the City and the Queen's person'. They included the Trainbands (trained bands) of London, comprising civilian volunteers who were drilled and exercised in military duties in their spare time. They were 'officered mainly by Gentlemen of the Artillery Garden' (The Honourable Artillery Company) 'the best disciplined of all the trainbands'. One of them was Captain Martin Bond, Captain of the Aldersgate Ward Company in London's North Regiment – the family who gave their name to London's Bond Street.

They marched into camp at Tilbury 'with cheerful countenances, courageous words and gestures, leaping and dancing'. Others had earlier joined the Fleet.

The Queen issued orders to the Court for the following day. 'We'll go to Whitehall for tonight. Tomorrow we will go down river to Tilbury to inspect the troops.'

They embarked on the State barge at Whitehall steps, escorted by the Yeomen of the Guard. Crowds lined the banks of the Thames as she made her stately journey past The Tower, Isle of Dogs and Barking Reach to Tilbury. There, in a dress of white velvet, she mounted a white gelding and proceeded to where the troops were drawn up, one page holding her reins, another her steel helmet. She was met by the Commander-in-Chief, her old favourite, the Earl of Leicester, accompanied by Sir John Norris, 'the most accomplished soldier of the day', and other commanders, including Essex. She carried out her review and, after a short service, departed for the night with close attendants to stay in a house conveniently near.

The next day she returned to the camp and addressed the men in words Bess committed to heart: 'Let tyrants fear. I have always so behaved myself that, under God, I have placed my chiefest strength and safeguard in the loyal hearts and goodwill of my subjects; and therefore I am come among you, as you see, resolved, in the midst and heat of the battle, to live or die amongst you all, to lay down for my God, and for my kingdom, and for my people, my honour and my blood, even in the dust. I know I have the body of a weak and feeble woman, but I have the heart and stomach of a King and a King of England too, and think foul scorn that Parma, or Spain, or any Prince of Europe should dare to invade the borders of my Realm; to which, rather than any dishonour shall grow by me, I will myself take up arms, I myself will be your General, Judge and Rewarder of every one of your virtues in the field . . . .'

Bess's heart filled with pride. How could any nation fail, she thought, with such a leader?

Their stay in Essex continued for a week. News came of the enemy's final annihilation with small loss to England in ships and men (other than the sickness which always raged at sea). There were more bells, bonfires and rejoicings throughout the Kingdom.

The troops dispersed and Leicester hurried back up North. He had not time even to say his farewells to the Queen but wrote her a letter on the way expressing his wishes for her good health and a long life. The Queen and her retinue returned to London. They had barely arrived when news came of Leicester's unexpected death. Bess was there when the Queen was told of the death of her former lover, her 'sweet Robyn' with whom she had for so long been so close.

'Ma'am, we have terrible news for you. Please brace yourself for the worst.'

She showed acute alarm. 'Is it the Armada back? Or something happened to Lord Essex?'

'Neither of those, Ma'am. No. My Lord Leicester is dead.'

She said nothing for a few moments. There was silence. Then: 'Thank you for breaking this so gently. Now leave me, all of you. I will call when I want you.'

They filed quietly out.

The Court was unable to gauge the depth of her reaction to this loss. There were the victory celebrations to be arranged. To be in the centre of activity, the Court took up residence in Somerset House. The scenes of jollification included tournaments – still in the vogue – cock-fighting and bear-baiting, horse-races and games. It culminated in a service at St Paul's Cathedral, an impressive building, even without its spire which had been destroyed by fire some years before. (Six decades later it was to be burnt down completely in the Great Fire and replaced by Wren's domed magnificence – itself to be in the centre of an enemy inferno.)

Bess described the occasion to her brother. 'You should have been there, Arthur. The Court retinue alone must have been half a mile long, stretching the whole length of Fleet Street and half the Strand. The Queen led in the State Coach drawn by two white horses. I was in the next coach. The crowd was more dense than anyone had seen before. We passed the beautiful St Bride's Church with the four curious pinnacles on its tower. We could hear further to the east the Bow Bells of St Mary-le-Bow in Cheapside "the most famous peal in all Christendom", ringing their heads off. The Bishop of London received her at St Paul's. She knelt, rose and as she went inside said a prayer out aloud. She gave the address herself. She told us how grateful we should all be for the victory, how brave and steadfast everyone had been, and how we should thank God for deliverance from slavery to the Spaniards. We would have fought them on land, she said, till the last man and woman dropped dead. No price was too great for freedom, freedom for ourselves and our children, freedom from tyrants especially. But our brave sailors had seen them flee. We must never relax our vigilance. There would be more testing times, and the Nation must never fail. Thanks be to God.'

'She's a remarkable woman,' said Arthur. 'But like so many of them, sooner or later she might go too far.'

'How can you say such a thing? She's marvellous. Anyway, we dined in state with the Bishop. When we came out, the crowds were as thick as ever, cheering and shouting. The guards had to force a passage down the street. Our procession was lit with torches as we went back to Somerset House. It was a day I wouldn't have missed for anything.'

'Don't forget it was I who got you your place in Court.'

The Queen never missed a main chance financially. To ensure payment of Leicester's outstanding debts she instructed the Privy Council to confiscate all his land in Warwickshire, including Kenilworth Castle which she well knew from ceremonial and other visits in earlier days – when William Shakespeare as a youth might have been among the fair-goers.

Ralegh and Sir Richard Grenville were away at sea. They had been deployed to watch the western approaches in case of a further attempt at invasion. But the Armada was still struggling down the west coast of Ireland, so they returned to port.

Ralegh paid a fleeting visit to the Court. The antagonism between himself and Essex immediately flared. Whereas Ralegh had had a role, albeit minimal, against the Armada, Essex had been cheated of any active part whatever in the battle. This rankled. In the hearing of the Court attendants but not of the Queen, he taunted him. 'Skulking in Ireland and Cornwall, while the rest of us prepared for the Spaniards. Very wise.'

Ralegh made to draw his sword but was restrained. 'That's not so, and you know it. I'll be at your service tomorrow at first light, and teach you a lesson.'

'That suits me admirably,' replied Essex. As Ralegh turned and left, Essex exclaimed to the company: 'He'll regret this, you'll see.' At the thought of a duel, Bess was scared. But she need not have worried. The Privy Council stepped in and forbade it on penalty of both being sent to The Tower. The Queen never knew about it.

7

'All This For A Song'

Portugal was England's oldest ally. They had been competitors in world exploration, in which Portugal had led everybody. The threat to England was from Catholic Spain, now by far the most powerful and wealthy nation. Spain had annexed Portugal and their leader, Don Antonio, was trying to stage a comeback. In 1589 the Privy Council, the Queen in the Chair, decided on reprisal. A combined force of two hundred ships and sixteen thousand soldiers was to land in Portugal and reinstate Don Antonio. Sir Francis Drake and Sir John Norris were to be the Fleet and Land Commanders. Ralegh was given permission to take part.

The force assembled at Plymouth. 'Call them soldiers,' he said scathingly. 'They're the scum of the earth – court idlers, jail-birds, ruffians and tramps.'

Essex had been forbidden to get involved. However, he was determined not to miss this chance of adventure and glory, so he rode in disguise to Plymouth. He was on the high seas with his friend, Sir Roger Williams, second-in-command of the infantry so-called, before the Queen's order stopping his departure could be executed.

The Queen was furious. 'This is outright disobedience. I don't blame Essex. It's the fault of Drake and Norris. They can pay for this expedition out of their own pockets. As for Williams, I'll have his head off.'

Word of this came to Williams. His reaction was untroubled. 'I have no doubt the darling will have got over it by the time we get back.'

Drake and Ralegh, with their experience of combined operations, advised that the best plan of attack would be to sail up the Tagus, forcing their way through any naval defences and storm Lisbon, the capital and seat of Government. Essex, whose inclusion in the council of war was a disaster, over-bore their advice. He urged an assault from the landward side. He was backed by Don Antonio, a feeble leader at the best of times. Norris went along with the plan.

It failed disastrously, as Ralegh later reported.

No Elizabethan set off on enterprises with exclusively altruistic motives. There was always the ulterior intention of personal profit. Ralegh captured a well-laden ship as a prize but to sail it back he had to use some of Williams's men. When they docked at Plymouth, an argument arose.

'Thank you, Sir Roger,' said Ralegh, 'for the use of your men. I will take over now.'

'Take over what?'

'Why, the ship. My prize.'

'That prize is mine,' Williams insisted. 'If it hadn't been for my men it would never have reached here. It belongs to me. My Lord Essex will confirm it.'

But Essex was no help. He had gone to ground, fearing the Queen's wrath. He was nowhere to be seen when Ralegh went to the Court to report to the Queen. Williams had better sense than to press his claim with her threat hanging uncertainly, even if not seriously intended, over his head.

Her first question before Ralegh could begin his account of the operation was: 'Where's Essex? He's going to get a piece of my mind when I see him.'

'Well, Ma'am, I must put a word in for him, although you know what I think of him. The attack was a complete failure – a farce almost. They made a bad plan. He's impetuous. But it was a brave attack. My Lord Essex deserves credit. He was the first to land. He leapt out of the boat and waded ashore with water up to his shoulders. What an example to the troops. They hardly met any opposition. If it had not been for our rabble of soldiers and the numbers who deserted or were sick, it might have succeeded. At least we sank a great many ships, two hundred in the Tagus alone, and took sixty prisoners.'

'What about Don Antonio?' she asked.

'The Portuguese have no time for him, as I said. He's no leader.'

He did not consider it relevant to add that his own share of the booty had been some £4,000.

'Well done. By the way, I spotted one of the fellows from your ship wearing a rather attractive embroidered waistcoat, obviously a prize. It's just what I've been looking for. I'll send someone to relieve him of it. But that needn't be your concern. Before you go,' she added, smiling, 'I have a little present to show my affection for you.'

She handed him a gold chain. He bowed and said, 'Ma'am, I am overwhelmed. Whatever I do, it is with no thought of reward. I will treasure this always.'

He took his leave of her and strutted out with great satisfaction. He had been rehabilitated. He was once more in her good books.

Bess happened to be about to go in, having been summoned to attend on the Queen. As he came out their eyes met, his penetrating, hers wondering. He stopped, transfixed. She saw his look of astonishment. They said nothing – for a moment. Then he collected himself.

'I haven't seen you in Court before. Have you been here long?'

'Quite a while, Sir Walter. But you wouldn't have noticed me. There are several of us.'

'Not noticed you indeed,' he exclaimed. 'How could I possibly not? May I ask – what is your name, my dear?'

'My dear,' she thought. 'This must be a dream.' She told him, 'Elizabeth Throckmorton. Most people call me "Bess".'

'What an attractive name, "Bess". It suits you. If I might ask another question – have you many friends in Court?'

'Quite a few. Lady Mary Darcy is my best friend. She's a cousin of mine. Then there's . . . .'

He laughed. 'No, I mean men friends.'

She smiled. 'No, Sir Walter. As you must know, we are under oath to her Majesty. We are forbidden to have close friends, if that is what you mean. Not that I have wanted one,' she added hastily.

He felt a great desire to kiss her. There was nobody else there. But that would have been disastrous. He must pass it off as though nothing had happened.

We must have another word sometime,' he said. He looked at her for a few seconds, smiled, then departed, head high, swinging along proudly, gold chain dangling from his hand.

She, for her part, was overjoyed. A new world had opened

up, perhaps, for her. The rest of the day she walked on air.
So did he.

But the Queen was pining for Essex, who was well aware that biding his time would increase her obsession for him beyond endurance. He knew this from her response a year or so before, when she had made a curious offer, couched in cautious terms, hinting at matrimony. He had put her off by referring her attentions to her former favourite Leicester. Sure enough, it was not long before she begged him with scarcely veiled humility to rejoin the Court. He swaggered in and came straight to the point. 'I gather you gave that renegade a gold chain. He'd already feathered his nest. He wraps you round his little finger.'

'That's not fair,' she objected. 'I wouldn't let anyone do that – not even you. I'll give you two gold chains if you like.'

Re-established, he could again throw his weight about even more outrageously than before.

Ralegh was already in trouble. His ship *The Roebuck* had intercepted, boarded and looted a Flemish ship. Had it been Spanish it would have been fair game. This understandably gave offence to the Flemings. A diplomatic incident was only averted by an order from the Privy Council to reimburse the losers. Ralegh protested vehemently:

'The Council must be out of their senses. They were nothing but Spanish goods sailing under a spurious Flemish flag. These people are Spaniards in disguise. The Dutch are only interested in themselves and their profit.'

This reaction did nothing to endear him to the Establishment. He had to pay up.

To pile on the agony, his private fleet also seized two French ships, which by no stretch of the imagination could have been deemed enemy vessels. The Privy Council once again avoided embarrassment, but only just, by ordering him to return the products of this escapade and compensate his victims.

Here were two sources of potential friction with two friendly powers. The Queen might have overlooked them, seeing that her Council had taken appropriate action. She had regard to the considerable gains she made from pillages of enemy property. It was not always possible to draw a precise dividing line.

But Essex would not let it rest or allow an opportunity like this to go by without all its possibilities being squeezed out.

'Look what the fellow's up to now. He'll have us at war with France and the Low Countries. He's out of hand, an utter menace.'

'I wouldn't put it as forcefully as that,' she protested.

'It's dead serious, believe me. This Court is not big enough to hold the two of us. Either he goes or I do,' he expostulated.

'I will have a word with him,' she replied meekly.

'Give it to him straight and hard,' he urged.

Her rebuke fell between the two extremes. Ralegh was in no mood to compromise.

'It's Essex again. I know it. He's always trying to trip me, the stripling. He should be put firmly in his place.'

'You are speaking of a Peer of the Realm, I would remind you,' she said reprovingly. 'You get above yourself sometimes. You had better go and reconsider your unreasonable attitude.'

He did. He bowed and swept out, pausing only to say a terse farewell to Bess. She had been sewing at the far end of the room during this heated exchange and was anxiously awaiting its outcome.

Having packed up his requirements at Durham House he again departed for Ireland. The Court, except for a minority, expressed approval. He had been dismissed, as they understood it from Essex, and banished to Ireland. They said to one another: 'My Lord Essex has again driven him out of Court to Ireland. He asked for it.'

When Ralegh heard this allegation, he denied it emphatically. He had gone to Ireland 'to see to his prizes'.

Action was the infallible antidote to frustration. He set about surveying his lands and checking up on progress to date. Botany had been a hobby of his. He never failed to bring back, or have brought back, from his expeditions some exotic tree, plant or vegetable that might be of medicinal, culinary or general use at home. Many failed in the strange habitat. But some flourished. He planted cedars in Cork and yellow wallflowers and a species of cherry from the Azores in several places.

He took the opportunity now of implementing the promise he had made on his previous visit: to introduce the settlers to an unusual species of vegetable from Virginia.

They were reassured to see him again. They had felt isolated, opening up their farms in hostile territory. The quiet conditions could revert.

'So you thought I had deserted you, did you?' he said to them. 'Far from it. I am keen to make this a successful colony and I want to see you flourishing. I have brought over the plant I spoke to you about. It's a sort of apple, but it doesn't grow on trees. It is in fact a vegetable and grows in the earth. You plant it a few inches deep – not too deep – depending on the soil and in three months it multiplies ten times or more. It's very popular among the natives – and the settlers like yourselves – in Virginia, I can tell you.'

They examined these objects dubiously. They were unlike any they had seen before – like brown apples. 'What do you call them? How precisely do you sow them?' they enquired.

'They're called "potatoes",' he explained. 'Place them in trenches a foot wide and nine inches deep. Space them a foot or so apart and cover them with earth to form a ridge. Or if the ground is hard and rough, just pop them in and cover them with earth ridges. They must be earthed up, otherwise they're green and poisonous. You can plant them early in spring, if they're an early variety, or the main crop a little later.'

'And then what?' they asked.

'When you dig them up, you can boil them, bake, roast, fry them, mash them up – anything you like.'

They were handed out and his instructions were followed. The first to dig his up omitted to observe the directions. He washed off the soil and, recalling that they were said to be like apples, proceeded to bite one. The taste was most unpleasant. He spat it out and decided that the crop was, as he thought it would be, a waste of time and effort. The others, however, persevered. After cooking them, they were agreeably surprised by their delicious flavour and filling capacity. The potato in Ireland, to become its staple crop, was born.

Ralegh ventured to Dublin, a journey not so hazardous as it had been. Peace, for the time being at least, prevailed beyond as well as within the Pale. An object was to renew acquaintance with one of his fellow combatants earlier at Smerwick, Edmund Spenser, Secretary to the Lord Deputy (now Sir William FitzWilliam), at Kilcolman. He was making his name as a poet – a popular pastime in that era.

'I thought I'd look you up, Edmund,' Ralegh said. 'I don't profess to write poetry to your high standards, but I have a few efforts you might like to look at.'

'Delighted,' was the reply. 'You really are an extraordinary fellow, Walter: soldier, mariner – you notice I didn't say pirate – I know your quick temper and sharp sword.' They laughed. 'Also a bit of a botanist. A landowner. Now poet. You amaze me. You must be an expert juggler too with all this going on. Let me see what you've written.'

'Here's an epitaph I did for Sidney, my great friend and yours.' (Sir Philip Sidney). 'Fatally wounded, dying with thirst but, given a cup of water, handed it to one of his men lying wounded beside him: "Take it, my friend. Thy necessity is yet greater than mine".'

'Valour indeed,' replied Spenser. He read the first verse aloud:

> 'To praise thy life, or wail thy worthy death,
> And want thy wit, thy wit high, pure, divine,
> Is far beyond the power of mortal line
> Nor any one hath worth that draweth breath.'

He read the next fourteen verses to himself. When he had finished, he commented: 'Yes. I like it. It shows promise. He would have liked it too.' He laughed. 'No. I'm joking. It's first rate. Now I'll show you some stuff I'm writing. It's not nearly as good as yours. I thought I might call it *The Fairy Queen*. It's really about you know who.'

'I know her well. Too well for my health sometimes,' Ralegh said ruefully.

'Oh! What's this about being kicked out of Court?' Spenser asked.

'That's rubbish. A rumour spread by Essex. I know we had our differences. The Queen and I, that is.'

'Tell me about these differences.'

'They're the usual sort of ups and downs. It's down at the moment.' He went on to relate recent events at Court.

Spenser listened attentively. 'That will be excellent copy for my poem. I'll use it, if I may. Naturally, I will use false names and allegories. And please keep me posted with the sequels. That will help the flow.'

'I'll do that. But be careful. I don't want to land in any more bother. I'll tell you what: when I go back, which should be before Christmas, come with me, and I'll arrange an Audience.

You can then tell her what you've written. She loves poetry – particularly if it's about herself.'

While he was in Dublin, he made a point of button-holing FitzWilliam. True to form, he told him all the mistakes he was making in his administration of Ireland – lack of support for the settlers, not being firm enough with the kerns and so forth. As a large landowner, he could command attention. But this infuriated the Lord Deputy, who told him so in unmistakable language.

Ralegh was unrepentant. He resumed land reclamation, draining bogs and planting trees. The work on Lismore Castle was going well. It promised to be a fine building when fully restored.

But many of his tenants, taking advantage of his eclipse at home, had stolen back quietly to the West Country, abandoning their farms. He was subjected to various pinpricks by way of illegal infringements of his property and business interests. In spite of his protests, the Lord Deputy would not give him the help he sought. He told his kinsman Sir George Carew, President of Munster:

'If in Ireland they don't consider me worth respect, they're deceiving themselves. Incidentally, the Queen thinks you're longing to see her. So do so.'

Ralegh was as good as his word. He took Spenser to Court and introduced him to the Queen. She received him graciously. 'I have heard many people speak of your poetry, Mr Spenser. Perhaps you would like to read me a little.'

'Willingly, Ma'am. I must say how grateful I was to Sir Philip Sidney, my first sponsor. Now Sir Walter has kindly taken his place. I will read some of one I have written entitled: "Colin Clout's come home again", which I have dedicated to him:

    His song was all a lamentable lay
    Of great unkindness and of usage hard,
    Of Cynthia, the Lady of the Sea,
    Which from her presence faultless him debarred,
    And ever and anon, with singults* rife,
    He cried out, to make his undersong,

---

* – sighs

'Ah, my love's queen and goddess of my life!
Who shall me pity, when thou dost me wrong.'

She was highly amused. 'I won't ask who Cynthia is – or the homecomer, Walter! Have you written anything else?'

'I have started another, Ma'am. I'm calling it *The Fairy Queen* – it's about the Legend of the Knight of the Red Cross.'

'What a charming title. Would you please read me some.'

He read the first few verses as far as the following:

> 'Upon a great adventure he was bound,
> That greatest Gloriana to him gave,
> (That greatest glorious Queen of Fairy land)
> To win him worship, and her grace to have,
> Which of all earthly things he did most crave.
> And ever as he rode, his heart did yearn
> To prove his puissance in battle brave
> Upon his foe, and his new force to learn;
> Upon his foe, a dragon horrible and stern.'

She was entranced. Ralegh was delighted.

'You have set it down so well,' she enthused. 'You must carry on the good work. I know how hard put to it you poets are. When villains like Sir Walter here are coining it, you poor fellows sit in a garret day and night writing. I am going to grant you a pension of £50 a year, which should be a help.'

'Ma'am, you are too generous. I cannot thank you enough.'

'Water, send for Lord Burghley. He should come and hear some of this for himself.'

He was duly summoned and entered rather resignedly.

'Listen, Spirit,' she told him, 'to more fascinating verse than you have ever heard before. Read a few verses again, Mr Spenser, if you please.'

He did so. Burghley listened carefully and at the end commented: 'It sounds acceptable to me. This gentleman obviously has talent.'

'Acceptable, talent,' she repeated. 'It's stupendous. It will survive for all time. I've awarded him £50 a year to help him along. Please see to it.'

'What? All this for a song? I can't believe it,' he protested.

'More than a song, my Lord,' she replied, 'an English treasure.'

After leaving the Queen, Ralegh said to his friend:

'Just wait here a moment, will you? I have some business to see to.' He had been looking out for Bess and she had just come into the room. He went over to her.

'My dear, I have missed you so much. I daren't write. How are you after all this time?'

'Very well, thank you, Sir Walter.' She had wondered if he might have had second thoughts and ignored her. She need not have worried.

'Listen,' he said, looking round carefully to make sure nobody was looking (other than Spenser, who didn't matter):

'To write would be too risky. But see if you can steal away to the backstairs as soon as you've settled her Majesty after dinner and I will be there. I'll be dressed like one of the servants.'

'I'll do my best.'

They swiftly went their own ways, he taking with him Spenser who told him, feelingly, 'I can't say how much I owe you for this, Walter. I'll see you get a suitable tribute. It was indeed a most rewarding afternoon. For both of us, may I say? It looks as though there might be something for you too, eh?'

'Please don't breathe a word about it,' he urged. 'There would be heaven knows what to pay if anyone suspected. They're a vicious bunch on the whole, with a few exceptions. This is no primrose path, I promise you. How it will end I really don't know.'

'I will be silent as the grave. But it will be just the theme for my *Fairy Queen*. Which reminds me,' he added, chuckling, 'what about that poem you slipped into Lady Laiton's pocket not so long ago? It started:

> "Lady farewell whom I in silence serve
> Would God thou knewest the depth of my desire,
> Then might I hope, though nought I can deserve,
> Some drop of grace would quench my scorching fire".

'That's hot stuff, is it not? And it finishes:

> "But yet amongst those Cares, which Cross my Rest.
>
> This Comfort Grows, I think I love thee best".'

Ralegh's reply was short: 'That's long since over and forgotten.'

From the height of elation, Ralegh could as easily fall to the depth of despair. His pedestal status with the Queen had taken a knock. His achievements had been considerable but a coveted accolade, to be sworn a privy councillor, eluded him. He could not understand why. It is not easy to see one's own short-comings in the eyes of others. He often leapt before he looked. He set down his frustration in a poem which includes the following lines:

> Whom care forewarns, ere age and winter cold,
> To haste me hence, to find my fortune's fold.

This must be his urgent quest – his fortune's fold.

That night, when the company were absorbed in their usual card and other games, Bess crept down the backstairs and paused in the shadows, away from the light of the lanterns round the court-yard. He straightaway emerged from a passage nearby leading into the garden shrubbery.

'Along here, my dear,' he whispered. Taking her arm he led her along the dark pathway to a seat in the arbour beyond. The touch of his hand was almost more than she could bear. She shivered.

'You must be cold, my sweet,' he said. 'Here, have my cloak round you.' – which gave him the excuse to put his arm round her shoulders. Her head nestled on his shoulder.

The shivering was not from cold. He for his part had never known the longing he now felt.

'I am so happy,' she said. 'So happy, that words cannot describe it. You must have met many girls more attractive than I. Why are you making this fuss of me?'

'Because I love you. I have only just got to know you, but that is enough. I have never met anyone who had this effect on me. I feel as weak as water – that's funny. That's what the Queen calls me sometimes. "Water". At other times, she has other names. So have the rest of them.' He laughed.

'Don't take any notice of them,' she said indignantly. 'But you weak? I can't believe that.'

'I wouldn't have believed it myself. But that's the effect you have on me. There's only one cure for it!'

He held her more closely and kissed her gently. He felt a strange tenderness. For her, it was the heaven she had dreamt of. Her lips were soft and yielding and for a few moments they were in another world.

They were brought to their senses by the sound of voices and of footsteps crossing the lawn. They kept very still. They could see the dim outline of two figures which passed close to them and on through the garden, their voices receding until all again was silent.

But the spell had been broken. They became alive to their danger. To be caught would be disastrous.

'My darling Bess,' he said urgently, 'we must go back before they miss us. I promise you my eternal love, I swear.'

'And I have loved you,' she replied, 'ever since I first saw you. Long before you noticed me. So you have my heart already to do with it what you will.'

He squeezed her hand. 'We must see one another again soon. I will find a way. Trust me. I will do all I can.'

A quick kiss, and they went in by different ways.

Only her shining eyes would have given her away had anyone sufficiently observant noticed them.

Meanwhile, with the Queen Essex could do no wrong. She gratified his every whim. Old enough to be his grand-mother, she was infatuated. He took full advantage of it. None of the Court dare cross him.

One evening she called him over and said, 'We'll have cards in my room tonight, shall we? Let's go up now.'

'I'll be with you in a moment. You go on. I have something urgent to sort out.'

The Queen's Musicians had been playing a pavan. Bess loved dancing. She moved gracefully to the measured rhythm of lute, recorder, trumpet and pipes. It was about to give way to a cushion dance. This involved vigorous capers and certain amorous advances. He was resolved to take part. A particular young lady had attracted his attention.

The Queen withdrew. The music commenced, its metre speeded up. Bess took her place. He joined her. As the dance proceeded and the excitement increased, he edged nearer and nearer to her. She tried to avoid contact but he pressed ever more closely. He persisted despite her lack of reciprocation. She was in a dilemma. He was a good dancer. That was beside the point. To snub someone of such standing, particularly the Queen's favourite, would be unthinkable. But she must do nothing which gave the impression of leading him on.

As the dance finished, he seized her arm. 'Your name is Bess, is it not? Bess Throckmorton.'

She nodded. He whispered in her ear: 'You are the most beautiful maid in this room, do you know? We must get better acquainted. There's no time like the present. Get your wrap and we'll go out for a little fresh air. It's stuffy in here, don't you think?'

How to counter this unwanted invitation taxed her wit. How was she to be firm but give him no cause for complaint? She replied: 'I must stay here. The Queen could call at any time.'

She could see that some of the others were eyeing them curiously, mischievously. They knew well what was happening.

'You needn't worry about her. The old girl's in her room, waiting to play cards. She can go on waiting.'

She thought again. 'But I daren't go out, my Lord, I promised her I wouldn't stir from this room.'

He nearly overflowed with frustration. He was not used to being rebuffed. He managed to restrain himself. 'Very well. But look forward to hearing from me again, my dear.'

There was no one she could turn to for help. The searching questions put to her as soon as the Earl had left to join the Queen she parried. One or two ribald suggestions she ignored. When she told Mary of her misgivings, all she did was laugh and say: 'Lucky you.' She felt she must somehow tell Ralegh.

She succeeded in having a quick word with him on one of his fleeting visits. He was furious.

'I'll murder the fellow, Queen or no Queen. I'll challenge him to fight it out. This time they won't stop us. I'll see he doesn't do that again.' She tried to restrain him, but he brushed her protestations aside and said tenderly: 'You mean all the world to me, my sweetheart.'

'Do be careful,' she pleaded. She wished now she hadn't told him. 'Please don't do anything rash.'

But it proved not to be necessary. It would be good copy for Spenser.

Sir Francis Walsingham had been sorely tried, as had Lord Burghley, over the occasion and aftermath of the Queen of Scots' execution. In April, 1590, he died. It had been largely due to his vigilance and intelligence network that the plots against Queen Elizabeth's life had been discovered. This, and the anxiety of the Spanish Armada, had led to his subsequent illness and hastened his death. He was replaced as Secretary of State by Sir Robert Cecil, Burghley's son. He was unprepossessing in appearance, small in stature (Elizabeth nicknamed him 'Pygmy', much to his disgust), deformed, but a shrewd and cunning operator. Government would be in his hands for the next twenty-two years.

A thunderbolt struck the Court, with wide reverberations. Essex, with neither consent nor knowledge of the Queen, suddenly married Walsingham's daughter, Sir Philip Sidney's widow Frances. The Queen's fury with them both knew no bounds. She was distraught. Her trusted lover had deserted her for another. He was banished from the Court – not that in the atmosphere then prevailing he would have wished or dared to show his face. But he was involved later that year in a military expedition to Rouen. Owing to his indecisiveness the engagement was inconclusive.

While Essex was abroad Arthur, not knowing of anything amiss, sent Bess some letters to pass on to Essex, which she duly did.

Ostracism lasted six months. Ralegh romped back on the stage with no competitor and was a source of solace to the rejected wooer. He commiserated with the Queen and endorsed her critical comments on his vanquished rival. He was cock-a-hoop. This could have contributed to his undoing. He decided to follow up his success by cajoling from her the prize on which he had long set his heart. She had asked him one day: 'Tell me, when will you cease to be a beggar?'

'When your gracious Majesty ceases to be a benefactor,' he retorted.

'You're a mercenary rogue,' she replied, laughing.

Acquisitiveness was a characteristic of the Elizabethans from their leader down. His quest was for a castle in this country. Since his visit to Sherborne that had been his first choice. It would give him a seat of status and beauty comparable with any in the land. He had angled for it at every suitable opportunity, but bided his final cast for the right moment. This had now come.

'Ma'am,' he explained at the end of a card game she had won, 'here is something which may interest you.'

It was an exquisite jewel, a gold brooch set with rubies,

diamonds and pearls, one of his prizes from a captured Spanish carrick. It was worth in the region of £250. It was gleaming and glittering and Elizabeth was fascinated.

'It's incredible,' she exclaimed. 'What are you proposing to do with it?'

'It has occurred to me, your Majesty, that it could serve as an inducement – if I may use that word – to persuade the Bishop to part up.'

'Which Bishop?' she asked.

'Why, the Bishop of Salisbury to be sure.'

She exploded with mirth. 'What – that Castle again? And why not? They get away with so much, these Churchmen. Once in the pulpit, it goes to their head. They don't spend a farthing, you tell me, on that noble building. I'll see what I can do.'

She told Burghley of her intentions. He was in no state of health to object, particularly as he could see her mind was made up. He knew nothing of any jewel bait.

Following the Reformation, the manors of Sherborne and adjacent parishes had been leased by the Bishop to the Duke of Somerset, without reservation of rent. They had been recovered in Queen Mary's reign from his assignee on the grounds that the lease had been extorted by undue influence. In 1577 Queen Elizabeth had brought pressure to bear on John Piers, the then Bishop, to lease Sherborne to her, to pass on to one Dr Thomas White. Her assignment to White and the head lease had been later cancelled.

The Bishopric of Salisbury had been vacant since 1589 when Piers had been promoted to Archbishop of York. There had been many seekers after this highly desirable See, as Ralegh well knew from his intelligence sources.

A deal was struck. 'The See of Salisbury is yours,' she told a compliant Churchman, John Caldwell, 'with a small proviso: you will have to lease me Sherborne again. That's only fair. It merely restores the *status quo*.' He could have asked, '*Quo* when and what?' That would have been imprudent. Ralegh had briefed her well.

It would have taken a rare Churchman to have refused such an offer. He was appointed and the lease to the Queen – for ninety-nine years at a rent of £200.16s.1d. per annum – signed, sealed and delivered.

He had no sooner taken up his Seat at Salisbury when the lease was transferred to Ralegh. He saw at once the source of this wily intrigue and realized he had been 'had'. He never forgave himself.

What did that matter? Ralegh was achieving the 'Fortune's Fold' for which his poem had revealed his long hankering.

He wasted no time in getting his brother Adrian over to Durham House.

'I've done it,' he chortled. 'Wonder of wonders. Sherborne Castle is mine – as good as. You remember what I told you?'

'Only too well – and the tumble,' he laughed. 'Congratulations.'

'We'll ride down and have a look at it, as soon as the lawyers have done the paper-work.'

8

'Otherwise My Heart Will Break'

In May, Ralegh was ordered to send a pinnace from Plymouth out to Lord Henry Howard patrolling the Channel entrance, with a warning that Spain had despatched another armada and that it had been sighted off the Scillies. Ralegh himself had to see to the Portsmouth fortifications, for which experience at Portland had qualified him. It turned out to have been a false alarm.

Early in June, the Court were in residence at Nonsuch Palace, in Surrey, the Queen's centre for hunting, a favourite sport of hers, being a keen rider. It was her best-loved country house, set in the midst of wooded parkland, built on the lines of a French Renaissance chateau. It was long, and had castellated battlements and tall, slender chimneys. At either end there were octagonal towers surmounted by onion-shaped turrets and in the centre a like turret.

Bess had had a happy morning, which included arranging the flowers in the Queen's bedroom, Privy Chamber and Presence Chamber. From her childhood she had always loved flowers and had assumed a willing responsibility for them in the palaces.

That evening the Queen was in an excellent humour. Although hunting was not in season, she had had a good morning's ride, her Council had been co-operative, and an enjoyable dinner had followed. Ralegh had performed his Captain of the Guard duties impeccably. She was pleasantly tired after a day of activity.

'I'm having an early night tonight,' she announced. 'I don't wish to be disturbed.'

This gave Ralegh and Bess a reasonably clear field, so long as they used elementary caution. The company were engrossed in dancing, songs and games and did not observe first Ralegh, then Bess, slip quietly away.

It was a warm, starry night with a full moon.

'My brother Adrian would prefer a new moon, I fancy. He would augur something from this, I have no doubt.' Then: 'We'll find somewhere a little more secluded tonight. And we're not tied to time.'

They made for a small wood some distance from the house. The light in the Queen's bedroom was burning. No doubt she was reading, Bess said.

'Maybe that other Robyn – Hood – dallying in the greenwood with Maid Marion,' he offered. 'That would give her food for thought.'

They both thought that a great joke – 'So long as you weren't referring to me!' Bess said, laughing.

All the sweet smells of summer were around them. An owl was hooting from a nearby oak. A cuckoo called, beguiled no doubt by the bright moonlight into thinking it was day. A nightingale started to sing in the wood. She felt overcome by it all, and told him so. 'In such a romantic setting,' she said.

Their feelings, so long suppressed, were too pent up for conversation. He held her close and stroked her hair.

'My darling,' he murmured, 'we are alone, really alone together at last. It has been unbearable not being with you.'

'I feel the same. How I have longed for you, counted the hours,' she replied.

'I love you, my sweetheart. I will take you with me, wherever I go. We must get together, for ever, where no-one can separate us.'

They kissed, at first gently, then passionately. His desire was stronger than her resistance. She made a half-hearted attempt to pull herself away but he smothered her faint cry of protest with kisses. She felt her senses reeling in an over-pouring of the most overwhelming joy she had ever known. She lost all will to resist.

They continued to cling together without speaking. Then they heard a scuffling and scraping in bushes behind them. She started up. But he reassured her. 'Only the deer. Perhaps they've been copying us,' he added, stroking her arm soothingly.

'Oh dear,' she sighed. 'I don't know how it all happened.'

'It had to,' he replied.

They made their way back slowly, hand in hand.

'I'm frightened,' she said, 'a little. But I don't regret what we did one little bit.'

'I will stand by you,' he said, 'come what may. This is the beginning of our story. We will see it through together.'

They went in separately. Their absence had not been observed.

One of Ralegh's drinking companions was Christopher Marlowe, a hard-living, hard-swearing young man of ready wit and a fund of stories. They had much in common and developed a close friendship. They roamed the London streets together and were often at the playhouse. They knew all the leading taverns well. They shared literary interests. They were together one night at The Mermaid Tavern, Bread Street. It was where they frequently forgathered with Ben Jonson and other poets and playwrights. Shakespeare was also a regular customer. Marlowe produced a sheet of paper, saying: 'Cap this if you can, Walter.'

'What is it?' he asked.

'A little thing I've writ on a current theme,' replied Marlowe. 'I'm calling it "Passionate Shepherd to his love".'

'With your experience,' Ralegh commented, 'you've chosen an apt subject. Read me some, and I'll have a go.'

They ordered two more pints and Marlowe began:

> Come live with me and be my love
> And we will all the pleasures prove,
> That hills and valleys, dales and fields,
> And all the craggy mountains yields.

He read six verses in all, the sixth as follows:

> The shepherds' swains shall dance and sing
> For they delight each May morning,
> If these delights thy mind may move,
> Then live with me and be my love.

Ralegh listened intently: 'That's splendid. I can't hope to get anywhere near matching, let alone capping it.'

There was time for another round before he said:

'Here's my feeble effort for the first and last verses of the Nymph's reply to the Shepherd.'

If all the world and love were young,
And truth in every shepherd's tongue,
These pretty pleasures might me move
To live with thee, and be thy love.
But could youth last, and love still breed,
Had joys no date, nor age no need,
Then these delights my mind might move,
To live with thee and be thy love.

Marlowe laughed. 'I like it enormously. But I don't know whether to laugh or cry. You're not all that old, you know. Not past it yet. Cheer up and have some more beer.'

A week later found Ralegh and Essex allied in a rescue mission. Neither were Church or Churchmen lovers. Essex was well-known as a Puritan. Ralegh was still gleeful after the fast one he had pulled over the Bishop of Salisbury, but was not saying too much about it because the legal work had not been transacted. He and Essex joined in coming to the rescue of a noted Puritan clergyman by the name of John Udal. He had unwisely criticized the Bishops in his sermon from the pulpit. He had said, 'They care for nothing but the maintenance of their dignities, even though it entails the damnation of their own souls or those of millions of others.'

The Church establishment were affronted and determined to have the ultimate revenge. He was charged with that excellent State stand-by, High Treason, and sentenced to death.

Essex consulted Ralegh: 'This fellow Udal has been an idiot. But it's monstrous what these fat-bellied bishops have done to him. The Queen won't have anything to do with me, but if you care to speak to her on his behalf, I'll drop her a line to back you up.'

'I agree,' said Ralegh. 'If he were a Catholic it would be different. But he's sound, solid Protestant, absolutely right in all he said but, as you say, a fool to say it. I'll see her tonight.'

Their combined efforts saved Udal. The sentence was commuted to one of imprisonment, perhaps terminating in emigration or exile to the newly discovered Virginia.

The same year, plans were drawn up for assembling a fleet to proceed to the Azores and intercept the Spanish Silver Fleet. Ralegh was appointed Vice-Admiral under Lord Thomas

Howard. Shortly before it was due to sail the Queen sent for him.

'Water, you're not going,' she ordered.

'Ma'am, and why not? It's a great opportunity and I know I would serve my Lord Thomas well.'

'I don't doubt that. But I'm not letting you go. It would be too risky. I'm sending your cousin Sir Richard Grenville in your place.' She was adamant.

It was an expedition that was spoken of as an epic of bravery. The Spanish fleet came upon them when they were anchored at the Azores close inshore, replenishing their supplies of water and taking their sick ashore to recover. Lord Howard managed to slip through the cordon but Grenville refused to abandon the men he had put ashore. His ship, *The Revenge*, was thus the last to weigh anchor. The towering galleons took his wind and he was becalmed in the middle of them. It became a fight to the death which went on for fifteen hours. Wave after wave of boarding assaults were repelled. The ship was awash with carnage from the concentrated cannonade. At the end Grenville was mortally wounded and had no alternative but to surrender. He was taken aboard one of the galleons and died three days later.

It was as well for Bess that Ralegh had been held back from the expedition. Her monthly cycle had stopped. She found herself with no appetite for food. Not knowing quite what was the matter but fearing something very much out of the ordinary, she wondered whom she could ask. The Court physician? No, he was too prying and his discretion could not be relied on. Her mother? She was too far away – and might not be particularly sympathetic. She suddenly thought of her old friend Elizabeth, the former Lady Elizabeth Brooke, now married to Privy Council Secretary, Sir Robert Cecil, Burghley's son, and living near Blackfriars.

She decided to act when the Queen enquired kindly after her health and said, 'My dear, you're not looking your usual self these days. You're pale and listless and not eating properly. I'll send the physician to examine you. He's very good, you know.'

'A very good spy too,' she thought. 'Ma'am,' she replied, 'thank you ever so much but I'm all right. Only a bit of a cold. It will soon get better.'

'Very well. But if it doesn't we must do something about it.

Vital to look after our loyal maids in waiting. I have such faith in you. You are one of my most trusted girls.'

Bess received this accolade with mixed feelings, but betrayed no sign of anxiety. She could be tough and determined when it was called for. She hurried to see her friend that same day. As soon as they had exchanged greetings, she explained her problem, also stressing the need for secrecy.

'Naturally, my dear Bess. I would not dream of letting you down. I won't even tell my husband. Indeed, he would be one of the last I would tell. The fat would undoubtedly be in the fire.'

'Why, whatever do you mean?' Bess asked.

'I mean, my little innocent, that it wouldn't surprise me – don't be shocked at what I'm going to say – if you were not about to have a baby.'

'What? That's terrible. However could that have happened?'

'I feel you would be the one to answer that question, my dear, not I,' Elizabeth replied drily.

'Whatever shall I do? What will the Queen say? She'll have me in the Tower.' She was utterly overcome.

'I won't ask who the lucky man was. But you had better tell him and make sure he pays up.'

'I'm too afraid to tell him.'

'Why? It's his doing as much as yours. You do as I say, and see him as soon as you possibly can. I can't give you any medical advice, obviously. But I believe this sick feeling will pass after a while. You'll have to think up a good excuse to leave Court while you're having it – in fact, before the signs become too apparent.'

That evening, she whispered to Ralegh that they must have an urgent talk. He half guessed, horrified, what it was probably about, so by the time they met he had thought out a scheme.

'My darling Bess, I said I would stand by you and I will. The first thing we must do – what I have wanted to do all along – is get married. It's only fair to our little one. I know a clergyman who'll do it. He can be trusted to keep his mouth shut – unlike some. Then we must get you away – but leave that to the last minute. You couldn't be away too long. They would suspect something. On the other hand, you must go before it becomes too obvious.'

'I'm so frightened,' she said.

'What – a strong-minded young woman like you frightened? Nonsense. You mustn't be. Unless you mean frightened of the Queen?'

'Yes, that. And having it.'

'You must be cheerful,' he urged. 'Remember I will never let you down. I'll make you up a mixture the American natives use, to see if it helps. Take it at night when you go to bed. Get yourself as hot as you can to sweat it out.'

His measures failed to have the desired effect. At any moment the cause of her disability would become apparent.

Mary had likewise been concerned with her looks and low spirits. 'Are you sure you're all right, Bess?' she asked. 'Several people have remarked on it – including one or two with rather nasty tongues.'

'They would. All I need is some time off. I'm overtired, that's about it. If anybody else says anything, tell them it's no more than that, Mary,' she implored.

'Very well. As you say. But I'm not at all happy about you.'

In her tribulation she was comforted by the assurance of Ralegh's support. When all was said and done, that was what really mattered. It had its bright side. It would have brought them together more intimately than she could ever have thought possible.

He made all the necessary arrangements. They were married in secret. After the brief ceremony, he kissed her and said, 'My Bess – Lady Ralegh.'

She returned to the Court. Her brother must be told as soon as he could be contacted. She and Arthur had never kept secrets from one another. This was a case where, although she could not have discussed symptoms, he might be able to help the cover-up. On 19 November, she called in to see him at his house in Mile End.

'Arthur, I have something important to tell you.'

'It must be serious for you to come specially, Bess. What's the problem.'

'I'm married.'

'You're jesting!' he replied.

'No, I'm deadly serious. We were married the day before yesterday.'

'Whoever to?'

'You'd never guess. Walter Ralegh.'

'That's the most astonishing thing I've ever heard. Married? Ralegh? And we knew nothing about it. Have you told mother?'

'No, not yet. I haven't told anybody.'

'What about the Queen?'

'She doesn't know. And she mustn't, either,' she added.

'I should say not – phew! Why all the hurry, anyway?'

She paused, then said: 'What do you think?'

He was flabbergasted. 'I would never have believed it possible. What could have come over you? – perhaps not a very sensible question.'

'I love him, Arthur. I have loved him from when I first saw him. I adore him.'

'At least he did the honourable thing,' he said, doubtfully.

'He loves me too, I know it.'

'Well, that's a blessing anyway. What about dowry?'

'It has never been mentioned.'

'That doesn't sound like Ralegh,' he commented. 'He worships the shekels. And spends them as soon as he gets them. Or even before he gets them. So I hear.'

'So do you, Arthur.'

'Yes,' he agreed. 'I suppose we all do. We pawn to live, half the time. The question is, where do we go from here? I will do all I can, you can rest assured of that. When's it due?'

'Late in March.'

'You must have it in my house here. That will be far enough out of London – a bare mile or so – but accessible. We'll find somewhere for you to stay in the meantime. Make an excuse – or better still, see my doctor and he can write to the Court saying you've been taken ill and mustn't be moved. I'll collect your things. We'll try that. Meanwhile, I must go and see Ralegh. We must draw up a settlement for you.'

'I am most grateful, Arthur. I knew I could rely on you.'

'As always – Lady Ralegh.'

Ten days later, Arthur went to see Ralegh. He had returned to Durham House from his Lord Lieutenant's duties in Cornwall and a check on Cornwall and Devon's coast defences. His return had been delayed by Stannary Court duties. As Lord Warden of the Stannaries, he was required to sit in judgement in suits arising from the tin mines. These cases involved such matters as disputes among the tin miners themselves, squabbles with owners of land adjacent to the mines, boundary disputes, sale price of tin and so forth. The Court sat on a tor on Dartmoor, and as presiding Judge his seat by ancient prerogative – uncomfortable duty, rather – was a high, flat rock of granite. The Court sat in the open whatever the weather or time of year. He could not get back to London quickly enough.

'I believe you may remember me, Sir Walter. I am an occasional Court visitor, and we did meet on one occasion.'

'My dear fellow, of course I know you. Throckmorton. I know of you too as a most affectionate brother in whom my darling Bess has the utmost faith. With sound reason, I have not the slightest doubt. I can, of course, guess why you have come.'

'I have been wondering how I can help,' Arthur explained. 'Bess must have the baby in my house at Mile End.'

'I cannot thank you too much. I will meet all the expenses, you may be sure. We're in a tight corner and no mistake. We'll have to wait and see how it works out. In the meantime we mustn't tell anyone. We'll talk about the settlement later.'

Ralegh could see his 'Fortune's Fold' slipping through his fingers unless he moved quickly. He had another word with the Queen.

'They seem to be taking a long time with the Sherborne lease, Ma'am. I was hoping to get it through this year so that I might have the great joy of a visit from your Majesty in the spring.'

'The West Country's a long way for me, Water. So you needn't worry on my account.'

'Still, it's a valuable post in our Western defences, Ma'am. It needs abundant repair. The Bishops have let it fall into ruin.'

'Very well, I'll ask the Council to speed things up. Lawyers take their time, as you know.'

'And our money, Ma'am. Our peace of mind too.'

She laughed. 'You're right there – devious as corkscrews and all well-cushioned. I'll see what I can do.'

Arthur also had an audience with the Queen just before Christmas.

'I'm glad to see you, Mr Throckmorton. How is your sister? We miss her. It's not like her to be unwell,' said she sympathetically. 'She is such a healthy young thing, so full of energy.'

'Thank you, Ma'am. She is as well as can be expected. She is in the capable hands of an aunt in Chelsea, and in the care of her own doctor. As Christmas is almost on us, my sister and I wondered if you would care to accept this little gift, which we would deem a great honour.'

'A waistcoat, I see,' she said, examining it with interest. 'Beautifully embroidered. Thank you and kindly thank Bess for me. The last time I saw anything like it was one that a good-for-nothing courtier had as a Spanish prize. I exercised my proprietary rights,' she exclaimed with a triumphant laugh.

He called again on New Year's Eve. 'Ma'am, just to tell you that Bess – my sister that is – thanks your Majesty very much for your good wishes. She is coming along nicely and has put on weight, but the doctor says it will be three months or so before she is well enough to resume her duties.'

'Poor little thing. I will make it my business to come along and see her. I invariably visit my officers and attendants when they are indisposed. And Chelsea's not so far,' she said helpfully.

'That would be more than kind of you, Ma'am. But,' he added hastily, 'she is required to be in complete seclusion. There has been talk of plague in the area. Visitors are being kept right away.' All this was true.

'As bad as that.' She was clearly upset. 'Dear me, give her all my best wishes for a speedy recovery, won't you?'

'Thank you kindly, Ma'am. We wondered if you would do us the honour of accepting this little New Year's gift.'

'A pair of ruffs. That is noble of you. Thank you both. And I wish you a very happy New Year.'

With Ralegh the Queen was as good as her word. The lease was duly executed. When he read it through he was not all that pleased with its terms, but they would do. He sent a quarter's rent to the Dean and Chapter of Salisbury and contacted his brother.

'We're in, Adrian old boy. The lease is signed and I've paid the rent. So we'll go down and have a look at it. A little secret for your private ear – promise?'

'Yes. Why, what is it?'

'Don't laugh. I'm married.'

'I don't believe it. Why weren't we invited?'

'It had to be done in a hurry.'

'I can believe that,' Adrian replied. 'Who's the lucky – or should I say the unlucky – maid, the first Lady Ralegh?'

' "Maid" is right. She's a maid-in-waiting – Bess Throckmorton.'

'Jove. That's asking for trouble, isn't it? Does the Queen know?'

'No. And she mustn't find out,' replied Ralegh firmly.

'How the devil do you imagine you can keep it dark? It'll be all over London.'

'We're doing our best to hide it. She's in Chelsea staying with an aunt at the moment. She'll have it at her brother's house at Mile End.'

'So, I might have guessed it. There's a tiny one involved, is there? Now I understand. Very careless of you, Walter. You're old enough to know better.'

They couldn't help having a chuckle.

'It's not really like that at all,' Ralegh assured him. 'She's a lovely girl. I love her. She loves me – surprising, isn't it! It had to happen sooner or later. It's come sooner. God knows how long we can keep it quiet. I'm going to see her tonight. You and I are for Sherborne tomorrow.'

He went unescorted on horseback to Chelsea and was shown in to Bess.

'How are you, my sweet?' he asked, kissing her. 'You've grown quite a big girl since I last saw you.'

'Oh Walter. It's not funny. It's lovely to see you. Did anybody see you come?'

'No. I came by myself,' he assured her. 'Only Adrian knows about it. He's totally reliable. An excellent brother to have, as is yours.'

'Every time I feel it kicking I think of you. If only we could be together,' she said wistfully.

'If only. But then,' he went on, 'if I were abroad on campaign, we wouldn't be able to see one another, would we? Or if I were in prison.'

'Don't say that. It makes me shiver. Let's make the most of it while you're here.'

'A small surprise for you – not so small in fact: Sherborne is ours at last. A magnificent castle – somewhat dilapidated but we'll soon put that right. It's in lovely countryside. As soon as you're well I'll take you down there to see it. You'll love

Sherborne, Bess – a little gem of a country town.'

'That will be wonderful. To be together in our own home.'

The following day the brothers with escort set off for the West Country, along the road they knew so well. As they passed through Salisbury Ralegh raised his arm in salute towards the Bishop's Palace and called out, 'Thank you, my Lord Bishop. Always at your service.'

When they drew near Sherborne Castle and they approached the gatehouse a face vaguely familiar to Ralegh appeared. They dismounted and Ralegh exclaimed: 'Good heavens. Look what the tide's washed up – if it's not Meere I'll eat my hat. What the devil are you doing here, may I ask? You're on my property.'

'I know it's yours, Ralegh. We've been expecting you.'

'Sir Walter to you, my man,' he replied peremptorily. 'Adrian, this is Meere – John Meere – one of those law chaps I was with in Chambers. In the Temple. They were an unattractive conceited selection. But he took the first prize.'

'That's a bit hard, Walter,' Adrian admonished. 'You must make allowances, Mr Meere, we've had a long ride.'

'That's perfectly all right. I fully understand. Yes, Sir Walter, we've been looking forward to your coming. I know we didn't always see eye to eye in London, but that's a long time ago. And please remember, my brothers and I were there because we had to take our law seriously. I know you all thought us bookworms and court-case grovellers, but it was different for you. I hope we can let bygones be bygones.'

Ralegh softened. 'Very well. I'm sorry I was curt. I had no right to talk to you like that. But what are you doing here?'

'I am – or rather, have been – bailiff for the Church authorities, keeping an eye on what was their property. My family have been legal practitioners in these parts for generations,' Meere explained.

'In that case,' replied Ralegh, 'you may continue to do so, if that is your wish. I will make you bailiff for the Sherborne Hundred and we'll work out a plan together to get this heap in better order.'

'Shall I show you round, Sir Walter?' Meere asked.

'No. We won't be staying long. We'll only have time for a quick look.'

Meere coughed apologetically. 'You will let me have my

appointment in writing, won't you, Sir Walter?'

'Don't you take my word for it?'

'Yes, most certainly. It's only for the records,' he explained.

'I'll put it in hand,' Ralegh agreed.

'Thank you. Welcome to Sherborne and have a good journey.'

After he had left, Adrian said: 'He doesn't seem too bad a fellow.'

Ralegh disagreed. 'I wouldn't trust him as far as I can throw this horse. But I'll give him the benefit of the doubt – for the time being anyway.'

The Castle was a heap. It had been a splendid building and could be made so again. But it had been allowed to fall into disrepair from years of neglect.

'I'm going to make a few changes here, Adrian,' he said, 'make no mistake about it. This road can go for a start.'

'What do you mean?' Adrian asked. 'It's an old highway – from time out of mind. The Ancient Britons used it – the Durotriges I believe they called themselves in Dorset. It's sacrosanct.'

'It's the wrong side of my Castle. It'll have to go. I'll move it over there,' pointing to the north side of the Castle wall.

They left the horses cropping on the verge under the eye of their escort and went over the bridge and drawbridge crossing the moat. Ralegh examined the curtain wall.

'They knew how to build in those days,' he exclaimed. 'Look at the thickness of it. Built by Bishop Roger of Caen – that is in Normandy in case you don't know. One of the brave old fighting Bishops – a sound breed, not like the feeble slitherers we have today.'

Adrian grinned and did not disagree. They inspected the tall gatehouse and walked up the stair turret to look through the windows on its second and third floors. They crossed the courtyard and went up to the first floor of the keep. By another circular stair they entered and looked round the chapel, whose window decoration indicated its Norman origin.

As they came away, Ralegh said, 'It's all very grand, but I can't see Bess wanting to live in it – too damp and draughty. Anyway, we'll see what it's like when the masons have worked on it.'

Back in London Christopher Marlowe came to him with

exciting news. Adrian was staying with Ralegh at Durham House. 'I've a producer for my play,' he announced – 'the one I told you about: *Dr Faustus*. It's having a private showing tomorrow. I've a seat for you if you'd care to come.'

'Well done old chap,' replied Ralegh. 'Could I possibly bring Adrian? It's just up his street. You'd love it, Adrian: necromancy, magic, Lucifer, Mephostophilis, power and all the delights you can imagine. It could be your autobiography, Christopher. The sting's in the tail, is it not: dream to nightmare?'

'By all means come too, Adrian,' said Marlowe.

It was to be a sell-out. His name was made.

The Azores operation of the previous year had whetted appetites. The task now was to send another expedition against the Spaniards and intercept and seize their Treasure Fleet – the Indian carracks – before it reached home port. This was to be followed up by storming Panama's pearl reserves. Ralegh himself was putting up all the money he could lay his hands on. He was to be both its Admiral and the chief entrepreneur. He entered into bonds at interest with London jewellers to help finance his investment. Fifteen ships were assembled. The Queen put in two ships and £1,800 as her share of the adventure, the City of London £6,000. Ralegh was risking his all.

She could bear the absence of Essex no longer. She summoned him – or entreated him to come – to Court. As he went in to see her, she wept copious tears, telling him: 'I could not stand any more of it. I have missed you so much. Why did you do this to me, when you knew how fond I was of you – and I thought you were of me?'

'I am,' he assured her, 'I promise you. But I felt so sorry for Frances, losing her Philip Sidney, as she did, so tragically. I felt sure you would understand.'

This lame excuse was only partially accepted.

'Understand? I was devastated. Don't ever mention that woman's name to me. I want you back here please, now. But I don't want to see her again. She can stay buried in the country and on no account come back to Court.'

Burghley's comment on hearing of the restoration of Essex to the Court and the Queen's good books was: 'He has one friend, the Queen; one enemy, himself.' This was not strictly accurate

– all the Londoners loved Essex, as did his great body of retainers, for his youthful exuberance, arrogant enthusiasm and open-handed luxury.

The continued absence of Bess had induced the Court to draw conclusions. Mary had her leg pulled unmercifully. She had already guessed the nature of her cousin's indisposition.

'How big is she now, Mary? Has it arrived yet? Who is the happy father? When did you tell her what it was all about?'

Mary denied all knowledge of these allegations, which she could truthfully do as Bess had never confided in her, although she recalled, in retrospect, the earlier symptoms. The whisper then went round the Court after endless speculation and a process of elimination, that there could only be one possible father within their circle – Ralegh.

He was working feverishly down river to get the fleet in shape and away – the quicker the better. A reasonable absence at sea and a successful venture might soften the edge of the Queen's wrath when she learnt of this treachery on the part of two trusted servants. From his headquarters at Chatham he was having difficulty in assembling crews. His Vice-Admiral was the deterrent – Sir Martin Frobisher, known for his exceptionally severe discipline. Ralegh reported to Cecil how he was 'barely able to survive, rowing up and down the Thames with every tide between Gravesend and London. The weather too is putting everything back.'

Bess went by night from her aunt's to Arthur's house at Mile End to await the event. Ralegh was at full stretch, nor could he take any risk of detection, but he crossed the Thames the following night to see her.

'How are you, my dearest? I hope you're being properly looked after. I am only too sorry I shan't be with you when it happens. I aim to get away any day now. I shall be thinking of you.'

'Leaving me to face the music on my own,' she replied, but jokingly, rather than reproachfully. A nurse, but no doctor, was in attendance. The fewer the number of people in the know, the safer.

He was summoned, in the middle of all this activity, to the Queen, who came straight to the point.

'I know how devoted you are to this expedition and you've put a lot of money into it – as I have and many others. But I am not going to let you yourself sail. I'm not risking it. You're too valuable here. I know it will be a disappointment and you can justifiably say I always step in to stop you taking part in these enterprises. But that's my decision.'

His reaction was two-fold: relief that the rumours had evidently not reached her and that the suspicions behind the curious or knowing looks of the other courtiers had not come to her notice – or had they, perhaps? Secondly, that his temporary avenue of escape was being blocked.

'Ma'am, I will naturally do anything you say. But could I have your permission please to go part of the way with them, otherwise they'll say I'm leaving them in the lurch?' he pleaded.

'Very well. Fifty leagues and no more. I am appointing Sir John Borough in your place as Admiral. Your ship *The Roebuck* can be his flag-ship. The Privy Council agree.'

Cecil, eyes and ears everywhere, could not fail to hear the rumours flying around and taxed him with them in a letter sent down to Chatham by a special messenger. 'The Council require your bond to cover the sailors' wages without delay. And what is this I hear about you wanting to get to sea to save having to get married? I should like to know precisely what is going on.' Cecil's wife, Elizabeth, could have given him the answer.

Ralegh replied on these lines: 'We have nearly finished our preparations. I agree – I have no alternative, have I? – to the Council's request that I enter into a bond to cover wages during the voyage. But I would like to put it on record that I have already entered into many bonds to finance this expedition. Besides, her Majesty told me she would pay her share and that my Lord Admiral would pay his and that I would be left only with the cost of my own ships.

'I have told her Majesty that if I can persuade the men to sail under Sir Martin Frobisher, I will return after fifty or sixty leagues. I have been lent *Disdain* for the purpose.

'I am certainly not trying to get away for fear of getting tied up with marriage. If so, I would have told you. I protest before God that there is no one on the face of the earth that I would be tied to. Please do what you can to suppress this malicious rumour.'

This was strictly correct – the marriage had already taken

place. He was already tied.

Cecil's comment when he received this was: 'Has he not, in his hurry, left out the word "rather" before "be tied to"?'

On 29 March Bess gave birth to a son at Arthur's house between two and three o'clock in the afternoon. He sent an urgent note by footman across the Thames to Ralegh, giving him ten shillings for the cost of his journey and to keep his mouth shut.

Adrian Gilbert called to see her but Ralegh's erstwhile friends who were in the know, kept out of the way. They feared the wrath to come.

Arthur discussed with Bess the question of baptism, and who should be asked to be god-father. Arthur knew Essex from military contacts as did Bess from the Court. His advances were something of the past. He had been more subdued since his marriage and ostracism from, and rehabilitation in, Court. They felt that the sharp differences between him and Ralegh, who had in their tempestuous characters much in common, had softened. As the Queen's restored favourite, his support at Court when the blow fell could be useful and he might be flattered to be asked. It might secure his co-operation. His wife's first husband, Sidney, had been a friend of Ralegh. It was a chance worth taking. They could rely on his confidence, they felt. Ralegh did not dissent. The baby was baptized as Damerei Ralegh on 10 April. The godparents were Essex, Arthur and a cousin Anne Throckmorton.

Bess returned to Court on 27 April and resumed her duties as though nothing had happened. The baby had been put out to nurse with some of Bess's relations at Enfield, Middlesex. She was heartbroken to be parted from her child – their child. Had he not been the bonding factor? She thought of him continually, with emptiness and an ache in her heart. But there was no alternative. They must keep their heads down till the tempest passed over. The world must be kept at bay with courage and a brave face. Her husband's future as well as her own was at stake.

She brushed aside the searching questions of her inquisitive colleagues with a laugh, and told them what they could do with their ribald comments. Even Mary was persuaded that her suspicions had been ill-founded. The Queen was pleased to see her back in good health.

'I'm so glad you've recovered, my dear. I would have come to see you but your brother persuaded me otherwise.'

Bess curtseyed and expressed her gratitude. This was brazen effrontery, in effect an act of perjury toward the Queen whom she had sworn to serve faithfully – although the oath did not say 'exclusively': a legal oversight, perhaps.

Ralegh was making his final preparations at Falmouth. They had intended to sail early in February but were held up for three months by bad weather. His elder brother Carew had provided *The Galleon Ralegh*. The Earl of Cumberland had fitted out a fleet for a privateering expedition of his own which he planned to co-ordinate with that of Ralegh.

They set sail on 6 May. Ralegh was only supposed to go as far as the coast of Spain and then return home. He went considerably further, to stave off the day of reckoning and hopefully seize a prize. The hope was unfulfilled. He sailed back to Plymouth from where he sent his friend Browne to London announcing his return.

Arthur had been acting on behalf of Ralegh and Bess over the marriage settlement. Browne, after delivering his message, and Sir George Carew, Ralegh's cousin, called in on Arthur and signed and sealed the deed. The nurse brought Damerei down to Mile End and as soon as Ralegh returned a week later to London, took him at night to Durham House where he saw him for the first time.

'So you are the little one to carry on the line,' he murmured. 'He's a tough-looking little beggar, nurse. If only your mother could be here too. Look after him carefully, won't you. We'll all be together soon – I hope.'

But the secret had to come out. The arrival of a baby at Ralegh's house, however well concealed, could hardly fail to generate gossip. He had enemies enough to ensure that such delicious news was brought to the ear of the Queen.

At first, she refused to believe it. Then she sent furiously for Cecil. 'I have never known such an insult. They've both flouted their oaths. They were the two I trusted above all others. They've done these disgraceful things behind my back.'

The thought passed through his mind that they would have been unlikely to do them in her presence, but he kept it to himself.

'Did you know it was going on, Elf?'

Cecil winced. He hated this tag but was stuck with it.

'Ma'am, had I known I would have told you. I would have put a stop to it – gone to every length to avoid affront to your Majesty.'

'First Leicester, then Essex, now Ralegh double-crosses me – with one of my own maids, which is the last straw. They must be punished – severely.'

'What have you in mind, Ma'am?'

'House custody, for a start. We'll decide what to do with them later.'

'You mentioned my Lord Essex, Ma'am.' He paused. 'You let him come back.'

'That was altogether different. And he had six months' dispatch to Coventry.'

'Very well. I will do as you say.'

Ralegh was committed to Cecil's custody and forbidden to stir from Durham House; Bess to that of the Vice-Chamberlain, Sir Thomas Heneage. Both were apprehensive, more so as some weeks went by with no hint of their fate. They were ordered not to communicate with one another.

Arthur and his elder (simple) brother William were told to report to Heneage. He explained, unnecessarily, the gravity of their sister's offence.

There was widespread joy among Ralegh's numerous enemies at his sudden fall from grace. It had only been a matter of time they said. For them it had not come soon enough. It was a well-merited settling of old scores – pride and fall.

Ralegh, even if down, was not out. He wrote bitterly to Cecil to complain, not of his treatment in London but of that in Ireland by the Lord Deputy FitzWilliam. He told Cecil how pleased FitzWilliam had been to learn of Ralegh's disgrace, that in his absence he had taken the opportunity of inventing a debt of £400 for rent due to the Queen and had ordered the Sheriff to distrain on his Munster tenants, seize their cattle and sell them unless the money was paid by the following day. Ralegh insisted that all Munster scarcely had that amount of money and that the debt had only been fifty marks, which had been paid.

'The Sheriff took five hundred milch cows from those poor people, some of whom had only two or three, and that to provide milk for their wives and children, in a strange country in which they had just been encouraged to settle. He has thrust me out of a castle in a lawsuit between me and Richard Wingfield (Deputy of the Lord Treasurer). This was a castle of the Queen's which I had spent five years rebuilding – Lismore – and manning with Englishmen, in which the Lord Deputy has now put a rebel – a castle moreover in the most dangerous part of Munster.'

He also complained about the quality of the soldiers then stationed at Youghal. 'A base fellow named O'Dodell commands a band of soldiers there costing the Queen £1,200 a year without ten good men in it. Our poorest people muster for threepence a day, while these soldiers do nothing but spoil the country and drive away our tenants. At three days' notice I could raise a better band whenever the Queen needed it. I care not for life or lands, but it will be no small weakening of the Queen's sovereignty in those parts and no small comfort to the ill-affected Irish, to have the Englishmen driven out of the country.'

This was followed in quick succession by more letters to Cecil: 'My loving friend, pray send me news of Ireland. I hear that three thousand are in arms in the boroughs, including young O'Donnell and the sons of Shane O'Neill. I wrote to the Queen about it ten days ago' (somewhat indiscreet perhaps) 'but she laughed at my conceit. Your cousin the doting Lord Deputy has dispeopled my land. I am like a fish cast on dry land, gasping for breath.' This last sentence succinctly summed up his frustration.

The Queen had held back from striking the final blow. Despite the strength of her feelings she might still have relented had either Ralegh or Bess shown signs of contrition. But no apology came nor any expression of regret. Both had their pride. Each was loyal to the other. Neither would express any regrets. They were not sorry, neither would they feign sorrow even to save their skins. Bess, despite having no dowry, had won a fine husband: a national hero, the Queen's man; and he a lovely, devoted wife who would stand by him.

There was virtually no alternative but to send them to The Tower – in separate rooms: this was no honeymoon hotel. From there Ralegh continued his tirade. His mood varied between defiance and despair. He could see the Thames from his window. Looking out one morning he watched miserably as a royal procession of boats and barges, headed by the Queen, and decorated with flags and bunting, passed by on their way down river. He turned on his keeper, cousin Sir George Carew, and complained: 'This was only done to torment me. It's like dangling an axe over my head. I can't stand it any longer. Let me disguise myself as a boatman, borrow a boat and row after them – anything to get a look at the Queen – otherwise my heart will break. I'll come back.'

'I'm very sorry, Walter,' his cousin replied, 'I must obey orders – which are to keep you here safe and sound.'

This was heard by another relative, Sir Arthur Gorges, who was standing nearby laughing his head off. But it took a more serious turn. Ralegh drew a dagger. Carew did likewise and the couple set to like madmen. At first, Gorges failed to see the daggers. As soon as he did he stepped in, greatly alarmed, to separate them. He succeeded in doing so at the cost of getting his knuckles and fingers cut and bleeding. He did his best to reconcile them, but Ralegh would have none of it. Gorges described the scene to Cecil later. 'Sir Walter swears he'll hate Sir George for the rest of their lives for stopping him from seeing the Queen whom he doesn't know if he'll ever see again.' Cecil smiled.

Ralegh wrote again to Cecil sardonically: 'Please ask the Queen to sign the bills for the Guards' coats. My heart was never broken till this day, when I hear the Queen is going so far away.' She was off on a Progress. 'She whom I have followed so many years with such great love, in so many journeys, and am now left behind in a dark prison. She rides like Alexander, hunts like Diana, walks like Venus. Sometimes she's singing like an angel, sometimes playing like Orpheus.'

Cecil laughed out loud when he read these compliments. They all knew that the Queen had a harsh, somewhat shrill, singing voice, although she could play the virginals well. If Ralegh hoped they would melt her heart, he was deluding himself. She was immovable.

Bess also wrote from The Tower. Her mood was more philosophical than his. One letter was to a friend living at Copt Hall. In her enchanting phonetic spelling which Arthur had never been able to correct, she expressed her hope day after day of being freed, but that she would not wish it unless Sir Walter were told and approved, nor if it would harm him to hear of her release. She acknowledged a kind letter she had had, by the hand of the correspondent's good lady, from Lord Cobham. (Cobham was her friend Elizabeth Cecil's brother.) But she wondered what would become of her when she was set free. The plague had subsided. And 'we are true within ourselves, I can assure you. Ever assuredly yours in friendship, E.R.'

She relished her new signature.

Ralegh continued to organize his business and maritime activities, despite his unsalubrious surroundings. He wrote to the Lord High Admiral, Lord Howard of Effingham, (of Armada fame) on outstanding seafaring matters. A ship they had been about to send out on an enterprise, *The Great Susan*, would have to be vacated and its provisions unloaded because he, Ralegh, was the only one who could have made her ready for sea, if he had been at liberty. (This perhaps was gentle pressure for intercession on his behalf.) The soldiers and mariners who had brought back prize ships were clamouring for their pay, but he was not allowed to speak to them and check their claims with his records to sort out the deserving from the rest. Could they please be allowed to come and see him?

But his spirits were at a low ebb. During the morning walk he was allowed with his Keeper, he exclaimed as they were passing the lions' enclosure, 'Let me myself feed the lions.' This suggestion was not accepted.

On return from her Progress, the Queen asked Cecil: 'What news of Ralegh? Any apology yet?'

'I regret to say not, Ma'am,' he replied, 'but there was a curious incident in The Tower which might amuse you.' He gave her an account of the brawl and the incident which occasioned it. She listened with satisfaction.

'So he's really feeling it. Good. I would suggest that what you've told me would support a charge of treason or attempted murder. What would the Attorney say, do you think?'

'I hardly consider it would stick, Ma'am,' he replied. 'It lacks evidence of malice aforethought.' It often paid to pour oil on troubled waters that could otherwise spread unacceptably. 'Maybe a charge of assault? The King's Bench had an interesting case of assault. A man drew his sword and said to his opponent: "If it were not Assize time, I would run you through". This was held to be an assault even though he didn't strike him.' No more was said about it.

Jesuits in Europe were grasping their opportunity to besmirch Ralegh's reputation further. They accused him of atheism. This stemmed from his habit of frank discussion of any and every subject, be it religion, politics, the art of war or any other topic of interest. The fact that a particular friend of his was the mathematician and logician Hariot added to their indignation, however baseless.

Lord Howard, who had great respect for Ralegh, offered to mediate with the Queen. He thanked him but discouraged any further approach on his behalf. The decision had been to disgrace him, he explained, and any more pleading to her Majesty would only make matters worse.

9

'*I Am Still The Queen Of England's Poor Captive*'

Early in September the Queen closed the Meeting of the Council and withdrew, taking with her Cecil and the Lord High Admiral.

In her Privy Chamber she threw herself into a chair, exclaiming: 'I've never known them so niggardly as they were this morning. To get a few coins out of them is like getting blood out of a stone. Where are we with the £1,000 loan from the City of London?'

Cecil replied: 'Ma'am, they're more than happy to advance it – at interest, naturally – but they humbly request the mortgage of a Kent manor to ease the formalities.'

'Isn't the word of a Queen enough?' she demanded. 'I suppose we have no alternative. Talk about lawyers' red tape. More expense into their coffers. Please go ahead and give it them. Now my Lord Howard, what is the latest of the Spaniard Adventure?' she asked.

'Ma'am, we have made the best capture ever, as I told the Council – the *Madre de Dios*,' he replied. 'The most brilliant piece of work ever. Before Ralegh (if I may mention his name) left the Fleet – off Spain – on your esteemed order – he divided it into two squadrons. One he put under Sir Martin Frobisher to watch the Spanish coast; the other under the substitute Admiral Sir John Borough to cruise by the Azores. Borough's flagship, as you commanded, was Ralegh's *Roebuck*. A great Portuguese carrack, *The Santa Cruz*, hove into sight. *The Roebuck* and the Earl of Cumberland's ship were about to take it on, when they were all scattered by a sudden storm. They regrouped and headed it off, but too late. Their crew set fire to it. That as you know is the King of Spain's standing order when escape is impossible.'

'Now tell us about the other ship,' she ordered expectantly.

'Ma'am, it all worked out well. We picked up *The Santa Cruz* crew and saw they were treated well. They told us about even more richly laden carracks heading in our direction to meet a pre-arranged escort of Spanish men-of-war. This is why Ralegh, anticipating their plan, had placed Frobisher to block their mainland ports.

'On 3 August one of the carracks came in sight, the Portuguese *Madre de Dios*, a seven-decker bringing home Spanish Governors from the East Indies and wealthy merchants. It was laden with treasure. After a fight lasting from ten o'clock in the morning to two o'clock the following morning, it was boarded. Our soldiers are reported to have done more damage than necessary. They would no doubt argue that they had no alternative. It is now under escort for Dartmouth. But the weather's terrible.'

'Well, my Lord, keep us informed. Talking of Ralegh: has he been pestering you to ask me to let him out?'

'No, Ma'am. Quite the reverse,' he assured her. 'He beseeched me not to offend your Majesty any further by pleading for him. He calls it all an "unfortunate accident".'

'Some accident,' she declared indignantly. 'Tell me as soon as this ship docks.' When Howard had departed she asked Cecil 'How's the prisoner doing?'

'He says he's more weary of life than his enemies are that he should perish. He's also worried about the plague coming back in The Tower,' he replied.

'Good. It'll teach him a lesson. He keeps flooding me with poetry. The latest he calls 'The last book of the ocean to Cynthia' – that's meant to be me – yards of it: one hundred and thirty-one verses. Listen, I'll read you the first and last verses:

> Sufficeth it to you my joys interred,
> In simple words that I my woes complain,
> You that then died when first my fancy erred,
> Joys under dust that never live again.

'I question the "first my fancy erred" bit. Now the last verse. It's about love. You wouldn't know much about that, little Elf, would you?' she quipped shrewdly. (She alternated this 'affectionate' form of address by 'Pygmy' – later used regularly by her successor James.)

Cecil squirmed, and protested. She guffawed, and continued:

> To God I leave it, who first gave it me,
> And I her gave, and she returned again,
> As it was hers. So let his mercies be,
> Of my last comforts, the essential mean.
> But be it so, or not, th'effects are past.
> Her love hath end; my woe must ever last.

'I wonder if he really means it,' she said thoughtfully.

'He's his own worst enemy,' Cecil emphasized. 'Adept at making enemies. But he's an able servant. His were the brains behind this Portuguese prize we've captured. I should say, "Spanish prize in a Portuguese ship".'

The *Madre de Dios* was taken into Dartmouth on 8 September. News of its fabulous treasure on board soon spread far and wide. It included gold, jewellery, gems, musk, amber, porcelain, calicoes, damasks, silks, pepper, spices and drugs. The captors assumed rights of self-help to the spoils. Local Devonians and Londoners with an eye to quick profit swarmed into Dartmouth. Articles bought from the sailors changed hands the same day for five times the price paid. The dockside was like a St Bartholomew's Fair. Drastic steps had to be taken by or on behalf of those who had equipped, launched or underwritten the expedition, to safeguard their share.

An edict was issued that no pillage would be held lawful until the whole had been brought into port and assessed. Warrants were issued to the Bailiffs of Devon and Cornwall to stop all those making their way from Dartmouth and search their trunks, packs and bags.

Ralegh heard of this with both interest and exasperation. It could be, if properly played, the key to his freedom. He was also being deprived of his due reward. He wrote to Burghley explaining how the Queen might profit from the capture, an idea put in his head by Carew whom he had fought over his close confinement. Burghley went to see the Queen, taking his son Cecil with him.

'I have had a letter from Ralegh, Ma'am,' he told her. 'He says, quite rightly, that he was the greatest adventurer in this operation; that he estimates £20,000 as his one-tenth share of the catch; that you, Ma'am, contributed £1,800 and a couple of ships; that he would assess your share at £80,000; and that if God had provided it for his ransom he hoped your Majesty in your abundant goodness would accept it. He also says that if his imprisonment or his life might do your Majesty more good, he would ask neither for liberty nor his right to go on breathing.'

A silence followed, broken by the Queen. He had struck the perfect chord.

'Cecil,' she said, 'I assume you have talked this over with your father. What do you make of it?'

'Ma'am, if I might be so bold as to say so,' he replied, 'he's not much use to us in his "unsavoury dungeon", as he puts it. He's had some weeks there. The men, certainly those in the West Country, believe this is all his doing, even though he wasn't there at the kill. They don't like the thought of his being kept locked up. But more to the point we need him on the spot —'

'He is "on the spot",' she interjected. They laughed. She heartily, they dutifully. He went on, 'He's needed down in Dartmouth to curb these mutinous sailors and get things under control; help salvage and sort out the prize. My concern is to safeguard your well-deserved share, Ma'am.'

'I heard from Sir John Hawkins,' Burghley added. 'He was emphatic that Ralegh is the only one who can deal with this business. I am told there's chaos in the ports, all scrambling for what they can get. Only he carries weight with the locals.'

'That's no doubt what Ralegh says too. He probably told him to say it.' She knew Ralegh better than he realized.

'In this Ma'am,' Burghley assured her, 'he has your interests at heart, as we all have.' They also had their shares in mind.

'There's a trick in it. Just an excuse to get himself out of The Tower. But very well. He shall go down to Devon, but under escort, as a State prisoner, you understand. I'm not letting him off. If he behaves himself, he can go home to Durham House when he gets back – so long as my share is a fair and proper one; of which I shall be the judge. But still in confinement, make no mistake about that.'

'And, Ma'am,' asked Cecil, 'what about her?'

'Who do you mean "her"?' she said, knowing full well.

'Your maid. She's still in The Tower.'

She paused for a moment. They were talking of her successful rival. Then replied: 'I will let her out. But in my own good time. When I do, keep her right away from me.'

On the way, Burghley voiced his relief. 'It was a near thing, Robert. But we made it. That was a masterly touch from Ralegh. We'll need to watch him. He'll trick us if he can. So I want you to go ahead and see how the land lies before he gets there. Keep me informed.'

Cecil left London that afternoon with his body-guard of servants. They stopped the night at Hartlebury at an inn he knew. After dinner he wrote his first despatch, suggesting how the spoils might be divided. He pressed on, reaching Dartmouth on 19 September, from where he sent his second report. Everyone he had met carrying a bag or sack within a radius of seven miles from Plymouth or Dartmouth smelt of the Indies' merchandise, particularly musk, spices and amber. He sent an urgent request to Burghley to send him back by the bearer a commission under seal to apprehend and examine on oath all mariners, townsmen and strangers who since the ships docked had bought or sold goods which might have come off them; and to make enquiries in London to ascertain which jewellers and goldsmiths had gone down to the West Country 'to see of what stones and pearls her Majesty has been robbed'.

In the meantime he had assumed that he had the necessary authority to use strong-arm tactics. He reported: 'It took my committal of two innkeepers to prison to persuade the stubborn folk here to divulge the source of their acquisitions'. They had no doubt profited from centuries of experience in salvaging wrecks, as had their neighbours to the West, at times encouraged. He went on: 'I found a bag of seed pearls in a Londoner's house and I have given orders for every bag and parcel of mail from the West Country to be searched. Unfortunately a lot of the birds have flown – jewels, pearls and ambergris. I found one rough sailor with a chain of orient pearls, two chains of gold, four great pearls of the bigness of a pea, four forks of crystal, four spoons of crystal set with gold and stones, and two cords of musk. A corporal had a large bag which, when we opened it, found it contained rubies. Another had three hundred diamonds; yet another a bag of diamonds as big as his fist. But the saving I am securing for her Majesty will more than repay the cost of my journey – and it hasn't been an easy journey: fouler roads and more obstinate people than I have ever come across. Please tell her Majesty that in the course of my search I came across an amulet of gold and a fork of crystal with rubies, which I am keeping for her.'

When the jailer unlocked his door the morning after Cecil had left London, Ralegh assumed that it was for his exercise walk. To his surprise he had with him The Tower Lieutenant Governor. 'I have here a Council order,' he informed him, 'you are to be released from here, but to remain in custody during her Majesty's pleasure, to carry out the instructions detailed in the paper enclosed with this Order. You've to read it, Sir Walter, and comply with it in every respect. You will remain under escort and Mr Blount, whom you know, will be your keeper. You will obey him unreservedly.'

Ralegh read his instructions: to proceed without delay to Dartmouth, under escort, report to Sir Robert Cecil on arrival, track down and guard the Spanish prize and draft proposals for its equitable distribution.

'That's straightforward enough,' he commented. 'I'll start this morning. But, first, what is to become of Lady Ralegh? I'm not leaving her here on her own, in this dreadful, degrading place. And for God's sake, why am I not allowed to see her?'

'My orders are my orders,' was the reply. 'It was, as you know, a direction from the Queen. But I can set your mind at rest on one score: your wife is well and, considering everything, cheerful.'

'Thank the Lord for that. Could I see her before I go?' he asked.

'It would be more than my job was worth to allow it, much as I would like to. I would find myself in your shoes. But you can send her a message, if you say nothing about it.'

His message was of necessity brief.

> 'My dearest Bess, I am pining for you, as I trust you are for me, and I long with all my heart to see you again. But it is not to be yet. You should not have been here, nor I, although mine was the fault – the cause, I should say. There was no fault.
>
> 'I am still a prisoner, but I have orders to go to Dartmouth and sort out the prize. So farewell, my darling Bess. Look after yourself for all our sakes. I

long to see you and our little boy soon.'

He and his keeper, Mr Blount, and a retinue of his servants set out along the Great West Road.

They stopped at Hartlebury for the night. The innkeeper, whom he likewise knew from previous visits, greeted him with the comment that a number of grand persons had been putting up there during the previous week or so on their way West. Asked if any he knew were among them he replied: 'The Council Secretary was here last night.'

'Was he now,' said Ralegh. 'Sir Robert Cecil, you mean?'

'That's him. In a great hurry too.'

'So are we.' Then to Blount he commented: 'They've sent him ahead to spy out the land ahead of me. Anyway, we'll be close on his tail.'

The highway degenerated into a rough track, churned up by the tread of thousands of horses, including packhorses, sheep and cattle. They had to deviate where the way had become founderous after heavy rain. Over Salisbury Plain the white, chalky mud presented a slippery hazard. They welcomed the wide main street of Andover to rest their party.

They pressed on, past the tall spire of Salisbury Cathedral to Shaftesbury. There they were still busy building their cottages from the stone of the dismantled Abbey. At Sherborne a fleeting glimpse of his Castle was all he would allow himself, thankful that the lease had been signed just in time. 'That is where I would sooner be,' he told Blount, 'breathing fresh Dorset air. It's like nectar after the foetid atmosphere of The Tower. We don't really value our freedom until it's taken from us.'

They arrived at Dartmouth on 20 September. Word of their coming had gone ahead of them. At the dockside a hundred and forty of his former servants were there to greet him. The sailors swarmed round him with shouts of joy. His brother Sir John Gilbert wept as they met.

Cecil was standing by and saw this spontaneous reception. He was amazed. He wrote in his next letter to Burghley, 'I never saw a man have more difficulty in quieting them in all my life. But his heart is broken. Whenever he is congratulated on regaining his liberty he replies: "No, I am still the Queen of England's poor captive." I told him to keep quiet – we don't want a riot on our hands. Nor do we want to lessen the respect they have for him, which is beyond belief and will help us. I do grace him as much as I may, for I find him marvellous greedy to do anything to recover the conceit of his brutish offence to her Majesty. But you should hear his rage at seeing the spoils squandered. I can't help laughing, as you would.'

Ralegh was exasperated at the incompetence and waste, and loss of their hard-won gains. The rich store included jewels, spices, ebony wood, tapestries, and silks and satins, amassed by the governors and merchants on duty or business in the Indies, much of it taken or pressurized from the natives and their chiefs with little scruple. Cecil and Ralegh headed a group of Commissioners appointed with the terms of reference of collecting, guarding and preparing proposals for partition of the proceeds. Even after the plunder this still amounted in value to around £140,000.

They pursued their task with zeal. As the Acting-Admiral Sir John Borough might have said, with overmuch zeal. He had left Dartmouth some days before. His job was done. But he had heard of their diligent search so he returned late one night and offered to open up and let them look inside his chest. As they reported to Burghley and the Lord Admiral, they found only china, taffetas, damasks and quilts.

They also examined the brother of Captain Crosse, one of the Captains, closely. It transpired that Crosse's ship, *The Foresight* (well-named, Ralegh commented) had docked not at Dartmouth or Plymouth but further along the coast at Portsmouth. They were there for five days before formally reporting their return to England: ample time to unload and spirit away captured material, although it could not be proved. Sir John Hawkins had been even more circumspect. He had sailed his ship *The Dainty* round to Harwich – and great bags of cinnamon were reported as finding their way from Ipswich to London's Lombard Street.

The haggling over the division of the treasure now began in earnest. The custom in privateering expeditions such as this was to divide it into three parts: one third for the owners who had supplied the ships; one third to the victuallers; and one third to the officers and crew who had carried out the operation. It was indicated that Ralegh and the Earl of Cumberland should each have £36,000. Ralegh protested vehemently. 'My expenses, which I had to meet from my own pocket and in fact had mostly to borrow at interest, came to no less than £34,000. That would leave me with a bare £2,000 to show for it. It was due to my ship *The Roebuck* that the *Madre de Dios* was boarded and captured intact, and neither allowed to escape nor set on fire and scuppered. I gave my sails and cable to get the carrick home or she would have sunk or foundered off the Scillies. It was I who masterminded the whole operation; I who lost more men than anybody else. When interest payments are taken into account my £2,000 becomes a £2,200 loss.

'The City of London on the other hand,' he went on, 'have netted £6,000 profit as their share over an outlay of no more than that. In the case of my Lord of Cumberland his expenses only came to between £17,000 and £19,000, netting him some £17,000 to £19,000 profit. This is particularly unfair because his ships were strictly not part of the main Fleet but were on a prize adventure of their own, although they had the advantage of linking up with the main body. Not that they did not acquit themselves valiantly, I am not saying that. They fought well. But my resources were at the disposal of her Majesty. Also, Cumberland had already had a substantial share of the pillage. His ships on arrival at Plymouth had had a dockside sale at the port of diamonds, rubies, musk, ambergris and other stuff. Ships of his including *The Dainty, Dragon* and *Foresight* also ran into other ports and sold off their booty, much of the rest and its proceeds disappearing up North. Moreover they were not searched by the Commissioners (of which I was one) whereas mine was subjected to a detailed scrutiny by Sir Robert Cecil.'

The Queen was one who gained substantially in reward both for authorizing it all and for her contribution in kind by the way of ships. The wheeling and dealing was symptomatic of most of these quasi-piratical, quasi-national security and fortune-seeking expeditions. The huge size of this prize, the largest ever, was what distinguished it from others. On the same lines as Ralegh's protest, a complaint was also made by Sir John Fortescue, Burghley's Chancellor. He drew attention to the desirability of what he termed 'a small measure of honesty'. He warned that unless Ralegh, Cumberland and the rest of the adventurers were adequately rewarded they might not be induced to take part in the future.

However, the eventual outcome was to Ralegh's advantage. He had wisely under-estimated his return. The Queen had had a satisfying share. He returned to Durham House and was formally released from custody in December. An appropriate letter to the Queen expressed contrition, grateful thanks and promises of faithful service.

Bess had had a less stormy sojourn in The Tower than he. Her yearning for her child and agony of separation from her sweetheart outweighed misgivings over the break of relations with the Queen. But she took her enforced captivity calmly. It must end sooner or later. She made friends of The Tower ravens who called at her window daily for food. She accepted their reproving nods with amusement. They were spontaneous friends from the outside world. She was also allowed visitors. And she had won her man. He had now earned his freedom.

She was allowed to rejoin him just in time for Christmas.

10

Fortune's Fold

They had a family get-together at Durham House over Christmas and the New Year. Arthur, his wife Anna and family and his and Bess's mother Anne joined them. Relief was reflected in the celebrations, in which Ralegh's servants joined.

Bess's first concern on being released had been to go up to Enfield and see Damerei and make arrangements for him to come home. But the child was poorly so it was decided that they would pick him up the day after Christmas. Late Christmas night they received an urgent summons. He had developed a fever and was very ill. They went over at once. They sat beside his cot holding hands and saying little. The doctor was sent for again. There was nothing more he could do. Before day-break the end had come.

For the first time Bess gave way to tears. 'It was all my doing,' she sobbed. 'I should have stayed with him and not gone back to Court.'

'You mustn't say that, my dear; fevers come from nobody knows where. How much worse it would have been for him in The Tower, where they had the plague. Blame me rather for having given you him.'

'That I will never do. It was he who brought us here together.'

Ralegh felt it deeply: his heir, born in tribulation, torn from them as they were emerging back into the light. Only in poetry can the depth of love, sorrow, hate, remorse be expressed. The first verse of a poem he wrote read:

> My first born love, unhappily conceived
> Brought forth in pain, and christened with a curse
> Die in your infancy, of life bereaved,
> By your cruel nurse.

Ralegh now had to see to his Parliamentary duties. He had been returned as Member for a small pocket-borough in Devon with few electors who were therefore readily accessible. The hustings were no problem. The Goverment needed more money. This was to subsidize Henry IV of France against Spain, to pay for armies in France and the Netherlands and the costs of war at sea. Mention of Spain never failed to inflame Ralegh, a reaction he shared with Essex. The Queen and Cecil had a more measured approach. But Ralegh's eloquence in the House of Commons suited their purpose in securing votes for more taxation. His warnings of Spain using ports of Brittany or landing places in Scotland from which to launch assaults were convincing. There was some talk of a conference with the House of Lords to discuss how best to levy the taxes but the Commons were up in arms against any encroachment on their prerogative, finance. An ill-timed speech by Cecil recommending consultation with the Lords was thrown back in his face. Ralegh produced a compromise which satisfied the House, that a meeting should be arranged to discuss the subject in general terms but with no mention of tax or subsidy. This was adopted unanimously. It went some way to modify the critical attitude which his recent troubles had inspired.

In another debate he pressed the arguments for an open declaration of war which would have had the rewarding effect of legalizing privateering. He reminded the House that even since that session of Parliament had assembled, Spain had captured some thousands of their mariners; that the Dutch, who had cornered most of the world's trade, were supporting the King of Spain, private profit being the only motive behind their international relations.

On another occasion religious questions came before the House. The Archbishop of Canterbury, Dr John Whitgift, had initiated steps to limit the activities of the Puritans, in which he had the Queen's backing, by strengthening the measures against sectaries. Ralegh opposed them, enlarging on the danger of juries being influenced by religious prejudice and convicting innocent people merely for entertaining non-conformist beliefs. His opinion of juries when political or religious issues were involved: 'Crowds are like dogs. Dogs do always bark at those they know not and it is in their nature to accompany one another in those clamours.'

He had made his mark on Parliament before its dissolution, speaking his mind with eloquence.

Spring was on the way: what better time to show Bess his – their – 'Fortune's Fold'?

'It's time we left London and headed for the country, Bess. How would you like to meet Sherborne?'

'That would be exciting. How soon?' she asked.

'We can leave at the end of the week. We'll stay at Bath for a few days on the way. I need to take the waters. That infernal Tower and its damp walls has given me the ague. The hot springs may put it right. They'll do you good too, Bess.'

They made for Bath with escort and retinue and had their health sessions, in his case unsuccessful. They then headed for Sherborne. They could see, as they rode down the long slope from the north, the Abbey tower nestling square and solid at the foot of the town. In a setting of glorious countryside, it evoked the spirit of the England they loved best. 'I'll show you round later, Bess,' he said, 'we'll make for the Castle first and settle in.'

On their entry to the town the Abbey bells rang out – the ringers had been promised a whole two shillings for this display of warmth, word of their coming having preceded them. The roads were lined with spectators curious to see their new lord and his lady and to acclaim one whose reputation in the field and at sea, and in his native Devon, was widely known.

'He can be an absolute terror,' some were saying; others, 'He looks after his men well. They'll do anything for him.'

The procession crossed over bridge and drawbridge and into the Castle courtyard. He pointed out to her its various features with pride, but some misgiving. As a stronghold for defence or attack it was superb. As a residence it left much to be desired. It had been designed for strength not comfort. He could guess what her reaction would be.

'It's a fine building. But where do we live? It looks cold, damp and draughty. But I mustn't be critical. I know how you love it.'

They installed themselves in the domestic area dominated by the keep. Stone steps led up to their rooms. Ralegh himself saw that the horses were fed, watered and stabled and the staff housed. After the journey and good dinner, quickly prepared, they retired more than ready for the first night's sleep in their new domain.

The following day he showed her the estate. The Castle walls were alight with valerian and wall-flowers. Nearby marshy ground abounded in wild fowl and marshland blossom – ragged robin, fritillary, marsh marigold. Early bulrushes were spiking through. The river flowed past bright and clear from hills to the north-east. On the surface of protected pools near the banks floated yellow and white water lilies. 'This is the Yeo. It runs down to the Tone and Parrett, to the Somerset wetlands and Athelney,' he told her, 'where Alfred the Great hid from the Danes and burnt his cakes. He owned my birthplace in Devon.' Two kingfishers flashed past with scintillating plumage and skimmed the surface of the water. A moorhen bobbed across to his nest in bushes at the side.

Beyond, to the south, was scenery unsurpassed anywhere. A wide expanse of meadowland sloped up gradually to a ridge thickly wooded with oak, beech, ash, birch and elm in bright green feathery dress of spring. 'Oaks such as these are the timber for our ships,' he said. The woodland was ablaze with a carpet of bluebells, primroses and celandine which had folowed close on spring's harbinger, the snowdrop. A light breeze from the sea blew in over the Dorset Downs. A vestige of mist was drifting away up the valley. Woodpeckers were busy tapping. Skylarks sang above their heads. High up a pair of buzzards soared and glided. A cuckoo called from an adjacent copse.

'It be two days after Wareham Fair, Zirr Walter,' stated a woodman working nearby.

'Oh! How do you know that, pray?' he was asked.

'It be the first cuckoo of the year, Zirr. Always comes then, you zee,' he explained.

Ralegh and Bess laughed. 'What a remarkable almanac,' she exclaimed, 'and what about this mass of white blossom in the hedges?'

'Ah! That be the sign of a blackthorn winter, my Lady. Sharp winds and rough weather.'

'That doesn't augur very well for our draughty quarters,' Ralegh said to Bess.

The meadows were studded with a myriad of hues – cowslips, ox-eye daisies, purple-tipped grass. Shepherd's purse and campion sheltered in the hedgerows.

'This must be the loveliest place I have ever seen,' she

exclaimed. 'If I can spend the rest of my life here, in this gem in this glorious county, I ask for nothing better.'

'That goes for me too,' he said.

The following day he introduced Meere to her. 'Morning, Meere. This is my bailiff, my dear. He is a lawyer and has been around here all his life.'

'How do you do, Lady Ralegh. Welcome to our town. I hope you have found everything to your satisfaction,' he said.

'Thank you, Mr Meere. Yes. But I wouldn't call the Castle luxurious, would you?' she replied.

'It does need some fixing,' Meere admitted.

'You did what I ordered from London, I take it – to cut down any matured timber to repair it?' Ralegh asked. He thought it unnecessary to add that the instruction had been written from The Tower. Meere confirmed that he had.

Ralegh went on: 'Look, Meere: I'm appointing you Keeper of the Castle, Overseer of Woods and Receiver of Rents. We'll discuss terms next time I come down. How would that suit you?'

'Excellently, Sir Walter. Thank you. I already have the books and I know all the tenants,' he replied.

'Are you married, Mr Meere?' Bess enquired.

'Yes, Lady Ralegh. You might be interested to know that my wife is a kinswoman of the wife of my Lord Essex.'

Ralegh snorted. 'So the poison spreads as far west as this, does it!'

'You're forgetting,' Bess chided him, 'that he was our son's godfather – and that she was your friend Sir Philip's wife.'

'Yes, of course. I withdraw that remark, Meere. My Lord of Essex and I don't always see eye to eye, you understand. But we look forward to meeting your wife.'

They were overjoyed with their new acquistion. This did nothing to inhibit him from pouring out a list of complaints to Cecil about its state of repair in a letter on sundry matters before they returned to London.

'I am writing from my "Fortune's Fold",' – and proceeded to proffer his counsel on current issues, including Spain and Ireland, where he warned of dangers and advocated a firm line. 'My advice is given in all good faith. Remember how the Trojan soothsayer cast his spear against the wooden horse and shouted: "It's hollow – have a look inside and see what they've hidden there." But he was laughed at.

'Her Majesty should think it no small dishonour to be saddled with such a beggarly nation, with neither arms nor fortifications.' The King of Spain was not seeking 'Ireland for the sake of Ireland but to raise troops of beggars at our backs and force us to look over our shoulders while he knocks our brains out.' The Earl of Argyll in Scotland should be recruited to keep Ireland's Ulster in check; he himself had been forced to withdraw his Munster settlers since the Government were not prepared to send over a few troops to protect them; the cost of keeping up Sherborne Park was beyond his resources and required Treasury subsidy; could he be allowed to volunteer as a hand on a frigate that was having to recruit West Country fishermen as pilots, while he was buried in Sherborne 'in his "Fortune's Fold". Every fool knows that hatreds are the cinders of affection' – he would be more than delighted to be made a sacrifice on those terms.

Meere introduced him to the details of his financial transactions with the town. He was the first layman to hold and exercise the Lordship of the Manor of Sherborne. Meere reported having received on his behalf two shillings by way of 'knowledge money' from the Governors of Sherborne School (acknowledging him as Lord of the Manor). The School had been founded in 1550 by Letters Patent of Edward VI. Their premises were an old building within the precincts of the former monastery, then standing empty, north of the Abbey, which had once been a 'schoolhouse'. The lease from Sir John Horsey included also a 'plumbhouse', gardens and adjacent land. It was secluded from the street. (In the next century the leasehold was erected into a freehold.) The Governors also paid Meere for Ralegh eight shillings a year for the under-lease to them of the shambles, stalls and standings in the market-place which, to supplement the School's income, they let out to stallholders. There were numerous other rents which Meere listed precisely in his books.

Restive Ralegh might be in this quiet countryside and frustrated at being ostracized from the swim of exciting national events, but he had his duties in Devon and Cornwall which he saw to with his usual vigour. There was the challenge of organizing this large estate. He also enjoyed with Bess the tranquillity of their peaceful surroundings. He put his emotions as usual in verse:

> Blest silent groves! O may ye be
> Forever mirth's best nursery!
> May pure estates
> Forever pitch their tents
> Upon these downs, these meads, these rocks, these mountains
> And peace still slumber by the purling fountains,
> Which we may every year
> Find when we come fishing here.
> and
> Where winds sometimes our woods, perhaps, may shake,
> But blustering care could never tempest make;
> Nor murmurs e'er come nigh us,
> Saving our fountains that glide by us.

Was it while he was sitting in a stone seat composing verse, smoking a soothing pipe of tobacco, that his manservant passed by carrying a pitcher of spiced ale: horrified to see clouds of smoke surrounding his master, used his presence of mind to dowse with the ale the source of the smoke?

Bess was supremely happy. She wrote to Cecil sending her love to her great friend Elizabeth, his wife, and telling him, 'Every day this place amends, and London grows worse and worse.' She was essentially a country girl and lover of nature.

They decided that the old Castle was too uncomfortable as a residence. 'We'll build ourselves something grand, in keeping with these gorgeous surroundings,' he declared. 'Something spectacular, out of the ordinary.' He took her over to an old hunting lodge to the south. 'We'll use this as the core for our new building. I'll get plans drawn up at once.'

Work started almost immediately on a building of rich red Tudor brick with the panorama Bess so admired stretching before them to the woodland along the hill crest.

Her personal servants brought with them from London were Christopher Harris and Mrs Hull; his were Bell, Myers, Fulford, Smith (the cook), John Layton, William the butler, Jockey, Peter Venn, Bromback and Smith (the cook's brother). Bess explained to her husband that she would need to engage some local girls. The Castle staff had hitherto been exclusively male. A few days later she told him she had engaged someone. 'I've taken her on the recommendation of two charming people you haven't met yet – Mr and Mrs Moyleyns of West Hall. She lives in Long Burton. She's been a dairy-maid with them for quite a while. Here she is in fact, so you can see her for yourself. Jane Foot is her name.'

She appeared to be about the same age as Bess. As their eyes met he started. So did she. It was more than their eyes that had met some years before at the fair. Bess was called to the kitchen where Smith the cook had a problem. Ralegh was the first to break the short silence. 'That was a night I have never forgotten,' he said. 'Did it work out all right for you?'

She giggled. 'Yes, Sir. It was Pack Monday night and my parents didn't expect me home any earlier. As for the boys – there was nothing they could say, was there?'

'Well, the less said now the better,' he laughed. 'It's a pleasure to see you again.'

'Nothing will ever pass my lips, Sir,' she promised him.

For the first time they could remember Bess and her brother Arthur quarrelled. She had been outspoken about the Queen's refusal to have her back at Court. He was naturally having to watch his step. Critics of the Queen would hardly serve him in good stead. While the Raleghs were away Arthur, having spent a night with friends in Colchester, Essex, went down to Sherborne. He had a look at the Town and called in at the New Inn for a drink before going on to the Castle, where he would be staying in their absence. One of his escorts told the Landlord his name: 'Begging your pardon, Sir. Would you be any relation of Lady Ralegh?' he asked him. 'Lady Betty we call her.'

'Yes. Her brother.'

'She's a great lady. Very popular hereabouts. Everyone loves her. Sir Walter himself stayed here once some years ago,' he added proudly.

'He's never mentioned it.'

'He enjoyed it here with the Fair on. He left very early in the morning.'

While at the Castle, Arthur gave Huckwell the guard five shillings and met Meere for the first time. Ralegh's man Hancock he knew from London. Early in the winter he made it up with Bess to her great joy. They were both stubborn, at times fiery, characters but devoted brother and sister. She relied on him – and on Cecil – when her husband was away. Ralegh's friend Hariot used to visit Arthur at Mile End. Knowing Hariot's love of tobacco, he gave him on one occasion a pouch of tobacco and papers to light it. Ralegh's men, John Shelbury of Sherborne, Wood and Knyvett also went there. Contact between the two households was close.

Ralegh's plans for using the timber on his Munster estates for wine-casks and pipe-staves were being held up by the Privy Council. There was a ready market for these in Madeira and the Canaries – and probably in Spain itself. Why not do a deal with the enemy if it brought in profit? But the Council had imposed an embargo on export and the large numbers of workmen he had sent to Munster for their making would be out of work and the timber rotted unless he could get it lifted. He went up to London and pointed out that to have to bring the men home would weaken the defensive position in Ireland.

He was back in Sherborne the following month, bombarding Cecil with letters headed 'from my Castle'. A hobby he and Cecil had in common was falconry. Ralegh was Ranger of Gillingham Forest, on the north-east border of Dorset, west of Shaftesbury. He spent a night or two in a lodge there. He was exercising a rare Indian falcon Cecil had given him. He reported: 'the bird is sick of the buckworm, and if therefore you will be so bountiful as to give me another falcon, I will provide you with a roan gelding.'

He told Meere: 'An improvement I have decided on: to enclose part of the marshy area and make it a water meadow and build the Castle wall round it. There's ample marsh for the wild fowl nearer the lodge. I want another fire-place in the gatehouse and some more windows and a new staircase in the keep. The present one is dangerous. Put it on the west side with a terrace at its foot. We'll also pull down St Mary Magdalene Church.' This was a little Norman church built at the same time as, and in the north-east corner of, the castle. 'That will require approval of the Church authorities and the Privy Council,' Meere demurred.

'Apply for it then,' Ralegh ordered, 'and move the road at the same time.'

'What – the ancient highway?' asked Meere, surprised.

'None other. What of it? It's in the way. It must go.'

'They'll make you replace the Church,' Meere objected.

'Very well. There's a perfectly good site further down in Castleton. Put it there.'

Meere told his wife when he arrived home that evening: 'He's a dominating, over-bearing bully. He'll come to regret it if I have anything to do with it.'

'You mustn't forget her Ladyship,' warned Mrs Meere. 'And for goodness sake don't cross swords with him. You'll destroy one another if you do.'

But Ralegh always looked after those worse off than himself. Bess was firm, indeed tough, but had a soft heart as he had for anyone in trouble. They went out of their way to intercede for a local woman named Eleanor Dyer. She had a complaint against the Master and Brethren of the Almshouse. She asserted to Ralegh and Sir Ralph Horsey that the Almshouse had wrongfully let an interloper occupy that part of the nearby Church House premises of which she claimed she was the rightful tenant. Ralegh took up the case and her claim was eventually settled by a money payment. Horsey had succeeded to his family estates at Clifton Maybank and elsewhere four years before. It was his forbear, Sir John, who had received from Henry VIII the grant of monastic lands, including Sherborne Abbey, which he had sold to the townsfolk of Sherborne and leased the premises to Sherborne School.

His mind was now directed to other matters. He was exploring the practicality of a full-scale expedition to Guiana. He believed this to be an El Dorado of great riches which could be won against minimal opposition. It had not been settled by Spain who had barely more than a trading post there. The natives were friendly and vastly preferred the English to the Spaniards at whose hands they had suffered extreme cruelty. He outlined his ideas to Cecil and he now confided them to Bess. He would establish an illustrious empire for her Majesty. Bess was sufficiently alarmed to write to Cecil herself knowing of his influence at Court and in the country.

She first thanked him for sending her down some tablets. Then: 'If I had lost my faith, I would have been lost, but I fear my mistress the Queen, if all hearts were open and all desires known, would be able to read her own destiny in the ordinary alphabet instead of having the difficult job of deciphering the clues. But we are both great believers, and flatter ourselves and direct our minds by wishful thinking.' She had hoped for the Queen's forgiveness. It was a forlorn hope. The Queen was as hostile to her as to the wife of the Earl of Essex – a woman scorned by two lovers. The ladies had been banished for ever.

She went on (phonetically as ever and poignantly): 'I hope for my sake you will discourage Sir Walter from his westward enterprise "towards the sunset" as he puts it. You great councillors are always producing new ideas and never settle down, whereas we poor souls who have bought sorrow at a great price are quite content to leave things as they are. So please stop him, and don't encourage him.'

Ralegh was still pressing an obdurate Privy Council for permission to export his barrels and pipe-staves from Munster – if not abroad, then to England. His constant journeys between Sherborne and Durham House were proving a strain.

One evening he was having dinner at Sir George Trenchard's house, Wolfeton, just north of Dorchester. His elder brother, Carew, who was staying at Sherborne, was also invited. When they had all imbibed rather freely Carew made an outspoken comment on religion. Horsey, also a guest, reproved him. 'Evil words corrupt good morals,' he asserted.

'And what danger will I incur?' demanded Carew.

Another guest, the Reverend Ralph Ironside, interjected somewhat pompously: 'The wages of sin is death.'

'But death comes to us all,' Carew objected.

'Not the death of the soul,' the clergyman stated firmly.

'Soul? What is that?'

'Better to find out how they can be saved, than be curious about its essence,' he warned.

Ralegh had been listening intently. There was nothing he liked better than a good argument. He commented: 'In all my studies at Oxford I never found anyone who could define "soul" satisfactorily.'

The Reverend Ironside, likewise at Oxford, bridled at this. He quoted a long-winded text from Aristotle.

'Too obscure and intricate,' Ralegh observed. 'Try again.'

Somewhat flustered by now he offered: 'A spiritual and immortal substance breathed into man by God, whereby he lives, and moves, and understands, and so is distinguished from all other creatures.'

'Yes,' replied Ralegh. 'But what is that spiritual and immortal substance?' The theologian was face to face with the scientist and logician.

'The soul.'

'That is no scholar's answer. It merely completes the circle. Let grace be said. That has more sense than this discussion.'

These possibly eccentric comments rankled with the Reverend Ironside. They bordered in his view on blasphemy. They were reported to the Court of High Commission in London. Cecil sighed in despair. But any possible chink in Ralegh's armour attracted numerous adversaries. He and his friend Marlowe were both suspected of atheism. (Marlowe indeed was actually charged with blasphemy. Before the trial could take place, to Ralegh's sorrow, he was involved in a fatal brawl at Deptford. A poet of great promise was lost.) Commissioners were set up to investigate the allegations, under the chairmanship of Lord Howard Viscount Bindon. It included Horsey himself, who could combine the roles of judge and witness. They sat solemnly at Cerne Abbas, also the site of a famous abbey, in March.

They took depositions from numerous witnesses. Called to give evidence were local people: Francis Scarlett (Vicar of Sherborne), Miss Elizabeth Whatcombe, Hyde (a town cobbler) and Robert Ashbourne (churchwarden and Sherborne School Governor). The Minister for Gillingham deposed that Ralegh's mathematical friend, Thomas Hariot, had questioned the Godhead and the Scriptures. The Gillingham Churchwarden, who had perhaps seen Ralegh the falconer in the forest on a Sunday, had heard that he was suspected of atheism. A curate from Motcombe, near Gillingham, had heard a similar report about Mr Thynne of Longleat. The parson of Wyke Regis, between Weymouth and Melcombe Regis (recently joined into one borough) and Portland had heard that one of his lieutenants at Portland, Lieutenant Allen, was a blasphemer who never went to Divine Service or sermons. Some Sherborne folk had heard that Allen and his men were atheists.

Ralegh and Carew looked in briefly at the hearing, then wandered off to inspect the ancient Abbey and the Cerne Giant, a huge Romano-British effigy cut into the chalk hill to the north of the village. 'If they spot us here,' Ralegh said jokingly, 'they will use it in evidence.' It was the scene of spring fertility rites from pre-Christian times which annually attracted the youth of the area.

The verdict sent up to London following all this hearsay evidence was inconclusive.

Between the night of the dinner and the investigation their 'Fortune's Fold' had produced the most desirable fruit they could have wished – a son, whom they baptized 'Walter' in Lillington Church on 1 November 1593 and affectionately called 'Wat'.

'You, little man, will one day have all this, and much more besides,' Ralegh exclaimed. 'We will treasure him, Bess.'

'That we will, my dear,' she assured him. 'He'll be your very image if I have anything to do with it.'

Shortly after, the new Lodge was ready for occupation. 'We must make a mark,' said Ralegh, 'to remind us and our successors when we came.' With one of his many diamonds he scratched his initials and a heraldic bend of fusils from his armorial bearings on a diamond-shaped pane of glass of a typically Tudor window. 'That will be there for all time,' he said, 'long after we, and little Wat here, are gone.'

'I'd rather not give that a thought,' Bess answered. 'We'd be better employed getting in the furniture.'

It was not only the house and furniture that she arranged. She helped him plan the garden. She brought from her old home a specimen of pink which quickly took root in the walls and window sills of the Castle and in the new Lodge garden, to which the staff gave the name 'Lady Betty's pinks'. He shared her enthusiasm for gardens. He referred to them as 'among the purest of human pleasures, without which buildings and palaces are but gross handiworks'. A ha-ha was dug to keep off the prolific red deer which roamed the woods.

He wrote to Cecil a good word for Henry Thynne who was in trouble for seizing a vessel from Bayonne belonging to the French and taking its load of cod.

The ship had since been returned, but £1,000 of the compensation was still outstanding. The parties involved were ordered to appear at Hampton Court on 20 October.

Following this, while attending Dorchester Assizes (in his official capacity) Ralegh wrote again to Cecil recommending that the Barry family, whose Castle in Ireland he had once taken, should now be rewarded as loyal subjects of the Queen – exemplifying his earlier advice for a firm hand.

In April of 1594 a Jesuit was caught in Lady Stourton's house. Trenchard, Horsey and Ralegh rode over to examine him. They found him to be 'Irish' and a 'villain' calling himself John Mooney.

Ralegh was then involved in upholding the Queen's absolute jurisdiction in Stannary matters. He urged Thomas Egerton, Lord Keeper of the Great Seal of England, to transfer a case brought by Plymouth Corporation against the tin-miners from the Court of Star Chamber to the Stannary Court. There it would be adjudicated by him, sitting on his granite seat on Dartmoor.

His intelligence network was active as ever. He sent a report from Sherborne to Lord Admiral Howard with up-to-date information about the Spanish Fleet received by his brother from a ship's master recently docked. The Spaniards had gone all out to get a fleet of huge ships ready and manned with soldiers, working on the Sabbath. They had occupied Brest. Could her Majesty be requested to let him serve in any capacity, as a poor mariner or soldier if need be, for no reward; and 'Attack is the best Defence'.

The following month he reported to Cecil that these preparations had been confirmed. Three Spanish men-of-war had chased an English ship with its prizes to the mouth of the Dart. There was obvious danger to the fleet then returning from Newfoundland. He again offered his services. These offers the Queen was not disposed to take up. He was still in the doldrums.

On hearing of the death of Bess's mother, Cecil wrote her a letter of sympathy. Ralegh was away on naval and defence duties and making preparations for the Guiana voyage which had been approved. Cecil did his best in his letter to cheer her up now that her husband was 'so busy'. He told her how much his wife, her friend Elizabeth, missed her company and of Ralegh's affectionate references to her when he called in to see Cecil in London. 'That', Bess replied, 'will increase if it were possible my love and respect for your absent friend, whom I will forever honour. I know it will be long before I see him again. Till then, I will fly to you with all my problems, my surest staff in his absence.

'I thank Lady Cecil for wishing me near her. My constant wish is to serve her and enjoy the company of you both. At the moment, a hermit's cell would be the best place for me, separated as I am from him.'

She may have gained this 'cell' idea from an anchorite's cell nearby in Castleton – or from a former anchorite's cell in the Abbey.

She also asked Cecil to press her lawsuit against the Earl of Huntingdon for return of her marriage portion which her mother had lent him. It was fruitless.

As an astute politician, Cecil kept his eyes and ears open. He was genuinely fond of Bess, as was his wife, and a friend of Ralegh. But it was each man for himself. He would not have been averse to making use of any gossip she inadvertently passed on from family chat. He was both skilled politician and statesman, a necessary prerequisite to survival. Ralegh, of great courage, genius in military strategy and original conceptions, master of language, lacked the vital ingredient for success in public life – ability to play the system.

He was now stationed on the Kent coast, held up by wind at the Foreland, 'forced to ride at anchor in the Downs, unless the enemy venture into the Thames'. He wrote to Cecil for instructions. He also inveighed against 'the priests of Salisbury', that is, the Dean and Chapter, referring to the Bishop as avaricious, 'a smooth, false knave demanding rent to which he is not entitled'. The Bishop had surely already been squared. Ralegh had given the Queen a jewel for just such a purpose.

The Bishop had a somewhat different view of their relations. 'Ralegh is the least deserving of men,' he complained. 'He has treated me unkindly and has wronged me, and I can do nothing to obtain redress. He has cut down the rent he pays for three of the manors he leases from the See, although I still have to meet the fee outgoings. He has refused to pay a penny of the acknowledgement money due on my consecration. He ignores all my requests for payment. Disgraceful, when you consider how much property he owns. I'm disgusted with the evil way he treats me and the shocking reports I hear of him.'

Actually, to help finance the Guiana expedition he had already sold his reversion to two of the episcopal manors near Sherborne, Long Burton and Holnest, to John Fitzjames of Leweston. He had never been entirely happy about conditions in the lease to him of the Sherborne Estates, over which there would now be a three-cornered argument. He decided to protect his estates from the various mishaps that might befall anyone like him in public life, including possible execution against his assets while abroad. He did so by conveying them to his son Wat. This was done without his wife's knowledge. He was then scared that it might come to light. If so, 'my wife will know that she can no longer have any interest in my living' and 'won't hesitate to tell me as much' without mincing words. Like most husbands, he treated his wife's potential reactions with caution and not a little trepidation.

In September, as he was about to sail for Guiana, a severe plague struck Sherborne. Bess and Wat had to be separated and sent to different parts of the country for safety, to avoid joint contamination. Ralegh expressed his concern over this to Cecil who, with Lord Admiral Howard, had invested in this expedition.

To alleviate hardships from the plague, money was raised by the Abbey and the wardens of the streets, fairs and markets for relief of the sufferers and for burial.

11

Search For Gold

Throughout December 1594 Ralegh was kicking his heels in Sherborne waiting for a favourable wind. He peppered Cecil with letters as usual on sundry matters and instructed his brother Sir John Gilbert to proceed with a levy of mariners to be ready to sail from Dartmouth. Seven ships were still held up in the Thames by adverse winds.

They set sail from Plymouth – with five ships – on 9 February 1595: no doubt to Cecil's relief. At the Canaries they seized a Spanish ship transporting firearms and a Flemish ship from which they helped themselves to twenty butts of wine. Arriving at Trinidad on 22 March they captured the town of St Joseph and took the Governor Antonio de Berreo prisoner. One of the pet diversions of Berreo and his henchmen was slow-roasting live Indians. But he was a devout Christian. Ralegh explained to him the purpose of their expedition, to explore Guiana. Berreo fired his imagination by telling him of a fabulous city in the interior called Manoa by the natives and El Dorado by the Spanish, the seat of a famous Emperor. He followed this with a caution. 'I advise you strongly to give up the idea.' Berreo warned: 'It will be a waste of time and effort and you will suffer endless misery.'

'I've been planning this for years,' Ralegh retorted. 'I'm certainly not giving up now after coming so far. If I did, back home they would call me a lunatic and coward.'

'There's another point,' Berreo pursued, 'we knew you were coming and there'll be a strong body of our troops, under the command of an officer by the name of De Vera, to greet you.'

The prospect of armed opposition did nothing to deter Ralegh.

'Thank you for the warning. We're going all the same.'

The crossing was about the same distance as from Dover to Calais, against high seas and a strong wind and current. When they landed they took on an Indian pilot named Ferdinando to lead them up the river Orinoco and into the hinterland.

Ralegh left the ships at anchor and detailed an exploration party of one hundred men. They set off up river in a galley drawing no more than five feet of water, a barge, two wherries and a ship's boat from Lord Howard's contributed ship, *The Lion's Whelp*. They took supplies for a month.

They soon found themselves in a labyrinth of rivers, tributaries of equal size which made it almost impossible to identify the main river. Their guide's knowledge proved to be very limited. To make matters more difficult there were a number of islands to confuse even further. The view ahead was restricted by tall trees and thick undergrowth. It was a nightmare of a journey.

But fortune served them a good turn. They spotted a canoe crossing the river ahead of them containing three Indians. Ralegh in his eight-oared barge quickly overtook them and found one to be a knowledgeable pilot who knew the rivers far better than their Ferdinando. They treated him with care. Even so, they ran into shoals, violent currents and rapids. The air was close and humid and it was impossible to find anywhere to land and have a rest. Twice the galley ran aground.

They accepted their pilot's advice to tie it up and take to the smaller boats which were of a size to navigate the narrower river which lay ahead. This, he said, would bring them to a large Indian town. For several days they rowed on, with no sign of the promised town. They began to suspect treachery. But suddenly they were in open country, with grassy plains, tall copses – and deer grazing at the water's edge.

By this time, because of the strong current the officers and gentlemen in the party were taking their turn on the oars, the sun was beating down and they were near exhaustion. Their food was finished and they only managed to survive on the birds they shot and the fruit they were able to pick.

Fortunately they came across a canoe belonging to a tribe of friendly Indians who replenished their bread supplies and took them to their chief, one Topiawari. The Indians' friendliness was due in part to their hatred of the Spaniards, who had treated them unmercifully, with many atrocities. Topiawari himself had been bound in chains and dragged along for seventeen days by Berreo until he paid a heavy ransom in gold. Their hosts loaded them up with provisions, including pineapples, the 'princess of fruit' Ralegh termed them. They also provided a pilot who knew that part of the river. Ralegh sang the praises of Queen Elizabeth. He showed them a picture of her 'which they admired and worshipped'.

But their troubles were not over. The river – the Caroni, a tributary of the Orinoco – suddenly rose. It took a whole hour to row a stone's throw. It was impossible to go any further by water, so Ralegh divided his company into small exploring bands, he and his friend Laurence Kemys leading two of them. Their object was to locate the gold mines of which he had heard reports.

His description of the territory was enthusiastic. 'We came across waterfalls as high as Church towers. I never saw a more beautiful country – hills, valleys, winding rivers, green grass plains, hard sand for marching, whether on horse or foot; deer crossing every path. Birds were singing on every tree with a thousand tunes, cranes and heron, white and crimson carnation on the riverside. Every stone we picked up had the promise from its appearance of gold or silver.'

They discovered a rock face of quartz interlaced with veins of gold. They hewed off sizable lumps to take back with them for analysis. However, their resources were inadequate to continue the search for the mine. They understood it to be only a few miles distant but the route to it lay through thick vegetation. They returned to Topiawari's headquarters to report the result of their search and replenish supplies. He proved most helpful and urged them to stay.

'When you come next time, make a firm alliance with the tribes,' he advised. 'Berreo made the mistake of forcing his men through without first making peace with the natives. They set fire to the dry savannah grass and engulfed the intruders. We hate the Spaniards for what they have done to us. I beg of you to leave some of your soldiers behind to protect us.'

'That would not be possible, I fear,' Ralegh replied. 'But I'll see if any of them would like to stay behind.'

Two in fact did volunteer to do so. One, Francis Sparrey, was the servant of one of his captains, the other a boy named Hugh Goodwin who decided he would like to stay to learn the

Indian language.

Topiawari ordered his people to help in every way they could, particularly with food. They loaded up in a scene which reminded them of an English market. Ralegh gave his men strict orders.

'Everything you take must be paid for. And there must be no liberties with the native women. We are their protectors.'

To a specially helpful young man they gave the name of 'Harry the Indian'. They became greatly attached to him, and he to them.

Their return down river with the strong current behind them was speedy. They covered one hundred miles a day. They called in at another town, on what happened to be the local feast day. The tribe were gathered together, passing round drinking pots and the worse for drink. They fed their visitors with generous hospitality.

They reached the sea to find a storm raging. They had to leave the galley anchored in the bay while Ralegh and some of the others, including his cousin Grenville, took the barge out to sea. Hugging the coast of Trinidad they eventually joined up with their ships at anchor – 'never a more joyful sight'.

The intention had been to sail on to Virginia and liaise with the settlers. That proved out of the question owing to the dreadful weather – they were totally reliant on fair winds and weather. Instead, they called in at a couple of Spanish settlements and loaded up with the victuals they seized. This was legal under his Queen's Commission, which empowered him 'to do us service in offending the King of Spain and his subjects to the uttermost power'.

They returned to England in August, the crew intact. Ralegh had the nuggets of gold-flecked rock assayed by refiners and assay-masters in Wood Street and in Goldsmiths Hall. They confirmed that it was indeed gold.

Ralegh made his formal report to the Queen and Council. 'Guiana,' he assured them, 'is a country that still has its maidenhead. It has never been sacked nor has its earth been tilled. Its graves haven't been pillaged and despoiled in the search for gold nor have the mines been pillaged. The images in their Temples are still intact. It has never been invaded by an army in strength, nor occupied by any Christian Prince.'

In answer to the questions about religious practices he said:

'They are an ignorant people and have bloody sacrifices and worship idols. They are ripe for conversion to the true Christian God. They have suffered untold cruelties at the hands of the Spaniards. They would welcome us – and would make an excellent colony for her Majesty.'

The Council were impressed, while discounting the report by the exaggeration factor they associated with Ralegh.

After completing his official business he hurried down to his new Lodge. Bess greeted him with joy and relief.

'We're clear of the plague now, thank goodness,' she told him. 'Little Wat is back with us.'

'Let's have a peep at him,' he said.

'Don't wake him, dear, please. He's just dropped off,' she cautioned.

He tip-toed over and looking in his cot exclaimed, 'He's a fine young fellow. You're doing wonders. He'll make a first-rate soldier one day.'

'I hope not,' she replied.

It was soon business as usual. One of his men who had been sailing in Spanish waters, in a small bark, anchored in Lyme Harbour. This was a haven well protected by the Cobb which Henry VIII had reinforced with a substantial grant.

'Sir Walter, there are any number of French ships held up in Spanish ports,' he reported urgently, having sped to Sherborne. 'Spain is preparing a fleet to invade Ireland any day now.'

'Well done. I'll let London know at once. Go down to the kitchen and see Smith the cook. Ask him to give you a good meal – and wash it down with a big pot of ale. I'll see you again before you go.'

He sent this news by special courier to Cecil, offering to provide a pinnace for £40 or £50 to spy out the land in Spain and stressing the urgency. 'There aren't many Ministers who get on with things.' ('Is he getting at me?' thought Cecil to himself.) He also enquired about launching another expedition to Guiana.

Three days later he received Cecil's reply which so far as Guiana was concerned was non-committal. Cecil was sent a response within one hour of receiving his letter. 'The mineral wealth of Guiana is colossal. Do persuade her Majesty to make sure no-one ruins the enterprise or lets pilferers get in first.' He was referring amongst others to Robert Dudley, son of the Earl of Leicester, who had already sent out a ship on his own account. 'I hope I would be thought worthy of directing an operation on which I have laboured at my own expense and of governing the country which it is I who discovered. It won't cost her anything. I have sent a bark there to reassure the natives and encourage them to hold out against any other nations who approach them. If it so happens that men are scared of serving under me because of my disgrace, I would like someone else to take it on, to make sure that the Queen does not lose what she could otherwise gain.'

He went on: 'Besides gold you will find diamonds and pearls there. I instructed Peter Vanlore' (a leading London Jeweller and money-lender with whom he had many dealings) 'to let you see two stones I gave him to test. He did not think much of them, but I am having them re-tested by Pepler, a skilled assayist who is here with me at Sherborne – as is my brother Adrian Gilbert.'

He added: 'I have sent you an amethyst, carnation in colour. Even in the East Indies there aren't more diamonds than in Guiana. I have here a sparkling jewel which, if not a diamond, exceeds any diamond in beauty – which I dare not risk letting go out of my keeping.'

All this was calculated to arouse Cecil's acquisitive instincts. But he knew Ralegh better than to be rushed into hasty decisions.

Ralegh proceeded to write a book for publication entitled *The Discovery of the large, rich and beautiful Empire of Guiana, with a Relation of the Great and Golden City of Manoa, which the Spaniards call El Dorado, and the Provinces of Emeria, Arromaia, Ampaia and other countries, with their Rivers adjoining*. He dedicated it to Lord Admiral Howard and Cecil 'who stood by me in the darkest hour of my adversity'. It was soon to become a best-seller in England and in every major European language.

Bess and he took their communion in the Abbey ('the resting place of Saxon Kings,' he told her) at her insistence 'to offer up thanks for your safe return and to use our seats' – and, for herself, a prayer: for no more foreign voyages. After the service he conducted her on a tour of, as she put it, 'a most beautiful church with its variety of architecture and feeling of friendship: sufficiently large to be impressive but not so large as to be impersonal.'

As they wandered down to the east end a racket started up beyond the east wall. The Vicar, Francis Scarlett, was standing by respectfully in case his assistance should be required by the Lord of the Manor and his Lady.

'May I welcome you, Sir Walter, in happier circumstances?' Ralegh explained this to Bess, laughing. 'He was a witness last time we met – at the Inquiry at Cerne Abbas.'

The noise was coming from the other side of the wall.

'Whatever is it?' she asked.

'I do apologize, my Lady,' he replied, 'it must be the two boys staying with the Headmaster. There's only a thin partition between the Abbey and the house they've just built for him. They have to keep quiet during services but then they let themselves go.'

'Who are these boys?' Ralegh asked.

'Sir Ralph Horsey's. Nice lads but boisterous.'

'I'll pull his leg next time I see him,' Ralegh told them.

'One item I should mention that may interest you,' the Vicar added, 'the tenor bell Cardinal Wolsey gave us is in full swing.'

Before returning to the Lodge they were shown the old school-house which it was explained had been the Almonry School of the pre-Reformation Monastery leased from (and later to be granted in fee simple by) the Horseys.

'In these delectable surroundings,' commented Bess, 'who could ever fail to learn?' a question which of course invites varied answers from past and present victims.

Ralegh followed by upsetting Meere. He told him about their visit to the School. Meere thought he might impress his chief.

'My grandfather was one of the very first Governors,' he boasted.

'Was he now?' Ralegh replied. 'That reminds me. I thought you might like to be relieved of one of your responsibilities. You have more than enough to cope with. I'm making my brother Mr Gilbert the Castle Constable. He has more time on his hands than you. I expect you'll be pleased, Meere.' (Knowing that he would be outraged.)

'Far from it, Sir Walter. But if that is your decision, I must naturally accept it.'

He would have been out of turn to inform, or remind, Ralegh of Adrian's reputation as 'the greatest buffoon in England' – but also a merry companion, which Meere could never be.

Ralegh received a letter from the Privy Council as the Officer-in-Charge of Devon's, Cornwall's and Portland's defences. It set out their plans in the event of attack by Spain. Their idea was for Devon forces to reinforce Cornwall. As soon as he received it, he roared with laughter and called Adrian over. 'Those folk in London want their heads examined. It's a novel conception that one county should reinforce another. Full marks for that. But Devon couldn't back up Cornwall. The only bridge over the Tamar is seven miles up-river from Plymouth. There would be unacceptable delay and Devon herself would be exposed.'

'What about ferrying them over?' Adrian suggested.

'Impractical. You would need an enormous number of small boats which wouldn't be at hand and they could be intercepted. Again, for Cornwall to support Devon if the latter were attacked would be equally difficult and in addition leave Cornwall entirely exposed for the enemy to occupy as soon as they gathered what was happening. Moreover, it would provide them with a base with no land to worry about between there and their home bases in Spain. Then again, Cornwall has no horses which could be put into service – there aren't any horses in Cornwall.' They grinned. 'Again, Cornwall has a seaboard on two sides and is narrow with a long coast line. Its south coast has some of the best ports in England, which would be vulnerable.'

'What's your solution, Walter?' asked Adrian, somewhat bemused at this analysis.

'I shall reply forthwith to their Lordships.'

Bess, who had been listening, interjected. 'For goodness sake, put it politely. You'll get their backs up otherwise, blundering in.' Bess was constantly having to defend him for being too outspoken.

'I shall employ my usual tactful language,' he assured her. 'Yes, I shall tell them it is for me to obey, not to question. I will point out the disadvantages in what they are proposing. I will explain that reinforcement from Somerset would be comparatively simple. The ports of Cornwall and Devon on their north coasts are difficult of access, only possible at high tides. I will remind them that Somerset is a very rich county, full of horses as well as carriages which could be brought into service and that it has many rich gentlemen: unlike Cornwall whose meagre resources such as it has consist of tin works.'

He wrote accordingly, finishing up: 'I crave pardon for my presumption and humbly take my leave.' 'How does that sound, Bess, my dear?'

'A great improvement.'

'I'd better let Cecil see it first.' So he sent Cecil a letter enclosing it to read. 'I am sending it unsealed. When you have perused it would you please ask your footman to deliver it to Durham House. My man Hancock has my seal and he can then return it to you formally for their Lordships.' He had prefixed his letter to Cecil with another reference to Guiana. 'Please let me know whether we are travellers or tinkers; conquerors or novices. If the winter is allowed to go by, there can be no chance of victualling in the summer, and if the operation is slowed down, farewell Guiana forever. How did you like the white stone? I have sent for one of each. As soon as they come, you shall have them.'

Four days later he wrote an urgent letter to the Lord Admiral, Howard of Effingham. Sir John Hawkins and Sir Francis Drake were staging an attack on Panama. News had come through to Ralegh of a fleet embarking from Spain to destroy them. He advised: 'Send two small caravels or pinnaces to warn them. If the Spanish Fleet catches them while their soldiers are still on land, the ships at anchor and those berthed at Panama will be lost. The cost would be small while it would save heavy loss in ships and men. It would be quickest to send them from Weymouth or Plymouth.' (He also took the opportunity of again urging Guiana.)

But it was too late. Hawkins had been surprised by five Spanish men-of-war and was dead. Drake died two months later. The attack had failed.

Authority then came through for the requested voyage to Guiana. He put the expedition under the command of Captain Laurence Kemys. It comprised two ships, one lent by Cecil whose father Burghley helped with a contribution of £50.

The Queen still showed no interest.

12

Winning Through

Spain was still smarting from the defeat of their Armada. Intelligence came in of the build-up of a hostile naval and military force at Cadiz. This was Spain's main naval base. Strategically located just west of Gibraltar, it guarded the entrance to the Mediterranean and provided a launching base for the Atlantic. It was well fortified.

Spain's wealth stemmed from their domination of the East and West Indies and Peru but the constant flow of treasure and produce was continually harried by privateering sorties from England, their arch-enemy. The French and Dutch posed a far smaller threat to them.

The plan was to destroy England as a maritime power, subjugate her and restore the Roman Catholic religion. They established close links to this end with the Earl of Tyrone in Ireland.

The Queen moved with caution. It was one thing to have sporadic operations which did not involve the public purse. Full-scale military action was a different matter. She weighed up the risks and cost. Levies were ordered, then cancelled.

Ralegh, having as instructed raised levies in Cornwall and Devon, no light task, was told to stand them down.

Essex took exception to her appreciation of the situation. He expressed his views forcefully at a Council meeting, the Queen in the Chair.

'Ma'am, procrastination is getting us nowhere. Before we know where we are we shall have the Spaniards at our throats. No-one but a lunatic could fail to see it. It shows a disgraceful lack of courage. We should strike before they get in first – as Drake did when he singed the King of Spain's beard.'

'Are you accusing me of cowardice?' she asked.

'No, Ma'am, but of, if I might say so, indecision. I've offered to lead an assault on Cadiz before they've completed their preparations. The only reaction I get is "wait and see".'

'My Lord Essex, you go too far. The meeting is closed.'

On his way to the Queen in her Privy Chamber Cecil was stopped by Essex. 'I know, Cecil,' he said, 'I went too far. Please ask her pardon and apologize for me to the Council. But you must agree it needed saying.' To Francis Bacon he said: 'If my hands are not tied, I know that God has great work for me to do.'

Cecil passed on the apology. The Queen asked him: 'Was he right, do you think?'

'I agree we mustn't move too hastily, Ma'am,' he replied tactfully, 'but time is against us. He's right to remind us of Drake. It put off the Armada for a year and gave us a breathing space. If we did launch an attack on Cadiz we could seize their treasure fleet at the same time.'

He knew this aspect could help resolve her mind.

'Very well. We'll call the Council and go ahead.'

Essex expressed his regrets in person. He had another demand. 'We must bring Ralegh into the command. His experience will be invaluable.'

The Lord Admiral, Howard of Effingham, supported him. 'His knowledge of sea operations is second to none.'

The Queen allowed her tentative objections to be overruled. She was secretly pleased.

The objectives were threefold: first, to assemble a fleet and army and destroy the King of Spain's ships and magazines at Cadiz; secondly, to take Cadiz; and thirdly, to intercept the carracks and merchant fleets from the Indies.

'There will be joint commanders,' the Queen ordered. 'You, my Lord Admiral, will be in command of the fleet; you my Lord Essex, of the soldiers. Absolute secrecy must be observed till you set sail.'

The reaction of Essex to his secretary was: 'I will see this through, or from being a General become a monk at an hour's notice.'

Ralegh down in Sherborne was ordered to raise the levies again. He was delighted to know that he was to be included and that he would be one of the Council of War. It could be his big chance to be rehabilitated with the Queen and Court. He was still her Captain of the Guard – non-operational.

Bess was less keen. 'I'm pleased for your sake. But it will be highly dangerous. I shall be alone again, I suppose. It's been lovely having you around. I believe you've been happy too.'

'I have, my dear,' he assured her. 'But there's work to be done. This is great news.'

He first saw to the levies, which meant a journey to Devon and Cornwall and then was off to London to help assemble the fleet and raise levies in Essex and Kent.

He, Bess and Wat, with some staff, put up at Arthur's house in Mile End, which was a convenient base and meant that they could all be together. Arthur was to be included in the operation. The Commanders were all absorbed in preparing the invasion force. Lord Admiral Howard reported that Lord Thomas Howard, the Vice-Admiral, Sir Walter, Rear-Admiral, and he were busy from eight in the morning at their staff headquarters office and that 'even after dark Ralegh and I are constantly up and down the Thames organizing the fitting out of the fleet.'

They were finding it difficult to recruit. Ralegh, trying to do so along the Thames and the south coast, complained to Cecil: 'As fast as we press men one day to join, the next day they slip away and say they refuse to serve. They've no respect for our Queen. It's more than I can cope with, rowing up and down on each tide between Gravesend and London.'

Cecil sent a puirsuivant to look for him with an urgent message. Ralegh told Cecil: 'He had to chase round the Kent countryside looking for me, because I was at a village a mile from Gravesend, hunting runaway mariners, and dragging in the mire from alehouse to alehouse. I can't write any reports to our Generals, because I can't get any paper.'

He still found time and paper, however, to bombard Cecil with letters and requests. He sent four on 3 May. One, written from Blackwall, was to seek the assistance of the Controller of the Admiralty in raising men. Another, from Mile End, had no connection with the business in hand. It was to recommend one Hugh Broughton, a friend of his, for the Irish Bishopric of Lismore and Waterford, in the Diocese of the Archbishop of Cashel, Meilor McGrath, no friend of Ralegh. The third recommended a Charles Cartie, an old servant, for a grant of land in Ireland. These were followed by a letter asking Cecil to stand surety for him for the sum of £500.

The following day he wrote again about recruiting difficulties, saying he would call on him at Blackwall if the strong wind persisted: two days later another letter, this time in support of a kinsman who had incurred the Queen's displeasure.

The Lord Admiral tried to contact him at Dover. But he was still at Mile End recruiting unwilling sailors. Essex was understandably restive at the delay. He was ready with his soldiers at Plymouth and suspicious as ever of Ralegh's motives. He told his officers: 'If the winds are the same there as here he has all the wind he needs to sail out of the Thames and down the Channel to here.' Was it that he had some cunning design as, for example, to take sole command of a smaller fleet, using the excuse that the Queen would be happy to save expense?

But by 26 May Ralegh was at Plymouth with the fleet assembled. He made his peace with Essex. As Sir Anthony Standen, a follower of Essex and no friend of Ralegh put it: 'He showed a mixture of cunning respect and deep humility.' An argument arose over precedence between Ralegh and Sir Francis Vere. Who was to be fourth in command? Vere was Marshal of the Army and in no way prepared to give way.

The argument was resumed at dinner. Arthur Throckmorton was there. He had been allowed to join the fleet as a gentleman volunteer and was dining with the four Commanders and that of the Dutch force which was also taking part. Arthur, with the best of intentions and worst of tact, supported his brother-in-law. He took exception to one of Vere's derogatory remarks about Ralegh and told him what he thought of him in forceful terms. For flaring up and not controlling his quick temper Arthur was ordered from the table, dismissed from the service and placed under guard. Ralegh was blamed for the incident as having recruited him and encouraged his outburst: a promising augury for the forthcoming battle.

However, as a gentleman volunteer as distinct from a member of the regular forces Arthur could not be dismissed or be made subject to military discipline. So his status was restored the following morning. On the question of fourth Commander precedence, a compromise was reached: Ralegh authority at sea, Vere on land.

The complement was as follows:

Seventeen Queen's ships, seventy-six hired ships (for transport) plus pinnaces and small craft.
A Dutch squadron of twenty-four ships.
6,424 English sailors, 6,530 English soldiers.
2,600 Dutch.

Other principal Commanders were: Sir George Carew, Sir Conyers Clifford, Sir Robert Southwell, Sir Anthony Ashley, Sir John Wingfield, Robert Dudley (the Earl of Leicester's son).

Before sailing Ralegh still found time for two more letters to Cecil. One recommended a William Hilliard for a Prebend in Exeter Cathedral. The other was in favour of John Randall, Vice-Admiral of Dorset, for an appointment. In the middle of momentous events he still considered his friends and their interests.

Essex had two men hanged at Plymouth for insubordination, as an example. The Fleet got under way on 1 June.

Bess was staying with her sister-in-law Anna at Mile End while their husbands were away. Captain Kemys returned from his Guiana survey and reported to Bess immediately on his arrival. The Spanish had built a fort at the mouth of the Orinoco and another at the junction of the Caroni to defend the passage to the gold mines. He had found the Spaniards more unpopular than ever with the natives. He said he had surveyed and charted the coast and rivers between the Amazon and Orinoco, recording creeks and obstructions and taking depth soundings with plumb-lines in likely shallows. Hariot the mathematician who had accompanied him was preparing maps of both Ralegh's voyage and that of Kemys.

She passed this information on to Cecil and told him: 'They daren't land anywhere because of the Spaniards and they came back with nothing.' This last piece of information was disappointing.

On 19 June the Fleet rounded the high, rocky promontory of Cape St Vincent. Ralegh exclaimed to his men: 'See, they have their lookouts up aloft. Cadiz will know within the hour.'

Ralegh's squadron and that of the Dutch were then detached and ordered to go ahead and anchor outside Cadiz Harbour entrance to prevent any ships inside from escaping. 'You will stop all ships trying to leave the harbour,' the Lord

Admiral ordered. 'But you will not fight, except in self-defence, without further orders.'

The following day the remainder of the fleet anchored three miles west of Cadiz. Reconnaissance established the extent of the Spanish naval strength. It was reported to be considerably larger than their own:

> Fifty-nine tall ships, including the four massive galleons: *St Philip*, *St Matthew*, *St Thomas*, and *St Andrew*.
> Some nineteen or twenty galleys.

The whole harbour and its forts were heavily fortified. Howard and Essex, Joint Commanders, called a Council of War to formulate their plan of assault. To try and force the harbour with their ships would put the fleet in jeopardy: the size and disposition of the Spanish fleet and the harbour defences would make this impractical, they concluded. The strategy decided upon therefore was to attack the town of Cadiz itself by pincer landings on the peninsula, the main thrust being on the Caleta, a sandy spit west of the town. Having captured the town, the fleet would then force its way into the harbour.

Returning to the main fleet having posted his ships as ordered, Ralegh was horrified to find that, in heavy swell, Essex was disembarking his soldiers. The strong south-west wind was making this a hazardous operation. Some of the boats with soldiers in them sank. After a swift appreciation of the position he sped over to Essex and exclaimed to him and his subordinate Commanders: 'This is utter folly. You'll never get away with a land attack. The losses will be fatal. You'll be going in without any fleet support. The Spaniards can obviously see what you're up to. The men would be sitting ducks. If the ships did manage to penetrate the harbour there wouldn't be any soldiers left for an assault on their ships or their land. Most of them would be drowned, shot or sea-sick. See how the sea's running. This doesn't stand a chance. The ships must force a way in first and seize the four galleons. Your army can then land with our back-up and no problems.'

Essex saw the force of his argument. The difficulty his men were having in disembarking was only too apparent. He responded: 'It wasn't my idea. It was my Lord Admiral's. The town has to be taken before the fleet moves in.'

The others also supported Ralegh. Essex told him to go over to the Lord Admiral Howard's flag ship, *The Ark Royal*, and convince him that the course proposed was suicidal and put forward his own plan. He jumped into his skiff and went over.

It was no light matter for a Commander fourth in rank to urge the countermanding of orders and substitution of an entirely different plan, particularly when the operation was already under way. Howard's instinctive response was that this was impertinent Ralegh showing him up for incompetence. But he had the breadth of character and vision and respect for Ralegh's opinion to think again. He had the evidence of his own eyes that Ralegh was right. The small boats still afloat were heaving and tossing in the swell, to the alarm of the soldiers in them. He agreed to the change of plan.

Ralegh, returning to his ship, passed Essex, eagerly watching him to know the decision: 'As eager now,' Ralegh said, 'for a sea fight as earlier for a land attack.' He called out to Essex. '*Intramus*, we're going in .' Essex flung his plumed hat into the sea with a shout of joy.

The soldiers were re-embarked – itself no easy task – and the ships made ready for battle. These strange manoeuvres puzzled and encouraged the Spaniards. At home rumours spread of disasters to the fleet. London resounded with the cry 'Ralegh drowned'. Bess feared the worst.

Little Wat would never tire of asking his father to tell him about the fight. He would listen agog, as would his young friends when they came to play. 'Tell us, Daddy., how you beat the Spaniards': his own childhood mirrored, when he sat at the feet of mariners on the Devon shore and drank in their anecdotes of adventures in far-off lands. Those tales were to colour his whole life, and Wat's. Bess, listening nearby, would have a look of pride mixed with anxiety and foreboding.

His narrative proceeded: 'By then it was almost dark. So it would not have been possible to attack that night, despite pressure on me to do so. The details still had to be settled and on who was to lead the attack. So at ten o'clock I sent a despatch to my Lord Admiral with my plan. First, we would bombard the galleons. We would then deploy two fly-boats with soldiers, to board them before they could set them on fire and scuttle them, which would cheat us of our prizes.

'My plan was adopted. They all wanted to be leader. But it

was decided that I should lead in my ship *Warspite*. Supporting me were to be *The Mary Rose*, commanded by cousin George; *The Lion*, by Southwell; *The Rainbow*, by Vere; *The Swiftsure*, Captain Crosse; *The Dreadnought*, by Sir Conyers and Alexander Clifford; *The Nonpareil*, Dudley; twelve ships sent by the City of London and some fly-boats. Our fleet was moved upon my advice closer to the Harbour entrance.

'My Lord Thomas Howard decided to take over command of Dudley's *Nonpareil* in place of his own flagship *Mer-Honour*, one of the largest, which was kept in the rear. However much I respected the Lord Admiral it was my plan and I was not taking any chance of losing the lead to him or anybody else. So at first light I weighed anchor and headed for the Spanish Fleet.

'A powerful fort, Fort Philip, commanded the harbour. The curtain sea-wall was lined with guns. The four royal galleons were drawn up just outside, and guarding the mouth of the harbour. Under the wall and to our right flank were ranged seventeen Spanish galleys. At anchor inside were forty other ships which we later found were bound for Mexico and other places. As soon as they saw me moving, the four royal galleons did likewise, as did three great galleons from Lisbon, three frigates (which were used also to carry treasure) and two well-armed argosies. The four moved to position under Puntall fort, closer to the harbour mouth which was a bare mile wide. The frigates were to their right. The Lisbon galleons and argosies were drawn up behind them. The seventeen galleys we later learnt had been ordered to interlace in groups of three the large ships.

'I sailed into the middle of them. I was bombarded from Fort Philip and by the guns on the curtain wall. The galleys then opened up on us. I ignored them. I shouted to my men. "They're no more than wasps". What did I do? I gave them a few blasts on our trumpet.' This never failed to raise a loud laugh from his young audience. He went on. 'The galleys moved to take up position in support of the galleons so I loosed off a few cannon at them. But the *St Philip* was my main target. It was their leading ship. Also, I was determined to revenge the loss of Sir Richard Grenville and his *Revenge* five years before at the Azores, even if it cost me my life. He had been heavily outnumbered. The *St Philip* and *St Andrew* had been two of the

Spaniards' men-of-war. I anchored close to them and pounded away. I had been ordered not to board till the fly-boats came up with the soldiers.

'My Lord Admiral, Lord Howard of Effingham, had decided that the sea was too clogged up with ships to get *The Ark Royal* up front and had joined Lord Thomas Howard in *Nonpareil* which with *The Lion*, *The Mary Rose*, *Dreadnought*, *Rainbow* and *Swiftsure* sailed up and anchored close behind me. Towards ten in the morning, my Lord General Essex became impatient. He could hear the gunfire and didn't want to miss the fun. So he went aboard *Swiftsure* and forced it up near my *Warspite*. But I made sure I stayed in the lead.

'For three hours I exchanged cannon shot with the *St Philip* and *St Andrew*, with volleys as thick as musket shot. The flyboats with the soldiers still hadn't come. So I went over to *Swiftsure* and urged my Lord General to get them at once, otherwise my ship would be sunk. If not, I told him, I would have to board from *Warspite* with the men I had, orders or no orders. "To burn or to sink are an equal loss and I must face one or the other", I said. He replied, "That would be much too dangerous. It would risk the Queen's wrath". This was a step she never sanctioned. The risk of being at close quarters with much larger vessels was too high. I persuaded him there was no alternative. Bear in mind that this was in the heat of battle, with metal flying around and the din of explosions, cracking and crashing timbers and splintering rigging. He told me: "I will back you up, upon my word of honour, if you go ahead".

'My meeting with Essex lasted about a quarter of an hour. What do I find on return to *Warspite*? That I was third in line instead of first. So I slipped anchor, sailed through until I was ahead of the other two and anchored athwart the channel to stop any more jockeying for position. My Lord Essex then sailed up to position number three, just behind *Nonpareil*. Then – and this will make you laugh – Vere, when he thought our backs were turned, secretly sent a man to tie a rope onto my ship's side to pull himself level with me. "Look out, Sir Walter", my look-out shouted over the noise, "he's put a rope on us". "I'll be blowed (or some such words)", I said. "The wretched fellow (I used a stronger expression really): Cut it", I ordered. Which they did. He fell back.

'By then, although we were much smaller, we had had the

better of the exchange of cannon fire. Our size gave us an advantage. We could shoot up to them but many of their guns were too high to shoot down at us. A cannon ball crashed into the woodwork beside me and my leg was a mass of large splinters and a bloody mess. But I didn't notice the pain – until later. The fly-boats still hadn't appeared. This wasn't surprising as the sea was running high and there was a fierce wind. But this also meant that we couldn't get alongside the galleons and tie up to board. So I ordered my men: "Lay out a warp and we'll shake hands with her". This we did, onto the *St Philip* under strong covering fire and fastened it to its side. This tied the two ships firmly together. We prepared for boarding. My men crowded on deck, armed with swords and knives, ready to spring over the gap as soon as it had narrowed sufficiently. They were eager for battle, all set to swarm over the *St Philip*.

'It was not to be. The *St Philip* took fright. Instead of fighting back, she slipped anchor and ran aground. Before we could board her they set her on fire, as I had feared. Flames were soon engulfing her, and there were deafening explosions as the ammunition blew up. The men tumbled out in heaps as thick as coals poured out of a sack into many ports at once. The *St Thomas* followed suit. It was a dreadful scene. They leapt into the water half burnt or grievously wounded, or hung by ropes over the ship's side. They drowned. The scene was hell on earth, the like of which I had never seen before.

'But we succeeded in boarding the other two galleons, *St Matthew* and *St Andrew*. We seized them before they could blow them up. The battle at sea was virtually over. Victory was ours. We spared the lives of the survivors. But the Flemings, who had done little or nothing in the fight, slaughtered them mercilessly until either I or the Lord Admiral were able to put a stop to it. The rest of the Spanish fleet was duly dealt with. Now came the task of landing the soldiers and storming Cadiz itself. My wound was too bad for me to run along with them. But my men did their best for me. They carried me ashore on their shoulders and the Lord Admiral sent me a horse. I suffered an hour's agony riding into the town. The wound was very painful and I could see that any moment it would be squashed in the crowd. There was an unruly tumult of yelling soldiers in a frenzied search for what they could find. So I had myself carried back to the ship. There were few left with the fleet: they were all busy sacking Cadiz. I was only too glad to rest my leg.

'All in all our light ships captured or destroyed thirteen enemy men-of-war and seventeen galleys. We were able to rescue all their English prisoners who had been slaving in the galleys. The Spaniards also lost forty merchant vessels. The Earl of Essex celebrated the victory with a service in Cadiz Cathedral. He had behaved most valiantly, without pride or cruelty and gained great honour, as I told everybody when we returned to England.'

A large number of hostages were taken. The cost to their families of redeeming them was considerable. Those who did not pay were kept in Bridewell Prison. The Council of War decided by a majority that holding on to Cadiz would be more trouble than it was worth. So the inhabitants were carefully put on ships and taken to St Mary's Port away from the town. Most of Cadiz was then razed and the forts and fortifications destroyed. All Europe agreed that everyone had been treated humanely. As Ralegh said: 'The King of Spain was one of the first to acknowledge the merciful way we treated them.' He also told his hearers: 'This was the greatest loss the King of Spain has ever suffered.' It indeed signalled the start of the long-term decline in Spain's fortunes.

Arthur had more than redeemed himself from his earlier misdemeanour. He acquitted himself so well in the taking of the town that Essex gave him a knighthood on the spot. Essex and the Lord Admiral handed out some sixty of them.

Ralegh lost no time in sending a despatch to Cecil back in England. At his behest Arthur detailed Sir Anthony Ashley to be its carrier.

There was something of a muddle over the spoils. The Council of War had been in two minds over whether to seize cargo or destroy the ships, cargo and all. The Seville merchants offered them two million ducats to redeem it. While they were debating the question, much of it was whisked away. In a report to Cecil, Ralegh said that had his advice been taken the entire fleet would have been captured with all its contents. It was also discussed whether the English fleet, or part of it, should proceed westward to head off treasure ships due soon. He advised against it because of the state of the ships, men's sickness and the weather. Malicious tongues put this down to his anxiety to get his plunder home.

Nevertheless the participants in the operation did quite well out of it. They succeeded in diverting the greater part of the prize into their own possession. The official return bore little relation to the actual acquisition. The Spaniards estimated their loss in merchandise alone at four million ducats, not counting ships and guns and the town's buildings.

The authorities back in England were well aware of the likely fate of the spoil. They even apprehended Ashley, despite being the bearer of urgent dispatches, and interrogated him about goods he was suspected of concealing between his docking in Plymouth and arrival in London.

Ralegh's expressed reaction was: 'What with ransom of prisoners and capture of prize the Commanders did well out of it. All I gained for my pains were poverty and pain. If God had spared me that blow I could have won a grand house.' In fact he did not do as badly as he liked to make out. He came off better than most. His declared spoils alone amounted to £1,769 worth in plate, pearls, gold ornaments, Turkish carpets, tapestries, wines and a chest of books.

Oxford University also did well. The Bishop of Cadiz had an excellent library. This was carried away and formed the nucleus of the Bodleian, Oxford.

Ralegh and Arthur took five days to sail home. They went straight to Bess at Mile End. Ralegh's praises were sounded publicly and in Court. The reports on the part he played were corroborated by the Lord Admiral. The three were invited to a feast at Knole (the house and estate presented by the Queen to her cousin, Thomas Sackville, Lord Buckhurst and 1st Earl of Dorset, with whom Ralegh was on good terms) to celebrate the triumph in its picturesque setting in the Kent countryside. Dismounting in the Green Court they were escorted through the Great Hall, up the Great Staircase and into the grand room at the top where they dined in state.

Bess and he were in Sherborne by mid-August. Shortly afterwards Essex landed back from Cadiz at Plymouth. As he rode through Sherborne on his way to London, the Abbey bells were rung in greeting and congratulation. Ralegh was one of the first to welcome him. They had been successful comrades in arms.

Cecil reported the public applause for this significant victory to the Queen and summarized the operation.

'Do you mean to tell me,' she exclaimed, 'that the total winnings are no more than the ridiculous figure you've given me?'

'Well, Ma'am, it was a great victory,' Cecil tried to explain, 'and there was a limit to what they could do with a comparatively small force, bearing in mind the numbers on the other side.'

'What are they asking for, Burghley?'

'We calculate that Lord Admiral Howard should receive £5,000 and Ralegh £3,000. Essex put in £22,000 of his own money. He ought to be allowed the prisoners' ransom money.'

'You're being hoodwinked,' she said unsympathetically.

'I think not, Ma'am,' Burghley protested. 'I'm the first to guard the Treasury coffers, as you know. But if I might suggest with great respect, it will be widely considered unfair to augment Treasury funds excessively. We must be reasonable.'

'What do you say, Cecil? You've heard your father's views.'

'Ralegh has expressed the hope that your most excellent Majesty will take his labours and endeavours into account. He says he has no other riches but that hope,' replied Cecil.

'He always was a good talker,' said the Queen briefly. 'Anyway, they've all lined their pockets and they're getting nothing more. So that's that.'

13

Ups And Downs

In January 1597, Cecil's wife Elizabeth died. Bess was heartbroken at the loss of her closest friend whom she had seen constantly whenever she was in London. She expressed her sorrow and sympathy to Cecil and assured him of her willingness to help in any way she could with his little boy, William, who was slightly younger than her Wat.

Ralegh wrote him a touching letter of condolence from Sherborne. 'It is true that you have lost a good and virtuous wife and I myself an honourable friend and kinswoman. But there was a time when she was unknown to you. She is now no more yours, nor of your acquaintance, but immortal, and not needing nor knowing your love or sorrow. Therefore you shall but grieve for that which is now as then it was, when not yours: only bettered by the difference in this, that she has passed the wearisome journey of this dark world, and has possession of her inheritance.

'She has left behind her the fruits of her love, for whose sakes you ought to care for yourself, that you leave them not without a guide.... I believe that sorrows are dangerous companions, converting bad into evil, and evil into worse.... The mind of man is that part of God which is in us – which, by how much it is subject to passion, by so much is it further from Him that gave it us....

Yours ever beyond the power of words to utter.'

By an ironic twist of fate it was the association of himself and Bess with Elizabeth Cecil's two brothers, Henry Brooke (Lord Cobham) and George Brooke, that was to prove Ralegh's undoing.

A family quarrel reared. His brother John had died. His nephew, Sir John Gilbert the younger, had complained bitterly that his share of spoils from an adventure had been insufficient. Ralegh rebuked him sharply. 'It were a strange conceit to think a nephew should be considered as bestowing a favour for going to war with his uncle – you being then of no ability. My estate being so far in debt, I could not neglect a son and wife. There is more land to descend to you than any of mine. I would be ashamed to have any man know of your ingratitude. As for your fortunes, fear not that I will labour to lessen them; for I will not hereafter look after them. And when mine shall be at their worst, yet they shall not need your help, whatever you have done to mine. Your uncle, Ralegh.'

Local affairs now demanded attention. He had taken a lease of fishing rights a few years before in a stretch of the Yeo, together with meadow pasture from one Thomas Swetnam and his nephew Laurence. Having diverted water on laying out the lodge garden he no longer needed the fishing and surrendered the lease accordingly.

After his enforced absence from Court his overtures to Essex paid off. His rival could hardly fail to give credit for the unstinting praise over Cadiz from his former adversary. Essex was the essential, if reluctant, avenue to the Queen's favour. The national acclaim for both of them may have influenced the Queen. In May Ralegh was allowed back to Court. Essex was not there to signify approval nor was he present at the beginning of June when Cecil re-introduced him to the Queen. Ralegh could not know that her change of heart was due in some measure to Cecil who had found himself in need of a balancing weight against Essex. Cecil in his turn did not know that Ralegh had been subsidizing Essex to help meet the heavy cost of his land forces and fondness for military exercises. This had gone some way to encourage the softening of former objections to Ralegh's reconciliation with the Queen. He entered the Presence and knelt before her.

'Welcome back to us, Sir Walter,' she said to him formally but adequately. 'You have been away a long time.'

'Ma'am, it has been an age. I would have flown to you had you lifted your little finger. I have dreamt every hour of the day for this moment,' he replied feelingly.

'You are still my Captain of the Guard,' she informed him. 'You will attend as such from now on.'

He took up his duties with gusto. He filled a number of

vacancies in the Guard, with the due formalities of oaths of allegiance to her Majesty. Nothing was said of Bess despite her pleadings. He had the wit to avoid any subject which might jeopardize his newly-regained favour. He accompanied the Queen to the Privy Council meeting later that morning. The Court were not slow to observe the resurrection of the old Ralegh as he swaggered in from then on to the Queen's Privy Chamber. That evening she graciously invited him to accompany her in her ride round the Park. His star was surely in the ascendant again – but always subject to the vagaries of his impetuous and short-sighted whims and obsessions. He was in and out of Court so often that he was commonly known as 'the tennis-ball of fortune which she was delighted to sport with'.

Down in Sherborne Adrian Gilbert was lording it over the Castle. This had given him a real job, he thought. He was well-liked by the locals who enjoyed his sense of fun and knew they need not take him too seriously. He enjoyed his pint. He had put on weight with good living. But as Ralegh discovered when he and Bess came down from London he and Meere, his deputy, not reconciled to being replaced, were constantly putting one another's backs up. 'He's always niggling at me for spending too much,' Adrian complained, 'but you wouldn't believe what it costs to keep this old heap wind and weather proof, let alone have a bit of comfort.'

'I thought for a moment you must be talking about yourself,' laughed Ralegh, poking him in his well-covered ribs. 'Anyway, you needn't worry about that,' Ralegh assured his brother. 'He's a little swine at the best of times. Not surprising with his Essex connection.' A little less of Adrian's bonhomie and more of Cecil's cool appraisal would have served Ralegh far better in dealing with someone like Meere. 'I wonder he didn't keep that quiet. What's new in Sherborne?'

'I had a queer experience the other night,' Adrian said. 'I saw a ghost.'

'Pull the other one,' Ralegh retorted. 'There aren't such things. Hariot would say you're crazy.'

Bess interrupted. 'Don't you be so sure, Walter. More things are possible than we can ever imagine. Tell us about it, Adrian.'

'There are odd goings-on in a house near the Abbey,' he explained. 'It used to be a monks' dormitory but has been empty some while. I posted myself in a cottage opposite. At about midnight I, and the couple I was keeping watch with, saw the light of a candle appear in an upstairs room. It moved across the room and back again with no sign of anybody holding it, three times in all. We went over, crept in – and something whizzed past our heads, hit the wall and shattered. Then an object crashed to the ground beside us. We lit our lanterns. I was feeling pretty shaky, I can tell you. The floor was covered in broken crockery, with a large painting of an old monk in the middle of it, undamaged. What do you make of that?'

'Over-indulgence in liquor I would say,' Ralegh offered.

'You shouldn't joke about it, Walter,' cautioned Bess. 'You remember that night when we were both woken up at Durham House in the early hours by the sound of two lots of running feet? They came closer and closer and then we both heard dreadful pummelling going on just below our bedroom window. We hopped out of bed. We could see where, but not what, the noise was coming from. We stood there listening and watching for a while, Adrian. Then Walter quietly opened the window to see what was going on. The window made a little squeak – and the noise suddenly stopped. We looked at the spot first thing next morning expecting to find something horrid. There was nothing there.'

'The window needed oiling,' Ralegh said.

'These are no joking matters,' warned Adrian. 'I take them seriously. There's a lot we don't know about – even you, Walter.'

'Your light was probably that old monk having a bit of fun. Wanting a nun maybe.'

'A poor joke that,' reproved Bess. 'You should treat the subject with less levity. It's time we went to Church again. We pay for our seats – although we don't have to. We ought to use them.'

Ralegh sent for Meere to receive his report and give him further instructions. He showed him some sacks of potatoes. 'I don't suppose you've ever seen anything like these before, Meere. You wouldn't, because you never go anywhere,' he taunted.

Meere ignored this quip. 'Whatever are they, Sir Walter?'

'They're called potatoes. They come from my far-off colony

Virginia. Named after her Majesty, you know.'

'Whatever do you do with them?' Meere asked.

'Plant them, my dear fellow: about two or three inches below the surface and, hey presto, three months later they've multiplied a dozen-fold. They've taken off on my Irish estates, I can tell you. Give them to some of our tenants. Tell them they must put them in on Good Friday.'

'That's a variable date,' Meere pointed out.

'No matter. That's when it must be. We'll make it a good old Dorset custom. They must earth them up in ridges.'

Spring was on the way and with it another offensive against Spain. Secret meetings had taken place at Cecil's house between him, Essex and Ralegh. It was decided to send another offensive expedition. During its preparation Cecil invited them to The Rose Playhouse on the South bank by Southwark bridge, down-river of its rival The Swan, to a staging of William Shakespeare's *Richard the Second*. The printed play the following August was an expurgated version but the one they saw included the abdication scene. It would have infuriated the Queen had she known. She was ageing and ever more sensible of her increasingly precarious position. The three were highly amused at this episode with its current implications.

'My Lord Essex,' said Ralegh, 'you would make an excellent young Bolingbroke – good old Henry IV to be.'

'And you my father, old John of Gaunt?' replied Essex. 'And Cecil here can be the venerable Duke of York, perched on the fence. And Elizabeth is ready-made for her rôle.'

They all thought it a huge joke. 'But the beauty of the verse,' exclaimed Ralegh. ' "This precious stone set in the silver sea . . . . This blessed plot, this earth, this realm, this England . . ." I would give everything I have to write such lines.'

A fleet of three squadrons was assembled at Plymouth with Essex as Commander-in-Chief combining (unusually) the offices of Admiral and General. Lord Thomas Howard was Vice-Admiral and Ralegh again Rear-Admiral. It included the galleons *St Andrew* and *St Matthew* captured at Cadiz. Essex was guest for a night on *Warspite* with Ralegh who reported to Cecil: 'My Lord Essex will sleep well tonight. I am a good watchman at sea.' They sailed in July but violent weather forced them back with losses. They eventually got away on 17

August. More bad weather disabled the two Spanish galleons, less manoeuvrable than the smaller English ships. Ralegh's *Warspite* had to put into Lisbon for repairs. He rejoined Essex and the rest of the fleet at Flores in the Azores.

Ralegh was a voracious reader. He always took a supply of books with him when he went to sea. On the bridge in the daytime, the ocean all around, and in the watches of the night, he used the time otherwise on his hands in study. His general knowledge became phenomenal.

A report came through that their main objective, the Spanish silver fleet, was due shortly at the Azores where they were lying in wait. Essex split his force into three. He ordered Ralegh to join him at Fayal and set off ahead of him. Ralegh, with his superior navigational ability and seamanship, arrived there first. For three days he lay at anchor in the harbour waiting for Essex as instructed. It was deemed an affront to commence battle without the Commander-in-Chief. On the fourth day, as Essex had still not appeared, he and his officers took stock of the situation. The inhabitants could be seen strengthening their defences and carting possessions into the interior. They accordingly decided to launch their attack. They scaled the cliffs and fought their way to the town against the Spaniards' resistance, plundering it and spending the night there in comfort.

Essex arrived the following day. Ralegh rowed out to meet him. Essex, after a perfunctory greeting, accused him of disobeying orders. 'To engage without my express command, in my absence, and storm Fayal was a serious breach of discipline. That is an offence punishable by death.'

'I did no more than carry out my duty,' replied Ralegh. 'As I had been detached from the main fleet I was in effect the principal commander under your Lordship. There was therefore no question of my acting "without the Commander's orders".'

A henchman of Essex, Sir Christopher Blount, did his best to incite Essex to keep the argument boiling. It would otherwise have been dropped. Howard interceded and peace was restored. Ralegh's only significant haul from the whole operation was the capture of a carrick laden with a huge quantity of cochineal.

Bess meanwhile had been alarmed at the absence of news

and had told Cecil how worried she was. Her suspense ended in October when Ralegh returned, in poor health but intact. The weather had been so bad that he had not been to bed, or even in his cabin, for ten nights and days.

The only person to receive recognition was Lord Admiral Thomas Howard. He was created Earl of Nottingham, which gave him precedence over Essex, who withdrew from Court in a sulk. The Queen discussed the delicate situation with Howard.

'Essex is taking this badly, my Lord. Could we not bend the rules a trifle and let him, as your predecessor in time, keep his place in the rank?'

'Ma'am, that would be unconstitutional,' Howard objected. 'I couldn't accept it for a moment nor, I think, would the peers. It would create an undesirable precedent.'

Ralegh tried his hand at persuasion. 'For the sake of her Majesty's peace of mind, my Lord.'

'Not for that or any other spurious reason,' was the curt reply.

When they were on their own, the Queen told Ralegh: 'I'm extremely upset about this. The trouble is I can see both sides. But I want Essex back in Court.'

Ralegh had, unusually, a diplomatic solution which was bound, however, to upset Howard. 'If you make my Lord Essex Earl Marshal, Ma'am, that will automatically reinstate his precedence.' She thought this a good idea and acted on it.

Within the next fortnight Ralegh received reports of a projected Spanish attack on Cornwall. He passed it with top priority on to the Command Headquarters at Plymouth. The reports were confirmed and amplified by a statement from a Spanish captain whose ship was captured. Its armament was said to include field artillery, mules and oxen and a company of Irish. It was heading for Falmouth, but had been driven back by storms. A strong contingent of soldiers was sent to defend Falmouth. But the danger passed. The defences were stood down and peace reigned in the household.

There could be no better time for the Queen's Players, visiting Sherborne, to take over the Church House, at a rent of two shillings, to stage their performances. Might they not have played *The Merry Wives of Windsor* with a Falstaff reference to Ralegh's voyagings (of which Shakespeare like all England was aware) when sending his page to the two lady objects of his desire:

'Sail like my pinnace to those golden shores.'

Sherborne Lodge would have made an ideal lodging at the conclusion of their play. They could have been entertained by Bess and Adrian. Their host, genius in several spheres, could have interrogated them on the doings of his genius contemporary.

In the New Year the Earl of Southampton, Shakespeare's patron, ran into trouble. One evening when the Queen had retired early the Earl, Ralegh and another courtier were playing primero in the Presence Chamber. They were making too much noise and the Queen sent one of the gentlemen in waiting, Willoughby, to tell them to finish their game. Ralegh at once settled his account and went home. The Earl's reaction was the reverse. 'I resent your impertinence, Willoughby. I'll have you know you're addressing a peer of the realm not one of the servants. I'll remind you that you are no more than an esquire. I'll do as I please.'

'I'm only trying to carry out her Majesty's orders,' he protested. 'I must insist that you desist, my Lord.'

'The damn cheek of it. You can go to hell. This may help you on your way' – and Southampton dealt him a hard blow.

Willoughby did not take this lying down. In the tussle that followed he pulled out some of the Earl's precious locks. The Queen made a point of thanking him next morning when he had explained what all the commotion had been about.

Southampton then compounded his offence by compromising one of the maids-in-waiting, Elizabeth Vernon. As a courtier commented: 'Southampton's fair mistress doth wash her fairest face with too many tears.' But all turned out well – or as well as could be expected. He married her. But it was without the Queen's permission, which damned her Court career. She was dismissed.

It was Essex who had encouraged the marriage. He showed his contempt for the Queen by a rude gesture. She slapped his face whereupon he put his hand on his sword hilt and called her a 'King in Petticoats'. Devoted as she was, she could not overlook such behaviour.

A further irritant was conjured up on the Queen's birthday, 17 November 1598. Ralegh discussed with Bess the form his greeting should take, as befitting the Captain of the Guard.

'Something really colourful,' Bess suggested.

'Yes, I'll parade my company as a Guard of Honour in orange – orange plumes in their hats and orange favours.'

On the morning in question they marched, with Ralegh at their head, to the Palace to greet the Queen.

Essex, however, had learnt of Ralegh's intention. No sooner had the men taken up position than Essex arrived at the head of his company of vassals numbering upwards of two thousand and similarly arrayed, completely upstaging his rival – and so ridiculing his mistress. The festivities, ruined, broke up in disorder.

After further insulting behaviour, Essex was allotted the unenviable post of Lord Deputy of Ireland. He set off with excessive pomp and ceremony, inflaming his supporters. Contrary to the Queen's specific orders to take a firm line with the Irish rebels, in particular the Earl of Tyrone, he adopted a policy of moderation and tried to do a deal. This the Privy Council firmly overruled. Rumour spread that he was plotting an invasion from Ireland. Instead, he stormed back with a band of his followers without permission, in effect deserting his post. He was taken before the Council, placed in custody, then under house arrest, but released. He had unswerving support throughout from the Londoners, for whom he was in the nature of a hero. Ralegh was consulted by Cecil who, in view of the gravity of the situation, took advice from many quarters. He advised a steady hand with Essex, in Cecil's and the nation's interests, to bring him into line. The situation was complicated by intrigues with which Essex and his supporters had tangled with James VI of Scotland, with a watchful eye on the Queen's declining years. Ralegh tried unsuccessfully through Lady Essex to mend matters. Essex, forbidden to see the Queen, unceremoniously burst in on her one morning. She had barely started her toilet preparations. She had not even had time to put on her wig. They had a violent argument. He told her: 'the conditions you are imposing are as crooked as your carcass.' She was speechless with rage and humiliation. All the Court either heard or learnt of this affront. Her feeling of love for him was obliterated at a stroke. Ralegh shared the general horror. 'This will seal his fate,' he thought. His reaction was one of gloom, not triumph.

The Globe Playhouse had recently been built near The Rose and The Swan. He asked Bess if she would like to see a play.

'Women never go to plays,' she said. 'Well, hardly ever.'

'They can if they are escorted,' he assured her. 'Why shouldn't you have your entertainment?'

'I'd love to see inside The Globe,' she exclaimed. 'They say Richard Burbidge is playing – our leading actor now his father's gone. It's the last word in playhouses. They built it from the one north of the river they pulled down. Will Shakespeare and the Lord Chamberlain's men are putting on *As You Like It* and *Henry V*. I'll have a good laugh if we see the first. You can see yourself as Henry in the other.'

'And you?' he enquired. 'Rosalind – or Katherine? One married the Duke, the other the King.'

'I did better than either a Duke or a King,' she laughed. ' "It was a lover and his lass" . . . If only we were in Sherborne's meadows now.'

They settled for *As You Like It* the following night, weather permitting. It was fortunately a fine night: no fear of rain washing out the audience. The Globe Flag was flying. The play was on. The Thames watermen were doing a roaring trade as people streamed across. Bess dressed up for the occasion. She wore 'a dark coloured hanging sleeve robe, tufted on the arms with under it a close-bodied gown of white satin, flowered with black, and close sleeves down to her waist. Round her neck was a string of large pearls and on her fingers a ring of clustered diamonds and another of sapphire,' all precious as gifts from him.

They were shown through the tiring room, as a special privilege to avoid the crowds at the main entrance, and into their seats in the lowest gallery in the amphitheatre with the best view of the stage. They had been invited to sit on the stage itself – as some of the gallants chose. That would have been Ralegh's choice, but Bess preferred somewhere less conspicuous. The heat was soon trying and the smell of oranges and peppermint almost overpowering – particularly from those paying one penny in the pit. This did nothing to lessen Bess's excitement.

The trumpet blew – three blasts. The red curtain was pulled back. Orlando – indeed Burbidge – set the scene.

The play had a tremendous reception. As they were rowed

back to Durham House, Ralegh repeated:
>'Under the greenwood tree
>Who loves to lie with me.'

They laughed. The words struck a chord. Did they not remember a certain wood?

Then he fell silent. He recalled the last play he had seen, Christopher Marlowe's *Dr Faustus*. The hum of London and the rhythmic splash of the oars reminded him of happy hours he had spent with its author and other companions combing the streets and taverns and exploring the heights of literary achievement – or just having roistering fun.

'You know, Bess,' he said, 'I still miss Christopher. Only twenty-nine when he was killed. I loved him. I always will. I often think of him. A love with no sexual connotations, you see. He was totally honest. He meant so much to me. It is something sacred that will be with me always.'

The water lapped the bank as they stepped ashore and made their way the short distance to Durham House.

Ralegh was the Queen's trusted support. She resolved at his request to secure for him the freehold – fee simple – of the Sherborne Estates of which, as he pointed out, he was only the lessee. There were at least a dozen others who would have grabbed it if they could. The freehold was still with the Dean and Chapter of Salisbury. To achieve this she once again used the vacant bishopric as a lever. Her overtures to two aspirants to this office were unsuccessful. They would not accept the strings attached. With the third, her godson Henry Cotton who was a Prebendary of Winchester and one of her Chaplains, her scheme succeeded. For him this unexpected offer of promotion, unlikely to be repeated, was irresistible. The Dean of Windsor expressed his disapproval forcefully: 'To bargain for a bishopric is disgraceful and scandalous.' Cecil rebuked him for his opposition 'to Ralegh and to me that love him.' As soon as he was installed, Cotton saw to it that the Dean and Chapter vested the freehold in the Queen. She thereupon granted Ralegh, his heirs, successors and assigns the freehold of the Manor and Castle of Sherborne and the Hundreds of Sherborne and Yetminster on payment of an annual rent charge of £260 to the See of Salisbury.

As Bess and he looked out at the park from their bedroom window he mused: 'All this is really ours now, Bess, to do what we will with.' Meere said to him next day, disguising his true feelings: 'Monarch of all you survey, Sir Walter. You will now receive all these rents as the *dominus*. My congratulations.'

Cecil had been relying on Bess to advise him on the bringing up of his young son William. He was devoted to him, more than ever after the loss of his wife. Early in 1599 he asked the Raleghs to take William back with them to Sherborne for some fresh country air. He would have the company of their son Wat, then six years old. Down in Dorset Ralegh and Bess both took a hand in the boys' education. Bess dealt with the more practical aspects and the fairy stories. She did not get involved in their spelling lessons. He enjoyed taking them through their sums and their books. To learn to read early would open up a wide vista. He could thrill them with tales of adventure in foreign parts, of strange and exotic birds, animals and people he had encountered, descriptions of islands in the West Indies of surpassing beauty, battles at sea and on land and of frightening gales and storms. Little Wat was determined to follow in this great man's footsteps.

Ralegh was able to write reassuringly to William's father in the spring. 'Because I know you can receive no pleasanter news from here than of your beloved creature, I can tell you William is in good health. Whereas when I last wrote to say he was a little troubled with looseness, I thank God he is freed thereof and better in health and strength than ever I knew. His stomach, hitherto weak, is amended. He is eating well and digests rightly. I hope this air will agree with him. He is also better kept to his books than anywhere else:' reminiscent of a house-master's mid-term report to anxious parents.

The boys may have had reservations on the enforced study. But they could relax when Bess and he took them down to the river fishing. Catching sticklebacks, small trout and tadpoles and putting them into their pails was a supreme joy. They inevitably revelled in paddling in the water and soaking their shoes and socks. This took him back to his Devon childhood when all the days were sunny, which he relived with them beside the river or along the hedges searching for birds' nests; or, when a little older, hearing of their getting up to the sort of risky mischief of which parents never know anything: the joy of dreamy days that seem to go on and on but pass all too quickly, lived again with children – and maybe grandchildren.

April in a sense was a significant month. The Raleghs had become friendly with Henry Brooke, Lord Cobham, whom they had first come to know through his sister Elizabeth Cecil. The Cobhams had an ancestor, Sir John Oldcastle, Shakespeare's Sir John Falstaff in *Henry IV Parts I and II* and *The Merry Wives of Windsor*. It was said to be through their insistence, to avoid a blot on the family, that he agreed to change the surname in the play. Ralegh often went to Bath for the 'cure'. He wrote to Cobham hoping he and Bess would see him there and offering half the house he had taken. He also hinted at his wish to have the Governorship of Jersey which had recently fallen vacant. In the event Cobham had to cancel his planned visit to Bath because he was competing for the purchase of an estate, Otford Park. Ralegh wrote to him from the Pump Room saying how they missed him: 'My wife will despair ever to see you in these parts if you do not come now.'

They were all good friends. A new friend was the eccentric intellectual Earl of Northumberland who invited him to dinner at Sion House in Isleworth, Middlesex.

In September 1600 he achieved his latest objective. He was appointed Governor of Jersey. He sailed from Weymouth to take up his duties. Bess took the boys (William was still with them) to wave goodbye from the harbour. The weather was fine as he left but the crossing was rough and it took two days and nights. He was given a royal welcome on his arrival. It was a pleasant enough island but he estimated not worth a third of what he had been led to believe. Within two days he had written to Bess to tell her how he fared. He also sent a report to Cecil. He was making good the fortifications and restoring Mount Orgueil Castle, a sizable fort with the Normandy coast in view.

Bess wrote to Cecil telling him of William's progress. The boys had built up a close friendship. Cecil had written about a fire in their Durham House. She told him that if it had been any worse their 'meagre quantity of plate and other things would have been destroyed'. It meant they would lose Cecil's and Cobham's company and so would not enjoy that winter. She suggested Cecil might take over some of it. Her husband had spent hundreds of pounds on the upkeep of 'this rotten house'. But at least the Queen would not have to rebuild the Bishop of Durham's old stables.

William, she said, was putting on weight and enjoyed bathing. She loved having him with them. As she wrote:

'My cossin Will is heer, very will, and louketh will and fat with his batheing. This, wishing you all honnor and the full contentements of your hart.
I ever rest,
Your assured poure frind,
E. Ralegh'

Ralegh was a good family man – when he was there. William was fond of, indeed worshipped, them and stayed with them often. On one occasion they had sent him up to Bath for three weeks under a Dr Sherwood's care. On his return he wrote to his father in Latin (showing how his education had progressed): 'I am now returned to Sherborne in the best of health.' He also wrote to Ralegh likewise in London:

'Sir Walter,
We must all exclaim and cry out because you will not come down. You being absent, we are like soldiers that when their Captains are absent they know not what to do. You are so busy about idle matters. Sir Walter, I will be plain with you. I pray you leave idle matters and come down to us.'

Surely if that could not move Ralegh, nothing could.
On his return from a visit to Jersey they were joined at Sherborne by Cecil. The Governors of Sherborne School were dealing with the appointment of a successor to William Woode the Headmaster. To secure this post of prestige at least one applicant was not above offering financial inducement to the Governors, which was firmly rejected. Cecil by letter to them indicated his support for another applicant, John Geare, Master of Arts, Headmaster of Wimborne Grammar School, whom Ralegh likewise supported as did a number of the county gentry. In September, on Geare providing a sworn assurance that he had not given or promised any reward, he was appointed. The Governors managed to persuade Woode to vacate the premises, but not before Christmas. Geare had to rent a house in the meantime. His appointment secured a bonus for the School: he brought with him a number of 'gentlemen's sons' from the school at Wimborne, as boarders –

a practice not unusual in the country then or for the next couple of centuries or so.

The Governors were perhaps slightly uneasy over the circumstances in which the appointment had been made and the involvement of the Queen's Chief Minister and the Lord of the Manor. They wrote to Cecil putting on record their independence and impartiality; and the proper manner in which it had been done, all above board.

Early in November Ralegh was in Cornwall seeing to the interests of the tin-miners 'to keep a promise with these poor men in whom I have the utmost faith'. He sought to get another lawsuit by the powerful Corporation of Plymouth transferred from the Court of Star Chamber in Westminster to his Stannary Court. The case involved the diversion of a watercourse which threatened the closure of two hundred tin works.

Meanwhile the affairs of Essex had been going from bad to worse. His contacts with King James VI of Scotland had come to the attention of the authorities. He blamed Ralegh, Cecil and Cobham for all his troubles.

Cecil and Ralegh could see in him all the hallmarks of the irresponsible rabble-rouser seeking personal position at any cost – a potential dictator. He lacked, however, the essential ingredients of cunning and the back-up of intelligent advisers, together with political astuteness. Cecil had all three. Ralegh the first two, but not the third.

One of the Essex supporters was a cousin of Ralegh, Sir Ferdinando Gorges. It became common knowledge that an insurrection was brewing among Essex's conspirators. Ralegh decided to warn his cousin against it and invited him urgently to come and see him in Durham House. Gorges consulted Essex who instructed him: 'Meet him half-way across the river.'

Ralegh agreed to this and that night rowed himself out alone and met Gorges and his two companions. Ralegh warned him: 'You're going to get yourself in terrible trouble if you're not careful. You're playing with fire. They know what's going on. I don't know whether you know it, but there's a warrant out for your arrest. Get yourself back to Plymouth at once before there's any trouble. That is where you should be in any case as Governor of Plymouth.'

'It's too late,' he replied, 'I believe in the Essex cause. I'm up to the ears in it.'

'In what? enquired Ralegh.

'We have two thousand men standing by who will live or die for their freedom,' he told him.

'What? Against the Queen's authority?'

'It is because you and the rest have abused that authority that we are taking action. This will be the bloodiest day's work that ever was,' Gorges exclaimed.

'For goodness sake think of your duty and sworn allegiance,' Ralegh exhorted him. But it was a waste of time to argue.

While this was taking place Sir Christopher Blount, unknown to Gorges, was waiting in his boat at Essex Stairs. He had been unable to persuade Gorges to rid them of Ralegh so he decided to do it himself with some of Essex's servants. He pushed off from the bank and made for where they were talking. Gorges, who had half suspected something like this might happen, spotted him approaching. He pushed Ralegh's boat away and urged him: 'Get back quick.' As he complied, four shots were fired at him but missed. Other attempts by those in authority to dissuade Essex from his venture were rebuffed.

The rebellion started with Essex leading his large company of nobility and gentry, and others, up The Strand and into the City, all armed, to raise support from Londoners. Their exhortations fell on deaf ears. This was much further than most were prepared to go to support him. By then all the Government's defences were in place. Ralegh with his men was guarding the Palace. Barricades had been set up and troops posted. Essex was proclaimed a traitor. He realized his cause was lost and resolved to flee. But the London Trainbands who had earlier mustered against the Armada blocked his escape routes. Lud Gate was closed, bolted and chained. To get back to Essex House he had to go by boat to Essex Stairs. He intended to hold out in Essex House but Lord Charles Howard, the Earl of Nottingham, brought up heavy guns and compelled surrender.

Even at his trial in Westminster Hall Essex kept up his show of insolence. His illness may have had something to do with it, which included suffering from stone. When Ralegh was called to give evidence Essex exclaimed: 'What booteth it to swear this fox?' His crime was in effect making war against the

Queen. The death sentence was to be carried out at The Tower – mere beheading unlike the dreadful end for his misguided followers with lower social status.

Southampton grovelled and was released after a period in prison. Shakespeare's reaction to his patron is not recorded.

Ralegh as Captain of the Guard had to attend all executions for treason. Blount, before his turn at the scaffold came, called for Ralegh. 'I beseech you to forgive me for the wrong I did you,' he implored.

'I most willingly forgive you,' Ralegh assured him, 'and I beseech God to forgive you and to give you His Divine comfort.' Surely this was no cry of an atheist.

Blount then started to give the spectators his final address on this earth. The Captain of The Tower, in charge of the execution, interrupted him and ordered the executioner to proceed with his duty. Ralegh intervened. 'This is the sacred moment of his life. Pray give him the leisure of speaking his mind in full before going hence.'

When the turn of Essex came he had abandoned his hitherto disdainful air. 'I have been justly spewed out of this Realm,' he said. 'I can only say that Ralegh and Cobham were true servants to the Queen and State.'

Ralegh stood by near him, hoping he likewise would ask to speak to him. However, sensing that people round about might think he was gloating, he withdrew to watch from a Tower window. If, as some said, Essex did ask for Ralegh, the message did not get through.

As he watched, some onlookers saw him smoking and criticized him for what seemed to them revelling in a rival's downfall. He was in fact cast down with melancholy. He rowed back up the river sadly. He told Bess when he arrived home: 'This has been one of the worst days of my life. He could have been a friend but was eaten up with jealousy and ambition. He said not a word to me before he went. It was that terrible thing he said to the Queen that really cost him his life. He leaves my good friend Sidney's wife a widow for the second time. And what have I done in my life?' he asked despairingly. 'Nothing. I own estates. But half of them are worthless, the other half I barely have time to see. Virginia struggling, Guiana but a pipe dream, like its goldmines. I have served the Queen and the Council faithfully. I have shared in many of their meetings.

They have often sought my advice. But she has never made me one of them. Her sun is setting. What of my sun? The sky is full of dark clouds.'

At times like this only a loving wife can comfort.

14

Rogue's Writs

The loss of Essex hit the Queen more deeply than any, herself included, had realized. No alternative course would have been possible. There were many who regretted his passing and blamed her. She missed a courtier to whom she had once been devoted. He had not merited her devotion. She had been spurned. She took her frustration out on the Court, particularly her maids-in-waiting.

Down in Sherborne Ralegh was having more difficulties with Meere, a 'sly fellow'. He had never trusted him. Meere detested Ralegh and thwarted him whenever he thought he could get away with it. The last straw was finding Meere tracing his signature over and over on a piece of transparent paper from a document Ralegh had signed, for which no satisfactory explanation was forthcoming.

Ralegh discussed matters with his brother Adrian, then resolved on action. He summoned Meere and told him: 'As you know, I'm not at all pleased with your behaviour or with the way you're doing the job. I am therefore terminating your appointment as Bailiff from today,' he declared.

'You can't do that, Sir Walter,' Meere protested. 'You granted it me for fifty years, you remember, in writing. There are still forty-one to run.'

'Forty-one my foot. You'll go now and pass Attorney Robert Dolberry all the books,' Ralegh demanded. 'He's a lawyer I can trust.'

'Whatever you say, I am still the legal Bailiff for Sherborne. I shall continue to act as such,' insisted Meere.

'We'll see about that. There's another thing: that house you built just outside the Castle. You had no permission to build there, other than one you gave yourself. You'll have to vacate it.'

'It was vacant land, Sir Walter. Everyone, including you, knew where I was putting it and made no objection. I therefore had implied legal authority and I now have a prescriptive right.'

Adrian was standing in the background, enjoying the fun. He loved a quarrel and the more violent, the better. Bess did not share their blunt approach. 'It's his life's work,' she reminded them, 'and what about his poor wife?'

'It's hard on her, I agree,' said Ralegh. 'But it's no good being soft. She's a nice little thing, not like her sneak of a husband, but we mustn't let that influence us. There's plenty else to do in his legal practice. I'll bet he makes a fortune debt-collecting alone.' He published in the Abbey the dismissal of Meere and the appointment of his replacement.

The first test was when writs had to be served on behalf of the Sheriff. He was the Officer of the Crown for enforcement of law and order in the County, including the administration of justice. The Sheriff of Dorset was John Stocker. He and the prospective Clerk of the Peace, a lawyer named Philip Alexander, looked into the delicate issue which had reared suddenly in Sherborne. Ralegh summarized his case briefly and succinctly. 'I don't like the fellow. I don't trust him. I've dismissed him and appointed Dolberry.'

'I've no objection to Robert Dolberry as such,' replied Stocker. 'He's an extremely good lawyer – would you not agree, Alexander?' His companion nodded. 'He briefs for cases in the Assizes and Quarter Sessions,' he went on, 'and knows the ropes. That is not the point. He hasn't been legally appointed as Bailiff, nor could he be if Meere is the lawful Bailiff.'

'I'm Lord of the Manor. That should be enough.'

'No, with respect, Sir Walter,' said Alexander, 'it is not sufficient. It puts us in an impossible position. Just imagine: if we let Dolberry serve the writs and the Courts in Westminster Hall decide it's illegal, we shall all be in trouble: actions for trespass, false imprisonment, breach of the peace, tampering with the Queen's Justice and Lord knows what. Give it another thought, we beg of you.'

'Nothing doing. I've made my decision and that's that.'

But it was not 'that'. The legal advice to the Sheriff was that he had no authority to serve writs otherwise than by the duly appointed Bailiff. He was no mere servant to be dismissed at will. The fact that he had received his appointment from the Lord of the Manor was immaterial. He was the accredited officer responsible for an essential part of the Crown's administration of Justice. The Clerk of the Peace, as Alexander reminded him, held office for life or during good behaviour and the same principle applied to the Bailiff, at least for the fifty years of his term. He therefore forwarded the writs to Meere as usual and he duly served them as hitherto.

This incensed Ralegh. When the next writ arrived for service, Ralegh and his men, including Adrian, seized Meere, snatched the writ away and took it to Dolberry's office and handed it to him for service. Dolberry did not enquire too closely how the document had come into their possession. He proceeded to execute his assumed legal duty. He also had taken legal advice, which was to the effect that Lords of the Manor had legal powers at common law over-riding statute law and Royal Prerogative. (Lord Justice Edward Coke was similarly arguing on behalf of the common law against Charles I and his claims for the Royal Prerogative some thirty years later.)

Meere was satisfied that he was in the right. He knew he had the backing of the county authorities. He accordingly exercised what he considered his right as a Crown officer and arrested Dolberry, and locked him up for obstructing the course of justice. Ralegh boiled over when he was told about this unexpected development. He took his men at once to the town jail in Duck Lane, which ran from the bottom of Cheap Street to the river, forced open the jail door and freed him. Meere responded by obtaining a Sheriff's warrant for Dolberry's re-arrest which he flourished in front of Ralegh's face, saying: 'I would be obliged, Sir Walter, if you would kindly assist me in the execution of this undoubtedly legal and valid document.'

Ralegh was beside himself with fury at this impertinence. He marched Meere to the market place, got hold of the key to the stocks and locked his leg to it. He put the key in his pocket and stood over him triumphantly. A crowd had gathered as on all occasions when the stocks were brought into use. But this occasion was not to be missed. It made history – leading townsman physically trapped in public by Lord of the Manor.

There was a mixed reaction from the onlookers. There were no bad eggs or rotten fruit, but most of them enjoyed the sight of an unpopular local lawyer getting what they considered his deserts. Others were somewhat apprehensive of the outcome and more subdued, especially if they owed rent to Meere or his clients.

'He can stay there and sweat for a while,' ordered Ralegh. He was there for six hours before being released. Meere had been resolved before this to hold his own. He was now implacably bent on revenge. This was reinforced by the reception when he arrived home, besieged by townsfolk who knew the identity of his high-level sponsor in the background. 'Where is Lord Howard?' they shouted.

He retaliated by exhibiting a bill of complaint in the Court of Star Chamber against Ralegh, Adrian and the men who helped in the operation. In his complaint he listed the steps he had taken by virtue of his appointment as an Authorized Officer of the Court, with special reference to the alleged assault and false imprisonment. He summarized his case as both a criminal offence of obstructing the administration of justice demanding a penalty, and a civil tort to his personal detriment deserving of heavy damages. He served process on Ralegh, who ignored it, and this became a further item in his claim. He also sought a declaration that he was the lawful Bailiff, to be confirmed as such, and submitted that it was a proper matter for trial at the Dorchester Assizes before a jury of Sherborne freeholders.

Ralegh kept Cecil informed. Dealing first with details of national import he warned him of intelligence he had received of a Spanish fleet assembling at Lisbon with six to seven thousand soldiers for an attack on either Ireland or the Low Counties. He himself was not at all well. (Worry over these local affairs probably had something to do with it.) 'I meant to go to Bath, but fell sick and still am. Rogue Meere continues his knavery as violently as ever. He has issued seven writs out of the Exchequer against me and six against six other poor men' (Ralegh's helpers) – Meere was having a field day or days. Ralegh sent Cecil a pair of gloves from Bess who 'envied any fingers that might be wearing them, but your own', to be sent back if they didn't fit.

Meere was making so much commotion that he was bound

over by Sir George Trenchard and Sir Ralph Horsey and a number of other County Justices of the Peace for £40 to keep the peace. He was using all his legal experience and artifice and served no fewer than twenty-six subpoenas on Ralegh.

Bess unwittingly helped fuel the flames with some domestic information of her own which her husband did not hesitate to blazon abroad. Bess was quite fond of Meere's wife and of her young sister who had been living with the Meeres. She, although not married, was discovered to be about to have a child. Despite his wife's pleading he turned the girl out of the house having first relieved her of two hundred marks (presumably for her keep). This she had been given as her marriage portion.

Despite his local preoccupations Ralegh continued to prime Cecil with news from Spain. While in Weymouth he had received information from two Scotsmen recently in Lisbon. The objective of the fleet assembling there was, they said, to establish a plantation in Ireland. This had been confirmed by a Fleming. These reports proved to be well-founded. The fleet set sail and made for Ireland. On the way it chased three English pinnaces which had seized a large prize of sugar. It landed for supplies in an Irish port. It was then attacked by English ships, scattered and left for home, leaving behind a large number of prisoners.

Cecil again stayed with them in Sherborne. He was a lonely widower.

Ralegh's enemies, in particular the Howards, thought Meere a heaven-sent stick with which to beat an adversary who never missed an opportunity to get the better of them. They could see that he had a weak case. He had played into their hands.

John Meere's brother Henry, who had been reared in the same Temple bed, joined in the fray. He entered a plea in the Court of Star Chamber on behalf of his brother. He enlisted Lord Thomas Howard to bring pressure to bear on Cecil who decided that he had no alternative but to see John Meere for himself.

In August Ralegh wrote to Cobham, referring to 'those rogues, the Meeres,' and telling him of the latest turn of events.

Bess, while she sympathized, was exasperated. 'You brought all this on your own head and have got us a load of trouble.

Poor Mrs Meere. I feel sorry for her.' Cecil took the matter up with Ralegh by letter. 'Is it true,' he asked, 'that Meere's wife is a kinswoman of my Lady of Essex?' Ralegh confirmed in his reply that this was so. He stated that Meere some while earlier had hoped for support from Essex, but that he had had no time for Meere and would not even see him. 'But secretly,' he went on, 'he meant to use Meere for some mischief against me.' He could also have used him for forgery. 'For he writes my hand so perfectly that I cannot discern the difference.' If there were any nobleman, councillor or gentleman who would be content to be provoked by a servant, and suffer indignities from a villain put in his position by himself he, Ralegh, 'would be content to obey such a one's orders'.

At the beginning of October, exasperated beyond endurance, he confined Meere in the Castle gatehouse. From there, after a day or two, Meere wrote a contrite letter to Cecil. He admitted his violent speeches against Sir Walter, spoken 'furiously and foolishly'. He hoped Cecil would give it merciful consideration and take account of the time they were uttered. He expressed great regrets and would make 'such satisfaction as your Honour orders'. The gatehouse was no comfortable billet. If Ralegh had drafted the letter himself it could not have been more to his advantage.

Receipt of it by Cecil was preceded by a letter from Ralegh. It referred to Meere's 'villainous spirit': 'and yet a more cowardly brute never lived; that if he does not submit, he will triumph that he has worsted me and my friends.' This letter perhaps put Cecil in the right frame of mind when Meere's repentant letter arrived the following day.

Ralegh was still attending to his Parliamentary business. He was now a County Member for Cornwall. He was frequently in committee dealing with bills on sundry subjects: against lewd and wandering persons pretending to be soldiers or mariners; for paying the Queen's debts; for erecting houses of correction and punishment of rogues, vagabonds and sturdy beggars. He helped to procure the revocation of the tax on curing of fish, so protecting the interests of his West Countrymen. Cecil, Head of Government, was also Leader of the House. Ralegh opposed a bill for compulsory sowing of hemp for the rope-makers: 'Let every man be allowed to use his own discretion'. Market forces should be the criterion. With regard to the Statute of Tillage:

'Poor men cannot provide seed for as much corn as the law requires them to plough.' He supported freedom of trade but Cecil presented an alternative view which the House adopted: 'Whoever does not maintain the plough destroys the Kingdom.'

Ralegh submitted that it was not fair to make the poor pay as much in taxes as the better off. He urged the Commons: 'Do you call this equity of levy when a poor man pays as much in tax as a rich, while his estate is no better, or little better, than the figure at which it is assessed – while our own estates that are but £30 or £40 in the Queen's books are not a hundredth part of our wealth?'

He opposed, as a restriction on personal liberty, a measure which proposed that parish churchwardens should charge before the courts anybody failing to attend church.

He sometimes resorted to extremes to secure acceptance of his views. In the case of one division on a motion he had proposed, he won by a majority of one vote. An opposition member raised a point of order with the Speaker to challenge the vote.

'Mr Speaker, I beg to report an irregularity. An Honourable Member for Cornwall obstructed the division. He held back one of the Honourable Members from the "No" lobby by tugging at his sleeve.'

'Why, Mr Speaker,' explained Ralegh with contempt, 'it is a small matter to pull one by the sleeve. I have done so often.'

He was criticized in the House for exorbitant profits from his tin monopoly. He retorted: 'Before I was granted my patent the tin-miners were getting two shillings a week. I doubled it to four shillings. This allegation, Mr Speaker, I regard as an affront to her Majesty.'

He also served on a House of Commons committee set up for the purpose of restraining excessive apparel. He was surely its prime witness. But he was finding his stays on duty in Cornwall increasingly tedious and hard on his aches and pains.

The Howards meanwhile were not prepared to let the Meere weapon slip through their fingers. They continued to press Cecil, whom Ralegh was always anxious to please. Cecil had a quiet word with him over this tangling business. 'My Lord Thomas Howard' (Earl of Suffolk) 'has expressed an interest in this case. I'm afraid he's backing Meere, not you. He is convinced you are wrong in law. I'm not expressing any view either way. But I'm anxious not to upset him at the moment. I hope you understand.' The case rumbled on.

Bess and Ralegh were sitting in the garden when Jane Foot brought her the cloak she had sent for. 'Thank you, Jane,' she said, and turning to her husband: 'Jane's leaving us after all this time. She's getting married. You've been one of my most reliable girls,' she told her. He added, smiling, 'Lady Ralegh has always spoken highly of you. We must find you a present to remember us by.' He produced from his pocket a jewel the like of which she had never seen before. 'You may keep it, or sell it – whichever you prefer,' he said. 'We wish you both every happiness. If you make him half as good a wife as Lady Ralegh me, he will be a happy man.' She could not thank them enough, and added: 'I hope you won't mind me saying, Sir Walter: I do hope the nasty gentleman Mr Meere is put in his place. None of us like him.'

Some while later Ralegh had to go to Jersey on Governor duties. On his return he discovered that another Howard, Thomas, Lord Howard, Viscount Bindon, who had earlier chaired the commission at Cerne Abbas investigating Ralegh's alleged atheism, had been pursuing Meere's claims while he was away and that Ralegh's attorneys had been unsuccessful in applications for the trial of his case to be adjourned until his return. He complained about this underhand action while he was away 'in Jersey on her Majesty's business' and the refusal to postpone: 'a right and courtesy afforded every beggar.' He expressed his frustration to Cobham: 'I never busied myself with the Viscount's wealth; nor told her Majesty of his extortions or his poisoning his wife as is avowed. I have forborne to do so in respect for Lord Thomas Howard' (Suffolk) 'and because Master Secretary, Cecil, in his love for Lord Thomas has wished me to. But I will not endure wrong at so peevish a fool's hand any longer. I would rather lose my life. And I think that my Lord Puritan Periam' (Chief Baron of the Court of Exchequer) 'must think the Queen has more use for rogues and villains than for men, otherwise he would not, at Bindon's instance, have yielded to try actions against me when abroad.'

Lord Henry, Earl of Northumberland, was coming to stay with them at Sherborne and 'he will also meet us at Bath'.

With Elizabeth's closing years and everyone's fortunes and England's future on a knife-edge, he could well have done without this anxiety, stemming from an impetuous blunder into trouble with a weak case.

Bess wept.

15

Setting Sun

Ralegh's association with Henry Brooke, Lord Cobham, had become even closer in the past year or so. He, Cobham and Cecil were in constant touch, so much so that Essex had earlier accused them of ganging up against him.

Bess and Ralegh got on well with him. Her friend Elizabeth, Cobham's sister, had been quite close to him and she and her husband Cecil had entertained him regularly. Bess was not so keen on his brother George Brooke of whom they saw little. To Ralegh, Cobham appeared a useful contact. He was not only Cecil's brother-in-law. He was a peer and had friendly relations with the Queen, who conferred on him the important post of Warden of the Cinque Ports with imposing headquarters at Dover. He was convivial company at a party, quick and witty. He was also erratic, unreliable and an inveterate liar. They realized they had to take everything he said with a heap of salt, but what of it? He was good fun to have around.

When they went to Bath for the waters he was often with them. He used to stay at Sherborne Lodge. In August 1601 Cecil had tried to get in touch with him at Sherborne but on that occasion he had only stayed one night on his way to Cornwall. Ralegh forwarded on Cecil's letter. Bess and Cecil had, most unusually, had a difference some time before. Cecil said in his letter that he wanted to make it up, so Ralegh added a postscript to his reply: 'Bess returns you her good wishes, notwithstanding all quarrels.'

They had invited Cobham to stay again on his way back. Ralegh wrote: 'I hope your Lordship will be here tomorrow or Saturday, or else my wife says her oysters will be all spoilt and her partridge stale.' Ralegh apologized for not being able to be with him on a morning they had arranged. He had had to send some further particulars to the Court in connection with the complaints filed against him with the Justices by the two Meeres. Then: 'Have you taken up house at Bath, that we may go there? P.S. Bess remembers herself to your Lordship and says your breach of promise shall make you fare accordingly.'

Ralegh unexpectedly found himself in the position of a high-level reception party. He had come up to London to deal briefly with some business before returning to Bath. The Queen was on a Progress at Basing, Hampshire, home of the Marquis of Winchester. Suddenly there descended on London the French Duke of Biron who had been sent over with a retinue of four hundred attendants by King Henry IV of France to pay a complimentary call, unannounced, on the Queen. As he was known to be the King's favourite Ralegh considered himself obliged to do the honours.

He gave Cecil a report on his welcome. He took them to Westminster Abbey, with its historic tombs that never failed to fascinate – a microcosm of the history of this strange nation that against all the odds always seemed to come out on top, more by luck than foresight, they thought. He took them on a guided tour round London, including the Bear Garden and lions at The Tower which they enjoyed enormously. Londoners' mouths were agape to see this unusual band of foreigners gesticulating and chattering excitedly, and incomprehensibly, as they were shown the sights. 'I laboured,' he told Cecil, 'like a mule.'

He took them next down to Hampshire where they were invited to stay with the Queen at Basing Park.

'Water,' said the Queen, 'I would like my Lord Cobham to join us. He's the ideal person to help me entertain Frogs.'

'He's in Bath, Ma'am,' Ralegh explained. 'I will send for him at once.'

But Cobham was enjoying himself and had no intention of being disturbed. Ralegh was nonplussed at this cheeky rebuff to the Queen. He dared not tell her of Cobham's blank refusal to comply with her wishes.

'I've been in touch with my Lord Cobham, Ma'am,' he informed her. 'There is nothing he would like better than to attend on you but he is suffering extreme agony and daren't give up his treatment even for a day. He sends his profound regrets and apologies to you.'

Ralegh had another try at persuading him to change his mind, but added: 'I will support you whatever your decision. I will rejoin you in Bath presently. I am off to London to get myself fitted up with a suit to match these Frenchmen. They all wear sombre black, would you believe it?'

That Saturday night he saddled up and rode to London to order a plain black taffeta suit and black saddle – quite out of character. He was back two nights later with this acquisition, in time to complete her entertainment of their unsolicited guests.

Biron took the opportunity of tackling the Queen about Essex, whose sudden demise had astonished Europe.

'How did it happen?' he asked. 'You were always so fond of him.'

'Yes, I was. I still am. I miss him,' she replied. 'But he was a traitor. I had no alternative. He would have taken us all over. At the end, he refused to retract or express regret. As the Queen I could do nothing else.'

Biron could well ask. He had a personal interest in the subject. He himself was engaged in an intrigue against his own King, Henry IV. He likewise went to the scaffold ten months later. His talk with Elizabeth had taught him nothing.

Underlying all the façade of Court life and in anticipation of the likely imminence of the Queen's passing, there was a deadly undercurrent of intrigue, at which Cecil was the master. Each of the participating actors was unscrupulous in seeking self-preservation. He was the spider at the centre of the web, unspectacular but waiting and working quietly under cover to trap his prey and achieve his ends, irrespective of the fate of colleagues with whom he was ostensibly on excellent terms. The stakes were high. His interests in fact coincided with those of the nation whose stability depended upon a clear-cut succession to the throne. This was the key issue.

In the case of Ralegh and Cobham, the subject tended to be also one for open and incautious discussion of the advantages and disadvantages of the various possibilities. Cecil's mind was made up. The succession must go to James VI of Scotland. If the Scots had accepted him as their King despite rumours that he had been substituted for Mary's child lost at birth, he would be the strongest claimant to the English throne. But no word of contact must reach the Queen's ears. Ralegh he was not prepared to trust. He could not depend on his discretion or judgement and his close relations with the unreliable Cobham made him an added risk. Also he might prove a successful rival if allowed any rein.

Cecil was conscious of the influence of the Howards, peers of the realm and Privy Councillors as they were, with whom lay a deep reservoir of power accumulated over generations which transcended temporary reigns. It was essential not to antagonize any of them. An enemy of one meant an enemy of all – an elementary lesson Ralegh failed to learn. They must be courted. Cecil's moves had to be kept secret from the Queen and from the others, but he must have a collaborator. It would be too dangerous to act on his own. He well knew Lord Henry Howard, Earl of Northampton, as an utterly despicable character, but was satisfied that his well-known hatred of Ralegh would make him a reliable collaborator in confidential overtures to James VI of Scotland.

He also knew of Howard's Catholic leanings which had kept him on good terms with James's mother, Mary Queen of Scots, without overtly prejudicing his allegiance to Elizabeth. These amicable links (except in their religious aspects) had been maintained with Mary's son. Howard was also known to be friendly towards Spain. This appealed to James. He wanted peace at any price. He was James's 'my dear trusting Harry'.

Cecil and Howard conferred in secret. 'The Queen won't last more than a couple of years at the most,' said Cecil. 'There is only one person on whose discretion I can rely and that is yourself, my Lord.'

'What have you in mind?' Howard asked.

'We must make contact with James. He has the best claim to the throne, but it could go wrong.'

'Who else have you discussed it with?'

'Nobody,' Cecil assured him.

'Who do you think might muddy the waters?'

'Ralegh,' replied Cecil. 'And Cobham. Cobham's nothing. I should know. He's my brother-in-law. He's too unreliable. But Ralegh could be troublesome.'

'I agree. He'd better go the way of Essex, had he not? He's worse than Essex. An upstart, brags his head off. He wouldn't be above putting the knife in if it served his purpose.'

'I'm not sure we should go quite as far as that. Anyway,

James is our man. We'll get his people down to London and start things moving.'

They met James's envoy, Esme Stuart, Duke of Lennox, at Duchy House in The Strand in strict secrecy. A secret code was devised for correspondence, each of them, James included, being allotted a code number, as also were Ralegh and Cobham. 'Assure his Majesty,' Cecil told Lennox, 'that I desire nothing but peace for this nation.'

He took care to warn James (in code): 'The question of the succession is so dangerous to get involved in, it would set a mark in his hand forever that hatched such a bird.' He followed with a damaging attack on Ralegh and Cobham: 'It would be against their nature to be under your sovereignty. I do not check Ralegh in his light and sudden humours because he must not think I deny his freedom or his friendship and always contest what he says. But under pretext for his well-being I have dissuaded him from getting himself involved. So don't believe anything he says, even if he purports to speak kindly on my behalf. I wish I were free from offence for supporting, for private affection, a man whom most religious men utterly reject.'

The ground was carefully tilled and sown. The crop looked promising.

Cecil brought Ralegh's friend and kinsman George Carew into the plot with a device. 'My old friends Ralegh and Cobham are treating me very unkindly,' he complained. 'They are doing things behind my back. I make a pretence of not noticing it, so to all appearances we are close friends. But my revenge will be to heap coals on their heads. Can I rely on your complete discretion? They show their letters to everyone and cannot keep a confidence. It will serve you in good stead, I promise you.'

Carew went along with this, partly because of his disgust at Ralegh's fraternizing with Cobham while, as he had been persuaded, neglecting his old friend Cecil; partly because having been asked, it could have been more than his own future was worth to turn the offer down, even though it meant going behind his kinsman's back. Chief Secretary Cecil and Howard made a persuasive combination.

Their path was eased because James had already conceived a dislike for Ralegh. He knew him to be a manly, military man, which he could not abide. His agents had informed him that Ralegh had in his possession a tract entitled: 'Reasons why the King of Scots is unacceptable to the people of England.' He had rabid views on Spain. He also smoked tobacco. Nothing was easier than to poison his mind further in the coded correspondence with the derogatory fare, which he readily absorbed.

Howard pressed it home. 'The day of the Queen's death will be the day of their doom,' he affirmed.

The Earl of Northumberland was no lover of either Cecil or Howard. He could see what they were up to. He too was on good terms with James. He warned him not to be too trusting. 'Ralegh entirely supports your right to succeed to the Crown,' he asserted. 'He is hated and insolent, but he would do you neither good nor harm. He has his good points, and I advise you to keep on good terms with him. I don't want to see any man's hand against you.'

James thought there might be something in this. He was therefore in two minds over what to do. It could be that Ralegh after all was the one with influence and worthy of trust. Some of his advisors reminded him of the offices he held and of his undoubted military skills which might serve James in good stead. He decided to find out for himself. He again sent Lennox down to London, this time to sound out Ralegh and Cobham. They met at Durham House. The delicate question of the succession was broached. 'What his Majesty King James has asked me to find out,' Lennox informed them, 'is whether he can correspond with you on the various matters of State that are bound to arise between now and the Queen's departure, and whether you would be prepared to give him frank replies and keep him fully informed.' His hearers were unenthusiastic.

'If we were to consider it,' Ralegh replied, 'we should first need to be assured that any letters and reports would be kept strictly confidential. Our first duty is to the Queen and if she were to hear of discussion about her successor, things could become very difficult.'

'That is not quite the answer his Majesty was looking for. But I will pass it on to him.'

They had scented a trap whereas it had been intended as a genuine feeler. James's conclusion was that the two were probably hostile and would be unreliable confidants. He could not afford to take chances.

Cecil had been a little uneasy. Despite the apparently straightforward arrangements with James, Cecil knew that he had once had no time for him, as a friend of Protestants who had been his mother's undoing. His father Burghley had been one of the leaders primarily responsible. He himself had opposed a scheme by James to send troops into England and seize the Crown by force. He knew James had suspected his motives: was he in concert with Ralegh and Cobham plotting to place the Infanta of Spain – or perhaps the Lady Arabella Stuart – on the throne? Cecil had also been a main instrument in the fall of Essex, whom James liked even though he had referred to him as 'an unruly colt'. Howard had warned him of the contact between James and Ralegh, and that Northumberland was urging the suit of Ralegh and Cobham.

He need not have worried. Ralegh naively apprised him of this conversation, entirely trusting and wishing, perhaps deeming it prudent, to hide nothing.

'I sent Lennox away with a flea in his ear,' Ralegh boasted.

'Well done,' replied Cecil. 'I wouldn't trust them an inch. Our loyalty is to her Majesty. I would have replied similarly if the Scottish King had made that offer to me.'

'We had better tell the Queen, had we not?' Ralegh suggested.

'No. Leave things as they are. She would only suspect some weakness that had given the Duke of Lennox encouragement. Alternatively she might think you – we – were angling for thanks.' Howard was cock-a-hoop when Cecil told him about this latest twist. The ploy had been entirely successful. 'It is impossible for them to escape the snares,' he exclaimed with glee.

Nothing was easier now than to poison James's mind against the unsuspecting Ralegh in the coded letters. Cecil decided after a while to bring matters to a head by direct tactics. He had nearly been caught out by Elizabeth while deciphering one of these letters when she had come on him unexpectedly. She had expressed curiosity and he had had to dissemble and divert her attention elsewhere by pretending the letter smelt, while he hid it. She could not stand bad smells.

He informed James: 'I was surprised to learn that your Majesty had been in private conversation with Ralegh and

Cobham. That could not help our enterprise in any way and could do great harm. It was with difficulty that I persuaded Ralegh not to tell all to the Queen.'

'I thought you would have known about these approaches,' replied James. 'But I must say Ralegh has always spoken well of you. And can you tell me precisely what he has said against me? For my part I assure you that I have in you the utmost trust, and your honest confiding in me I don't doubt for a moment.'

'I admit he has not in so many words abused your Majesty,' Cecil conceded. 'He is far too clever for that. If he says kind words of me do not believe he means them. All religious men hold him anathema. But he must not know I deny his friendship.'

'What you tell me confirms that they are villains not to be trusted,' James assured him. 'Your suspicions and your disgracings shall be mine,' he promised him and Howard.

Cecil followed this with a letter to Bess. 'I would be honoured if you and your husband joined me for dinner tomorrow evening. I am inviting my Lord Cobham. You will be pleased with that I am sure. You are such good friends. By the way, young William is doing well. Would you care to take him with you when you next go down to your "Fortune's Fold"? He loves being with you and the Dorset air is so good for him.' No hint here of anything amiss.

They accepted both invitation and request readily. William was virtually part of the family.

There were curious religious interweavings through the political pattern. Essex had been a stern Puritan. Cecil dismissed Roman Catholicism as 'anti-Christ'. Ralegh was Protestant but not dogmatic. James was not a Catholic, unlike his mother, but expressed sympathy with them and did not ignore the possible support from their direction. Howard, a secret Catholic, did his utmost to encourage this liberal attitude. He told James: 'Such a Kingdom as England is worth allowing a Mass in a corner.' James replied: 'I have already told His Holiness the Pope that my personal gratitude when I am crowned King of England as well as of Scotland will make my accession a cause for joy among all Roman Catholics.' Cecil was aware of this exchange.

The Catholics themselves were divided. Many kept up secret

liaison with the King of Spain who they were convinced would uphold their religion if he were to be England's next monarch; others supported Ralegh in his out and out opposition to Spain and anything Spanish and whose constant theme in life was 'Death to Spain.

Ralegh could now see no future for his extensive estates in Ireland. With the exception of one prestige castle, Inchiquin, he sold them on Cecil's advice to Robert Boyle (later Earl of Cork) for one thousand pounds and put the proceeds into more privateering. Boyle had progressed swiftly. Twelve years before he had had only twenty-seven pounds to his name.

Ralegh also decided, in those uncertain times, to place his Sherborne estate outside the reach of the Crown and creditors should the worst ever befall and it were to become the subject of attainder or of confiscation for judgement debt or perhaps death in a duel. This would safeguard his family's succession. In April 1603, therefore, without telling Bess, he conveyed the freehold to trustees on trust to himself for life with successive remainders to his son Walter, to any future sons 'if God should send me any more', with remainder over to his elder brother Carew Ralegh, reserving the reversion, or remainder in fee simple, to himself and his heirs. Bess was to have a rent-charge of £200 a year for life. The deed was drawn up by Sir John Doddridge, Crown Counsel, later to become a judge of King's Bench.

The pleasure Bess found in Cobham's company was tempered when he re-married. His second wife was Katherine Howard, Countess of Kildare, one of her sworn enemies. Bess had renewed her approaches to the Queen for reconciliation. Lady Kildare had always been a powerful influence at Court and saw to it that the Queen's unbending attitude was maintained. Bess complained to Cecil. He sympathized but cautioned against being too critical. She told him: 'You know how unfavourably she has treated me with the Queen. It is true that I should not have mistrusted her without proof. But I never had any information to the contrary from you, nor indeed have I seen or heard from you since she did me that good office. For the honour I bear her name and my long acquaintance with her, I wish she would be as ambitious to do good as she is apt to the contrary.'

Cecil shrugged his shoulders. Where the ladies were falling

out, he like a sensible male was best out of it: except that they were useful sources of information which could be tapped.

Cobham was pursuing a game of his own which he kept to himself. One day he asked Ralegh: 'What do you say to a trip to the Low Countries? I've some business there to see to and we'll observe at first hand the latest state of the wars.'

Ralegh agreed readily. He never tired of re-visiting scenes of his earlier military activity and there was nothing like being on the spot to learn precisely what was going on.

Cobham had very different ideas floating round his fertile, feather-brained imagination. He was a long-standing acquaintance of the Count of Arenberg. The Count was Minister to the Joint Sovereigns of the Low Countries, the Archduke Albert and the Infanta Isobel, daughter of Philip II of Spain. Her claims to the English throne were supported by the Jesuits. He and Cobham had long had secret correspondence, their chief messenger being a merchant named La Renzi. They now conferred while Ralegh was occupied with an inspection of the local defences. Cobham arranged to visit Spain. They discussed a deal which, on the face of it, could have been of considerable financial advantage and secure the peace between England and Spain which Cobham had dangling before him as a coup, however unrealistic. Nothing was said of this to Ralegh.

Ralegh as Governor of Jersey had to pay an official call to inspect the Island's fortifications and look over the administration generally. He was pleased to find that the trade of cod and other fish between Jersey and Newfoundland, which he had initiated, was flourishing. Humphrey Gilbert, he thought, would also have been gratified. The Island's fragmented and complicated land ownerships, not dissimilar from those on the Isle of Portland, were also, thanks to him, being put on a register. He arranged to take Bess with him and invited Cobham to join them. He accepted saying: 'I'll fit it in with another visit to the Continent. I'll see you in Jersey on the way back.'

He was in fact going to Spain pursuant to the arrangements with Arenberg, to discuss the profitable peace deal. When he joined Ralegh on Jersey he informed him airily that his mission had been successful and mentioned the possibility of great gain in the offing. Ralegh's ears always pricked up when money was mentioned, but he laughed: 'Just another of your fanciful ideas. Let's take a ride round the Island. I'll show you over the castles and some of the fine beaches and a sight of the coast of Normandy. I'm making this a holiday as well as business.'

Cobham also made some flattering references to Arabella Stuart. 'That's a load of nonsense,' Ralegh affirmed. 'She's an empty-headed little thing. Mind you, she's attractive. She once joined us in Court – at dinner. My Lord Burghley was quite taken with her. She may be James's cousin and next in line after his sons but the throne, never. She'd never hold it down – nor get anywhere near it. James would see to that. So would a lot of other people. So forget it, if you ever had it in mind.'

'I don't say I have. But I know some who have.'

'Tell them to forget it.'

It made a good story at a dinner party they held that evening and raised a hearty laugh. But merely to refer to it with an audience was indiscreet. It could be misconstrued – perhaps intentionally.

The Elizabethans were courageous, adventurous, prepared to face the world and fight to the death for freedom. They scaled the heights of poetry, drama and literature. But they were greedy, self-seeking, and disloyal and ruthless if it served their ambitions. Survival depended on cunning. Captured prizes constituted a significant part of their income. Even in March 1603 Cecil was a partner with Ralegh and Cobham in another privateering expedition. He was their friend as well as an adventuring partner, they believed.

An action of Ralegh's which incensed Cecil and other Privy Councillors was a memorandum he sent to the Queen on the succession to the throne, a question with which he had no business to meddle. He refused to accept the fact that he was not one of the core establishment. He pointed to 'the dangers which might grow from the Spanish faction in Scotland'. She ignored it. He had presumed to involve himself in a delicate matter of high state – at the same time reminding her by implication of her impermanence. Realizing his blunder when he received no reply, he wrote again saying, 'You may, perchance, speak to those seeming to be my great friends, but I find little evidence of that or any other supposed amity. For your Majesty having left me, I am left all alone in the world and am sorry that ever I was at all. What I have done is out of zeal or love, but my enemies have their wills and desires over me . . . . I pray God that your Majesty may be eternal in joy and happiness.'

She ignored that also. She was probably in no fit state to do otherwise. The letter could do no good, and might do harm.

16

Trap Sprung

The Queen's last words to Parliament echoed through the land: 'Though God hath raised me high, yet this I account the glory of my Crown, that I have reigned with your loves.'

On 24 March 1603 she died. James was proclaimed King. The news was received calmly and reached him three days later. He proceeded south in his own time to claim his Kingdom. He handed out knighthoods on the way. At Newark he ordered summary justice to a young pick-pocket: 'immediate hanging from a lamp-post'. Coming from Scotland he had not heard of Magna Carta. A proclamation was issued at Cecil's instigation forbidding all those holding office to contact the King on his journey. It was vital to keep the ship of state on an even keel and on its planned course.

The people lining the streets to inspect their new King saw a tallish, thick-set, rather heavy-jowled man in his mid-thirties with fair hair and blue eyes who rode well. He enjoyed his feasting at every stop.

Ralegh was over-anxious to make his mark. He ignored the order and presented himself before James as Captain of the Guard. Lord Henry Howard was in close attendance on the King. He was taking no chances. The reception was cool. The ground had been well staked out. 'Sire, I have the honour to wait on you as your Captain of the Guard and Lord Warden of the Stannaries,' he explained. 'I offer you my loyal services and these offices I respectfully beg of you to renew.'

'That will be done, man,' James agreed. 'Captain of the Guard eh! If I had wished I could have taken this kingdom by storm.'

'I would God that had been put to the trial, Sire,' Ralegh replied.

'Why so?'

'Because your Majesty would then have known your friends from your foes,' he answered. Howard took this as a dig at him.

'Oh! Well, take yourself downstairs and I will send you a note to carry on what you are doing,' James told him.

'I'm greatly obliged, Sire.'

When he had left the room James instructed his secretary Lake (a spy of Cecil's): 'Give him his note speedily, that Ralegh may be gone again. I think of him very rawly,' he guffawed. Lake reported to his master Cecil: 'To my seeming Ralegh hath taken no great root here.'

On 3 May James dined at Theobalds which Cecil, who in ten days time was to be made Baron Cecil of Essendine, Rutland, had inherited from his father, Lord Burghley, five years before. 'I don't want him as my Captain,' James told Cecil. 'I was only too glad to see the back of him.'

'Of course,' Cecil replied, 'he had no right to force himself on you. It was against orders. Who have you in mind, Sire?'

'Sir Thomas Erskine. He was my close attendant in Scotland – where I was a King, remember,' James stated.

'Very good, Sire. If I can take the liberty of suggesting a small sweetener: perhaps you could let him off the £300 a year he pays as Governor of Jersey.'

Ralegh did not give up, although he realized he was in a corner. He arranged with Bess's young brother to be invited to dinner at Beddington Park, Nicholas's adoptive father's (Bess's and Nicholas's uncle's) house in Surrey. James was to be the guest of honour. Ralegh button-holed him and presented him with a pamphlet he had written entitled: 'Discourse touching on War with Spain and of the Protecting of the Netherlands'. James shrank when he saw its title but entered into what started as an amicable discussion. Howard was not there to queer Ralegh's pitch. So here was his opening.

'This is an interesting article, Sir Walter,' James commented. 'You must have given it a deal of thought. But you know, the Dutch are a load of rebels.'

'I agree, Sire, that they have only one object in life – money,' replied Ralegh.

'Well put, my friend. We must treat them with caution. The Spaniards too: handle them with care but keep on good terms.'

'If I might say so, Sire, you can't treat Spain with care. Fight them on land and at sea and flatten them. Attack, or they'll be at our throats again. I could raise two thousand men tomorrow at the drop of a hat, at no expense to your Majesty, and have Spain on its knees in a week,' he bragged.

He had mistaken his man. The Carews saw the sudden change in James's demeanour. He paled visibly and shook slightly. Ralegh, oblivious of his hearer's reception of his advice, continued in the same vein, unaware of the effect of what he was suggesting. James was a man of peace and compromise; a man who in his upbringing had been surrounded by violence during his mother's turbulent career. They stepped in hastily and diverted the conversation. As young Nicholas told his father afterwards: 'The monarch was not entirely unfriendly when Sir Walter opened up. But he was shattered. He could picture himself plunged into battle. He was frightened out of his wits.'

If there had been any hope of re-establishing himself, he had blown it. The machinery was grinding its way to crush a conspiracy in which the unsuspecting Ralegh's associates were deeply involved and in which he unwittingly was enmeshed. The predators were closing in on him.

The first blow came with their abrupt eviction from Durham House by its owner, the Bishop of Durham. Cecil had had this in mind for some while but it came as a bolt from the blue to the Raleghs. They were given a week to vacate. Commissioners were appointed under the chairmanship of Lord Keeper Sir Thomas Egerton to enquire into the tenancy and dilapidations. Ralegh protested: 'I have spent £2,000 of my own purse on this building. The meanest gentleman would have been given six months' notice; even an artificer three months. I, with a staff of forty, and twenty horses in my stables have to cast my hay and oats in the street together with my family within fourteen days.' But he could see how the wind was blowing and added: 'But if his Majesty thinks it reasonable I will obey.'

Bess's attitude was philosophical. 'I shan't be sorry to go but giving such short notice is an insult.' It was in fact extended to some months. 'But it may be just a mistake. I shall be glad to be away from this rotten house. It's been hideously expensive and difficult to manage. We shall be able to spend more time in Sherborne, Walter. It will be lovely to be back in Dorset.'

'There's something in that,' replied Ralegh. 'Green fields

instead of smoke and fog and the stench of foul gutters. I'm sure Wat would prefer it.'

Arthur who was present made no comment apart from expressing sympathy. He had a foreboding that even this modest optimism could be a delusion.

On James's accession the Count of Arenberg had been appointed the Archduke's ambassador to the English Court. He travelled over in the company of Lord Henry Howard. Any so-called secret correspondence with Cobham could have been divulged on the journey. Over-estimating the influence of Cobham he renewed his approaches concerning peace with Spain. Cobham had told Cecil before the Queen died of the discussions he had had with Arenberg. He tried to make a favourable impression as an international peacemaker on James as he came down from Scotland. He told him of their talks and enquired: 'Sire, what answer shall I make to the Count?' James replied curtly. 'You're more busy in this than you need be,' and said to Cecil: 'What does he think he is – a self-appointed Commissioner? He's getting above himself.'

Cobham now invited Ralegh to join him for dinner in his house at Blackfriars. Count Arenberg was also there. After dinner when Arenberg had gone Cobham told him a story about the large sum – half a million crowns – on offer from Spain for support of peace moves and toleration of the Catholics. 'I was offered this in Spain when I went over,' he announced, 'and Arenberg now confirms it. It could come from either Spain or Brussels. It wouldn't matter which, so long as it came. There could be £1,500 a year out of it for you, you know, merely for promoting peace. The recipients could include Privy Councillors also.' Ralegh thought this utterly unrealistic. But instead of refusing outright a bait which reflection might have indicated to be a trap, he temporized. His off-hand reply was: 'I would want to see the colour of it before I agreed.'

His private room at Durham House over-looked the Thames. He had a clear view of the river and the traffic passing up and down. On one occasion after Cobham had been with him he idly noticed him being rowed past, instead of to, his Blackfriars house and across the river towards St Saviour's. It was there that La Renzi, Arenberg's messenger and reputed agent, lived. He thought nothing of it at the time. There could have been any number of reasons for a call on the south bank.

There was a double conspiracy afoot. The Roman Catholics had assumed that James would honour his pledge to relieve them of their disabilities as soon as he became King of England. So far no steps in that direction had been, or seemed likely to be, taken. Two priests, William Watson and Francis Clarke, together with Anthony Copley, Brooksby and Sir Griffin Markham (a relative of Anthony Babington, executed for Mary Queen of Scot's plot), had entered into a conspiracy with George Brooke (Cobham's brother) and Lord Grey of Wilton (a fervent Puritan). They planned to kidnap the King from Greenwich Palace and bring pressure on him to relieve the Catholics. Ralegh knew nothing of this. There was also a supplementary plot. 'The King and his Cubs' were to be put to death and Lady Arabella Stuart proclaimed Queen and married to a Catholic to be selected by the King of Spain. Ralegh knew nothing of this either.

These underground, foolhardy activities were bound to be discovered by Cecil's intelligence network. Cobham played into his hands because of a letter he wrote inadvisedly to the Lady Arabella, who passed it on to the King, her cousin.

First Copley, then George Brooke were arrested, followed by Lord Grey and Sir Griffin Markham. Ralegh was not perturbed, since it was no concern of his. He and Bess were however astonished when they heard Cobham had been apprehended. 'I wonder what he's been up to now,' said Ralegh. No information was forthcoming. The last thing Bess would do was enquire of her old enemy, Lady Cobham.

On a morning between 13 and 15 July Ralegh was pacing up and down the Great Terrace at Windsor waiting to join the cavalcade which would be riding with the King in Windsor Park. It showed all the signs of being a good day. There was not a cloud in the sky and the sun lit up the grey stone of St George's Chapel and the red Tudor brick of Eton. There was the continuous passage of boats and barges up and down the Thames on business or pleasure. Ralegh was, as ever, dressed in his finery, a splendid figure of a man, booted and spurred for the morning's ride. Although no longer Captain of the Guard, he was still included in the royal escort. The King had just left the meeting of the Privy Council convened earlier that day and was expected any moment. Cecil came out onto the Terrace and told him: 'Walter, their Lordships desire your presence in the Council chamber. They have some questions to put to you. Will you come up, please?'

'Now, my Lord?' he asked.

'Yes at once. His Majesty will be riding without you.'

There was nothing in Cecil's demeanour to suggest any untoward circumstance. Their joint privateering expedition was still intact. There had been no words of difference between them or adverse element in their normal friendly relations. Bess and he had been guests at his dinner-party only a day or two before. 'Is this my big chance after all?' Ralegh thought. 'At last to achieve my ambition, membership of the Privy Council?'

He followed Cecil into the meeting with high hopes. The solemn atmosphere quickly banished his optimism. 'We are investigating serious matters,' he was told. 'You no doubt know what they are?'

'I know of no serious matters in which I have been involved,' he replied.

They put to him some details of the plot to kidnap James and his family. It was a carefully prepared operation with all the appearance of military efficiency. On a particular night all entrances to and exits from Greenwich Palace were to be placed under guard. The King was to be surprised in his chamber and he and his children seized.

'I know nothing of any of this,' he assured them. 'It sounds to me the most preposterous and wicked scheme I have ever heard of.'

They questioned him about the Lady Arabella. He agreed that he knew she would be next in line for the throne after the present royal family. He emphatically denied having had any contact with her whatever or with any of her advisers, if she had such.

'But you did know her, did you not?' he was asked.

'I met her once – at a Court dinner. She was twelve years old at the time,' he explained.

'You are a close friend of my Lord Cobham, are you not?' they pursued.

'I am indeed. In that respect I am in good company with my Lord Cecil whose brother-in-law he is, and whose first wife was my wife's best friend.'

'The circumstances of the origin of your friendship are immaterial. You see much of him, do you not?' they went on.

'I do. We dine and he often comes down and stays with us in Sherborne,' he agreed.

'And in Jersey?'

'He has stayed with us in Jersey.'

'On one occasion on his return from Spain?' they pressed him.

'That is so. I wasn't aware at the time that he had been to Spain. He only told me he had been on the Continent. That could include Spain of course.'

'Would you have been surprised that he had been on a visit to enemy country?' they asked him.

'Not necessarily. At the time there were no active hostilities between our two countries. Our trading ships were calling in at their ports and theirs in ours. I once took a ship into Lisbon for repairs after severe weather. I would have assumed he had been there on business. He had nothing to hide so far as I knew,' he assured them.

'Did he not call in at Jersey to give you details of a deal he had arranged? Was not that the purpose of his visit?'

'No. Certainly not. The only purpose of inviting him was holiday and jollification with us.'

'You know the Count of Arenberg, do you not?'

'Yes. He is the Low Countries' Ambassador.'

'My Lord Cobham is well acquainted with him, is he not? Has had much to do with him in the Low Countries and here?'

'Very likely,' he agreed. 'I don't know the details of their business but they have frequent conference, yes.'

'You know La Renzi, do you not?'

'I don't really know him. I have met him. He is a merchant and acts as the Count's messenger, I believe.'

'He is also a secret agent, is he not?'

'I have heard it said,' Ralegh conceded. 'I couldn't say whether he is or not.'

'You say you dine often with my Lord Cobham. Do you remember an occasion when you, the Count and La Renzi all dined together at his house at Blackfriars?'

'I recall one occasion when the Count was there. I cannot say whether or not La Renzi was there.'

'Did the subject of Spain crop up?' they enquired.

Ralegh jerked into realization of where this was probably leading. He paused before replying.

'We are waiting for your answer, Sir Walter,' they reminded him.

'I beg your Lordships' pardon. I am trying to refresh my memory. Spain was often a topic of conversation. It has, as your Lordships know, been a constant preoccupation of mine for many years. My dislike of that country, its King and religion, and of its cruelty toward the Indians in the Americas is well known.'

'Are you telling us that Spain was discussed at that dinner?'

'It could certainly have been.'

'Let us press you a little further on this. Did not the Count mention large sums of money that could come your way from the direction of Spain?' they asked.

Once again Ralegh thought hard. They were probing what he now could see was dangerous ground. However could they have tracked the details of a private conversation at or after the dinner table? Could it have been a Cobham servant? A Government spy, maybe? Or the Count himself? Or had they been questioning Cobham?

'Large sums of money, Sir Walter,' they repeated.

'I can honestly say that Arenberg made no such offer to me.'

'Well, if the Count didn't make such an offer to you, did he to my Lord Cobham?' he was asked.

'Certainly not in my hearing.' The examination was entering a sensitive area.

'The Count took his leave before you, did he not, and La Renzi likewise?'

'Yes, the Count went home. I repeat I can't remember whether La Renzi was there or not.'

'Leaving you and Lord Cobham alone together?'

'Yes. We no doubt had a final glass of sack before I left.'

'And a chat?'

'Naturally we were not sitting in silence.'

'A chat about the financial assistance the Count might be able to arrange – indeed, would be able to arrange?'

'My Lord Cobham did make some suggestion – completely foolish I thought – about rewards Arenberg had said he could produce for helping to procure peace with Spain.'

'Did not that strike you as curious – possibly treasonable?'

he was asked.

'I didn't take it seriously. It seemed to me unrealistic.'

'What reply did you give Lord Cobham?'

'I can't remember. I imagine I dismissed it out of hand.'

'Do you now? Let us help you a little to jog your memory. Did you not in fact say: "Show me the colour of your money and I am your man"?'

'I doubt it. If I did, it was meant as a joke and to show I didn't take the offer seriously.'

'So you may have said those words?'

'I could have done. To show my disbelief in the reality of so ridiculous and impossible a proposition.'

'Words such as that on a serious matter can hardly be said to be a joke, would you say?'

'By "joke" I meant an airy nothing that would raise a laugh but not deserve a moment's further thought.'

'But if a large sum of money could have come your way whose only condition of payment was to help bring about peace, might it not have tempted you?'

'If you put it like that, and if no harm could befall our King and country thereby, perhaps my reception would not have been different from that of anybody else I know – your Lordships included.'

'Quite so. And perhaps you knew, or suspected, that this so-called "peace" was to be achieved by an invasion from Spain on this island.'

'Certainly not. I would not have entertained the idea for an instant.' He could now see the intended end-product of his interrogation.'

'If there had been an invasion and the inconceivable had happened and it had been successful, the King would have been replaced by the Lady Arabella, would he not?'

'Perhaps. But what has that to do with me?'

'It would have followed this bribe to achieve the "peace" they had in mind: peace on their terms, that is.'

Their Lordships conferred and then told him: 'Sir Walter, you will return to your house and remain there till you receive further instructions.'

Back at Durham House he had to break the unwelcome news to Bess.

'I can't believe it,' she exclaimed. 'Whatever are they

playing at? They must know there's no one more loyal than you. If anything, too loyal.'

'I open my mouth too wide, that's my trouble. But Cobham's worse. He's hopeless. Always loudly indiscreet wherever he is and not giving a damn what he says or does. I should have seen the signs. The trouble is, we like having him around.'

The order came through for his custody in The Tower – grim lodging-house. He was given thirty minutes to pack and say his farewells. He stuffed some jewels in his pocket for conversion to cash when required. Bess smiled bravely, holding back her tears, fearful for the future.

'Look after yourself, my dear Bess,' he said. 'For our sake and little Wat's – not so little now, young man.'

'I'm big,' Wat said. 'I'll soon be as big and strong as you, Daddy. Where are they taking you?'

'To a grand castle – The Tower of London. I took you there, do you remember? It's only a little way down river, so I won't be far away. Look after mother while I'm away.'

'I will, Daddy. Will you be away long? You were going to take William and me fishing tomorrow, weren't you?'

'We shall see, Wat. We shall see.'

He kissed Bess goodbye. Their bright sky was covered with a black cloud. They clung to one another for a moment, not speaking. Then with a wave he had gone.

Wat asked his mother: 'Can William come and play, Mama?'

'I don't think so today,' she replied.

'Why not?'

'His father's very busy just now. I don't think he would let him.'

'That's not fair. He's my best friend.'

'So was his wife my best friend,' sighed Bess to herself. 'And we thought his father was, too. Now I'm not so sure.'

Ralegh tried to recollect details of any episodes he could call to mind about Arenberg or La Renzi. He suddenly remembered the occasion when Cobham, rowing back from Durham House down to Blackfriars, passed his own house and crossed over the river to the south bank. This was the area where La Renzi lived, he knew. He decided he must amplify his earlier statement by adding this small item which at the time had no significance. It was of no great consequence now, except that it indicated the possibility of Cobham communicating with La Renzi privately, rather than when he was present. He wrote to Cecil telling him of the incident.

Cobham was already in The Tower, as was his brother, George Brooke. Cecil discussed this letter with his colleagues to see what use they could make of it. Ralegh's lack of discretion and outspoken manner might well elicit damaging evidence. They decided to confront Cobham with it to soften him up. He took the bait. He flew into a rage, jumping to the conclusion that Ralegh was accusing him of treason, as had his brother George a few days before. The Brooke brothers would resort to any trickery to save themselves, even at the cost of ditching friends. Cobham retaliated by accusing Ralegh not merely of complicity in but of actually instigating shady transactions – the accomplice's recrimination for which they had been angling.

The inquisitors taxed Ralegh with this allegation. He denied it firmly. But realizing that Cobham had misinterpreted the letter, Ralegh compounded his blunder by sending Laurence Kemys to reassure Cobham that he had the wrong end of the stick and that in fact he had exonerated him as far as was in his power so to do. He added, unwisely, that Cobham could be happy in the knowledge that one witness alone was not enough to condemn a man for treason. There must be no fewer than two witnesses, so cheer up. Except for the hardened criminal, solitary confinement can distort the intelligence: he had unwittingly placed ammunition in his accusers' hands, since this came to Cecil's knowledge. A flimsy circumstantial case had been bolstered up.

Ralegh was in despair. It was common knowledge that a State trial almost inevitably resulted in a finding of guilt. This meant automatic stripping of all possessions. Nothing would be left for wife and child. His enemies would triumph. His family would be ruined and downfall complete. He wrote to his wife:

'My dear Bess,
    I cannot endure the dishonour to you and our child. If I had had a few more years I would have bettered your estate. You are young, forbear not to marry again. It is now nothing to me. You are no more mine, nor I thine. Take care you marry not

impulsively, but to avoid poverty and to preserve your child....

'I am now made an enemy and traitor by the word of an unworthy man, who proclaimed me to be a partaker in his vain imaginings.... But, my wife, forgive him everything as I do. God forgive Henry Howard, for he was my principal enemy. And for my Lord Cecil, I thought he would never forsake me in extremity. I would not have done it him, God knows.

'I know it is forbidden to destroy ourselves, but the mercy of God is immeasurable. In the Lord I always trusted, and I know that my Redeemer liveth.... I bless my poor child, and let him know his father was no traitor.... Let thy son be thy beloved, for he is part of me and I live in him.'

This letter was immediately followed by dinner with the Lieutenant of The Tower, Sir John Peyton. In the course of the meal Ralegh suddenly tore open his coat, seized a knife and plunged it into his breast, gashing it. His two servants grabbed hold of him before he could do himself any more damage.

Cecil was informed. He came over at once. The wound, not fatal, had been dressed but he was in some pain. Ralegh told him: 'All this is more than I can endure. And I am innocent, I swear it.'

If the action had been intended to shock, it succeeded up to a point. It was reported to James. His comment however was merely: 'Ralegh should be probed by a good preacher and persuaded to wound his spirit, not his body.'

Cecil later observed: 'He is now very well both in mind and in body.' This was correct. He had relieved some of his tension.

Cobham now had second thoughts – in the quiet, lonely hours in his room, a surge of conscience. He told Peyton's son who had looked in to see to his requirements: 'God forgive me. Ralegh has accused me, but I cannot accuse him.'

Young Peyton replied: 'He says the same of you: you have accused him, but he cannot accuse you.'

The interrogators were informed. Far from releasing Ralegh, their reaction was to dismiss Peyton and put Sir George Harvey in his place as Lieutenant of The Tower.

Direct communication between the two had been forbidden.

Security was now made even tighter. Ralegh thought of an ingenious way round it. He wrote out a letter to Cobham appealing to him to clear his name, put it inside an apple, which he had lobbed through Cobham's window. Cobham's smuggled reply, confirmed that Ralegh was as innocent of treasons 'as anyone living'.

Cobham then wrote another letter expressing remorse for having falsely accused Ralegh and gave it to the new Lieutenant. Harvey was in a dilemma. The fate of his predecessor had been ignominious removal from office for baulking the State's determination to get a conviction. While he was pondering what should best be done with this letter, his son did as Peyton's had done. He let Ralegh know about it. When he told his father what he had done, Harvey decided that, to protect his son, he must hide the letter till everything had blown over. Young Harvey was locked up, not for this but for divulging other confidential matter.

In Sherborne there was disbelief among the townsfolk as news spread of the mishaps of their larger than life Lord of the Manor. He had not had a great deal to do with the town itself but was respected and well-liked. In Devon and Cornwall the people were even more emphatic in his favour.

Bess was universally popular, a view Mrs Meere echoed.

'He treated you disgracefully,' she told her husband, 'but I am terribly sorry for poor Lady Ralegh. And the boy. Whatever is to come of it?'

But Meere would allow nothing to blunt the edge of his delight at this turn of events. 'It serves them all right,' he exclaimed. 'I hope they put a quick end to that insulting villain.'

He had the joy of knowing that he himself was one of the instruments of his tormenting chief's downfall.

Commissioners were appointed to examine Ralegh's part in the conspiracies – Lord Henry Howard (Earl of Northampton), Lord Thomas Howard (Lord Chamberlain, Earl of Suffolk) and Lord Charles Blount (Earl of Devonshire), together with Cecil. Ralegh insisted that he neither knew nor suspected either the involvement of Cobham or his intentions. He had had 'no suspicion of such a horrible purpose'. As for the allegations concerning money from Spain: 'God knows I have spent £40,000 against the King of Spain and that nation. I have served against them in person. I discovered the richest part of his Majesty's Indies; planted in his territories; offered his Majesty at my Uncle Carew's "to supply two thousand men to invade Spain, at no charge to him".' He went on: 'Your Lordships know I am guiltless of the "Surprise" intended for the King, that I never accepted money and it was never offered me for any ill.'

He later wrote to them denying two further allegations from Cobham: first, that it was he who had persuaded Cobham to go to Spain and bring back two hundred thousand crowns to him in Jersey; secondly, of planning to land Spaniards at Milford Haven, Pembrokeshire. 'Your Lordships know these to be false – if not, why had he not mentioned it at the outset? He was out to destroy me. Although, I must confess it, I am most worthy of the heavy affliction for the neglect of my duty in giving ear to some things and in hearkening to the offer of money.'

If he had hoped that this frank admission of some small measure of culpability would soften the Commissioners' hearts he was deluding himself. Innocent as he was, he was neglecting the elementary precaution of keeping his mouth (or pen) shut. He was instead providing useful scraps to prop up their case, otherwise flimsy in the extreme. For one so intelligent this was, to say the least, naïve.

17

'Justice Never So Depraved'

Ralegh was moved to Winchester. In the interests of the court this was to be the venue for the trial, there being plague in London. Special precautions had to be taken to safeguard him from the fury of the London mob who, despite risk of contagion, turned out in great numbers to abuse him during the journey from The Tower. The Government propaganda machine had worked well. How different was this reception from that of his West Countrymen!

The trial took place in Wolvesay Castle, Winchester. A group of scholars from the nearby college (where his brother Carew's second son, Walter Ralegh, had been a scholar up to the year before) waited to see the man of whom they had heard so much escorted in undeserved humility into the gaunt, forbidding former Palace of the Bishops. On 17 November 1603 he was brought before the Court of King's Bench composed as follows:-

> Lord Chief Justice Sir John Popham, presiding
> Lord Justice Sir Edmund Anderson
> Two puisne judges, Sir Francis Gaudy and Sir Peter Warburton
> Lay Commissioners also sitting were:
> Lord Cecil, Lord Henry Howard, Lord Thomas Howard, the Earl of Devonshire, Lord Edward Wootton, Sir William Waad, and Sir John Stanhope.
> A hand-picked jury was sworn.

The Attorney-General Sir Edward Coke prosecuted, assisted by Sergeants Hele and Sir Edward Phillips.

He was arraigned of high treason. The indictment charged

him with the 'Spanish Treason', that with Cobham and others he had conspired to place Arabella Stuart on the throne, for which purpose Cobham was to obtain five to six hundred thousand crowns from the King of Spain, to enable the said Arabella Stuart to establish peace between England and Spain, tolerate Papistry and enter into a marriage; and that he delivered to the aforesaid Cobham a book challenging the King's lawful title to the crown of England.

Included in the indictment were counts charging others, but not Ralegh, with 'The Priests' Treason' (to surprise and seize the King's person at Greenwich) and 'Lord Grey's Treason' (with one hundred gentlemen of quality to present the King forcibly with a petition and execute the Priests' Treason).

On his arraignment, Ralegh pleaded 'Not Guilty'.

The hearing was conducted rather like an after-dinner but acrimonious discussion over the port, ignoring rules of evidence. Some members of the court volunteered comments as witnesses to fact.

Ralegh objected that as he was not being charged with the last two counts it would be prejudicial to him to include them in his indictment. Coke argued that all charges were part and parcel of the same general accusation and that he was equally involved with the others in the statement by one of them: 'There will be no safety in England until the Fox and his Cubs are taken away.'

'Prove to me,' Ralegh protested, 'any one of these allegations and I will confess to all the indictment and that I am the most horrible traitor that ever lived, and worthy to be crucified with a thousand torments.'

Coke replied: 'I will prove all. Thou art a monster. Thou has an English face, but a Spanish heart. You incited my Lord Cobham, as soon as Count Arenberg came to England, to meet him. That night you supped with Lord Cobham and he brought you back after supper to your house, Durham House. Then the same night Lord Cobham went secretly with La Renzi to the Count and obtained from him a promise of money. After this it was arranged that Lord Cobham would go to Spain, returning via Jersey, where the two of you were to meet to discuss the distribution of the money. Your intention was to set up the Lady Arabella as Queen, deposing our rightful King. You pretended that this money was to further the peace with Spain – your "peace" meant Spanish invasion and Scottish subversion.'

Ralegh interrupted him. 'Let me answer. It concerns my life.' Coke refused to give way: 'You shall not.'

Lord Chief Justice Popham intervened in this exchange. 'Sir Walter, Master Attorney is still summarizing his general case. When he has called his evidence you will have your say.'

Coke jeered: 'Those shots struck home, didn't they?'

Popham, somewhat disconcerted by Coke's bullying tactics: 'Master Attorney, when you have finished this general outline, do you not mean to let him answer the particular charges?'

'Yes – when we deliver the proofs to be read.' Coke continued: 'If you provoke me, Sir Walter, it will be so much the worse for you.' Then, addressing the court and jury: 'Lord Cobham was never either a politician or a swordsman. But the invention of these treasonable schemes was the doing of a politician and their execution that of a swordsman. Sir Walter Ralegh fits both categories – and they fed on one another's discontent. But he took care never to confer with more than one person at a time because, he said, one witness can never condemn me. Ralegh received information in the Tower that Cobham had accused him and contrived that Cobham should retract his accusation. There was a pretence that Lord Cobham (who is, or rather was, until this matter came to light, Lord Warden of the Cinque Ports) and Sir Thomas Fare, (Lieutenant-Governor of Dover Castle), had offered money if a ship could be procured for Cobham to take refuge in France!'

Ralegh interrupted him: 'This is no evidence against me. If my Lord Cobham is a traitor, what is that to do with me?'

Coke responded: 'It was at your instigation, you viper. I will prove you the rankest traitor in England.'

'No, no, Master Attorney,' Ralegh protested. 'I am no traitor. Whether I live or die I shall stand as true a subject as ever King James had. You may call me a traitor at your pleasure. But I take comfort in it. It is all you can do. For you have given no grounds for any charge of treason.'

Popham tried to calm things down. 'Sir Walter Ralegh, Master Attorney speaks out of zeal for his service to the King. And you for your life. Be patient, both of you.'

Coke modified his tone, saying: 'I will now read my proofs relating to the conspiracy. On 20 July Cobham confessed he had had conference with the Count of Arenberg about procuring five to six hundred thousand crowns from the King of Spain and a passport for Spain; that he had intended to go to Flanders to confer with the Archduke before going to Spain, returning by way of Jersey; and that nothing further was to be done with the money until he had consulted Ralegh on its distribution to discontented persons in England. He was then shown Ralegh's statement and exclaimed: "Oh! traitor. Oh! villain. I will now tell you all the truth. I would not have been involved at all had not Ralegh pestered me." He spoke of plots and invasions – he could not remember precisely what. He said he was afraid that Ralegh, when he had him in Jersey, would betray him to the King.'

Ralegh missed a trick here which learned counsel, had such been permitted him, would have exploited. The visit to Jersey took place while Elizabeth was still Queen. Instead, he asked: 'Could I see this statement, please?' It was handed to him. He examined it, then said to the court and jury: 'This is all the evidence that can be brought against me. But now, I beseech you, hear me. I was examined at Windsor about this so-called treason, next of plotting for Arabella and, thirdly, of operations with the Lord Cobham. I was never a party to any of them. It is true I suspected him of exchanging intelligence with Arenberg. During the late Queen's reign he was in touch with him in the Low Countries, as my then Lord Treasurer Burghley and my Lord Cecil were well aware. I knew he knew La Renzi well from seeing him and Cobham together. When I thought they had both been to Count Arenberg together, I reported it. But my Lord Cecil told me to keep quiet about it, since the King would not hear a word spoken against Arenberg from the time he first came to Court. I therefore wrote to Lord Cecil warning that if La Renzi were not apprehended, whatever plot it was they were hatching would not be discovered; alternatively, if he were arrested, it would forewarn Lord Cobham.'

It is remarkable that, although Cecil was meticulous in filing all letters he received (as distinct from copies of those he sent), this letter is nowhere to be found.

'When my letter which I wrote in the Tower was shown to Lord Cobham he raged and spoke bitterly of me. But when he reached the bottom of the stairs he repented and, I am told, acknowledged that he had wronged me.'

Addressing the Attorney General, he said: 'Master Attorney, my Lord Cobham is not the babe you make him out to be. He can be uncontrollably violent. And why would I plot with a man like him who people neither love nor follow? I, too, having just resigned my high office as Warden of the Stannaries. I could see also that we must have the Kingdom of Scotland united with us, since some of our worst troubles come from there. As a united island we can face the world in trade or war. Divided, we could be no more than warring factions. We needed a quiet Ireland instead of the divisions amongst our forces there; a friendly instead of an antagonistic Denmark; good relations with the Low Countries.'

He continued: 'Instead of a lady whom time surprised we now have an active King. I would not have been so made as to turn myself into a Robin Hood, a Wat Tyler, a Kett or a Jack Cade. I also knew the State of Spain well – we having six times repulsed his forces: thrice in Ireland, thrice at sea. And I spent £40,000 of my own property in so doing. Their navy was down to some six or seven ships and most of their wealth from the Indies had been squandered. The Jesuits, Spain's imps, even had to beg at the church doors. When the King of Spain was trying to wheedle small sums for other states, how could he possibly have been persuaded to disburse six hundred thousand crowns to my Lord Cobham? Certainly not by my Lord Cobham. The Queen herself would not lend money to the Netherlands unless she had bonds with towns such as Flushing for security. Even the City of London wouldn't lend money to the Queen herself unless she mortgaged her land for it. And to show I am not "Spanish" I wrote a treatise to his Majesty the King setting out the present weak state of Spain and reasons for not concluding a peace.'

He went on: 'My close dealings with Lord Cobham were advising him on private estate matters. On one occasion I dealt on his behalf with the Duke of Lennox, ambassador in London to King James VI of Scotland as he then was, to procure a fee-farm from the King. I had for the purpose in my bosom £4,000 of Cobham's jewels – for as a baron of the realm he had great possessions: houses alone worth £5,000 a year, rich plate and furniture. Is it likely that I could entice a man of such fortunes to enter into treasons such as these? Not three days before his arrest he had spent £150 on books for his Canterbury house. He gave £300 for a cabinet which he offered you, Master Attorney, did he not? for drawing up the conveyance of his fee-farm. Is it likely that he would venture all this on some vague exploit? As for my knowing that he had conspired with Spain for Arabella and against the King, I protest before Almighty God I am as clear as anyone here.'

Another statement by Cobham was then read in which he declared that he and Ralegh had met in Jersey and taken 'advice of the people's discontents'. He had refused to sign it and urged that his status as a peer of the realm should be sufficient without signature. When pressed he had said: 'If my Lord Chief Justice says I am compellable and ought to do it, I will.'

Lord Chief Justice Popham, presiding judge, who was advanced in years, explained the part he had played: 'I came to Lord Cobham and told him he ought to subscribe. As he did so he referred to Sir Walter Ralegh as "the Wretch" "that traitor Ralegh". And surely the countenance and action of my Lord Cobham much satisfied me that what he had confessed was true and that he surely thought that Sir Walter had betrayed him.'

Coke also commented on what Ralegh had just said: 'I'm much obliged, my Lord. Lord Cobham did not act in the heat of the moment as you suggest, Sir Walter. He twice called for your letter, twice thought hard. He saw that his dealings with Count Arenberg were known and thinking himself discovered said: "Oh! wretch. Oh! traitor Ralegh". Also it is unlikely that he would condemn himself and his honour out of malice to accuse you. Again, Lord Cobham conferring with his brother Brooke two months before had said: "Sir Walter Ralegh and I are to take away the King and his Cubs". If he feared you would betray him, there must have been trust between you. And your discourse on Spain's poverty and your writing against the peace with Spain was your seeking but to cloak a Spanish traitor's heart. You say the evidence against you is but a bare accusation, without proof of circumstances or reason. I will satisfy them and will prove every circumstance of Lord Cobham's confession to be true.'

Ralegh responded: 'My Lords, I claim to have my accuser brought here to speak face to face. Though I know not how to make my best defence by law, I have learned that in case of treason a man ought to be convicted by the testimony of two witnesses, by statute. Surely you will not withhold my accuser, Mr Attorney. If you proceed to condemn me by bare inferences, you try me by Spanish Inquisition. If my accuser were dead or abroad it might be different. But he is living, and in this very house. Prove me guilty by one witness only, and I will confess the indictment. I stand not upon the niceties of the law. I beseech you, my Lords, let Cobham be sent for. If he maintains his accusation to my face, I will confess my guilt.'

Ralegh knew his man. So did Coke and Popham, Cecil and Howard.

Popham pronounced his decision in law. 'Proof of treason is a matter for the common law. By the common law one witness is sufficient. Nor is that witness's subscription necessary if it be otherwise attested by credible persons.'

Mr Justice Warburton observed: 'Many horse stealers would escape if they could not be condemned without witnesses.'

Ralegh demurred. 'Yet, my Lord, the trial of fact at common law is by jury and witnesses.'

'Not so,' replied Popham, 'the trial is by examination. If three conspire a treason and all confess it, there is no witness involved – yet they can all be condemned for treason.'

Ralegh submitted a comment on this ruling: 'I do not know, my Lord, how you conceive the law. But, if you affirm it, it must be the law for posterity.'

'No, we do not "conceive" the law. We know the law,' Popham asserted.

Ralegh tried again: 'Though the law, my Lords, may be as you state it, that is a rigorous interpretation. The King at his coronation swears to observe the equity and not the rigour of the law. As his ministers your Lordships are bound to administer the law with equity.'

Popham would not accept this proposition: 'Equity must follow the law. It must proceed from the King. You can only have justice from us.'

(It was to be two and a half centuries before all courts, whether of common law, equity or otherwise, were required to apply the principles of equity as well as those of common law.)

Cecil intervened. Time was getting on. 'Now that Sir Walter accepts my Lord's ruling that the accusation is sufficient I pray you, Master Attorney, proceed with your proofs.'

Coke continued. 'This dilemma of yours about two witnesses led you into treason. You thought to yourself: "Either Cobham must accuse or not accuse me. If he accuses me he is but one witness. If not, then I am clear". Cobham says he was to confer with you at Jersey on his way back from Spain. You yourself admit that you promised to meet him at Jersey, but only to make merry with you and your wife. Again, Cobham says that money was to be raised, but you say it was to be for furtherance of the peace.'

Part of the letter Cobham wrote to the Lords of the Council was then read out, including the statement: 'The last letter I wrote to Count Arenberg was asking him to get me a passport for Spain, and that if the King produced four or five hundred thousand crowns it would save him millions. The Count replied to say the money would be forthcoming, but how would it be distributed? Nothing was decided, however, and it was left for when the general discontentment gave rise to the occasion.'

Extracts of statements by Copley, Watson and George Brooke were read, including a reference to hearsay evidence indicating Cobham's and Ralegh's support for the Spanish faction.

There followed the reading of a statement by La Renzi which included a reference to Ralegh having supped with the Lord Cobham on the evening of the day on which Cobham had written to Count Arenberg; and that when a messenger from the Court brought a letter to Cobham, Sir Walter Ralegh was standing in the hall and later went upstairs.

Coke then gave Ralegh's statement of his reply to Cobham when he made the offer of part of the money to come from Spain: 'When I see the money I will give you an answer.'

Ralegh rejoined: 'Mr Attorney, you have seemed to say a lot but in fact nothing applies to me. You have come to the conclusion that I knew of the plots because I was to have part of the money. But you have the time completely wrong. It is true that my Lord Cobham spoke to me about the money and made me an offer. But it was one day at dinner at his house, sometime before the Count came over. He and I were arguing violently – he for the peace, I against the peace. He said that the Count, when he came over, would have strong enough arguments in favour of the peace to satisfy anyone. He told me, in his usual irresponsible fashion, what great sums of money could be given to some councillors for supporting the peace – naming Lord Cecil and the Earl of Mar. I told him he would make himself most unpopular if he did make such an offer. If after this Lord Cobham decided to join up with Lord Grey and others, what has that to do with me? I repeat. The offer was made to me before the Count came over. That to the others was made afterwards!'

Mr Serjeant Phillips put a question: 'Ralegh admits the point but tries to avoid it by distinguishing the times. You said it was offered you before the Count came over. That is untrue, for you, when being asked in examination whether you were to have the money from Cobham, replied "Yes" – and that you should have it within three days' – then in Latin: "No-one is presumed to lie when about to die".'

Howard put a pointed question: 'Give me any good reason why you listened to Lord Cobham on the matter of receiving hand-outs in matters you had no business to involve yourself in.'

'Could I stop my Lord Cobham's mouth?' Ralegh replied.

Cecil hinted next that he was in two minds whether Ralegh's request should not be favourably considered, asking: 'Sir Walter Ralegh is pressing for Lord Cobham to be brought face to face with him. If he is asking favours, they can only come from the one in a position to grant them. How can we, sitting here as lay commissioners, be sure that Lord Cobham should be brought here, unless the Judges accede to that course?'

Lord Chief Justice Popham ruled: 'The request cannot be granted. If it were, treasons could flourish.'

Mr Justice Gaudy added: 'The statute you speak of was found inconvenient in any case, so it was repealed by a later Act of Parliament.'

Ralegh resumed his argument. 'The common trial in England is by jury and witnesses. I would like to draw your attention to the story in the Old Testament Book of Daniel and Susanna, where innocence was vindicated. She was falsely accused and Daniel called the judges "fools" because "without examination of the truth they had condemned a daughter of Israel", and he discovered the false witness by asking them questions. I know the diversity of religion in the princes of our country in earlier days caused many changes in the law. But the equity and reason behind the laws still remain. If the statute law created by King and Parliament and the civil law, and God's word, require two witnesses, at least bear with me me if I only ask for one.'

Popham voiced his objection: 'That would open a great gulf to the King if we were to grant your request. I have never known of that course in a case of treason, writing and speaking to one another. There has been an exchange of information between you and Cobham, and what underhand practices I do not know. But if the circumstances do not agree with the evidence we will not condemn you.'

Ralegh pursued his point: 'The King only desires to establish the truth and would not take advantage of an unduly severe law. If a charge is merely one of stealing a few pence a witness must be produced. My Lords, let my accuser come face to face with me and give his evidence.'

Popham was adamant: 'You have no legal basis for such a procedure. Nor may any man accuse himself on his own oath.'

Coke was listening with barely concealed satisfaction and added: 'There is a presumption of law that a man may not accuse himself in order to accuse another. You are an odious man, for Cobham thinks his case is that much the worse because you are involved in it. Now to deal with the insurrections to be stirred up in Scotland.'

An extract was read from Copley's statement: 'Watson' (his co-accused) 'told me that a special person had told him that Arenberg had offered him one thousand crowns and that Brooke had said the insurrections in Scotland came from Ralegh's hand.'

This was not merely hearsay. It was hearsay on hearsay. Ralegh merely commented: 'Brooke has been taught his lesson.'

Howard bristled at this. He took this as an attack on himself. 'Brooke's examination was taken in my presence,' he declared. 'Do you infer it was I who taught him a lesson?'

Ralegh denied this vehemently. 'No, I swear I wasn't referring to any Privy Councillor. I only meant that, because he is short of money, he will juggle on both sides.'

Coke asked: 'Do you agree you stated: "The way to invade England is to begin insurrections in Scotland"?'

'I still think it. I have often expressed that as my opinion, in the course of discussion, to various lords of the council.'

'Now to the words "destroying the King and his Cubs",' Coke said.

'What a barbarous idea,' retorted Ralegh angrily. 'If there were unnatural villains who spoke such words, should I be charged with them? I will not hear of it. I was never false to the crown of England. I spent £40,000 of my own money against the Spanish faction for the good of my country. What grounds have you for bringing the words of those hellish spiders, Clarke, Watson and others against me?'

Coke spat out: 'You have a Spanish heart and are yourself a spider of hell. For you professed to call the King a most sweet and gracious prince yet you conspired against him.'

He read extracts from statements of Watson, Brooke and Cobham, one of which stated: 'Brooke thinks the idea of destroying the King was put in his brother's head by Ralegh.'

Ralegh repudiated this allegation: 'This is a lying, disgraceful and treacherous suggestion which I completely and utterly refute. If you produce scurrilous matter such as this as evidence you would have any man's life in a week.'

Coke had not secured much change there. He moved to another assertion. 'Now to the book. Cobham says: "I had from Ralegh a book challenging the title of the King to the throne. I gave it to my brother. Ralegh said it was foolishly written".'

'I never gave it him. He took it off my table. I was settling my estate affairs and had all my papers, including the book, spread out on the table.'

'There was some collusion between you in the Tower, was there not?' Coke put to him. 'For he, having said it undermined the King's title, proceeded to deny it.'

Sir William Waad interjected: 'First my Lord Cobham agreed it was against the King's title. Then he retracted what he had said. Then he retracted his retraction. But he always told me the drift of it was against the King's title.'

At this stage it was apparent to at least one of the jurymen that the questions and comments were irrelevant and one of them was heard to murmur to that effect. Coke pounced on it. He could see that his grip of the case was weakening. 'My Lords, I must object to Sir Robert Wrothe's interruption. He said the evidence is not material.'

Sir Robert Wrothe hastily denied it. 'I never said those words. Let Mr Serjeant Phillips say whether he heard me say them.'

A commissioner said: 'I confirm what Sir Robert has said.'

Popham asked: 'Why was the book burnt if it wasn't subversive?'

Ralegh replied: 'I never burnt it.'

Mr Serjeant Phillips challenged him: 'You gave him the book when he was discontented. Had it been before the Queen's death it would have been a different matter, but you gave it him just after he had had an audience with the King, when he considered he had a grievance.'

'Here is a book supposed to be treasonable. I never read it, commended it or recommended it. I will tell your Lordships how I came by it. I had it from a Privy Councillor's library. It was written about twenty-six years ago by a lawyer.' The Court stirred at this.

Popham asked him: 'From which Privy Councillor, pray?'

'I would prefer not to say.'

'You are here to answer any questions,' Popham warned. 'Which Privy Councillor?'

'From my Lord Burghley.'

Cecil had to think quickly at this somewhat alarming disclosure: 'You are talking of my father. You may remember that after he died, you wanted some maps and books about the West Indies,' he reminded Ralegh. 'But if you took other things besides you abused my trust. It obviously wouldn't have been surprising to find a book like that. For any book or libellous pamphlet having implications for the State could have been amongst his papers, since he was a Councillor of State. The same applies to me. But you were wrong to take it, Sir Walter.'

Cecil also drew attention at some length to his own views and to the former 'dearness' between him and Ralegh and the difficulty he had in dividing himself between his duty and his love.

'It just seemed to be included among the maps and books,' Ralegh explained. 'I only spotted it later when sorting them all out. Its theme was to justify the late Queen's proceedings against the Queen of Scots. I am astonished that my possession of it is now considered treasonable. It was just one of many such books in those days, freely available. How Lord Cobham came by it, I do not know. I remember it was on my table during one of his visits – and that was at a time when I knew nothing of his discontent with the regime.'

Howard followed this up: 'I clearly remember, when I was sent to take the Lord Cobham's confession, pressing him about that book. He suddenly blurted out: "It is an unhappy man who must accuse his friend. I had the book from Sir Walter Ralegh. He didn't say much about it but did tell me it questioned the King's title." Did you not in fact leave it on your table so that he could not fail to see it – and be tempted to take it?'

Popham (incredulously): 'Are you sure about this, my Lord?'

Howard withdrew this accusation: 'On second thoughts I remember now that the Lord Cobham retracted his account and stated that the book contained no reference to the King's title and that Ralegh had not given it him, but that he took it while Ralegh was asleep.'

Coke dealt with the question of the number of witnesses required for proof of treason: 'Cobham said that Kemys brought him a letter and reassured him that he need not be alarmed, for one witness would not be sufficient to convict.'

'This wretched man Kemys has been in close confinement these eighteen weeks,' Ralegh claimed. 'He was threatened with the rack to force a confession.' They all gasped at this. He went on: 'I never sent any such message. I merely wrote to Cobham to tell him what I had said to Mr Attorney about a great pearl and diamond I had belonging to Cobham.'

'This is a disgraceful suggestion,' Howard protested. 'Kemys was never put on the rack. The King ordered that there should be no violence.'

The other commissioners joined in: 'We swear this is the first we heard of this.'

'Was not the keeper of the rack sent for and Kemys threatened with it?' insisted Ralegh.

After a pause Sir William Waad coughed apologetically and explained: 'When Mr Solicitor and I examined Kemys we told them he "deserved the rack" – but did not threaten him with it.'

The other commissioners said in a chorus: 'We knew nothing of this.'

Coke read other passages from Cobham's statement. 'Kemys brought me a letter from Ralegh stating that he had been examined and had cleared me of all blame; that my Lord Henry' (Howard) 'had "expressed the view that because I was discontented I was likely to commit a treasonable act".' And that Kemys had given him a message from Ralegh 'that I should be reassured, in that one witness would be insufficient to secure a conviction for treason.'

'If Kemys said that,' Ralegh commented, 'he added it without authority. I never told him to say that.'

The court asked him to proceed with his defence: 'Pray tell us your version of events, Sir Walter.'

'I am accused,' he stated, 'of acts relating to Arabella and money from Spain. Allow me this one request, my Lords. Let Cobham, as he is both alive and in this building, as I have said, but be brought here to testify to any of these statements of his and I will confess the whole indictment and renounce the King's mercy.'

'Arabella is a kinswoman of the King. We must not allow her to be slandered,' Cecil objected, 'innocent as she is, innocent as I or anybody else here, by confusing speeches to the court. She did receive a letter from Cobham. Far from instigating her disloyalty she laughed at it scornfully and showed it to the King. How far Count Arenberg was involved is a matter for the State to decide.'

Howard asserted: 'The Lady Arabella swears she never had any part in these affairs.'

Cecil supported this, adding: 'Lord Cobham wrote to the Lady Arabella to see if he could come and see her and indicated that there were people close to the King who were working to disgrace her. She thought it was a trick. Brooke said his brother Cobham tried to persuade him to induce Arabella to write to the King of Spain. Cobham denies it.'

Ralegh repeated: 'It is the Lord Cobham who has accused me. If it weren't for his accusations there would be nothing in these charges against me. Ask him if I knew anything about the letters La Renzi brought him from Arenberg. Let me question him, who has my life at stake. It cannot harm him to be brought here. It is strange treatment if this request is not allowed me. There is no precedent for this refusal.'

Popham again blocked: 'Though Cobham seeks justice, the possibility of getting his old friend acquitted might move him to speak otherwise than the truth.'

Ralegh turned to the jury: 'It is alleged that I was his instigator of these treasons. Gentlemen of the jury, please note this. He said I was the cause of his miseries and the destruction of his house, and that the evil has befallen him owing to my wicked advice. If this is true, who else has he cause to accuse and be revenged on but me – and he is as vengeful as any man on this earth.'

'He is a party to the proceedings,' Coke insisted, 'and may not come. The law is against it.'

A joint trial would have elicited the facts.

'It is playing with words to refer to the law. I defy the law. I stand on the facts,' Ralegh replied.

Cecil intervened: 'Speaking as I have here so often today, people will think I like to hear myself speak. My affection for you, Sir Walter, was not extinguished but merely lessened following your misdoings. You know why my Lord Cobham cannot be brought.'

'He could be, my Lord.'

'Are you challenging that decision?' Cecil asked angrily.

'Yes. Here and now.' Ralegh knew from the turn of the proceedings that it was the only chance he had of clearing himself.

Coke tried another tack: 'You say that my Lord Cobham, as your main accuser, must come here to put forward his accusations – which you say he has retracted. That is a fact to be left to the jury. Let me ask you this. If my Lord Cobham affirms that you were the only instigator to persuade him to these treasons, will you stand or fall by that?'

Ralegh knew that if he could only get him there, the truth would come out. He would not have the courage or wit to stand by his false accusations face to face. 'If he will swear before God and the King that I knew anything of the Arabella matter, or of the money to come from Spain, or of the plot to seize the King, I will put my case on it.'

'If he puts it in so many words to that effect?' asked Howard.

'Yes. If he makes the basic point.'

'Suppose he says you instigated his dealings with the Spanish King, will the council not have another charge against you?'

Cecil warned.

'I will accept them all,' said Ralegh heatedly.

'Then pray to God,' exclaimed Cecil, 'and prepare yourself, Sir Walter, for I honestly believe my Lord Cobham will affirm it. With the exception of your misdoing I am your friend. Your evident passion, and the Attorney's zeal for the King's service, make me say this.'

Coke resumed. 'So far as Arabella is concerned, I explained that she knew nothing of the matter. It is patently obvious that Ralegh was involved in all these treasons. The jury have heard the evidence. There is one other person I am calling, one Dyer, a pilot, who while in Lisbon met a Portuguese gentleman who asked him if the King of England were crowned yet. He replied: "I think not, yet, but he soon will be". "No", said the other, 'that will never be, because his throat will be cut by Don Ralegh and Don Cobham before he can be crowned".'

Dyer was called and gave evidence accordingly on oath. Ralegh laughed unbelievingly. 'Mr Attorney, whatever inference do you deduce from that?'

'That your treason has wings,' retorted Coke.

'But if Cobham was involved with Arenberg how could it not be known in Spain?' Ralegh pointed out.

He was then invited to address the jury.

'Consider, gentlemen of the jury,' he urged, 'there is no cause so bad in law that learned King's Counsel cannot make out a good case: even against men of their own profession. Consider then my disability and their ability. But they can prove nothing against me. When all is said and done you see that my only accuser is the Lord Cobham who has since shed tears and repented his false accusation.

'Presumptions must surely proceed from prior or subsequent facts. In that regard I have spent £40,000 of my own money against the Spaniard. If I had died in Guiana I would not have had as much as three hundred marks a year left for my wife and son. I who have always condemned the Spanish faction am now strangely accused of supporting it.

'Now, if you would be content on presumptions such as these to be delivered to the slaughter – to have your wives and children thrown on the streets to beg for their bread – if you would be content to be so judged, then so judge me.'

Mr Serjeant Phillips summed up for the prosecution. 'This

matter is treason of the highest degree: the intention being to deprive the King of his crown. The particular treasons are these: first, to raise a rebellion and then, for this purpose, to stir up tumults in Scotland by divulging a treasonable book denying the King's right to the crown, the object being to take the life of his Majesty and his issue. Sir Walter Ralegh confessed Lord Cobham's guilt of all these treasons. The question is, whether Ralegh is guilty for joining with him or inciting him. If my Lord Cobham's accusation is true, he is guilty. If not, he is clear of blame.

'So, the question is, who is telling the truth? Ralegh has no answer but a bare denial – put with considerable wit.' It was evident Ralegh had impressed all his listeners. 'A defendant's denial must not influence the jury. Even in the Star Chamber or in the Court of Chancery concerning the question of title to land, a defendant's bare denial even on oath is insufficient evidence to absolve him. Therefore in a case of treason it is that much less sufficient. On the other hand, when one person such as Lord Cobham accusing another does not excuse but condemns himself his testimony is as strong as that of the verdict of twelve good men and true.'

Ralegh interrupted his address. 'If truth be constant and constancy be in truth, why has my Lord Cobham forsworn his earlier statements? You have not proved anything by direct proof. It is all circumstantial.'

Coke broke in. 'Have you finished? It is for the prosecution, the King, to have the last word.'

'No, Master Attorney, it is he who speaks for his life who must speak last,' protested Ralegh. 'I appeal to God and the King on this point, whether Cobham's accusation is sufficient to condemn me.'

'The King's safety and your acquittal cannot co-exist. I never knew a clearer case of treason.'

'I have never had conversation with Cobham since he came to the Tower,' Ralegh replied.

'Rubbish. You are the most confident traitor who ever came to the bar. Why did you take eight thousand crowns?' Coke almost shouted.

The court felt this hectoring was going too far.

'Do not bo so impatient, good Master Attorney,' Cecil requested him. 'Give him leave to speak.'

'If I am not to be heard patiently you will encourage traitors and discourage us,' Coke flung back. 'I am the King's sworn servant and must speak. If he is guilty, he is an odious traitor. If not, let him go free.'

He sat down in a dudgeon and would not go on till the court urged him to proceed. 'You had communication with Cobham within four days before he was taken from the Tower.'

He addressed the jury. 'Ralegh had an apple and pinned a letter to it and threw it in my Lord Cobham's window. It stated: "It is doubtful whether we shall be proceeded against or no. Perhaps now you will not be tried". The intention of this was to get a retraction of his accusation. It was Adam's apple by which the Devil deceived him.

'He also wrote: "Do not as my Lord of Essex did – take heed of a preacher. By his persuasion he confessed and so made himself guilty". Cobham did retract his accusation but could not sleep or rest till he had re-affirmed his statement. If this were not enough to prove him a traitor, the King my master would not survive the next three years.'

Cobham's letter was read, with two or three interjections by Coke: 'Is this not a Spanish heart in an English body?'

He continued: 'Damnable atheist. Ralegh has learnt some scripture texts to serve his purpose, false allegations. He counsels Cobham not to be led by counsels of preachers as Essex was. But he died the child of God.'

Some of the bystanders gasped at this in disbelief. Coke was taken aback. 'You were there,' he accused Ralegh. 'He died in fact for his offence against the law.'

Ralegh again spoke to the jury. 'You have heard a strange tale of a strange man. His accusations are enough to destroy. But the King and all of you shall witness by our deaths which of us ruined the other.

'With regard to the apple, I told somebody to throw it into his window with a note stuck on it as follows: "You know you have been my undoing. Now write three lines to clear me. Otherwise I will die, in the knowledge that you had wronged me". Why did he not inform me of his treasons if I was frank with him?'

'But what do you say now of the letter?' Coke asked.

'I say that Cobham is a base, dishonourable poor soul.'

'I throw that remark back in your face. But for you he would have been a good subject.'

Ralegh resumed his address. 'Gentlemen of the jury, I will recapitulate events in the Tower. Before my Lord Cobham left the Tower I was advised by my friends to get a confession from him. So I wrote to him: "You or I must go on trial. If I first, then your accusation is the only evidence against me". It was surely not out of order for me to beg him to speak the truth. His first letter was not good enough, so I wrote to him again and he sent me a very good letter. I then sent him word that I feared the Lieutenant of the Tower might be in trouble if it were discovered that letters had been sent – although I must emphasize that the Keeper of the Tower is not to blame for this. It could have happened with any keeper. So I wrote to him again saying: "It is now likely that you will be tried first." He replied: "It is fitting that you had such a letter". And here you may see it.' He handed it to the clerk of the court. 'I pray you to read it. Therefore whereas I am accused of being a traitor I will prove myself a true subject and honest man, and that Cobham is base, silly and perjured.'

This second letter Cobham had written retracting his accusation was read out aloud by Cecil: ' "To clear my conscience and free myself from the cry of your blood, I never had conference with you in any treason; nor was I moved by you to those offences of which I accused you. So far as I know you are as innocent of treasons against the King as anyone living. So God deal with me and have mercy on my soul, as this is true".'

He concluded: 'Now, my masters, you have heard both sides. I am wholly gentleman, wholly soldier. That produced against me is no more than an unsworn confession. This of mine is under oath and the deepest protestation a Christian can make. So please believe the one which has the most force.'

The clerk of the court ordered: 'Gentlemen of the jury, you will now retire to a convenient place in secret to consider your verdict.' The jury withdrew as, separately, did the judges and lay commissioners. Coke went out into the quandrangular courtyard to await the verdict. He was pessimistic, by no means convinced that the charge had been brought home to the jury, carefully selected though it had been. He voiced his doubts to Serjeants Hill and Phillips.

Ralegh sat on in the court-room, anxiety tinged with the hope that his plea had been successful, but knowing the dice were loaded.

Coke would not have admitted it but thought to himself: 'Ralegh made rings round us,' and that the jury would be out some hours. He was astonished when he was recalled after a quarter of an hour. 'We've lost,' he muttered. But on the way in he was given a strong hint that their verdict would be guilty of treason. He was astonished. 'Surely you are mistaken,' he exclaimed. 'I myself only accused him of misprision' (no more than knowledge) 'of treason.'

Their foreman, Sir Thomas Fowler, was asked for their verdict on the counts as charged.

'Guilty, my lords.'

'Is that the verdict of you all?'

'It is, my lords.'

The clerk of the court addressed Ralegh: 'Prisoner at the bar, is there anything you wish to say before judgment is passed on you?'

'Yes my lords,' he said, shaken. 'The jury have found me guilty. I can say nothing as to why judgment should not proceed. You remember Cobham's protestation that I was never guilty. I desire that the King should know the wrong done to me since I came here.'

'You have had no wrong, Sir Walter,' Popham insisted.

'Yes. At the hands of the attorney,' Ralegh replied. 'I desire the lords to inform the King of three things:

I never knew my Lord Cobham meant to go to Spain.

I never knew of any dealings with Arenberg.

I never knew of my Lord Cobham's arrangements with Arenberg or of the plot against the King.'

Lord Chief Justice Popham in his judgment gave full rein to his invective, and passed sentence of death by hanging, drawing and quartering.

Ralegh went over to that part of the bench where Cecil and the other lay commissioners were sitting. He spoke privately to one or two of them. 'Cobham,' he said, 'is a false and cowardly accused. He can face neither me nor death without acknowledging his falsehood. If pardon is refused let Cobham die first.'

He knew that a death-bed repentance by Cobham, eternity before him, would force out the truth and clear him. Did not John of Gaunt in that ill-fated staging of Shakespeare's *Richard the Second*, seen by him, Cecil and Essex together say:

'Where words are scarce, they are seldom spent in vain,
For they breathe truth that breathe their words in pain.'

'Would you please also request for me an honourable death by straightforward beheading?'

This they promised to do for him. Cecil was in tears – Ralegh had helped to bring up his son. Crocodile? relief? penitent? sorrow?

At the beginning of the trial everyone in court and most in London had believed Ralegh guilty. By the end, nobody believed it. Some members of the jury asked him to forgive them.

Ralegh wrote to Cecil: 'Your Lordship knows what I have been towards yourself and how long I have loved you and have been favoured by you; but change of times and my own errors have worn out these remembrances (I fear).' He included a reference to the King who 'as a true gentleman and just man owes me most merciful respect' as one 'most willing to have hazarded his life and future for him.'

He wrote also to the King – on Cecil's advice? 'I speak to my Master and Sovereign to assure him that I never invented treason, consented to treason or performed treason against him. Save me therefore merciful Prince that I may owe your Majesty my life itself; than which there cannot be a greater debt.'

On 18 November Bess pleaded with Cecil by letter. Its phonetic spelling (not reproduced) accentuates its appeal. 'If the grieved tears of an unfortunate woman may reserve any favour, or the unspeakable horrors of my dead heart reserve any comfort, then let my sorrows come before you. I know in my own soul that he does, and always has honoured and loved the King – far from wishing him harm. I most humbly beseech your Honour – even for God's sake – to be good to him. Pity the name of your old friend on his poor little creature of a son Wat, eight years old – that we may lift up our heads and hearts in prayer for you and yours. Let the whole world praise your love to my poor unfortunate husband. And God for His infinite mercy bless you for ever.

P.S. I am not able to stand on my trembling legs, otherwise I would have waited on you in person.'

On 29 November the priests Watson and Clarke were hanged, drawn and quartered. Ralegh wrote to Bess what he thought to be his last letter on the eve of the day assigned for his execution.

'You shall receive, dear wife, my last words with my last will in these last lines. My love I send you, that you may keep it when I am dead. I would not present you with sorrows, dear Bess. Let them go to the grave with me and be buried in the dust.

'First, I send you all the thanks my heart can conceive or my pen express for your many troubles and cares taken for me. Secondly, I beseech you for the love you bear me living that you do not hide yourself many days, but by your travel seek to help your miserable fortunes and the right of your poor child .... Love God and repose yourself in Him. Teach your son also to serve and fear God while he is yours.

'When I am gone, no doubt you will be sought by many, for the world thinks I am very rich. But take heed of the pretences of men and of their affections; for they last but in honest and worthy men. I speak it (God knows) not to dissuade you from marriage – for that will be best for you. As for me, I am no more yours, nor you mine. Death has cast us asunder. Remember your poor child for his father's sake, that chose you and loved you in his happiest times.

'Get those letters which I wrote to the Lords suing for my life. God knows it was for you and yours that I desired it but I disdain myself for begging for it. And know that your son is the child of a true man.

'My true wife, farewell. Bless my poor boy. Pray for me. May true God hold both of you in his arms.'

Before execution George Brooke withdrew his accusations against Ralegh about 'killing the Fox and his Cubs'.

James was staying at Wilton, just west of Salisbury, in Lord Pembroke's house the day before that appointed for the execution of the rest. He was in a good humour, cackling away to himself but would not disclose the cause of his merriment, which only Cecil knew. That evening he called his page John Gibb, a young Scottish groom of the bed-chamber, into his room.

'Laddie,' he said, 'you're to keep your mouth shut. I've a

wee bit of fun in store for the morrow, a bittie play. You're the only one I'm telling. Listen carefully. But not a word to a soul.' He explained the practical joke he had in mind.

At Winchester Bishop Bilson had been sent to see Ralegh that night as his confessor. He had found him orthodox and devout, but not prepared under any circumstances to confess any treasonable guilt.

The morning of execution dawned. A huge crowd gathered. Such was the public interest the roads within a ten mile radius were jammed and Winchester itself was bursting.

Sir Griffin Markham was first for the block. He had said his farewells and prayers and was ready for the axe which had disposed of George Brooke. Ralegh was at the window overlooking the scene.

Suddenly there was a commotion. A young man forced his way through the crowd and in a pronounced Scottish accent shouted: 'Save this man's neck.'

To the astonishment of the on-lookers, he pushed into the centre and thrust a paper into the hand of the Sheriff, Sir Benjamin Tichborne. He read it carefully then told Markham: 'You have two hours respite.' He was taken away in custody to the Great Hall, to try and fathom beside the Round Table the explanation for this unexpected turn of events.

Lord Grey's turn came next. He was brought out knowing nothing of what had happened. He turned over the straw with his foot looking for blood. He spent a long time in prayer. It started raining. The crowd were getting restive. They had already been cheated once. The procedure was repeated.

Next came Cobham. He however had almost certainly been told that morning what was in the wind. Instead of looking scared he was jaunty. This avoided his retracting, at the point of death, his accusation of Ralegh. Ralegh's request that Cobham should go first was fulfilled but frustrated. He expressed repentance cheerfully and affirmed his allegation.

Markham and Grey were summoned back from the Great Hall to the scaffold. The three were together asked by the Sheriff: 'Were you not justly tried and lawfully condemned?' They agreed dutifully and were told: 'His Majesty in his mercy has reprieved you'. They were led away.

There was a divided reaction among the spectators. A minority felt themselves deprived of their day out. The majority applauded the royal clemency which they assumed would apply to the fourth man whom they were sure was innocent. They could see him up at the window. He also had been a spectator of these events but could not make them out. He could hear nothing from where he was. So far as he knew his turn came next.

It did not come. Tichborne went over and up the stairs to Ralegh. He told him as he told had the others that his punishment had been commuted to life imprisonment.

Such was his reputation in the country and on the Continent that among some the outcome was attributed to Ralegh's wiles and money payments.

The establishment had triumphed. Their strategy had been successful. They had eliminated a troublesome competitor. They had extracted the last drop of revenge without the ultimate penalty which might have been on their consciences and could have rebounded.

He expressed gratitude in letters from Winchester to the King, Cecil and Council. To the King he re-affirmed his loyalty and gave 'humble thanks for your mercy which has been shown despite believing me to have been one of those intending evil.'

The Lieutenant of The Tower, Harvey, made overtures to secure his son's release from prison, to which he had been committed for trying to help Ralegh. He told Cecil by letter of Cobham's letter exonerating Ralegh 'Knowing how easily a man might be limed for treason I left my son to himself. I now enclose a letter from Lord Cobham dated 24 October manifesting his desire to justify Ralegh. I stopped it but my son told Ralegh about it.'

The young tend to have a keener sense of right and wrong, and courage of conviction, than their more cautious elders.

Harvey offered his resignation, but hoped it would be deferred for a year, as winter was such a difficult time of year to move. Cecil's reaction was, perhaps: 'Well done, Sir George.' Young Harvey was released.

James wrote a personal letter to the Archduke Albert: 'We thank you most affectionately for the sincerity and affection you have shown yourself to bear towards the conclusion of this peace and friendship by the choice you have made of such worthy and eminent instruments as are our cousin the Prince

Count of Arenberg and his colleague' presumably La Renzi, 'who, by their sufficiency, prudence and integrity have so conducted this important affair that we have received therein great satisfaction.'

Years later, as he was dying, Sir Francis Gaudy, one of the judges, who had always had Ralegh's trial on his conscience, affirmed: 'Never before has the justice of England been so depraved and injured as in the condemnation of Sir Walter Ralegh.'

18

Wolves Pounce

Conviction of treason meant automatic forfeiture by attainder of all Ralegh's possessions. He was divested of the remaining offices.

Meere and Serjeant Sir Edward Phillips (one of his prosecutors, later to become Speaker and Master of the Rolls) were appointed commissioners to deal with his Sherborne estate. They pounced on the Castle and lands and proceeded to sell the stock, fell timber and strip it. The Lodge was their next target.

Ralegh complained bitterly to Cecil, Lord Treasurer Lord Bathurst and other lords of the council: 'Meere vaunted and sent me word of this triumphantly.' Things could not have worked out better for Meere. 'It grieves me that so infamous and detestable a wretch as Meere is made a commissioner – who dares not show his face, having so many executions against him, and hath not forty shillings worth of ground in the world but of my gift and who now rooteth up all my coppices and promises to pay his creditors with the proceeds promised him out of Sherborne. He is spreading it abroad that someone of your Honour's has employed him to procure the remainder of all I have in the world from his Majesty and turn my poor wife, child and family a-begging.'

Ralegh asked the lords of the council to stay the sale of 'such poor stuff as remains in my house in Sherborne. The deed of conveyance is in the hands of my servant John Wood, now at Bath, so I cannot get my papers.' He set out a note of his income and debts. 'All my rich hangings I sold to my Lord Admiral' – Charles Howard, Earl of Nottingham – 'for £500. I had but one rich bed, which I sold to Lord Cobham. All my plate – which was very fair – is now lost or eaten out with interest at Cheyne's the goldsmith in Lombard Street. I humbly beseech you not to leave me to utter beggary.'

Cecil acted swiftly. This was going too far. He became his and Bess's protector. The danger from Ralegh averted, some natural affection and sense of obligation reasserted themselves. Had they not helped him in his low time after his wife died and devoted themselves to his son William? Also, he must avoid any risk of being charged with victimization. He had personally delivered Ralegh's letter to the King following his reprieve. He now ordered the pillage to stop. The Rangership of Gillingham Forest and Governorship of Portland he kept in Ralegh's family, giving them to his elder brother Carew. Bess and Wat were allowed to join him in The Tower. Despite its grand setting and view of the river and countryside, it was no first-class inn. But his apartments, in the upper storey of the Bloody Tower, were reasonably spacious. They enabled Bess and him to be together again.

Ralegh wrote his thanks. 'Due to your great favour I owe preservation of my movables which ravenous sheriffs would have seized had it not been for your letters. My last desire is to obtain the poor estate that remains, so that the life which your lordship hath stayed at the grave's brink may have wherewith to relive it, and that my poor child may be your poor creature for ever as I am.' He renewed his protestations at the injustices of his condemnation.

Ralegh's wine patent was likewise transferred to Charles Howard. He not only took over the patent income but claimed also the large sum in arrears which Ralegh had been unable to collect. A word from Cecil was needed before this claim was dropped.

There was an ironic twist. Peace with Spain was concluded. Cecil, Lord Henry Howard and others received secret and substantial pensions for life from the King of Spain, increased a few years later. This was unearthed in 1614 by Sir John Digby when in Madrid negotiating a projected marriage between the King's second son, Charles, and the Infanta of Spain.

In March the royal family with Court were to descend on The Tower. James had decided to liven things up with some entertainment. There had not been much fun since his Winchester joke. Ralegh prepared to make appropriate salutations. It was not to be. The day before the party arrived he and his fellow prisoners from Winchester were transferred to the Fleet prison. Kemys was allowed to join him. The Court enjoyed various diversions such as two mastiffs being put on to a lion and bull-baiting – similar to the entertainment Ralegh had provided for the French ambassador and his company the year before. When the visitors had left and the prisoners returned, plague broke out in the Tower. This could have stemmed from the river mists and water oozing through the walls, or from the concourse of the recent spectators. Bess and Wat had to leave in haste.

Ralegh and Bess renewed their pressure for the Sherborne estate. He told Cecil of the secret conveyance in trust for his son and brother drawn up just before Elizabeth's death, subject to his life interest. The life interest was undoubtedly forfeited by the attainder, vested as it was in himself. But the freehold and trust were a different matter. Accordingly, in July 1604 it was agreed that the property should be made over to trustees on behalf of Bess and her son by a sixty year grant of Sherborne and ten other Dorset and Somerset manors. Her plea for a pardon was turned down out of hand.

Ralegh followed this up with another letter to Cecil. He reiterated the plea for a pardon even if it meant being confined in the Hundred of Sherborne. He would even be content to live in Holland – where he might succeed in getting a job in the Indies. Or he could get himself attached to a bishop or nobleman. Perhaps Cecil could let him look after one of his parks for him. He would not break his undertaking to stay put. If he could not get to Bath his health would suffer.

These frustrated pleadings Cecil ignored. He had had enough. Some people were never grateful but always wanted more. Meanwhile he made a mental note to have the secret conveyance examined at the highest level. On 20 August 1604 he became Viscount Cranborne, and eight months later Earl of Salisbury.

Sherborne soon learnt of the good news that Lady Ralegh would be staying after all. The staff and townsfolk congratulated her. She was well liked by all classes. She had taken an interest in their personal problems. They knew her to be honest and straightforward. 'I thank you for your goodwill,' she told them. 'I shall spend most of my time in that magnificently horrible Tower. But I will come down whenever I can. I trust he will be able to join me one day – perhaps sooner than we realize.'

Ralegh was delighted that his trustworthy steward John Shelbury from Sherborne was to be one of the two trustees appointed to manage his affairs. He had leisure to write, and re-read, his poems. One was entitled *The Lie*:

> Say to the Court it glows
> And shines like rotten wood,
> Say to the Church it shows
> What's good, and does no good.
> If Church and Court reply,
> Then give them both the lie.

They were not for publication.

Sir George Harvey was still Lieutenant of The Tower. He confessed to Ralegh about withholding Cobham's letter. 'I did it to save my son,' he pleaded.

Ralegh, at first furious, was a philosophical pragmatist who had no wish to get on the wrong side of his jailer. He accepted his explanation with grace. What's done could not be undone. 'I would have done the same for my Wat,' he assured him.

'Look, Sir Walter, you are at complete liberty to use my garden for recreation – and do some gardening yourself if you feel so inclined,' he added laughing.

'I might well do that,' answered Ralegh. 'Thank you. And what about the little hen-house – I could put that to good use, I know.' He had in mind using the small shed as a laboratory for chemical experiments to occupy his time. He might even make substances for sale.

'By all means,' was the reply. 'You're welcome.'

Bess stayed with him more often than not, although she felt free to go out during the day. He encouraged her to do so. 'I want your life to go on normally as far as possible, my dear Bess,' he insisted. 'You must keep up with your friends and so must Wat. He must have company of his own age.' She took the lease of a house nearby on Tower Hill.

A preacher and three boys were allowed to join him, supplementing his staff of two servants. He was allowed visitors. They included Kemys, Shelbury, another trustee Sir Alexander Brett, Hariot, Peter Vanlore (jeweller and money-lender), a school master John Talbot, his surgeon and others.

Bess had no time for Vanlore. Ralegh had had many financial dealings with him, raising money for privateering expeditions and so forth. She felt her husband always had the worst of the bargain. On one visit Vanlore produced a bond which had not been honoured. Ralegh and Shelbury admitted they had forgotten all about it. Vanlore pressed him on it. Ralegh replied: 'As you know I've no ready money at the moment. But I'll sort it out. Leave it to me.' He spoke to Bess: 'You know the jewel the Queen gave me?'

'The sparkling diamond you're always reminding me of? Of course I know it.'

'I have to raise some cash to pay Peter,' he explained. 'He's dug up an old bond of mine.'

'How much for?' she enquired.

'£600 including interest.'

'What's the jewel got to do with it?'

'I'll have to let him sell it for me,' he confessed.

'I consider that monstrous,' she exclaimed. 'He's nothing but a shark like all those London jewellers, goldsmiths and money-lenders. I'm not going to let it go. He's always twisting you. You're too soft. Besides, that jewel means a lot to you – to us.'

However, he insisted. She swept out to her Tower Hill house to get it, brought it back and flung it at him saying: 'You needn't expect me this evening. I'm dining out and I shall be sleeping at home – if I can call it home.' She flounced off, furious.

Only £400 remained after the debt had been deducted. Vanlore's response: 'Sir Walter, you're the best payer of debts I know.'

It was two days before she called again. She had seen her doctor in the interval. 'Walter,' she said, 'I have some news for you.'

'Have you forgiven me, my sweet?' he asked.

'Of course. We'll forget all about it. It was only a trinket, after all. We'll buy it back sometime. We have a more precious jewel coming our way.'

'You don't mean – a brother for little Wat?'

'Not necessarily. It might be a sister.'

'My darling. God has been so good to us.' He kissed her tenderly.

But life in The Tower was telling on them both. He became unwell. He had difficulty in breathing and his left arm and side swelled up. He was even finding speech difficult. To cap it all, plague broke out again. As he reported: 'My child has lain these fourteen days next to a woman with a running plague sore, whose child also this Thursday died of the plague.' Bess had to take Wat and herself away. She petitioned James for some measures of relief, unsuccessfully. But he was allowed to sleep out in his garden shed to get away from the damp quarters and into the fresh air.

Their child, a boy, was born in February, 1605. He was baptized in The Tower Church of St Peter ad Vincula. They named him Carew after Ralegh's elder brother. It was a family name.

Bess, however, was getting desperate over money matters. The Sherborne deal had still not been settled. Expenses were draining their limited resources. On one of her visits she was more than usually distressed. She burst in with Wat and the new arrival Carew, crying and sobbing. 'What is to become of us? You're looking after yourself and doing nothing for us. We can't go on like this. I thought it was all cut and dried but we've heard nothing. What do you imagine I can live on? And feed these two children? Air?'

At another time he might have reminded her that the baby's food was already provided for. This was not the occasion for pleasantries. 'These things take their course, my dear,' he offered soothingly, 'I'll see what I can do to hurry things along.' He wrote to Cecil. He told him how unwell he was and went on: 'I shall be made more than weary of my life by her crying and bewailing when she hears nothing has been done. She has already brought her eldest son in one hand and her sucking child in the other, crying and berating me for having looked after myself and neglected them.' Her nagging had spurred him into action.

Cecil sighed, not always resignedly, when Ralegh's letters appeared among the pile on his desk. He saw James and explained the situation. 'Very well,' said the King, 'we must keep faith seeing that the conveyance was in my predecessor's time. Make out the grant to the wife and elder child so that we may be no more troubled by their pitiful cries. But on no account include the father.'

Ralegh expressed his gratitude to Cecil but at once saw financial possibilities which could benefit him even though he had been excluded. 'Sherborne would make an excellent seat for you, my Lord Cecil' (Earl of Salisbury as he now was and Lord Treasurer, undisputed head of government). 'It has a fine setting. It would save you the £10,000 it would cost you to build elsewhere.'

He could not arouse Cecil's interest. He would soon acquire a delectable park in Hertfordshire.

In November 1605 the Gunpowder Plot was discovered. Commissioners were appointed to see if Ralegh had had any part in the affair, Sir William Waad, one of his trial commissioners being one of them. They looked into possible dealings with the French ambassador. Ralegh had been seen to hand a package to Captain Whitelocke, a retainer of the Earl of Northumberland suspected of being a spy for France. Ralegh denied any sinister motive and explained the circumstances. 'I have no business with the ambassador. His wife, Madame de Beaumont, once called at the Tower in the company of Lady Howard of Effingham. The pale being down she waved to me and asked me for a little balsam from Guiana. I fetched a bottle of it from my still-room and gave it to Captain Whitelocke for her, he being with her at the time.' He went on: 'In the name of my many sorrows and causes, my services and my love to my country, I beg you not to suspect me to be knowing about this unexampled and devilish invention.' Of Lord Henry Howard, Earl of Northampton, he told Cecil (ignoring, or in ignorance of, the close contacts between the two): 'I would no more trust him than one of the corrupt lawyers. He took Cobham's place as Lord Warden of the Cinque Ports. And what does he do? Lets Catholics sail in, secretly.'

Harvey had been replaced as Lieutenant of The Tower by Waad. During Harvey's tenure Ralegh had been allowed a large measure of freedom. The garden shed was a useful laboratory and still-room as well as for sleeping out of doors. In the course of his experiments he had produced a cordial which became a medicine in great demand. He had also been permitted to walk on the ramparts. People would visit The Tower just to view the spectacle of this famed giant disporting himself and strutting up and down beyond the battlements. It was one of the sights of London. From them there were good views of the Essex, Surrey and Kent countryside. Waad put a stop to this. He reported to the Council. 'Ralegh flaunts and sports himself and struts the ramparts like a turkey-cock, boasting that your Lordships interviewed him to clear him of the plot charge, not to charge him. Lady Ralegh drives grandly in and out of The Tower in her coach.

Anyone is allowed to visit him.' He was again placed under close supervision, which was bad for his health and his morale.

His steward Shelbury was having difficulty in collecting the rent from land at Bishops Down, a hamlet south-east of Sherborne. The occupier had produced a lease purporting to have been granted and signed by Ralegh, to whom Shelbury showed it. There was no record in the books of a lease of this land and neither had any knowledge of it. It dawned on him that this was an example of Meere's craft, derived from practice of his signature.

But Meere's fortunes were in decline. As a tool he had long since been discarded by Howard, having served his purpose. He had lost all credibility in the town. In helping to destroy Ralegh he had indeed destroyed himself.

Bess went down to Sherborne two or three times to clean and tidy up the Lodge and see if all was in order. She spent a large amount of money on the garden she loved. The pinks she had introduced ('Lady Betty's pinks' as the locals called them) were flourishing. She found the armour in the house rusty, so had it scoured and polished. This caused some alarm. Rumour spread that she must be involved in rebellion and was preparing weaponry. It was noised all along the way to Salisbury that Ralegh's muskets and pistols were being made ready. It was quickly scotched.

There was another rumour, which raised the hopes of the folk of Sherborne, that he would be given his liberty during the sitting of Parliament. It came to nothing.

He was joined in The Tower by the Earl of Northumberland, Henry Percy, convicted for complicity in the Gunpowder Plot. They and their erudite friends and staff constituted a learned little band of intellectuals. They were regularly instructed by the celebrated mathematicians Hariot, Hughes and Warner.

These learned contacts were ideal for Wat. He was the

image of his father in looks, character and impetuosity. Although not by nature addicted to study – not uncommon with boys – he was intelligent and interested and had absorbed more than an average share of learning by the time he was fourteen. 'This boy's ready for Oxford,' Ralegh informed his wife one day.

'Oh! No, Walter. He's too young,' Bess objected. 'Give it another year.' Mothers tend to be reluctant to see their offspring go.

'We'll ask Hariot,' said Ralegh. 'He's the expert. What do you say, Hariot?'

'We were discussing him only yesterday, Sir Walter. With respect, Lady Ralegh, we all have no doubt that he could matriculate now.'

On 30 October 1607 Wat was sent not to his father's old college, Oriel, but to Corpus Christi. He was fortunate there in his tutor, theologian Dr Daniel Fairclough (alias Featley), a fellow of Corpus. He, being young himself, understood him – which one of the age of his parents, let alone grandparents, had they still been alive, could not possibly have done, as he constantly reminded them. Things were different from when they were young. Featley applied a gentle but firm curb – too firm for Wat.

'Mother, Featley's an absolute tyrant,' he complained. 'I get no freedom. He's always at me, telling me I have promise but don't work hard enough and could do better. I don't get any fun.'

'How terrible, my dear,' said Bess, horrified. 'He must be a nasty man. I never did like the look of him – much too enthusiastic. He sounds a proper bully. Mind you, I never did take to academics. They can be so cocky and self-righteous. I'll speak to your father.'

Wat heard this with satisfaction: he'd scored a bull first time – as he thought.

Featley's report to Ralegh had been rather different. 'I like your son enormously, Sir Walter. He has talent but he's lazy. You have to keep on at him. If he can learn to control his temper and channel his energy into positive directions he will do well. He has a good grip of his Latin and the Greek is coming along adequately. He's fond of music but prefers to pluck rather idly at his lute instead of getting down to music composition.'

'I know what you mean. You're doing a good job, Dr Featley,' Ralegh assured him. 'Keep at it. That's what he's there for. I had to snatch my education in spare moments. I would like his course in life made easier.'

'You are an understanding father, if I might presume to say so, Sir Walter. You and Lady Ralegh are obviously very fond of him – not surprising with such a likeable, if somewhat headstrong, youth. I will find out from his music master his daily exercises and will myself accompany him to make sure he does them.' He made no comment on the effect on Wat of the insalubrious home surroundings.

Firm father was more in his interests than tender mother – in the academic field, that is.

Ralegh tried to interest Cecil in another expedition to Guiana. He referred to some mineral stones he had had from the previous exploration. 'I have heard,' he wrote, 'that you had some doubt that you thought it was an invention of mine to procure my liberty. I assure you that it was collected in Guiana by me from an abundant supply near the river. I had no idea of its value and I happened by chance to show it to a refiner who was assaying another stone for me. Admittedly, I promised him £20 if he could find gold or silver in it – but he guarantees his assaying with his freedom or even his life.

'If it is decided to launch an expedition I would be happy to go as a private person in a ship under somebody else's charge. The cost would be £5,000 and if her Majesty the Queen, who is sympathetic, and your Lordship will bear two parts, I and my friends will meet the remaining third. Alternatively, if she or your lordship do not wish to join the adventure I will find some other way of meeting the whole cost and give her and you one half of the proceeds. We would melt down the ore into ingots before leaving, taking six pairs of great bellows and brick in ballast for the purpose. We would invade no Spanish towns, will only trade with the Indians and have nothing to do with the Spaniards unless they attack us.'

Cecil showed this to Queen Anne who was all in favour. She had a great respect for Ralegh. Cecil himself did not bite – was it not a trick to get freedom by one means or another?

As an admirer of Ralegh she had pleaded her husband James for clemency immediately after the trial and several times since. She had even taken her elder son Henry as a young boy to see him at The Tower. He was likewise impressed by this hero, who was so unlike the feeble men he met at Court. She renewed her efforts for Cecil's co-operation. 'I would be willing to meet my share, Lord Salisbury,' she said. 'It would let that poor man out of prison – for a while at least. Shall I ask the King for his approval?'

'Yes. Do so by all means, Ma'am,' Cecil replied. 'I will find my share if he agrees.' He knew the King would consult him before committing himself, as he did.

'The likelihood of finding anything worthwhile I rate very low, Sire. I told her Majesty I would be prepared to meet my share if you agreed. But I don't advise it. Trouble with Spain would be inevitable.' He might have had his annual secret subsidy in mind. 'We know they have at least two settlements there guarding the mines. Of course I wouldn't want to cause her Majesty any disappointment,' Cecil added.

Nothing more was said about it. Sometime later Ralegh made a similar approach to John Ramsay, Lord Haddington, offering him 'a journey of honour and riches – an enterprise feasible and certain. I am more in love with death than with falsehood. When God shall permit us to arrive, if I bring them not to a mountain (near a navigable river) covered with gold and silver ore, let my head be cut off and his Majesty to have £40,000 into the bargain.' Nothing came of this either.

Despite the instruction from James the grant of land to Bess and Wat had still not materialized. Cecil had sent the secret conveyance executed by Ralegh in 1603 to Chief Justice Popham and Sir Edward Coke for examination. They pronounced it invalid despite having been drawn up by crown counsel Sir John Doddridge. It was discovered that owing to a mistake either in drafting or engrossing, two lines of vital words had been omitted: 'that the trustees shall and will henceforth stand and be thereof seized to the uses specified.' In one sense this was a mere technicality. The intention of the conveyance was clear, to convey the land away from Ralegh personally to trustees, thus divesting him of the freehold interest. Unlike Ralegh the trustees would have been free of the attainder. In days however when formalities were all-important it was fatal to the intention. Popham ruled: 'the freehold remains wholly in the father – I think by the omission of the clerk in the engrossing' – words perhaps phrased to avoid offending his colleague Doddridge. Thus despite the clear intention the freehold as well as Ralegh's life interest passed to the Crown by virtue of the attainder.

Ralegh railed against the unfairness of this ruling. Surely it was inequitable. Do not the courts of Chancery administer equity? he insisted.

Coke's reply was brief. 'Equity must follow the law'. He upheld the common law against allcomers – even Parliament in the following reign, but it was in due course decided that this contention was going too far. It overrode some of the King's dictatorial alleged prerogatives but not the sovereign power of King in Parliament. He rightly claimed that the common law was a bastion of individual freedom. It could also be rigid in its implementation.

19

Royal Friend

Ralegh spent more and more time with his books, writings and experiments. He had constant discussions with Hariot and the various tutors imported by that other prisoner, the eccentric Earl of Northumberland. He achieved a wide reputation as a chemist. His still-house, the converted garden shed, served him well if not ideally for this purpose. He allowed himself no more than five hours sleep. He researched the classics and ancient history with care, remarkable in one who had had no formal education apart from intermittent undergraduate years at Oriel. His researches were directed to a book he was writing on the history of the world, the military aspects of which would have the benefit of a critical eye from personal experience in battle on land and at sea.

Prince Henry came to know him well. His mother, Queen Anne, had all along believed him innocent and tried to protect him. Her brother, the King of Denmark, would have welcomed Ralegh as his Admiral had he been able to secure his release, such was his international reputation.

Henry became a great friend. He never tired of visiting him in The Tower and listening to his anecdotes.

'Bess, you must come and meet this Prince,' he told his wife. 'He is one of the most charming young men I have come across. No wonder he's so popular in the country. He takes after his mother. His Majesty dotes on him too. He'll make a first-rate King one day.'

Henry was with him one morning in 1610 when Bess and Wat arrived. They had come on foot from where they had left the coach outside The Tower, it still not having been readmitted. She curtseyed, Wat bowed. The Prince greeted her with a warm smile. She saw before her a well-built, upright young man with broad shoulders, a kind face and eyes that seemed to see through her, old for his years, courteous. No wonder he is so liked, she thought.

'So this is your son, Lady Ralegh, of whom I have heard so much. You, I hear, have been working hard on your Sherborne gardens.'

'Yes, Sir. I am getting them in good shape. I hope to have the pleasure of showing them to you one day, your Royal Highness,' Bess replied.

Addressing himself to Wat (a year older than he) he said: 'And what are you doing with yourself?'

'I'm down from Oxford, Sir. I have my bachelor's degree. I'm off to The Temple soon, like my father, to get myself a smattering of law, before I go abroad,' Wat replied.

'You're a luckier fellow than I. What would I not have given to do just that? I get so little freedom or time to myself. I'm not permitted to do a useful job. If I make any comment when I see something going badly wrong, I get chastised. Freedom is a wonderful thing – wouldn't you say, Sir Walter? No, don't answer. That was an unkind question.'

Their younger son, Carew, was brought into the room by one of the servants and introduced. He was an earnest child, eager to please, full of fun but cautious in all he did. He loved books but enjoyed a good game too. He was an affectionate little chap who loved company but was careful of new acquaintances till he had weighed them up – unlike Wat who plunged in regardless. He could show, like the rest of his family, a sharp temper when aroused.

'So this is your young son,' and to Carew: 'Yours is a very good name – is it a family name?' 'Yes, Sir. My uncle's called it and my kinsmen too,' Carew replied. 'I see them sometimes.'

'You must be proud of your boys, Ma'am,' he said, turning to Bess, 'and I hope to be able to accept your Sherborne invitation one day.'

Shortly after this he was created Prince of Wales with due ceremony on attaining his sixteenth birthday. He had in mind building a ship of his own, having been fired by the enthusiasm of Ralegh whom he consulted over the project.

'Now I should like the benefit of your advice, Sir Walter. You know more about this than anybody. It needs to be a large ship.'

'How large?' Ralegh enquired.

'Well, larger than *The Victory*.'

'That could have drawbacks, Sir,' he warned. 'I'll tell you why. It would need deep water. Our channels silt up every year. Take the Thames, Portsmouth, Plymouth, Falmouth. Even Harwich. I remember when Falmouth had three feet more of water at the entrance than now, and Plymouth little less. A smaller ship of six hundred tons will carry as much ordnance as one of twelve hundred. The lesser will turn her broadsides twice before the greater can wind once, and so there is no advantage in an over-plus of ordnance. Also, over-long ships are more fitted for our seas than for the ocean – one hundred feet long and five and thirty feet wide is a good proportion for a great ship. I will send you details of the specification. Two decks and a half are ample. Don't have any structure above it except for a low master's cabin – men of the better sort and better breeding, unlike ordinary mariners, cannot stand the rolling and tumbling from side to side in ships that are too high. They prefer more steadiness and less tottering cage-work. Also, high cabins are dangerous, in a fight. You can get torn to bits with the splinters.'

'What about armament?' Henry asked.

'Take care to keep the great guns four feet clear of the water, otherwise they're useless at sea. It is dangerous too to leave the ports open. You remember *The Mary Rose*? That magnificent battleship being launched by Henry VIII – your great-great-great-uncle – from Portsmouth to fight the French. There was a sudden puff of wind and a little sway of the ship as it cast about. Her ports were only sixteen inches above the water. She sank within two minutes. What a catastrophe that was.'

'Will you put all this in writing for me please?' he requested.

'I'll put it all down when I send you the specification. I'll go further than that. I'll write you a paper which I'll call "The Art of War by Sea" and let you have it.'

Henry laughed.

'Is there no end to your writing, let alone all your other activities? I know you must have time on your hands but not enough surely for all you accomplish.'

'I've some other maritime works in hand. One is called "Discourse of the Invention of Ships": another "Observations concerning the Royal Navy and Sea Service". I've carried out research into vessels used by the ancient Tyrians, Rhodians, Greeks, Carthaginians and Romans; every maritime state's sea laws; naval tactics through the ages; ports and natural harbours all over the world; the influence of commerce on maritime strength; defensibility of coasts in various seasons of the year. These could be useful information for any naval power.' He made no reference to the poetry he was also writing.

'I'm utterly bewildered. When do you find time to sleep even five hours? I hate to say it: perhaps it's as well you are stuck in The Tower. If you weren't we would have none of the products of all this literary activity. But it's a terrible price to have to pay to exploit such skill – genius indeed, which is what it is. Now to a subject close to your heart. But you won't like what I'm going to tell you.'

'Oh! and what is that, Sir, may I ask?'

Henry explained. 'My father has promised Robert Carr who, as you know, is one of his unpleasant intimate male friends, all your Sherborne property. It was Cecil's idea. He was only toadying to the favourite. You've probably heard how popular he is at Court. I can't stand him myself – strictly between ourselves. But my father is besotted with him.'

Ralegh was shattered at this news. 'Our only hope is to see if Bess – Lady Ralegh – can move his Majesty. He did promise it all to her, you know, Sir. But nothing's happened. I understand why now.'

'Nothing's happened because Carr has said he wants it.'

'I'll write to Carr at once,' said Ralegh, 'and I'll get my wife to seek an audience. Thank you for warning us.'

Ralegh wrote to Carr: 'I beseech you not to begin your first buildings upon the ruins of the innocent – obtaining the inheritance of my children and nephews, just because the law says a few words were missing. I therefore trust, Sir, that you will not be the first to kill us outright, cut down the tree with the fruit and bear the curse of those who enter the fields of the fatherless.'

Bess succeeded in getting an audience with James. She threw herself on her knees at his feet and implored him to keep to his promise and let her and Wat have Sherborne. He was adamant: 'I maun ha' the land; I maun ha' it for Carr.'

He tried to make up for it by a grant for £8,000 and a pension of £400 a year during her life and that of Wat.

When Henry learnt of this he stormed into James in a fury.

'No one but you would keep such a singing bird as Ralegh in a cage.' Had it not been for Cecil and Howard, might not the cage door have been unlocked? 'And what's this I hear about Carr and Sherborne. You promised it to Lady Ralegh and her son. It's theirs by right. Only a lawyer's fault or quibble – or fiddle, I shouldn't wonder – stopped them keeping it by law. Now you've given it to this blackguard.'

'I didn't think you felt as strongly about it as that, my boy,' he replied feebly. 'And Robert Carr's a very good friend, and loyal. He'd do anything for me. I do wish you and your mother would try and get on with him.'

'He's a plague and everyone but you knows it. Anyway he's your affair and not mine. But I want Sherborne for myself. So you'll have to buy him off,' he insisted.

James loved his sons, especially Henry. He was one of the few who could argue with him. 'Dear me, I'll do my best,' he told him. 'I don't know what Carr will say. I'll tell him I had no idea you were after it.'

'Tell him to do as he's told if he knows what's good for him,' he demanded.

The upshot Henry related to Ralegh and Bess in some glee.

'My father's bought off Carr. It cost him £20,000. Serves him right. Sherborne's mine – or soon will be. I promise you, Sir Walter, that as soon as a reasonable time has elapsed or your release comes through – and mother and I are forever pressing for it – Sherborne shall be yours again – or, at least, Lady Ralegh's and Wat's. But say nothing of this.'

The news that after all Prince Henry would be their Lord seeped out and was received in Sherborne with joy. 'We're the Prince of Wales's men now,' they shouted. The Abbey bells were rung to celebrate the change from the short-lived rule of Carr. 'The Prince is a good friend of Sir Walter and Lady Betty,' they all said.

The 'knowledge money' acknowledging his seignory once paid to Ralegh was willingly paid to Henry. Their local draftsman and artist Charles Rawlings was commissioned to paint the Prince's arms and feathers, to hang in the Abbey. The Prince was enchanted when told of their reception of his lordship and with the romance of the old Castle. He would have welcomed the reverence for it and for the Abbey and town in later generations and perhaps shared the sentiments expressed in a verse composed within the Castle walls in a winter some centuries later:

> 'Its noble ruins stand defiant yet,
> Gatehouse thrust up against a lowering sky,
> Stark, leafless trees sere, swaying sentries set
> Around the Abbey Town's once watchful eye.'

The Prince next consulted Ralegh on plans for his marriage. 'I've told his Majesty I will marry whoever he commands. They have in mind a French or Spanish Princess. It's all part of the political game, of course, as you well know. Their favourite choice would be the daughter of the Duke of Savoy for me and her brother, the Prince of Piedmont, for my sister Elizabeth. What say you?'

Ralegh was in his element. 'Not at all a good idea in my view. The Princess Elizabeth, one of the precious jewels of the Kingdom, would be sent far away. How long could she live free from plots and treacheries of the Jesuits? Her children would either have to be brought up in a way directly contrary to her conscience or she herself driven to wound her conscience by forsaking her faith. She would be tied to a Jesuited Prince in a family of Roman Catholics always under the domination of France or Spain. He couldn't help us in war or trade with us in peace. A Spanish envoy could even become King of England.' He favoured a Protestant prince.

'In your case, Sir, similar considerations apply. A link with Spain would be inconceivable. Spain and England are irreconcilable. The wounds we have given Spain, the archdukes and the Pope are too many and too deep to be healed with a plaster of peace. It would also arouse the enmity of the Netherlands, with whom our need for friendship is paramount. What profit would there be from this alliance? A sum of money and a beautiful lady. But beauty was never so cheap in any age, and it is ever better loved in the hope, than when it is had.'

Henry laughed loudly. 'You don't mean that, surely?'

'I do indeed, Sir,' replied Ralegh earnestly. 'My advice would be: keep your own ground for a while and in no way entangle yourself with any marriage proposals. Keep them all in Europe guessing. If it comes to the choice of a French or Spanish marriage, choose the French every time.'

'I agree with all you say,' exclaimed Henry. 'Two religions will never live in my bed.'

On another occasion he asked: 'What is the state of our defences today?'

'Deplorable,' Ralegh affirmed. 'We're very weak. The Government won't spend a penny. I have known a time when one of her Majesty's ships could take on forty foreigners. Now they are well-armed and quite prepared to take us on one to one.'

Henry was full of Ralegh's fervour for Guiana. 'Virginia is ours,' Ralegh explained. 'I know the settlers find it tough. It will get better. If only I could be there. Treat the Indians fairly and they will reciprocate. Treat them roughly and they will get their own back. Guiana could be ours too if we went all out for it. The natives love us. They hate the Spaniards.'

'I'd be the first to come with you,' Henry enthused.

'I don't feel that would be permitted, my Prince. At least not until it were safe. Come to think of it, that might not be so difficult. What I have in mind is an empire like the Romans, ruled by his Majesty – you one day. It would bring us untold wealth as it does the Spaniards.'

'Tobacco too?' asked the Prince, laughing.

'It's in great demand, and costly.'

'Might I try some?'

Ralegh refused to entertain the idea. 'It would be more than my life was worth, let alone my future, if his Majesty heard that I'd been corrupting his heir with the nauseating substance, as he calls it. So I fear my answer must be "No",' he said firmly, 'much as I dislike refusing a Prince.'

'Now, this business of war, could we not do away with it altogether?' asked Henry. 'It's a fruitless loss of life.'

'Ideally, yes – but I must unfortunately disagree,' replied Ralegh. 'The necessity of war, which among human actions is the most lawless, has a kind of affinity and resemblance to the necessity of law. There would be no use for war or law if every man had the prudence to conceive how much of right were due both to and from himself – or to rest contented with what he already had. But seeing that conveyances of land cannot be made strong enough by any skill of lawyers without a multiplicity of clauses and provisos to secure them from contentions, avarice and the malice of false-seeming justice:' (as he knew to his own cost) 'so it is not to wondered that the great charter, whereby God bestowed the whole earth upon Adam has bred many quarrels in its interpretation. If only men could appreciate the great truth – that no man is wise or safe, except he who is honest.'

'As a man of the world, is there any other advice you can give me personally?' Henry asked. 'I do so, Sir, with deference to yourself and your rank. But since you ask, I will. Your youth, and the thirst for praise which I have observed in you, may mislead you to listen to charmers. Hear them not, oh! my Prince. Whatever some men would insinuate, you have lost your subject when you lose his respect. The soul is the essence of a man, and you cannot have the true man against his inclination and respect.'

As Prince Henry had quipped, from the point of view of the exercise of his talent, the frustration at being penned in The Tower was far outweighed by the flowering of his literary skill and intellectual endowment in those uninviting surroundings.

But he was in trouble again with Cecil. Interference in matters of state, with which he had no right to concern himself – as earlier with his unsolicited paper to Queen Elizabeth on the succession – brought a severe rebuke and close confinement for three months and Bess was ordered to leave The Tower.

Howard told Carr: 'We had a bout with Ralegh, bold, proud and passionate as ever. The lawless liberty in The Tower has given him too much scope. We will duly inform his Majesty,' knowing that Carr would be only too pleased to do so himself. 'But he has the sympathy of Prince Henry.'

Ralegh addressed a petition to his sympathizer, Queen Anne, in verse, of which the following are the first two and last two verses:

> My day's delight, my springtime joys fordone,
> Which in the dawn and rising Sun of youth
> Had their creation and were first begun,

> Do in the Evening and the Winter sad,
> Present my Mind (which takes my time's account)
> The grief remaining of the joy it had.

☆ ☆ ☆

> Who should resist strong hate, fierce injury
> Or who relieve the oppressed state of Truth,
> Who is companion else to powerful Majesty,
>
> But you, great godliest, powerful Princess,
> Who have brought glory and posterity
> Unto this widow land and people hopeless?

When the Prince next called Ralegh told him: 'I'm in the middle of writing a history of the world. Must do something in my spare time! I can't tell you how many books I've consulted in the past four years. Ben Jonson, bless him, has helped with the research. May I dedicate it to you, Sir? The first part is ready for the printer. Take it away with you if you like, and see what you think of it.'

He did so and returned it a few days later. 'Absolutely fascinating,' he declared. 'I shall be honoured to accept the dedication. I found the narrative of the Greeks, Persians and Romans exceptionally interesting. If you could put in a little more on that it would make even more enchanting reading.'

He went on: 'I can see the theme of your philosophy running through it from God's creation of the world. I find history absorbing. Is it of practical use, would you say?'

'It is not the least debt which we owe to history that it has made us acquainted with our dead ancestors,' Ralegh replied, 'and out of the depth and darkness of the earth delivered us their memory and fame. How can we possibly deal with the present and the future if the past is a blank?' He went on: 'We may gather out of history a policy no less wise than eternal; by the comparison and application of other men's past miseries with our own like errors and ill-deservings.'

'You lay emphasis on the omnipotence of God. You must have pondered deeply over this,' Henry commented.

'The justice of God,' Ralegh asserted, 'requires no other accused than our own consciences, which neither the false beauty of our apparent actions, nor all the formality which (to pacify the opinions of men) we put on, can cover up from His knowledge. You may recall that Euripides said, if anyone who in his life has committed wickedness thinks he can hide it from the everlasting gods, his thinking is far from well.'

'You portray the rise and fall of nations rather as waves on the ocean. Can you account for the continual change in this respect?' asked the Prince.

'All kingdoms and states have fallen either by outward and foreign force, or by inward negligence and dissension, or by a third cause arising from both,' Ralegh explained.

'You touch on the need for loyalty in a way that gives me the impression that there lies the basic core of your conduct.'

'You may well say that,' Ralegh agreed. 'Whatever I have been part of I have sought to give my loyal support. I know that I have lost the love of many people for my fidelity towards her, my Queen, whom I must still honour in the dust: though further than the defence of her excellent person I never persecuted any man.' He continued: 'But we must not forget, nor neglect our thankfulness to God for the uniting of Scotland to England; though they were severed only by small brooks and banks, yet by reason of long-continued war and the cruelties exercised upon each other they were infinitely severed in their relationships. This, I say, is not the least of God's blessings.'

'My father ought to be pleased to hear that,' Henry laughed. He added: 'You also propound a legal caveat, that the prisoner's confession must not be taken as evidence of the crime, unless some other proof inform the conscience of the judge.'

'That is so – he might for example be light-headed. Or tortured.'

'On a lighter note, from what you say, Jason's golden fleece was really a sieve – a sheep's fleece dangled in a torrent to trap grains of gold washed down from the Caucasus. You also doubt the likelihood of the Trojan wooden horse.'

'Yes, Sir,' agreed Ralegh, 'but they're wonderful stories.'

Henry pursued another theme. 'Mother and I did enjoy also your translations of Horace and Catullus – as good as, if not better than, the original Latin, I thought. For example, this Horace:

> Many by valour have deserved renown
> 'Ere Agamemnon: yet lie all oppressed
> Under long night unwept for and unknown;
> For with no sacred Poet were they blest.

And the Catullus:

> The sun may set and rise:

> But we contrariwise
> Sleep after our short light
> One everlasting night.

Very true. A solemn thought indeed. We never know when that night will start – which is as well. How I wish I could write verse such as yours. There are emotions – joy, love, sorrow, hate, fear – which can only be expressed in verse, are there not? You must have plumbed the depth of all in your life.'

'Horace was a rather conceited fellow, I feel,' commented Ralegh, 'and something of a braggart. It was he who wrote: *Dulce et decorum est pro patria mori*: translate that, Wat,' he told his son who had just entered the room.

'I'll try, father,' he replied dutifully – unusually: 'What a beautiful and noble thing it is to die for one's country.'

'Well done. And yet he it was who threw away his shield and fled from the field of battle.'

Next time, Henry arrived in some excitement. 'I have a piece of news that may interest you: my father has undertaken to see you are released at Christmas. Keep this to yourselves.'

Ralegh and Bess were overjoyed. They could not even tell Wat or Carew. Wat in any case was getting involved in scrapes, despite parental exhortations. He had all the answers. They were out of date, with no conception of the world of his generation. 'You're thirty years behind the times,' he reminded them. 'Things have moved on since you were young.'

'You've much to learn yet, my boy,' his father said. 'If you don't watch out you'll learn the hard way.' But Wat's was the normal youth's reaction. The tune changes twenty or so years later.

Prince Henry's ship was built at Woolwich by a leading shipbuilder, Phineas Pitt, in accordance with Ralegh's specifications. It was universally complimented. It was named *The Prince* and Henry planned to attend its launching by the Queen. The arrangements had to be postponed. He was never to see it launched. The gods from the pages of Greek tragedy struck again. His future could have moulded the fortunes of the Raleghs and indeed of the Stuarts. Instead, he felt a lethargy creeping on him and worsening daily. Whether it was from swimming in the Thames at Richmond after dinner or from walking in the damp night air, no one could tell. From being his vigorous, athletic self he felt overwhelmingly tired. A severe fever developed and he became delirious.

The Queen pleaded for him to be allowed one of Ralegh's magic potions, the great cordial for which he was famed. There was some delay while the request was considered by the Council. Eventually they agreed. But it was too late. He died on 6 November 1612.

The Raleghs' loyalty had been devoted to, and their fortunes linked with, this promising young prince. Ralegh summed up his feelings to Bess – and later wrote them into the preface to his *History of the World*: 'It is God that commands all, it is nature that is obedient to all. It is God that has all things in himself; nature nothing in itself. For I protest before the Majesty of God, that I bear malice to no man under the sun. For it was to the service of that inestimable Prince Henry, the succession hope, and one of the greatest in the Christian world, that I undertook this work. It pleased him to peruse some part of it, and to pardon what was amiss. It is now left to the world without a master.'

Bess in her tears could do no more than echo his sorrow. He had a final word: 'All the hope I have lies in this, that I have already found more ungentle and uncourteous readers of my love towards them although well deserving of them, than I shall ever do again. For had it been otherwise, I should hardly have had this leisure, in this Tower, to have made myself a fool in print.'

Ralegh had finished his *Art of War by Sea* – but the final version would never now be read by its intended recipient. Full of grief, he put it and its draft notes at the bottom of his cedar chest.

20

Gold To Dust

Robert Cecil, Earl of Salisbury, Lord Treasurer and Head of Government had collapsed and died in Marlborough six months before Prince Henry, on his way back to London from Bath, where he had taken the waters. He had no friends. Scurrilous verses were written of him and the cause of his death. He was only forty-nine. He had played his rôle ruthlessly. He had thrown the Raleghs overboard with a slender life-line. He had served himself and his family well – and his country safely.

Ralegh's arch-enemy Henry Howard, Earl of Northampton, died in 1614. He had been an accomplice with Carr's wife, née Frances Howard (Howard's niece) in the murder by poison of Carr's former close friend Sir Thomas Overbury. His involvement did not come to light until after his death. Carr in the meantime had been allowed to re-purchase Sherborne which had reverted to the Crown on Henry's death, for what he had been paid to release it and was created Earl of Somerset. Lady Ralegh received compensation of £8,000 together with a £400 annuity rent-charge for her life and that of Wat – which she always had the utmost difficulty in getting paid.

The appointment of Sir Ralph Winwood, who was friendly to Ralegh, as Secretary of State increased the hopes of his release. The delayed edition of *The History of the World* was published. It was a best-seller in England and on the Continent. James however had reservations about some of its allusions which he took personally, saying: 'It is too saucy in censuring the acts of Princes.' He ordered the Archbishop of Canterbury to suspend its further publication. This might have been because of certain principles it spelt out: for example, that the great English victories were won despite no advantages in weaponry; against superior numbers; by people who were neither savage nor effeminate; against nations who had had much more concentrated training in military discipline, often better than that found in England, who were never ready for war till it was forced on them.

James may have objected also to what he took as an impertinent reference to rulers: 'Kings and Princes neglect the advice of God while they enjoy life, but they follow the counsel of Death on his first approach. Death, which hates and destroys men, is believed. God who made him and loves him, is always deferred. It is therefore Death alone that can suddenly make Man know himself.'

Resumption of publication was eventually permitted provided Ralegh's name and picture were removed from the title page. It comprised as its first, and as it transpired its only, instalment, five enormous and detailed books.

James also suppressed another book of Ralegh's entitled *The Prerogative of Parliaments*. It set out dialogue between a King and a Privy Councillor (the office he never succeeded in achieving): 'The bonds of subjects to their Kings should always be wrought out of iron; the bonds of Kings unto subjects but with cobwebs' – a proposition which with the Stuart James surely struck a chord. James commented on Parliament: 'I am astonished that my predecessors allowed this monstrous institution' – his son Charles would have agreed. In fact Ralegh's book was aimed at protection of the Crown by mitigating the influence of bad advisers.

In September 1615 Arabella Stuart, who had also been confined in The Tower, died after a sad life of imprisonment. Ralegh sighed to recall the vivacious young girl at the Court dinner party when Lord Burghley had been impressed with her charms. How hard fate could treat some, however unjustifiably, he well knew. He was less than pleased however when the Privy Council issued an order that Arabella's jewels, which for some reason were in his possession, (he had a great fondness for jewels) should be seized by the Crown.

The Raleghs were having problems with Wat. He was a handsome young man with undoubted ability. He had not distinguished himself at Corpus Christi although he was fluent in Latin and a good debater. Affairs of the heart had more interest for him than affairs of the head. He had a quarrelsome disposition and in general little patience with academic work. His behaviour was even worse when he came down to London. Frustration at not being allowed at Court like his contemporaries no doubt aggravated matters. When a complaint came to him that his son had wiped an adversary's face with a turd Ralegh decided to take action. 'But hes's no worse than you were at his age,' Bess reminded him.

'That's as may be. At his age I was fighting. A taste of war would do all youngsters good, I say. They'd learn some discipline and leadership and broaden their minds. I suppose I was lucky. It was wonderful experience. The real thing.'

'What a dreadful way to get experience,' retorted Bess. 'What are you going to do about it?'

'I'm sending him over to France to sort his ideas out.'

'With whom?'

'Ben Jonson.'

She laughed derisively. 'That'll be a case of the blind drunk leading the blind.'

'Ben's not as black as he's painted. He has a good brain and he's a first-rate tutor,' he replied defensively.

'We shall see.'

It was Ben Jonson who, amongst others, had been helping him compile his *History* – between drinking bouts.

Wat's education may have improved. Jonson's habits did not. Ralegh received a report on their exploits which he showed Bess. 'What do you think now? I've no time for drunkenness, neither has Wat, believe it or not. I learnt my lesson early – good parties getting out of hand. I admit I stretch a point with Ben. But what do you imagine they've been up to now? Wat got Ben drunk, put him face up on a trailer, stark naked, and had some men tow him through the streets of Paris. To cap it, he pointed out Ben's private parts to the passers-by as being a more lively religious symbol than any they had.'

Bess burst out laughing. 'Just the sort of thing you might have done if you'd thought of it. Anyway, what did I tell you?'

'I'm getting them back home before anything worse happens.'

There was another contributory factor to Wat's violence. The heiress to Sir Robert Basset (great-grandson of Arthur Plantagenet, Sixth Viscount Lisle, a natural son of Edward IV) was Elizabeth Basset. She was the ward of Lord Cobham, and had an estate of £3,000 a year. With his consent and that of Cecil as Master of the Court of Wards she and Wat had been betrothed in their childhood. On the attainder of Ralegh and Cobham the engagement was broken. But their affection for one another continued and they grew ever more attached. They were childhood and teenage sweethearts. Demure, attractive, her heart was his. As with most wild young men, a loyal and devoted consort can steady them down. It was not to be. Against her will she was affianced to Henry Howard, a son of Lord Treasurer Thomas Howard, Earl of Suffolk, despite her and Wat's protestations, and they were married. A retainer of Suffolk's incensed Wat by an unprovoked comment about his lost love. They fought a duel in which his opponent was badly injured.

'Your mother and I realize, my boy,' Ralegh told Wat, 'how hard you have been hit over Elizabeth Basset. It was no fault of yours. But what is to be is to be. As Will said: "What's done is done and cannot be undone". Not much consolation perhaps. But, like it or not, I'm going to give you a word of advice about marriage.'

'Not all that again, father, please,' Wat retorted.

'No. This is not in the nature of admonition – merely ideas based on experience – strictly between ourselves, of course. Your dear mother might leap to the wrong conclusions. Women have funny ideas on this subject.' He went on: 'Noblemen I have known, of meagre build, have grown plump after getting married. They used to pull my leg and say I was different from other men who usually became lean after they were first married. My explanation was simple: "Why, there is no beast that, if you take him from the common and put him into the several, on his own with one mate, will not grow fat".'

Wat laughed – in relief as well as amusement. It was not going to be the kind of interview he had expected. 'I thought that might appeal to you, you villain,' said Ralegh. He consulted the sheaf of papers he was holding. 'I have written it all down, you see. I'm just picking out bits here and there. What about this: Bestow your youth so that you may have comfort to remember it when it has forsaken you – that's sound, if anything ever was. Now this one applies to you: Even if you cannot forbear to love, yet forbear to link. You may find another more pleasing than the first, second or third love. I like that.'

Wat offered no comment but waited to see what would come next.

'Be careful in your choice: don't marry for beauty only, lest you bind yourself for life to that which perchance will never last or please one year. Nor yet an uncomely woman, since as much regard is due at least to our own issue as to any other race of creatures; and comeliness in children is riches, if nothing else be left them.'

'I've no complaints on that score, father.' Ralegh looked up – to see if Wat was trying to be clever. But if he had intended a jest, he gave no sign of it.

'Be not sour or stern to thy wife, for cruelty engenders hatred; let her have an equal part of your estate while you live, if you find her sparing and honest. Watch the age gap, my son. Believe me, the young wife betrays the old husband; and she who had you not in your flower will despise you in your fall. Observe duties too. Do not leave your wife to be a shame on you after you're dead, but able to live according to your estate – especially if you have few children and those provided for.

'At the same time,' he continued, 'leave her no more than necessity requires, and that only during her widowhood; for if she loves again, let her not enjoy her second love in the same bed wherein she loved you – nor fly to future pleasures with those feathers which death has pulled from your wings.

'I've nearly finished.' He could see Wat getting restive. 'Bestow your youth that you may have comfort to remember it when it has forsaken you. While you are young, you think it will never have an end. But the longest day has his evening. Remember, you will enjoy it but once, that it never turns again; use it therefore as a spring-time, which soon departs, and wherein you ought to plant and sow all provision for a long and happy life. Defame no woman in public. Don't be found a liar – hateful to God and man. Seek not riches basely. Remember Pliny's injunction: "Wine maketh the hand quivering, the eyes watery, the night unquiet, lewd dreams, a stinking breath in the morning, and an utter forgetfulness of all things".

'So,' he concluded, 'there are a few points to bear in mind. I'll let you have a copy. In fact I might even get it published. For posterity. It's full of good stuff – whatever my dear wife might say.' He took hold of Wat's hand. 'Finally, my dear son, let God be your protector and director in all things.'

Wat was again sent abroad, this time to Holland and without Ben Jonson. His father had arranged papers of introduction to Prince Maurice who duly entertained him. His former duel adversary had likewise gone abroad and they had been seen together having on the face of it made up their quarrel. But their intention was to resume the duel as soon as the opportunity arose.

James was desperate for money. This coincided with a hint from Ralegh which may have reached him that he should not make the same mistake as Henry VII when he rejected a request from Christopher Columbus for support. His magnanimity was moved, or further moved, by pleas on Ralegh's behalf by Sir Edward Villiers and Sir William St John, brother and half-brother of Sir George Villiers (later Duke of Buckingham) who had long since replaced Carr as James's favourite. The two had each been paid £750 for the purpose by Ralegh. He wrote thanking George Villiers for speaking to the King.

A warrant for his release was issued on 19 March 1616. It was to take, in charge of a keeper, an expedition to Guiana. He was not to resort to the Court or to the Queen's or young Prince Charles's chambers nor to attend public assemblies. His release came a month before Shakespeare's death at Stratford-on-Avon.

His rooms in The Tower were vacated to make way for Carr's wife, the Countess of Somerset, who had been consigned thereto for Overbury's poisoning, as had Carr her husband. On the attainder of Carr's property Sherborne again reverted to the Crown and was conveyed on sale to Sir John Digby, James's envoy in Madrid. Her trial had been adjourned because she was pregnant.

Exulting in his freedom Ralegh walked all over London – although normally no walker by choice. As in his Islington days, he kept an ear cocked for the cry 'Gard lo', and a watchful eye for the slops that followed from upper floor windows. He visited Elizabeth's and her sister Mary's tomb in Westminster Abbey: 'Having filled the same Throne, they sleep in the same grave, in the hope of the Resurrection.' Bess and Carew moved out of their house on Tower Hill, glad to get away from the sombre precincts into the house he took in Broad Street.

He set about raising money for the expedition. James looked for great profits, convinced by Ralegh's assurances. Sir Ralph Winwood, Privy Council Secretary, was enthusiastic. He had considerable respect for Ralegh. During the preparations he invited him to several dinner parties where he met dignitaries from home and abroad, including the French Ambassador, the Comte de Marets.

Bess was determined to do all she could to help her husband launch the enterprise on which he had for so long set his heart. She called in the £8,000 compensation for the loss of Sherborne, which had been put out to loan. She sold her property in Mitcham, Surrey, for £5,000 to pay for his ship *Destiny*. It was a fine ship which the public flocked to see. Queen Anne was keen to pay a visit but James forbade it. There must be no visible royal involvement in this unpardoned adventurer's enterprise.

Co-adventurers were the Earls of Huntingdon, Pembroke and Arundel. They advanced £15,000. Huntingdon also put in two pieces of brass ordnance – but he still owed Bess her jointure loan of £500 by her mother which they had never managed to squeeze out of him. Ralegh's cousin and friend Sir George Carew (later Earl of Totnes) supported it. Some £5,000 was raised from Amsterdam and from London merchants large and small. For the past century or more London 'the flower of cities all' had grown in wealth and importance nationally and internationally. People had flocked in from all over England to find work and seek their fortunes – as had Shakespeare himself. One such were the Fatt family originating from the West Country to which they still had loyalties. John Fatt of Aldgate, like many small businessmen who supported the operation, was one of them. He like them had mustered with the trainbands at Tilbury to resist the Armada. The State subscribed £175 towards the cost of *Destiny* – but this was no more than the customary shipbuilding grant.

Ralegh approached his old friend and money-lender Peter Vanlore whom Bess could not abide. 'Sir Walter,' he said, 'you know you are my favourite debtor whom I could not refuse. My diamond merchant brother-in-law in Amsterdam, Sir Adrian Thibaut, and his friends will be pleased to help you. They will require security, of course, and a share of the profits.'

The gentlemen volunteers keen to sail on the expedition

found £30,000. They included his nephew George Ralegh; William Herbert (of the Pembroke and Montgomery families); Charles Parker (brother of the Lord Monteagle who had participated in the Gunpowder Plot); Captain North (brother of Dudley, Lord North) and Edward Hastings (brother of the Earl of Huntingdon). Sir John Ferne and Ralegh's faithful companion Laurence Kemys were among the ship's captains. The Netherlands provided some men and material.

The venture had support in high places. The stakes also were high. Many friends tried to dissuade him. They could see disaster ahead, they told him. But he was adamant. This was the adventure on which his ambitions had been centred.

Among the visitors allowed on *Destiny* was the sharp-faced, keen-eyed, persuasive Spanish Ambassador, Diego Sarmiento de Acuna, Count of Gondomar. His uncle, some twenty-eight years earlier, had been held captive by Ralegh (albeit treated well). Gondomar himself as a young man was likewise reputed to have been held to ransom by him. He therefore had a dual interest in Ralegh's fortunes. He reported back in detail to the King of Spain the preparations for the voyage, known to be headed for Guiana. He was on close terms with James and had ready access to the Court and to him in person, and to meetings of the Privy Council. He was something of a dandy. 'I have a deep admiration for your Court,' he told James. 'Your ladies are most beautiful. And several of them are kind to me. I am a great admirer of your country's craftsmen too. The skill of your goldsmiths and tapestry workers is beyond belief. Your writers too have great talent, although I must say some stray over the borders of heresy.'

He moved on to the main purpose of his interview. On instructions from Madrid he warned James: 'We are concerned at all this activity. I have been asked to remind your Majesty that by virtue of His Holiness the Pope's ordinances and our lawful possession, Spain is entitled to the whole of America, South, Central and North. Any attempt to usurp our authority would, I humbly submit, be an affront. In fact it would be an act of war.'

Any mention of violence always frightened James. His childhood memories were ingrained in him. But in his impecunious state he could not let this statement go unchallenged. Too much was at stake. Winwood had had some success in stiffening him up.

'I cannot accept your contention,' he replied. 'For example, Virginia is none of your business. Most of North America – at least on its east side – is unoccupied: except by ourselves and the Indians of course, and they're heathens. Guiana I am reliably informed is likewise occupied by heathen natives.'

'Has not your Majesty's intelligence – Ralegh's Captain Kemys and others – told you that we have fortifications on the coast and up-river and a settlement at St Thomas?' he enquired.

'I don't doubt that you have a trading post or two. But nothing more substantial.'

It was clear, however, to James and the Council that what Gondomar was telling him was already known fact. James knew he had to give.

'I don't wish to be unfriendly to your King. The expedition is purely a private one – nothing official about it – but I promise to keep him informed, in strict secrecy of course, of all its plans. I will also order them to do no hostile act towards your country.'

'I'm deeply obliged, your Majesty.' As well he might be. Every move of Ralegh from then on was made known to Spain well in advance.

The Government had mixed motives in authorizing the operation. James needed the gold Ralegh had promised. He also wanted a marriage of his son Charles with a bride of Spain's choosing, accompanied with a fat payment to him. So he must do nothing to upset Spain. The majority of the Council wanted to kill his marriage idea. Their preference, in which they were led by Winwood, was for an alliance with France to maintain, or secure, a balance of power. They knew also that the odds were in favour of a complete break with Spain as a result of the intrusion into what they regarded as their territory. Ralegh was caught either way. He was realizing his ambition. It would have required a Cecil to analyse and deduce the various permutations. He looked on it as any Elizabethan expedition would have been regarded: outward opposition to warlike action and delight in the prizes. But it was not as simple as that. This was not the age of the Tudors.

A Royal Commission was issued to Ralegh in August. It made him Admiral in supreme command. It was expressly subject to his not visiting the dominions of any Christian prince. Armed force was permitted, but only for defence. The inclusion of France was welcomed: if there were hostilities they could be explained away as a dispute between Spain and France.

Spain put forward a counter-proposal. They would offer no resistance and would indeed escort and give safe conduct to a journey to the gold-mines. This offer was unacceptable as Ralegh pointed out: 'It runs completely against our claim that the natives have ceded sovereignty to his Majesty the King of England. It would be interpreted as an acceptance of their constitutional claim that it was they who had the rights to Guiana. Anyway you daren't trust the Spaniards. Our traders were invited in to trade. They were wined and dined. After a month they were tied back to back and had their throats slit.' This was going back a quarter of a century.

Ralegh was still a convicted prisoner on parole. No formal pardon had been granted. The first draft of the Royal Commission was worded: 'Our trusty and well-loved . . . .' It was to have been under the Great Seal. Gondomar, informed as ever, took violent exception to it – perhaps scenting possible legal implications for Spain's old enemy. It was re-drafted, those words omitted and issued under the Privy Seal.

Ralegh consulted the eminent lawyer Sir Francis Bacon, Lord Keeper of the Seal (later to be Lord Chancellor), on the pardon question. 'You may have heard I paid the Villiers brothers each £750 to help my release. For the same again they would get me a formal pardon. What do you advise?'

'You have the Royal Commission for this voyage. That should be sufficient,' Bacon replied.

' "Should be" isn't quite what I'm looking for,' he objected. 'There's a lot of talk going round about me being an unpardoned traitor – awful words. What is the legal position? Ought I not to play safe and find the money somehow?' he asked.

'Money is the knee-timber of your voyage,' Bacon reminded him. 'Spare your money. You have sufficient pardon for all that is past already. The King under his Great Seal has made you Admiral and given you the power of martial law. While it could be argued to the contrary, in my opinion your commission is as good a pardon for all former offences as the law of England can afford you.'

But the commission, as Bacon apparently over-looked, was under the Privy not the Great Seal. Was popular lay public opinion a more reliable legal guide than the lawyers? £1,500 was a large amount to find in straitened circumstances with so many calls on the purse – but cheap for a life.

Bacon also asked him: 'What will you do if you don't find the mine?'

The irrepressible Ralegh surfaced (jokingly): 'We will look after the Spanish Fleet to be sure.'

'But then you will be pirates.'

'Oh no! Whoever heard of men being pirates if they seize millions?'

Ralegh explained to the authorities in detail for James's benefit all the plans, including lists of ships, personnel, armaments, places of call and dates. He supplied the chart of his route. Gondomar was given access to them, making good use of this indulgence and relaying the intelligence back to his masters.

The Earls of Pembroke and Arundel entered into sureties for his safe return to England, which he promised them he would honour.

Wat was still in Holland, duel pending. Ralegh told Bess – knowing nothing of his intention, which would have hastened orders to return: 'I'm going to take Wat on the trip. It'll be the making of him, his unique opportunity.' He overrode her maternal reservations and summoned him home. He appointed him captain of his flag-ship *Destiny*.

Secretary of State Sir Ralph Winwood was not so fearful as James and some councillors. His advice was: 'If you get the chance to capture the Mexican Silver Fleet, take it. And liaise with the French. I have already introduced you to their ambassador. The Count is a useful ally.'

Ralegh invited de Marets over *Destiny*. He assured him there was no foundation for the suspicion that he intended to attack French ports. He was thereupon given permission to enter them should the occasion arise and for this purpose was issued with a French commission by their Admiralty. But they declined the invitation to send ships to join in the expedition. They saw through this stratagem.

Like most Elizabethans Ralegh had always been a gambler. This would be the biggest throw of his life. Success – replenishing James's coffers – could put him back near the pinnacle; failure, ruin. Its outcome would depend as much on the luck of the cards he was dealt as on his skill playing them.

Wat could still be troublesome to his doting parents. Before setting off Ralegh and he had been invited to farewell dinners in London. He was as boisterous as ever and his father was hard put to it to keep him in order. When the last of these invitations came Ralegh told him: 'Thou art expected at dinner to go along with me, but thou art such a quarrelsome, affronting fellow that I am ashamed to have such a bear in my company.'

'I'll behave myself, father,' was the reply.

Half-way through dinner Wat, who was sitting next but one to Ralegh, told the company a bawdy story concerning himself and his father which he said he had been told by a casual female acquaintance. Ralegh, infuriated, smacked his face. Wat aimed back, but instead struck the man sitting between them, shouting angrily: 'Box away.' Twill come to my father anon.'

Very soon afterwards Wat, still bitter over his frustrated love, received news to restore his equilibrium and good humour. It was a message from Elizabeth Basset. She had been living apart from her husband Henry Howard with relations up North, having resisted his efforts to consummate the marriage. 'A wonderful thing has happened,' she told him. 'Henry died suddenly at table last week.' He went up at once to see her. She was as lovely as ever. They were overjoyed to see one another again.

'This is the best news I have had for years, my darling. Ever, in fact. We'll carry on where we had to leave off. I will come over the moment I get back from father's Guiana affair. I'm sorry I'm going now.'

'I will wait for you forever, my love,' she assured him tenderly. 'Take care of yourself for my sake – and yours, of course.'

The rest of the autumn, Christmas and the New Year were taken up with hectic preparations. At the end of March the Thames contingent of the Fleet sailed for Plymouth to link up with the rest and take aboard assayers, refiners and miners. As always there were last minute hitches. Bess later told her husband: 'Your Captain Pennington' of *The Star*, 'got as far as the Isle of Wight and couldn't go any further because he was short of groceries. He suddenly appeared in Broad Street on horse-back to get me to subsidize him – which I had to do.'

At Plymouth Ralegh learnt that Captain Whitney of *The Encounter* likewise could not pay for his supplies. Ralegh sold his plate to raise the required sum. Departure was delayed.

West Countrymen rejoiced at seeing him again after years of absence – not now at the helm only but Admiral. Bess took Carew down to Plymouth to see them off. She shared his delight at the men's reception of their old champion. 'You see how much they love you, Walter. Look after yourself. I will pray for you both ten times a day.'

'Goodbye, dear Bess. You have stood by me through all these troubles. Take care of yourself and of our Carew.' To his young son, then twelve, he said: 'Carew, my little man, be brave and look after your mother for me, won't you? We'll soon be back and all together again.'

'I will, Daddy. If anyone tries to hurt her I will fight them.'

'That's a good boy.' He kissed them goodbye.

-Bess paid a fond farewell to Wat. She was relieved that he and his father had made up the differences – as father and son – or daughter – must. She had not been told the details of their original quarrel, try as she could. They were setting off on a joint enterprise with unknown dangers ahead. She pictured in her mind her husband watching over the small boy fishing with his younger companion William Cecil on the banks of the Yeo. How big he had grown. How she loved him.

Wat was full of high spirits. He had everything going for him: captain of a ship, his lovely bride now to be his.

'Don't worry, mother. We'll bring back sacks of gold.'

Ralegh's eyes were misty as he and Wat stood there while Bess and Carew walked back to their coach outside the dock. One last wave and they were gone.

In a moment they were out of his mind. There was work to be done. He assembled the captains, gentlemen and mariners. 'We sail on the next tide. These are my orders which will be enforced rigorously:

Divine Service shall be read twice each day and God will be praised with a psalm when watch is set.

Blasphemers shall be admonished, fined for a second offence, then reported to me. For the Scriptures state: The curse shall not depart from the house of the swearer – much less from the ship of the swearer.

Search is to be made each night for careless fires, for there is no danger so inevitable as the ship's firing, which may also happen by smoking of tobacco between the decks.

All landsmen shall learn sea skills.

All firearms shall be kept clean and oiled.

Should any other ship be seen, keep together.

No ship of a friendly nation is to be attacked.

There is to be no feasting or drinking between meals nor health drunk at the cost of the ship.

Any coward to be disarmed and become a labourer for his fellows.

No woman shall be forced, whether she be Christian or heathen, on pain of death.

Take special care when God suffers us to land in the Indies to eat no strange fruits. Such fruits as you do not find eaten by birds on the trees or beasts under the tree you shall avoid.

There to be no sleeping on the ground, no eating of new flesh until it has been salted, nor of over-fat hogs or turkeys.

Take care not to swim in any river except where you see Indians swimming, for the rivers are full of alligators.

Nothing must be taken from the Indians by force, or we shall never get help from them. Treat them all with courtesy.

If you are told not to do a thing, you are to be told the reason.'

The fleet set sail on 12 June, 1617. Gondomar duly reported its departure, describing the men as of indifferent quality but the guns good. Spain made dispositions accordingly.

The gentlemen were of sound quality. Otherwise, the cards dealt to Ralegh were well below average. The men were described as 'drunkards and blasphemers and others which their fathers, brothers and friends thought it exceeding good gain to be discharged of with hazard of some £30, £40 or £50 – less than the cost of keeping them a whole year at home.'

Twice they were forced back by bad weather, first, into Plymouth, then Falmouth. After more gales they made for Kinsale Harbour in Ireland to refit. Ralegh was made welcome in Cork and entertained by his former enemies as well as friends. Lord Barry and Lord Roche called on him. Richard Lord Boyle, Earl of Cork, made a fuss of him and treated him as an honoured guest. It was he to whom he had sold the bulk of his Munster estates. 'What about some falconry while you're waiting for your ship?' Boyle asked him – an offer accepted with alacrity. It took him back to days in Dorset as Ranger of Gillingham Forest and Cecil's gift of a falcon. He visited his old home at Lismore. Their discussions ranged over current affairs, the expedition and outstanding matters arising from the conveyance of the land to Boyle. He helped him by providing evidence against a former partner, Henry Pine, to whom Ralegh had assigned the Castle of Mogelie. Their other partners had been Edward Dodge and a Fleming, Veronio Martens. Pine appeared to have failed to account for profits which, if due, would be payable to Boyle. Ralegh subsequently expressed second thoughts about this alleged debt. Boyle provided generous supplies for the fleet. Ralegh gave up any outstanding claims against the estate.

He was anxious to be gone. Weather was always capricious. Refitting completed, they again set sail on 19 August. It was as though time had stood still for twenty years. He was back on the poop deck, in solitary communion with the heavens, the ocean around him under a boundless sky, the soothing sigh of the wind in the sails, creaking spars and the waves furrowing at their bow. When all advice has been given and received it is the lone commander who on his own must make the decision. He kept a meticulous journal of their progress.

They reached Lanzarote, an island in the Canaries, on 7 September. Ralegh spoke to the Governor: 'We are only landing for water and victuals,' he assured him. 'We have no hostile intent.'

'That will certainly be arranged,' was the reply. 'You will want for nothing that the land affords.'

But instead of complying the islanders surreptitiously sent their goods into the interior. Three of Ralegh's men were murdered on shore. His captains urged retaliation. He refused.

'It would be against my orders from the King. There must be no violence. We have also to consider the English merchants trading with the island. Where would they be if we brought this load of trouble on their heads?' Instead, he sent a message to the Governor: 'If it hadn't been for my resolve not to offend my King I would have pulled you and your people out by the ears, so consider yourself lucky.'

However, one of his captains, John Bailey of *The Husband*, objected to being deprived of spoil. He seized on Ralegh's comment as an excuse to slip back to London and spread a malicious rumour: 'I am convinced that Ralegh has turned pirate.' This was proved to be a lie when an owner of one of the merchantmen for whom Ralegh had had particular care at Lanzarote, Captain Reeks of Ratcliff, arrived back in England. He exonerated Ralegh and confirmed his account of the incident. Bailey retracted his allegation and was imprisoned for his slander. But damage had been done. Spain made capital out of it.

An attempt to get supplies at another island was thwarted. Their landing party was ambushed and one of Sir John Ferris's crew killed. Ralegh and Sir Warham St Leger forced a landing and scattered the forty or so men opposing them, but it was clear there was no help to be had there and they left for the last island, Gomera. Here they had a stroke of luck. Ralegh sent the Governor a message: 'I promise on the faith of a Christian not to attack you. Our urgent need is water. I will land a small party of unarmed men. But if you attempt any treachery I will blow you to bits.' This overture was accepted. Ralegh himself went ashore and was introduced to the Governor's wife. 'My mother was English,' she informed him. 'She was a Stafford. I will see you get all the help you need. My husband will support me in this.'

'That is most kind, Madam,' he replied. 'Water is our main requirement. I thought you might like this little gift as a memento of our visit.' He gave her six pairs of gloves and some head-dresses. She in her turn gave him four sugar loaves, a basket of lemons, another of oranges, grapes, pomegranates and figs. He reciprocated with other gifts which included ambergris and a picture of Mary Magdalene. On saying their farewells and sailing they were given more fruit, white bread, some hens and plenty of water – and a written testimonial to their good behaviour.

Bess was having a problem at home with which Carew could not help her, getting the Government to pay the £400 annuity for Sherborne. She wrote to the Master of the Rolls, Sir Julius Caesar: 'My payment is daily put off by Mr Bingley. I should have received £200 at Michaelmas, most of it being due to poor men from Sir Walter Ralegh for his necessaries. I have not had a penny since he left.'

The fleet ran into violent storms. Fever took off a number of the men. There was then stifling heat. For two days it was as dark by day as by night. It was followed by a hurricane. Ralegh went down with severe fever. He would not have survived had it not been for the gift of fruit.

They sailed into the mouth of the Cayenne on 14 November. He sent Bess a letter 'with a weak hand' as he was recovering. 'In my delirium,' he wrote, 'I thought the sea was a green field and it was all I could do to stop myself jumping into it. Your son has never had so good health,' but added that they had had casualties.

Ashore a welcoming chief was Harry the Indian whom he had had lodging with him in The Tower for some two years and who now provided the supplies they needed. These included pineapples – described by Ralegh as the king of fruits, a description with which James later agreed – which he was at first too ill to eat. He told Bess: 'To tell you I might be King of the Indians here would be vanity; but my name has still lived among them. Here they feed me with fresh meat and all that the country yields; all offer to obey me. Commend me to poor Carew my son.'

By the same boat Ralegh also sent back formal reports. But in England he had been dealt another blow. It was during his attack of fever that unknown to him his friend, Council Secretary Sir Ralph Winwood died prematurely. He was succeeded by Sir Robert Naunton, no friend of Ralegh.

It was therefore Naunton who was the unsympathetic recipient of Ralegh's letter and outspoken reports addressed to Winwood. These were meticulously forwarded on to Madrid. Spain thus knew his every move and the state of his force.

Ralegh himself looked more dead than alive. The men were amazed to see him survive at all. Among the dead were Captain Piggott, his land General and John Talbot, friend and scholar who had lived with him for eleven years in the Tower. He was too ill to lead the expedition into the interior – another turn of the screw. But he was still very much in command. He drew up a plan for their operation and called his officers together.

'There are two gold mines, as you know. One, the first that was discovered but the more distant, is just beyond St Thomas.

The nearer one is to its east, about thirty miles before you get to St Thomas. Make your landing within striking distance of this mine. Only when you have found it are you to go on to St Thomas and see if you can set up a trading venture – particularly in tobacco. If our presence encourages the Indians to rise up against the Spaniards, so much the better.

'If the miners are unable to dig enough ore, or if they prove to be less valuable or more difficult to work than we think, at least bring back a basket or two of gold ore to prove to his Majesty that my design was not imaginary. If you find the Spaniards have sent a large force of soldiers to the Orinoco and that the river passage is strongly defended and you cannot make it without endangering my son, you yourself Captain Kemys and the other captains, take care how you land. It won't be easy. I know, a few gentlemen excepted, what a scum of men you have.'

He went on: 'You, Captain Kemys, will be in command of the force as a whole. You, George Ralegh, of the land forces. Captain Sir Warham and myself are both too ill to go. You, Wat, will be under George's command. Prepare five ships of shallow draught and take with you one hundred and fifty mariners and two hundred and fifty soldiers. I will proceed to the south coast of Trinidad at Puncto Gallo where you will find me, dead or alive – for run will I never.'

He bade Wat a fond farewell. 'Do everything Laurence and George tell you, my boy,' he said, 'and the best of luck to you.'

'You, too, father,' Wat replied.

While Ralegh sailed on to Puncto Gallo the exploration party proceeded as ordered up-river under Kemys's command with provisions for a month.

They were continuously peppered with musket shot from Spaniards firing from behind cover along the banks, clearly prepared for their arrival. Two of the five ships were held up, grounded in the maze of channels.

Kemys had been a close friend of Ralegh for many years. But he was essentially an academic and lacked his leader's skill and authority. He had led the charting expedition immediately after Ralegh's first voyage to Guiana but had never commanded a fighting group. As he had reported to Bess on his return from the survey, while Ralegh was engaged in the Cadiz battle, he had brought nothing back other than his survey charts – no prizes, to Bess's (and Cecil's) disappointment. They also missed Ralegh's influence with the Indians, who kept well out of the way.

Kemys discussed tactics with George Ralegh, Captains Cosmor, Charles Parker, Wat and others. 'If we land and make for the nearer mine, as Sir Walter ordered, we shall be shot to pieces in the forest,' he said apprehensively. 'It's ideal ambush country. Also, we don't know precisely where the mine is. But I do know where the other mine is: just above St Thomas. We had better make for that.'

Captain Parker advised caution but none of them disagreed with the course now proposed. Although it would be a departure from orders, a local commander is in the unenviable position of having to make decisions in the light of circumstances as he finds them. This is the dilemma that can face the general or admiral, lance-corporal or petty officer, general manager or clerk. The overall objective was to find gold or at the least to get hold of gold ore samples for analysis. The further mine could be the bird in hand.

Instead of landing, therefore, they continued up the Orinoco to within three miles of St Thomas and landed some troops. The three ships went on and anchored opposite the town. Since Kemys's last visit this had developed from a mere trading post to a substantial settlement. He also thought it was now further down-river than on his previous voyage.

The town garrison opened fire on them. The fire was not returned. The troops who had landed down river had just retired for the night when they were attacked by a small Spanish patrol. There was confusion for a few minutes. They were rallied by Wat who led them up to the town at top speed. Confronting the Governor and his company he cried out: 'Come on, my hearts. This is the mine. They that look for any other are fools.'

In the brave tradition of his father he rushed forward, sword in hand, ahead of his pikemen, not waiting for supporting fire from his musketeers. He and Lieutenant Plessington, who went forward with him, each slew an opponent. Two more were slain by one of their men, John of Morocco. The more experienced Captain Parker, not far behind them, was horrified at what was to him a foolhardy act. Wat was hit by a musket shot. He pressed on regardless of his wound and struck at a Spaniard armed with a musket. The Spaniard (named it was later ascertained Erinetta) reversed his weapon and rammed Wat with its butt end. He fell, mortally wounded, shouting his last orders to his men: 'Go on. Lord have mercy on me and prosper your enterprise.'

He and Captain Cosmor were among the only five English casualties. The Governor was one of the only five Spanish casualties – perhaps killed by his own men who it was learnt had been planning a revolt. The Spanish garrison withdrew to the forest.

Kemys was devastated. 'How can I ever tell Sir Walter?' he exclaimed. 'He'll never get over it. Neither will I. He will blame me for the loss of his son. We must give them a full military funeral and bury them in the church.' With reversed muskets, trailed pikes and muffled drums, and banners outspread, they were buried before the high altar. He sent a report forthwith to Ralegh. The two ships previously stuck down river then rejoined them.

Back at Trinidad Ralegh had first tried to trade with the Spaniards. They replied to his friendly approaches with a volley of shots which killed two of his skeleton force. He ignored it and sailed on. Much of his time was spent pursuing his hobby, botany, looking for rare plants and for those with medicinal qualities. Because of the treacherous currents he did not stay in one place but cruised around the island. He was anxious. He had been baulked when close to the summit of his enterprise. He had had to leave it in much less reliable hands. The outcome was unsure. He could only wait and hope.

One afternoon a canoe of Indians came past. He stopped them in case they had any news. 'Yes, master,' one of them replied, 'there was a fight. The English attacked a town and two of their captains were killed.'

He was horrified. He sent out parties each day for any further information they could find, fearing the worst.

Meanwhile in St Thomas, they found Ralegh's fleet inventory, in his own handwriting, together with a copy of one of Gondomar's reports and instructions from Spain for deploying defence forces. That there were gold mines in the vicinity was evidenced by the fact that the most sumptuous houses in the town belonged to the gold refiners. They seized large quantities of tobacco, together with Government papers and account books.

Kemys made attempts to proceed to the mine up-river from St Thomas but ambushes by the Spanish troops proved too much. George Ralegh was more adventurous. He went some three hundred miles further up the Orinoco but likewise sustained constant casualties from sniper fire. On his return Kemys invited the Spaniards to come to terms. They refused. Having lost more than half his force he had no choice but to evacuate the town, setting it on fire as they left. The tobacco was loaded and on 14 September they withdrew down river. This was to the despair of the Indians.

That same day Kemys's report reached Ralegh. He was overwhelmed to receive confirmation of what he had most feared, Wat's death. The meticulously kept journal of what was to have been a historic voyage closed at that moment.

Kemys reported to him immediately on return. He emphasized Wat's bravery and described his burial. He gave him details of the operation from start to finish. Ralegh heard him out in silence. Then he burst out angrily: 'My orders made it clear that you were to land thirty miles down river of St Thomas. How was it you were so near the town at all?'

'Sir Walter, it would have been suicide to land where you said. We were being shot at and the men picked off all along the river. We would have been ambushed in the forest and shot to pieces. We had no alternative but to go on. Besides, I didn't know precisely where that mine lay.'

'By your folly you have undone me. My credit with King James is wounded past recovery. And what have you to show for it? Nothing but losses in men dead. And some tobacco,' he added derisively. 'Not even an ounce of gold. Not a single lump of ore. You didn't get anywhere near either mine. Seeing that Wat was slain, I wouldn't have minded if you had lost another hundred men so long as you had reached the only object of the whole expedition – and saved my credit with the King.'

'I couldn't get through. I did my best,' he pleaded.

'You will have to answer to the King and Council why you pulled back having got so close. And why set fire to the town? I wouldn't like to be in your shoes. You've made a complete mess of the operation. If only I hadn't been laid low by fever. I trusted you and you have failed me. You're a coward and incompetent.' It had been a complete disaster.

'I'll go to my cabin, Sir Walter, and draft my report,' he replied miserably.

'Bring it to me as soon as you have done it.'

He spent the rest of the day and the following day writing his version of events. He brought it to Ralegh's cabin to show him. Ralegh read it, critically and despondently. Then: 'I will have nothing to do with this. I don't agree with it. You'll have to do better than that.'

Kemys felt desperate. He had failed his master and friend. He had let everybody down. He had been responsible for the death of the young man he had known from a child. He had proved too small for the task and had failed as a leader in the emergency. He knew also that his leader would have to live with the nightmare that he, too, admiral of the fleet, had failed. All in life that he had strived for had come to nothing. A black cloud came over him. 'I will go back, Sir Walter, and produce something to satisfy you,' he said, and returned to his cabin.

He it was, this fellow of Balliol, writer of Latin verse and polished English prose, who had stuck by Ralegh through thick and thin. He had lived with him in The Tower, had faced the rack on his behalf without giving way. It had been by a stroke of bad luck that he, not his chief, had been in command. He had been faced with a situation with which only a leader of Ralegh's ability could have coped. He had done his best. It was not good enough.

Shortly afterwards Ralegh heard a pistol shot from a cabin above him. He sent his boy up to see who had fired it. Kemys called down to him: 'It was only me. I fired a round out of the window to clean my pistol.'

After a couple of hours, puzzled at the silence, Ralegh sent his boy up again. He went inside Kemys's cabin. He found him lying on his bed in a pool of blood, a knife through his heart. A rib had been chipped where the bullet had missed its mark. Papers were scattered on the floor in shreds. Had the shot been a cry for help?

21

Judas Traps

Ralegh's immediate concern was to send his report back on the abortive attempt 'to find the gold mine' and on his own movements during the operation. He addressed it as before to his friend Sir Ralph Winwood as Secretary of the Privy Council. He still had no means of knowing that he had died and been replaced by an enemy, Sir Robert Naunton. In his letter he made special mention of those officers worthy of his Majesty's praise. He also wrote bitterly about James's own part in the business. 'For it pleased his Majesty to value us so little as to command me, on my allegiance, to set down under my hand the country, and the very river by which I was to enter it; to set down the number of my men and burden of my ships; with what ordnance every ship carried; which being made known to the Spanish Ambassador, and by him in post sent to the King of Spain, a despatch was made by him and his letters sent from Madrid, before my departure out of the Thames.'

He wrote next to his wife: 'My dear Bess, I was loth to write, because I know not how to comfort you; and, God knows, I never knew what sorrow meant till now. All that I can say to you is, that you must obey the will and providence of God.... Comfort your heart, dearest Bess, I shall sorrow for us both. I shall sorrow the less, because I have not long to sorrow, because not long to live.... The Lord bless you and comfort you, that you may bear patiently the death of your valiant son.'

This is perhaps all he meant to say. But he could not restrain himself from pouring out the bitterness at the deception behind the scenes and the fumbling and inefficiency when he was compelled by illness to cede command of the up-river culmination of the expedition. He wrote of the existence of other mines and declared that none of the mines near the town could be worked 'because under a Spanish law the Indians cannot be forced' (although they could be tortured) 'and the Spaniards themselves would find the work involved too hard – whatever that *braggadocio* the Spanish Ambassador may say – which I can prove by record books.'

Ralegh called his captains together. 'I'm going up the river myself,' he told them. 'I will find the mine, or lay myself beside my son. There is gold there. I intend to prove it.'

But he was an unlucky, albeit able, commander. They had lost faith in him. They sensed that there was an awful fate in store when he returned to England, unpardoned as he was. 'It's hopeless,' they told him. 'Spanish reinforcements are arriving every day. It would be a massacre.'

He became desperate and reckless in his efforts to persuade them to further action. 'We will do as we would have done in the old days. We'll seize the Spanish Plate Fleet. We will go back with something to show for our money. They'll be easy pickings.'

But these were no longer the golden days of Elizabeth when extrovert buccaneers could swoop on Spanish ships and help themselves, with no questions asked provided Queen and Government received their cut.

'We would be condemned as pirates,' they objected. 'The King would have the spoil and we would be hanged.'

'No fear of that,' Ralegh tried to reassure them. 'I have a French commission to seize anything west of the Canaries.'

'And I,' endorsed Sir John Ferne, 'authority to harbour at Brest and do a deal with France, and our own country.'

They were not convinced. The decision of the Council of War was to make for Virginia and Newfoundland to refit and replenish supplies and return to England. Two of the captains opted out and went off on a pirating expedition of their own. Ralegh was determined to return to England. He had given his word on this to his bondsmen before setting off. At one stage of the argument violence was offered to him by some who as wanted criminals had no desire to return. He was forced to agree that they would be dropped off in Ireland.

At Court while awaiting news of the expedition, James promised Ambassador Gondomar: 'If Ralegh has been guilty of any offence against your King or country I will hand him over to you to deal with.' Gondomar was congratulated by his

Government for this unparalleled coup.

The news of St Thomas reached Madrid before London. He burst in on James: '*Piratas! Piratas! Piratas!*' he shouted, and stormed out. There was consternation in the Court.

Ralegh's letter to, as he supposed, Winwood arrived some two or so weeks later by Captain Roger North, who had been sent ahead. He did not help by critical reports on both his commanders, Ralegh as well as Kemys. Loyalty was no established creed in either Elizabeth's or James's time. The fact that the only spoil was tobacco, valuable as it was, would only add fuel, James being a hater of this 'drug'. By the attack on St Thomas the King's Peace had been violated. More important, James's plan for marrying his son Charles to a Spanish Princess was in jeopardy. This marriage was to be accompanied by the dowry of at the very least £500,000 and jewels, a demand made earlier on behalf of the Crown by James's envoy in Madrid, Sir John Digby, the new owner of Sherborne. Gondomar assured James that if the Ralegh business was managed to Spain's satisfaction Madrid would still support the marriage he so earnestly sought. If not, English claims in commercial and other matters would get short shrift from the Spanish courts and creditors would get no redress from Spanish debtors.

They were taking no chance of letting slip this opportunity of settling long-standing scores with their old enemy.

James at Greenwich Palace ordered the Marquess of Buckingham to reply: 'His Majesty would have your Excellency assure the King of Spain that he will be as severe in punishing them as if they had done the like damage to an English city; if Sir Walter has returned with ships laden with gold taken from him or any of his subjects, I will return them and they will suffer punishments as such crimes deserve.'

The journey home seemed endless. The bright hopes of the outward voyage were sunk. No Wat with him now for company, alone, no one to cheer him up, his only music the wind moaning through the sails. They had a rough passage. Three of the ships docked in Ireland, at Kinsale, as promised. *The Destiny* arrived on its own at Plymouth on 21 June. Bess hastened down to join him; words could not express their relief at being reunited or the sorrow which accompanied it. 'We must tell Elizabeth Basset,' she told him. 'I did not dare do so till you came. Everything was ready for the marriage.'

Elizabeth was heart-broken: cheated yet again of her childhood sweetheart. Not even a portrait to remember him by. It was some years before grief allowed her to marry again, this time to William Cavendish, Duke of Newcastle. He told close friends: 'I would never have married her had young Walter Ralegh been alive. I believe her, before God, to be his wife. For they were married as much as children could be.'

Ralegh spent the next fortnight dealing with fleet business, following which they left for London with their escort of servants and accompanied by one of his most loyal captains, Samuel King. They had had no indication of anything amiss although they knew there must be problems ahead.

It was a sunny day with a light breeze. Trees and hedges were in full leaf, willow-herb lit up the verges and Ralegh drank in the fresh air of his native Devon as they rode along the way they knew so well. 'How much easier life would have been if I had never taken this road,' he said to Bess. 'But it would have been dull. And I would never have met you.'

'That might have saved you a heap of trouble,' she smiled.

'It would have deprived me of a heap of joy.'

They had barely gone twenty miles, almost to Ashburton at the edge of Dartmoor, when they were met by Sir Lewis Stukeley, Vice-Admiral of Devon. He was one of the shady characters in public life. He came from an ancient Devon family, being Sir Richard Grenville's nephew and a distant relation whom Ralegh had helped in the past.

'I have orders to arrest you, Sir Walter, and your ships,' he told him. 'Needless to say I regret this very much. Will you please accompany me back to Plymouth?'

So long had elapsed since his return to England, the hope had been growing that all would be well. Bess put a brave face on it. They were steeled by experience. They had been through it before and survived. But this could be worse.

As they retraced their steps Stukeley told his prisoner and Bess: 'I do apologize for this, Lady Ralegh, but I have no alternative but to carry out orders. Let's hope it won't be for too long.' He added: 'I haven't a formal warrant yet from the Council, Sir Walter, but I'm sure you wouldn't wish to take advantage of that technicality. I hope you will look on me as a friend, and indeed cousin, not as your gaoler.'

Ralegh laughed bitterly. 'I'll do my best,' he replied.

'Certainly I won't give you any trouble.'

'Now – what did you manage to bring back with you? Any gold, or jewels?'

'Nothing like that. Not even a basket of ore, although there was plenty around which the bunglers missed. No. But I have a big load of tobacco.'

'That's interesting.'

'Yes,' Ralegh went on, 'it's all locked up. It will be worth a great deal.'

'I'll take you to your lodging,' Stukeley said. 'You'll be staying with friends in Plymouth. It's all been arranged – with Sir Christopher and Lady Harris. While you're settling in I'll go and have a look at this tobacco.'

Their host (a kinsman) and hostess took great care of them. Their stay lasted something over a week. Any unwelcome visitors were kept away. Carew had been brought down from London. He was thirteen years old, earnest and precise. Ralegh looked at him fondly. He had grown since he last saw him. Although gentle by nature, he was determined and with his father's – and Wat's – fiery temper.

'Your mother tells me you've been looking after her like a man since I left.'

'Yes, father,' he replied, 'and every day we moved your ship across the map you left us. Was it very hot where you were?'

'Yes, very hot. And I was extremely ill. But I'm better now. Are you doing all your studies as I told you?'

'My tutor says my Latin's the best he's seen in anyone of my age.'

'Well done, keep at it. Our Wat, bless him, had to be pushed and bullied before he'd get down to it. We'll have you up to Oxford before you're much older.'

'Don't make the boy go away too soon, Walter,' protested Bess. 'He's my protector.'

'You're a fine boy,' said his father, putting his arm around him, 'and just like your mother.'

'And like you, father.'

'Of course you are.' He kissed him tenderly. Bess watched with tears in her eyes.

Sir Christopher pressed him for his own safety to escape to France before it was too late. He refused to entertain the idea. 'I gave a solemn promise to my sponsors, Lords Arundel and

Pembroke, that I would return. I must not let them down.'

'But this is a question of your life. You owe it to Bess and Carew. You have friends in France. James won't live for ever. You can come back then. In any case, you have returned, so you wouldn't be breaking your bond.'

He took a great deal of persuading but eventually their entreaties overruled his objections. Reluctantly he asked Captain King to hire a ship to take them to France.

'That's the most sensible thing I've heard since we landed,' King replied. 'I'll be delighted.'

The ship anchored half a mile off shore. He said his farewells and they set off in a rowing boat to join it. He still felt it against his better judgement. He had never been one for turning tail. 'My Wat didn't,' he thought.

When they were within two hundred yards of the ship his earlier decision prevailed. 'It's no good,' he exclaimed. 'I'm sorry. I'm going back.' King's pleadings fell on deaf ears. They turned and rowed back. The ship remained at anchor for two days in case he changed his mind, then sailed away.

The Raleghs moved into the house of another kinsman, Drake, where they were equally welcome. Stukeley had been in no hurry to take his prisoner up to London. He had been spending his time profitably and methodically, taking over and selling the substantial cargo of tobacco and other stores – and pocketing the proceeds. But on 25 July a peremptory command came from the Council ordering him to London forthwith. They were to be accompanied by another unsavoury character, a French physician (or quack) named Manourie, a Government agent planted on him by Stukeley. He wormed himself into Ralegh's favour with discussions on chemistry, known to be of particular interest to him. He undertook to help him with medical advice and treatment, particularly as he still had the effects of fever.

Once again they took to the road, no longer hopefully. Bess viewed the future with a foreboding which he shared. Young Carew could see they were in trouble. He looked anxiously from one to the other for any sign of cheer. He, silently, shared their worry, which can strike a helpless young person hard.

They stayed a night with another member of the Drake family at Musbury, near Axminster. The following day, Sunday, they stopped off for a break at their old friends the

Horseys at their noble house at Clifton Maybank. Their destination for that night was a village three miles north-east of Sherborne, Poyntington.

As they topped the rise leading down to Sherborne the Abbey bells were pealing – but not this time for them. Seeing the square tower in the valley below reminded Ralegh of the carefree ride he and Adrian had had as young men, when all life lay before them with its joys, sorrows and imponderables. This was indeed a heavy home-coming. The few curious onlookers were galvanized into activity when they realized who it was, but they had passed through before the excited inhabitants could wave in sympathy to their well-loved Lady Betty and former lord.

The Castle was as he had left it, solid defence against disorder, uncomfortable residence. He and Bess paused for a moment. There to the south was the monument of their creation, Lodge and garden in beautiful parkland setting, trees they had planted thrusting up in the woods on the ridge beyond.

Manourie was close behind them as they contemplated the scene. Ralegh said to him: 'All this was mine, and it was taken from me unjustly. I wish Sherborne well. I can't wish him' – the new owner – 'well. But I won't wish him harm. The law has taken its course. That will be the concern of my beloved Carew.'

They moved along narrow lanes to a house on the outskirts of Dorset they had known in happier days, Poyntington Manor, and clattered into the courtyard. They were greeted by their hosts and hostess, John Parham and his son and daughter-in-law, Sir Edward and Lady Parham. She was a first cousin once removed of Ralegh, Sir Edward was an old friend. He had received a knighthood (as had Bess's young brother Nicholas) at the beginning of James's reign. He now owned the house. 'We were so grieved to hear of your misfortunes, Sir Walter,' Mr Parham said. 'The people hereabouts couldn't believe it. We are honoured to welcome you, Lady Ralegh.'

They introduced Carew. 'Good evening, Sir. Good evening, Sir Edward, Lady Parham. I hope you are well, Sir.'

'We are very well, thank you my boy,' Mr Parham replied. 'We haven't met before, have we? I trust you are as well as you look, too.'

'Some years have passed since we saw you last,' said Lady Parham. 'You will recall that Edward was tangled in the trial in which you were dealt such injustice, Walter. He was acquitted. You can imagine my relief.' Bess could indeed.

'It is an honour to have you with us,' said Sir Edward. 'We will never forget it. As our house would hardly be large enough to contain all your company,' he went on, 'we have reserved accommodation for your attendants in two inns in Sherborne, The George and The New Inn. I am sure they will be well looked after. I do hope you will be comfortable here.'

Ralegh smiled ruefully at this unexpected reminder of youthful adventures. 'We are grateful to you and we shall be more than comfortable in these hospitable surroundings,' replied Ralegh.

This charming old house was built of grey stone. It was long, had tall hexagonal chimneys and mullioned windows. It nestled in the middle of the village near the headwaters of the Yeo which flowed through the garden, a favourite haunt of the kingfisher. It was the essence of tranquillity in gathering storms.

A cheerful fire blazed in the dining room, it being a cool evening, and Bess could once again admire the moulded ceiling beams of the drawing room before they retired for the night. It was there that, to Ralegh's surprise, Sir John Digby, resident at the time in his Sherborne Lodge, called in to see him.

'I thought I should let you know, Sir Walter,' he said, 'that the threat to you is not from the common law. It is from the civil and admiralty laws of piracy. Your defence should therefore be directed to that aspect. I hope this advice may be of some help.' They received him civilly and thanked him for his kind offices.

They resumed their journey early the next day. As they left Wilton and approached their next stopping place, Salisbury, Ralegh felt a little sick. Stukeley put it about that he must have been poisoned the night before. He dismissed this as nonsense. But it gave him an idea. 'Give me a vomit – an emetic, they call it now, I believe,' he ordered Manourie. 'It will be good to evacuate bad humours. It will also make me look even more ill than I am and give me time to write my defence for the King and Council – perhaps even pacify his Majesty. I can also write to my friends and get my affairs in order. Otherwise as soon as I get to London they will have me in The Tower and cut off my head. There is no other way I can do it except by feigning sickness. Your medicine can do it without arousing suspicion.' The only other person in the subterfuge was Bess. If she thought it a crazy idea she knew better than to argue with him.

Ralegh had chosen Salisbury because he had learnt that James would be visiting the city. At the inn he pretended to be dizzy and struck his head hard against a timber beam, to the alarm of his servants. The following day he sent Bess and her retinue, Carew, King and all but a few of his servants ahead to London. As soon as they had gone he gave a realistic imitation of dementia. Stukeley sent Manourie into him. He administered the required emetic and, on his patient's versatile instructions, a concoction that made his skin burst out into purple blotches to simulate leprosy. This scared the wits out of Stukeley who hastened to get a message to old James Montague, Bishop of Winchester. He was in his colleague Bishop's palace at Salisbury. Unknown to Stukeley he was on his deathbed. Three reputable doctors were called in to examine Ralegh. They pronounced themselves baffled by these curious symptoms – not knowing they were the product of earlier experiments in The Tower. They were emphatic that he must on no account be moved. Ralegh and Manourie enjoyed the joke. Ralegh naturally made it worth his while – not knowing that he was serving two masters.

The trick achieved its object in giving him time. With great concentration and little sleep he wrote *Apology for the Voyage to Guiana*. He explained that England had a better claim than Spain: the natives had ceded it to England. It was a desirable colony for its gold, other minerals and agricultural potential. He developed these themes in detail. He reiterated the events of the previous months. Any action they had taken against the Spaniards had been forced on them by self-defence. Defeat had been the lot of many Princes and Generals. He refuted the piracy allegations in their entirety – Digby's advice had been apt. 'I hope the Ambassador does not esteem us for so wretched and miserable a people as to offer their throats to their swords without any manner of resistance.'

He had hoped for an audience with James. In this he was disappointed. Stukeley was curtly commanded to bundle him off to London. An order from the Council was issued for his committal to The Tower.

James, hearing of Montague's plight, hastened to visit the old bishop. It was he who had translated James's Latin writings. He surprised the King by a plea on Ralegh's behalf. 'Very soon now, your Majesty, I shall never see you again. I have just one favour to beg of you. Sir Walter Ralegh often used to upset me by what he said and did. But he was well respected by your predecessor Queen Elizabeth and has done many noble things in his time. Please save his life. Let him die in peace and not come to an untimely death.'

Digby stepped in again. 'This man is ill,' he said. 'That was evident when I called to see him at Poyntington. He is worse now. The Tower would be disastrous for him. He should be allowed to go to his London home in Broad Street, at least for a while.' This was agreed.

The journey continued through Andover, Whitchurch, Hartford Bridge and Staines. News of his coming had preceded him. Crowds turned out to see this figure of national, indeed international, stature.

Unknown to him, Captain King had renewed efforts for his escape. The possibility of fleeing was in his own mind. His reasoned overtures had had little or no effect. The net was closing. He had honoured the assurance of his sponsors to return to this country. At Staines he broached the idea to Manourie and said: 'It would be impossible to get away without Stukeley's co-operation.' He took out a beautiful jewel powdered with diamonds, saying: 'This is worth £150. Tell him I'll give him £50 on top of it.' Manourie did so. Stukeley put it in his pocket and said: 'Tell him I accept his proposal, that nothing can be done for the moment, but we'll arrange something when the opportunity offers.'

The international aspect came to the fore when they arrived in Brentford. The French Embassy interpreter, La Chesnée, called on him at the inn where they were staying to tell him that the Ambassador Le Clerc wished to see him with an offer of safe refuge. The French, unlike their English counterparts, recognized his value as a military leader, despite his age, against their Spanish adversaries. It was only at the last minute that they had pulled out of the Guiana expedition. They were also angling for a marriage, French instead of Spanish, for

James's son, Charles. In this they were encouraged by James's wife, Queen Anne. The Government noted the French contact. They hoped to catch him out in an act of treason. But Ralegh politely turned the offer down. He had been told of King's moves for escape.

Manourie had by now been withdrawn before his duplicity came to light. Ralegh arrived home in Broad Street on 7 August. A large company of friends and servants were there to greet him. He was allowed unrestricted liberty. Two nights later the French Ambassador called in person with La Chesnée to renew the invitation before all his friends – and Stukeley – and to provide a ship for the purpose. He replied: 'I am, as I said before, most grateful for the offer. My intention is however to go by way of an English ship.'

Stukeley was reporting back regularly to his superiors. The cat and mouse stalk proceeded, the victim unaware of his immediate predator. Stukeley was instructed to humour him and profess support. 'I have, as you know, a great affection for you, Walter, and I will not only help you escape, I will come with you.' He had had the £50 and the jewel. The Government were still looking for a watertight pretext to execute The Tower committal warrant. With the help of a relation, a courtier named William Herbert, he set up a trap.

On the night appointed for escape, Ralegh put on a false beard and, with his page, went down to Tower dock where a wherry had been drawn up. Stukeley and King made their way there by different routes. They were to join a ketch lying off Tilbury commanded by Hart, once a boatswain of King's. Hart had been recruited by a former Tower servant of Ralegh's named Cottrell. They were both in the trap plot. A short distance down the river bank, hidden in the shadows was another wherry, containing the courtier Herbert and Sir William St John and a large crew. St John it was who a year or so earlier had accepted money to assist Ralegh's release from The Tower.

Ralegh and his party cast off, Stukeley in high spirits, the other subdued. 'Have I not shown myself to be an honest man?' he quipped to King as they rowed down the river in the dark.

King, unlike Ralegh, had never fully trusted him. 'I hope you will continue so,' he replied doubtfully.

They had not gone far when the second wherry pushed off. Ralegh spotted it. At first he did not take much notice of it, until it changed course and, to his alarm, followed in their wake. 'We've been betrayed,' he exclaimed. Then to the boatmen. 'Would you carry on rowing if any of them tried to arrest me?'

This scared them. 'We can't go further than Gravesend,' they answered. 'The tide's too strong.' He took some gold coins from his pocket. 'Will this help you?' he asked.

Stukeley took the coins and added his exhortation. 'It was a bad day when I risked my life helping someone so suspicious as you,' and to the boatmen: 'I will kill you if you don't keep on rowing.'

Their pursuers continued to follow. By the time they were below Woolwich Ralegh decided his suspicions were well-founded. He ordered the men to row to the shore. Still trusting Stukeley he said: 'Lewis, I am your prisoner and content to be so.' He took some more gold pieces from his pocket saying: 'Thank you for what you have done. Take these.' Stukeley accepted them and put his arm round him affectionately.

They landed at Greenwich, as did the other wherry. As soon as they had disembarked, Stukeley announced: 'Sir Walter Ralegh, I arrest you and Captain King in the King's name. I commit you into the charge of these two men of Sir William St John's escort.'

Ralegh was thunderstruck. 'Sir Lewis,' he said, 'these actions will not turn out to your credit.' Then quietly to King: 'Look, my friend, you have done more than enough. You must save your own skin. Don't mind me. Pretend you knew all about this treacherous plot to trap me.'

'Sir Walter, whatever happens,' he replied, 'I will stand by you. If I'm to be in trouble, so be it. I went into it with my eyes open.'

Ralegh took his hand, and said nothing. They were taken to The Tower. At the gate King was ordered to leave. He protested. His place was at his friend and master's side. They insisted.

Ralegh, his comrade in arms, tried to cheer him up. 'You have been my true friend. You need be in no fear of danger. It is I only who am the mark shot at.'

22

'Stars Must Fall'

A miscellaneous assortment of articles was taken from him at The Tower by Stukeley. They included: a naval officer's gold whistle, set with diamonds; sixty-three gold buttons with diamonds; a diamond ring given him by Queen Elizabeth; a sprig jewel set with stones, a ruby in the centre; a Guiana idol of gold and copper; a gold wedge of 22 carats; a gold bar; gold chain with diamonds; diamond ring; a silver seal with his arms; jewel set in gold; £50 in gold coin; jacinth seal in gold with a Neptune carved into it, with Guiana ore attached; a lodestone in a scarlet purse; a Guiana ore sample; silver mine samples; charts of Guiana, the Orinoco and region, with description; and a chart of Panama. He also had ambergris which he was allowed to keep. He refused to hand over a gold-cased miniature portrait of Bess set with diamonds except to the Lieutenant of The Tower, Sir Allen Apsley, a friend.

James's comment on hearing of this episode was: 'He was a coward to be caught so easily. He could easily have escaped from so slight a guard.'

The Queen remained his loyal friend. But she was powerless, and dying. He had sent her verses before. He sent her another poem which included the following verses:

> Oh! had Truth power, the guiltless could not fall,
> Malice win glory, or Revenge triumph,
> But Truth, alone, cannot encounter all.

> But if both God and Time shall make you know
> That I, your humblest vassal, am opprest,
> Then cast your eyes on undeserved woe.

> That I and mine may never mourn the miss
> Of Her we had, but praise our living Queen

Who brings us equal, if not greater bliss.

She tried to use George Villiers, the King's favourite, as a go-between for mercy, but it was useless. She was no more successful than the late Bishop of Winchester. Cecil's old spy, Sir Thomas Wilson, was planted on him as his keeper by Naunton, to secure his confidence and evidence.

Whether or not due to the timely warning from Digby at Poyntington about the thrust of the prosecution, nothing Ralegh said gave any indication of the piracy they aimed to prove.

Wilson represented himself as a friend rather than keeper. 'You are in a tight corner you know, Sir Walter. I am sorry to see you here again. I will do all I can to help. My advice is to be perfectly frank with me.'

Recent experience had taught him to be on his guard. 'I always am frank, ' he replied. 'At times too frank. But I have nothing to add to what I have already said and written. I will not weary you by repeating it.'

They had long conversations. But if Ralegh was outspoken, he said nothing that would assist the prosecution. He spoke the truth, and that showed no evidence of offence. Wilson still pressed. 'His Majesty will pardon you if you tell all you know.'

'My dear fellow, I have told it. It's no good trying to put words in my mouth that I don't intend to say.'

Ralegh was in far from the best of health. He wrote to Bess describing his ailments and praising the care shown him by his assistant keeper, Edward Wilson. She returned his letter with her (phonetic) reply:

> 'I am sorry to hear amongst so many discomforts that your health is so ill. 'Tis merely sorrow and grief that with wind hath gathered into your side. I hope your health and comforts will mend and mend us for God. I am glad to hear you have the company and comfort of so good a keeper. I was something dismayed, at the first, that you had no servant of your own left you, but I hear this Knight's (i.e. Apsley's) servants are very necessary. God requite his curtesies; and God, in mercy, look on us.
> Yours
>   E. Ralegh.'

Bess herself was under house arrest between 20 August and 15 October.

Attempts to establish collusion with France were abortive. An investigation into their alleged French involvement merely upset France and did nothing to implicate Ralegh. When the Council questioned and suspended the ambassador, his reaction was that Ralegh was only in prison to please the Spaniards, that prior to that he had been at liberty and that anyone had been able to visit him at home.

By 24 September Ralegh's patience had run out. He wrote to the King. He reiterated his forbearance in avoiding acts of revenge against the Spaniards or in attacking towns which he could have taken with ease. 'If it were lawful for the Spanish to murder twenty-six Englishmen, tying them back to back and cutting their throats, when they had traded with them a whole month and came to them on land without so much as a sword amongst them all – and that it may not be lawful for your Majesty's subjects, being forced by them, to repel force by force – we may justly say "O miserable English".' His poor estate had been spent, he had lost his son, suffered illness and misery, voluntarily given up his liberty. He had been warned by his mutineers that his life was at risk. 'But I believed more in your Majesty's goodness than in their arguments.'

James had assured Spain of his willingness to send Ralegh to Madrid for his trial – and execution – despite strong reservations expressed by members of the Council. He would have no mercy from the Spanish Inquisition – Cadiz would be belatedly avenged. The English public would not stomach it. As it turned out, Spain herself foresaw too many complications. Her Council of State formally decided it would be better to have him executed in England.

The Lord Chancellor, Sir Francis Bacon, and the Chief Justice, Sir Edward Coke, drew up at James's request their recommendations for subsequent proceedings. There was a choice, they considered, of alternatives: trial for his recent activities or an informal hearing before the Privy Council, judges and nobility, he already being civilly dead. Death would result either way. The latter alternative was rejected out of hand. 'It would make him too popular, as was found at Winchester,' James reminded them, 'where by his wit he turned the hatred of men into compassion for him.'

A compromise, to sit in private, was decided upon. On 22 October he was brought before the tribunal selected. The Attorney-General, Sir Henry Yelverton, followed by the Solicitor-General, Sir Thomas Coventry, outlined 'faults' before, during and since the last voyage. The statement of Stukeley and Manourie was quoted: 'My trust in the King has undone me'.

Ralegh pointed out that the King himself had never believed him guilty in 1603 of treason. He had been freed to go to Guiana. James himself had commented that he would never wish to be tried by a Middlesex jury. One of his judges, Mr Justice Gaudy had, on his death-bed shortly before, said of his trial that never had English Justice been so depraved and injured. That his intention had been to mine gold was evidenced by his taking with him miners, mining tools, refiners and assaying equipment, which had cost him £2,000. He emphasized that he had made no attempt to escape until long after his arrest by Stukeley. His clumsy feigning of illness at Salisbury was no more than King David had done when the occasion demanded. He did agree that he had told his men that if the mine failed 'We will take the Mexican fleet', but that this otherwise light-hearted comment was to counter a possible mutiny and hearten his company to make another attempt to find the mine – and that in fact the Mexican fleet had not been touched.

He had relied on the King's magnanimity. That was why he had never thought twice about returning. He denied making any critical comment about the King and repeated his constant loyalty.

Bacon summed up by condemning his attack on Spanish soil and announced that his sentence would be death.

He was brought formally before the Council on 24 October. There were obvious legal objections to sentencing for any alleged crime or crimes of the previous six months, lack of evidence or identification and the fact of its being unconstitutional as a legal tribunal being some of them. The only legal justification for sentence was the 1603 conviction for treason. They confirmed that the sentence was to be execution. His only request was to be beheaded as befitted his status, not hanged. This was granted.

There were still legal objections to be overcome. No constitutional court had pronounced its verdict. It could still be argued in law that Ralegh's appointment as Admiral of the Guiana fleet, conferring as it did the power of court martial and summary trial and execution, amounted to a sufficient pardon for the old conviction, even if not under the Great Seal. Accordingly on 28 October he was brought up formally before the Court of King's Bench at Westminster Hall. He was shaking with ague and had omitted to comb his curling white hair. An old personal servant offered to do it for him. He replied in the Devon burr which had never left him: 'Let them kem it as have it' and smiling ruefully: 'Peter, dost thou know of any plaster to set a man's head on again when it is off?'

The court had assen.bled. For the first time it was a court conducted with proper formality and respect. The judges, resplendent in their robes, saw before them a man who had been a legend in his own time, whose name would go down as one of the nation's heroes; a man of splendour, brave to the last, victim of his own convictions and strength of personality – and of a double-dealing system.

Yelverton, subdued and as affected as now were the judges, presented a courteous appraisal: 'Sir Walter Ralegh hath been a statesman and a man who in regard of his parts and quality is to be pitied. He hath been a star at which the world hath gazed. But stars may fall, nay, they must fall when they trouble the sphere wherein they abide.'

The Clerk of the Court read out the former conviction and judgment. 'Have you anything to say why judgment of execution should not be given?'

He replied, weak with his ague: 'What I did was in defence against the Spaniards' assault – .' The Chief Justice, Sir Henry Montagu, interrupted, saying gently: 'You are not here for any offence committed on your voyage but for your conviction of treason in 1603.'

'That judgment was so many years ago I hope it will not be strained to its lengths to take away my life,' he urged. 'All I can say, my Lords, is this: since it was his Majesty's pleasure to grant me a commission to proceed on a voyage beyond the seas, wherein I had martial power over the life and death of others so, under favour, I presume I stand discharged of that judgment. By that commission' – he might have added 'on the advice of my Lord Bacon when I could otherwise have taken remedial action' – 'I gained new life and vigour; for he that hath power over the lives of others must surely be master of his own. Under my commission I undertook a voyage to do honour to my sovereign and to enrich his kingdom with gold of the ore whereof this hand,' raising his hand, 'has found and taken in Guiana. But the enterprise, notwithstanding my endeavours, had no other issue than what was fatal to me – the loss of my son and the wasting of my whole estate.'

'Treason can only be pardoned by specific words, not by implication.'

'I must accept that. But many, including his Majesty, would witness that I had hard measure.'

'You must accept that the verdict then cannot now be challenged.' Sir Henry continued: 'Your faith has been questioned but I am satisfied that you are a good Christian, for *The History of the World*, an admirable work, testifies as much. Fear not death too much, nor too little; not too much, lest you fail in your hopes; not too little, lest you die presumptuously. As the Attorney-General has rightly stated: "You have lived like a star; and like a star you must fall when the firmament is shaken".' Then: 'I pray that God may have mercy on your soul. You are hereby condemned to death by beheading' – described with its legal technicality.

Among urgent petitions sent to James for clemency was one from Carew, horrified and frightened at the impending loss of his beloved father – he who, despite all the difficulties had cherished, comforted and directed him, and on whom he relied for guidance and support.

'Please Sire,' he wrote, 'spare the life of my poor father, sometime honoured with many great places of command by the most worthy Queen Elizabeth, the possessor whereof she left him at her death, as a token of her goodwill to his loyalty.'

But Naunton already had the death warrant drawn up ready for signing. James signed it, saying, 'Make sure he is out of this world early tomorrow morning.'

23

'If The Heart Be Right'

Ralegh was taken to the gatehouse of St Peter's Monastery, Westminster. On the way he met an old friend from Cheshire, Sir Hugh Beeston, and asked him: 'Will you be at the scaffold tomorrow morning, Hugh?'

'I hope so. It is the least and most I can do, Walter my friend.'

Ralegh smiled forlornly. 'I do not know what you will do for a place. For my own part I am sure of one. You must make what shift you can.'

Throughout the evening friends came to see him. To some he said: 'The world itself is but a large prison, out of which some are daily selected for execution.'

He forced himself to be cheerful. His kinsman Francis Thynne's advice was: 'Do not carry it with too much bravery. Your enemies will seize on it if you do.' He knew Walter and his brazen façade of old.

'It is my last mirth in this world. Do not begrudge it me. When I come to the sad parting you will see me grave enough.'

One of his visitors was the Reverend Robert Tounson, Dean of Westminster, a royal chaplain, young, enthusiastic and businesslike. He soon found he had a man with nothing of any alleged offences to confess and good and lawful reason for all his actions. He said afterwards: 'When I began to encourage him against the fear of death, he seemed to make so light of it that I wondered at him. When I told him that the dear servants of God, in better causes than this, had shrunk back and trembled a little, he denied it not. But yet he gave God thanks that he had never feared death . . . . I wished him not to flatter himself; for this extraordinary boldness I thought might come from some false ground. If it sprang from the love and favour of God, and the hope of salvation by Christ and his own innocency, then he was a happy man. But if it were out of any humour of vainglory, or carelessness of death, or senselessness of his own state, then were he much to be lamented.' He continued: 'He satisfied me then, as I think he did all his spectators at his death.'

They discussed Guiana and the breaking of peace with Spain. 'How could I break peace with a King who within these four years took divers of my men, bound them back to back and drowned them? As for burning the town, it stands upon the King of England's own ground. I did him no wrong in that.' He could have added that he was two hundred miles away at the time, having been at death's door and had had to delegate command. But he at no time shirked responsibility for his subordinates' actions, even though against his orders.

The young clergyman shook his head and left. This character was unlike any within his previous experience. Then on to the next: his diary later referred briefly to this meeting as among one of a number of busy engagements that day.

Bess came for what they knew would be the last time they would meet. For a while they clung closely together, saying nothing. He pressed his lips gently against her hair, then his cheek against hers. They must not talk of the morrow. But there were still outstanding matters to be dealt with.

'My darling,' he said: 'I have written down a list of things to be seen to. These two widows need help. You remember their husbands who died in our service, one has lost her only son also. If we don't help her, she'll die. There's all that tobacco of mine Stukeley took at Plymouth and sold. He still hasn't accounted for it. He's a cheat. He also filched ten gold pieces off me, pretending to be a friend, just before he arrested me. You must get these back. The rest are all on the list.

'Next, most important of all, my dear Bess, we must clear my name, for your sake, for little Carew's – and for posterity. We have been unlucky, we have been slandered and vilified. But I have always tried to do my duty to God, King, the Country and you. In trying to clear my name I have been blocked with granite. If I am forbidden my right to make a speech on the scaffold you must do it for me, otherwise no one will ever know the truth. Stukeley and Manourie in particular made up a pack of lies. They are scoundrels. Here are all my papers: we have plenty of friends who will set it all down. You will do this for me, dear Bess?'

'Yes. I will do whatever you say. I will see your name goes down as a great Englishman. But they will never know how wonderful you are. I love you dearly. My dear, dear husband.' In her anguish she could hardly get out the words. She had been a truly loyal wife – soon to be a sorrowing widow.

'We must be brave. Ours has been a life of ups and downs, has it not?' he said.

'I treasure the "ups". The "downs" fade beside them.'

'How is our Carew? How I miss him. It has broken my heart not to have you both with me. And our dear Wat. You must see Carew gets up to Oxford. My old College Oriel perhaps, or Wat's Corpus Christi. Perhaps Wadham. Be advised by his tutor. Give him my love and a kiss . . . ' and after a pause: 'Of all the blessings in life, love is the greatest. It is love which obeys, which suffers, which gives, which sticks at nothing.'

A bell in Westminster Abbey struck midnight. She knew she must go and leave him quietly to himself. She told him so, and added tearfully: 'I have obtained permission of the Lords of the Council to bury your body.'

He smiled. 'It is well, dear Bess, that thou mayest dispose of that dead, which thou hadst not, always, the disposal of when alive.'

She smiled also, through her tears. They had a last kiss. The Carews, waiting outside, took her to their home.

In the quiet of the night, under the eyes of the Abbey and St Margaret's Church, he wrote in his Bible his final poem – his own epitaph – and left it at the (as he wrote it) 'Gate howse':

> Even such is tyme which takes in trust
> Our yowth, our Joyes, and all we have,
> And payes us butt with age and dust:
> Who in the darke and silent grave
> When we have wandred all our wayes
> Shutts up the storye of our dayes.
> And from which earth and grave and dust
> The Lord shall rayse me up I trust.

The well-intentioned Reverend Tounson returned towards dawn. Ralegh had composed his thoughts and his mind was at peace.

'You surprise me,' Tounson commented, puzzled at his composure. 'I've never known anything like it. You don't seem at all worried about your future. In fact you look and sound cheerful and merry.'

Ralegh laughed. 'What point would there be in being gloomy?'

'Would you like to receive the sacrament now?'

'Willingly.'

After that he exclaimed: 'It can always be said that I died an innocent man.'

'Consider what you are saying,' Tounson reproved him. 'Men don't die innocent. You are questioning the justice of the realm.'

'I accept that by the course of the law I must die. But I stand on my innocence in fact. The King himself and all who heard my answers thought I was truly innocent. The King himself agreed that he had never heard of me saying a word against him.'

'Then misfortune has caught you justly,' Tounson retorted, 'if not for sin that people could see, then for sin you had kept dark. And what about my Lord Essex? It is said that you were the instrument of his death. If so you should ask God's forgiveness.'

'I am as innocent of that as of the other matters. My Lord of Essex was fetched off by a trick' – of which he told Tounson in a whisper – perhaps referring to the locking of London's gates by the authorities to prevent his escape.

His confessor, still shaking his head, bade him farewell, and left.

Looking through his window Ralegh could see a clear day and a pale autumn sun with its rays faintly reflected in the Thames. Boats were proceeding about their normal business. He ate a good breakfast and smoked a final pipe.

When the moment came to go down, a cup of sack was brought in to him, which he accepted with thanks.

'Is it to your liking, Sir Walter?' the bearer asked.

'I will answer you as did the fellow who drank of St Giles's bowl as he went to Tyburn. "It is a good drink if a man might tarry by it".'

A great crowd of spectators had gathered on this sharp October morning. The day had been chosen, and early, because it was Lord Mayor's day when the pageants in London might be expected to attract large numbers who might otherwise have come to see this spectacle. Notwithstanding, large numbers had assembled. All shades of society were there: men and ladies of rank and those of the humblest. On the balcony of his kinsman Sir Randolph Carew stood Lords Arundel, Doncaster, Northampton and Oxford. Lords Sheffield and Percy sat on horseback. Also there were Sir John Eliot (a later victim when fighting for Parliament's freedom), Sir Edward Sackville, Colonel Cecil, Sir Henry Rich and the Dean.

Ralegh was dressed in a satin doublet with under it a black-wrought waistcoat, black taffeta breeches, ash-coloured silk stockings and a wrought black velvet gown. He wore a hat with a night-cap of cut lace under it.

As he was led down to the scaffold by the two sheriffs and the Dean they had to force their way through the on-lookers. Among them was a very old man with a bald head. 'Why have you come out on such a cold morning as this?' Ralegh asked him. 'Is there anything you want?'

'Nothing,' was the reply, 'but to see you, Sir Walter, and pray God to have mercy on your soul.'

Ralegh took the night-cap from under his hat, saying, 'I can make no better return for your goodwill than this,' throwing it to him. 'You need this, my friend, more than I.'

A fire had been lit at the foot of the scaffold to keep the sheriffs warm while waiting. 'Come down and warm yourself, Sir Walter,' they invited him.

'No, thank you. I want no delay because this is my third day of fever. If I show any weakness, I pray you attribute it to my malady, for this is the hour of the day I look for it.'

He took off his hat to all those present and especially his many friends, saying: 'I thank God of His infinite goodness that He hath sent me to die in the sight of so honourable an assembly, and not in darkness.' His voice was however too faint to reach those furthest away so, trying to speak more loudly, he added: 'I will strain myself, for I would willingly have your honours hear me.'

Lord Arundel called out: 'We will come over to the scaffold.'

Many shook hands with him. He proceeded with the address he had hoped he would not be forbidden to make, the gist of which was as follows: 'There are two main points which as I conceive, have hastened my coming hither of which his Majesty hath been informed against me. The first, that I had some practice with France. And the reason why his Majesty had so to believe was, first, for that, when I came to Plymouth I had a desire in a small bark to have passed to Rochelle; and after that because the French agent came to my house in London. But, as ever I hope to see God, or to have any benefit or comfort by the passion of my saviour, I never had any practice with the French King or his ambassador or agent; neither had I any intelligence from thence; neither did I ever see the French King's hand or seal, as some report, asserting that I had a commission from him at sea. Neither, as I have a soul to save, did I know of the French agent's coming to my house, till I saw him in my gallery.

'It is not now a time either to fear or flatter Kings. I am now the subject of death, and the great God of Heaven is my sovereign before whose tribunal-seat I am shortly to appear. And therefore have a charitable conceit of me. To swear falsely is an offence; to swear falsely is a great sin. So to call God to witness an untruth is a sin above measure sinful. But to do it at the hour of one's death, in the presence of Almighty God, before whom one is forthwith to appear, were the greatest madness and sin that could be possible.

'The other matter alleged against me is that I should have spoken some disloyal, dishonest and dishonourable words of the King. Mine accuser is a renegade Frenchman who, having run over the face of the earth, hath no abiding place. This fellow, because he had a merry wit and some small skill in chemical medicine, I entertained rather for his taste than his judgment. He perjured himself at Salisbury; revealing that, the next day, the contrary of which he avowed to me the day before. But by the same protestation I have already made, and I hope for my inheritance in Heaven, I did never speak any disloyal, dishonourable or dishonest words of the King. If I did, the Lord blot me out of the book of life. He is our anointed sovereign. Nay, I will now protest further that I never thought such evil of him in my heart; and therefore it seemeth somewhat strange that such a base fellow should receive credit.

'Touching Sir Lewis Stukeley, he is my countryman and kinsman; and I have this morning taken the sacrament with

Master Dean, and I have forgiven both Stukeley and the Frenchman. Yet this much, I think, I am in charity bound to speak of it, that others may take warning how they trust such men. Sir Lewis Stukeley hath justified before the Lords that I told him my Lord Carew sent me word to get me gone when I first landed. I protest, upon my salvation, neither did my Lord Carew send me any such word, neither did I tell Stukeley any such matter. He accused me again, that I should tell him that my Lord Carew and my Lord Doncaster would meet me in France, which was never my speech nor my thought. Thirdly, he accused me that I showed him, in a letter, that I would give him £10,000 for my escape. I never made him an offer of £10,000 or £1,000. If I had had half so much I could have done better with it. I did show him in a letter that if he would go with me his debts should be paid when he was gone. For as to my seeking to escape, I cannot deny it. I had advertisement that it would go hard with me. I desired to save my life. And as for that I did feign myself sick at Salisbury, and by art made my body full of blisters, to put off the time of coming before the council. I hope it was no sin. The prophet David, a man after God's own heart, did feign himself mad, and let the spittle fall down upon his beard. I find not that recorded as a fault in David; and I hope God will never lay it to my charge. I hoped by delay to gain time for obtaining my pardon.

'But Sir Lewis Stukeley did me a further injury which I am very sensible of, however it seem not much to concern myself. In my going up to London we lodged at Sir Edward Parham's house. He is an ancient friend and follower of mine, whose lady is my cousin-german. There Stukeley made it to be suggested unto me, and himself told me, he thought I had some poison given me. I know it grieves the gentlemen there should be such a suspicion entertained. And as for the cook who was suspected, having once been my servant, I know he would go a thousand miles to do me good.

'For my going to Guiana, many thought I never intended it, but intended only to gain my liberty – which I would I had been so wise as to have kept. But, as I shall answer it before the same God before whom I am shortly to appear, I endeavoured, and I hoped, to have enriched the King, myself and my partners.' (Gold was discovered in great quantities some two and a half centuries later.) 'But I was undone by Kemys, a wilful fellow, who seeing my son slain and myself unpardoned, would not open the mine and killed himself.' He paused for a moment. This was a bitter memory. He had lost a son to whom he was devoted. He could not blame Kemys for this – except that he was in the wrong place, against orders. His hitherto loyal follower had found it all too much for him, blundered and then failed to have the courage to carry out the whole object of the expedition. He had not brought back even one bucket of ore as evidence. On top of that he had fired the town. He could not forgive him. It had been the undoing of them all. But he would not dodge responsibility or plead defence of incapacity through illness. He had been commander, for good or ill. He moved on to the next event in his statement, to clear up any misunderstanding.

'It was also told the King that I was brought by force into England, and that I did not intend to come back again. I protest that when the voyage succeeded not and that I resolved to come home, my company mutinied against me. They fortified the gunroom against me and kept me within my own cabin; and would not be satisfied except I would take a corporal oath not to bring them into England until I had got the pardons of four of them – there being four men unpardoned. So I took that oath. And we came into Ireland where they would have landed in the north parts. But I would not because all the inhabitants there are redshanks. So we came to the south; hoping from thence to write to his Majesty for their pardons. In the meantime I offered to send them to places in Devon and Cornwall, to be safe till they had been pardoned.'

He turned to Arundel, saying: 'I am glad that my Lord Arundel is here. For when I went down to his ship his Lordship and divers other were with me. At the parting salutation his Lordship took me aside, and desired me freely and faithfully to resolve him in one request, which was whether I made a good voyage or a bad, yet I should return again to England. I made you a promise and gave you my faith that I would.'

Arundel confirmed this: 'And so you did. It is true that they were the last words I spake unto you.'

Ralegh continued: 'Other reports are raised of me touching that voyage, which I value not . . . . I will yet borrow a little time of Master Sheriffs to speak of one thing more. It doth make my heart bleed to hear such an imputation laid upon me.

It was said that I was a persecutor of my Lord of Essex and that I stood in a window over against him when he suffered, and puffed out tobacco in disclaim of him. I take God to witness that my eyes shed tears for him when he died. And, as I hope to look in the face of God hereafter, my Lord of Essex did not see my face. When I suffered I was afar off in the armoury, where I saw him, but he saw not me. And my soul has been many times grieved that I was not near unto him when he died, but I understood afterwards that he asked for me, at his death, to be reconciled to him. I confess I was of a contrary faction. But I knew that my Lord of Essex was a noble gentleman and that it would be worse with me when he was gone. For those that set me up against him did afterwards set themselves against me.'

If this was the gods' revenge for hubris, if over-weaning pride had triggered his downfall, the retribution exacted, as the Greek tragedy drew to it close, at the hands of their puppet James, was grim.

He knelt in prayer. 'I have many, many sins for which to beseech God's pardon. For a long time, my course was vanity. I have been a sea-faring man, a soldier and a courtier, and in the temptations of the least of these there is enough to overthrow a good mind and a good man.' He emptied his mind of all worldly thoughts and prayed: 'I die in the faith professed by the Church of England. I hope to be saved, and to have my sins washed away, by the precious blood and merits of our Saviour Jesus Christ.'

He rose. The Sheriffs cleared the scaffold of all except themselves, Ralegh, the Dean and the executioner. Ralegh showed no sign of fear. He removed his hat, gown and doublet, tried the axe with his thumb and commented to the Sheriff: 'This is a sharp medicine; but it is a sure cure for all diseases.'

The executioner spread his own cloak on the ground for him to kneel on, having first knelt before him and asked his forgiveness. Ralegh laid his hands on the man's shoulders, saying: 'I grant it willingly before God.'

He took his place on the block. The headsman asked him if he wished to face east. He replied: 'If the heart be right, it is no matter which way the head lies.'

His friends urged him to face east. He agreed. He was asked whether he would be blindfolded. He replied: 'Think you I fear the shadow of the axe when I fear not the axe itself.' Then,

'When I stretch forth my hands, despatch me.' To all those within hearing he gave a final farewell and said: 'Give me heartily your prayers.'

He closed his eyes. His lips moved in prayer. He stretched out his hands. The diamond ring he was wearing sparkled. It had been given to him by Queen Elizabeth. The executioner was too overcome to wield his axe.

'What dost thou fear? Strike man, strike.'

The axe fell. Twice. But the first blow had finished his life. A shudder and groan went through the crowd.

24

Restored In Blood

Ralegh's body was delivered to Bess in a black mourning coach. His head was in a bag of red velvet.

Bess and he had once discussed Sherborne Abbey as their choice for burial. That would no longer be appropriate. Distraught, she wrote to her young brother, Sir Nicholas Carew. Having been adopted by his childless uncle he had inherited the Beddington estate in 1611 – scene of Ralegh's untimely talk with James. Her spelling had not improved:

'I desiar, good brother, that you will be plessed to let me berri the worthi boddi of my nobell hosban, Sur Walter Ralegh, in your churche at Beddington, wher I desiar to be berred. The Lordes have given me his ded boddi, though they denied me his life. This nit hee shall be brought you with two or three of my men. Let me here presently. God hold me in my wites.'

He would thus have been buried in a small country churchyard, as was another English hero at his wish three centuries and a half later, in Oxfordshire. It was decided a more magnificent tomb was called for. His body was buried instead in the chancel, near the altar, of the church in sight of which he had died, St Margaret's, Westminster – a stone's throw from the Queen to whom he had hitched his star.

Bess had his head embalmed. She treasured it all her life (she lived till 1647) as did Carew thereafter. It was buried when Carew was buried, in 1666.

Stukeley became known as Sir Judas. He was ostracized from society. He and Manourie were arrested for the offence, at that time capital, of clipping gold coin over a long period. He was found guilty. He died a lunatic in isolation two years later.

At the instance of the council a slanted statement, termed an apology, was published to explain away the events leading to Ralegh's execution. It was drafted by Lord Francis Bacon, and James supplied his contribution. The public rejected it. They were indignant, enraged at the injustice committed in the name of the law. The groan spread over the country. Ralegh was mourned. Their champion was no more.

Bess moved into the Parish of St Martin-in-the-Fields. She carried out her husband's wishes for Carew's education at Oxford. He entered Wadham College. He was a presentable young man, straightforward, eloquent, devoted to his mother, as he had been, and remained to his father. He was balanced in his approach. He was determined to do all he could to reinstate the family name and recover the estate.

In 1621 a bill was introduced in the House of Lords to restore him in blood. It was passed by them and the House of Commons and in 1624 submitted for the Royal Assent. This was refused. The bill therefore fell. It was to be very many years before the constitutional convention was established that assent could not be withheld from a bill which had passed both Houses.

Relations were doing all they could to help Carew and Bess regain their status. One of them, William Herbert, Earl of Pembroke, introduced Carew to Court as the next step in this process.

James for years had nursed an obsession that his son Charles would oust him. He was now heard to say ominously of Carew: 'That boy appears to me like the ghost of his father.'

This came to Pembroke's ears. Were these the shades of Macbeth's Banquo? He knew, as they all did, his Shakespeare. 'My boy,' he told Carew, 'you must travel. Quickly. Go abroad and don't come back while the King is still with us.' Carew took this timely advice.

James died the following year. Carew returned. He bent his energy to the task of restoring the family in blood and so recovering the estates. Charles, now King, sympathized. But he had a dilemma. Owning Sherborne then was the family who had also rendered – and were in the future to render – faithful service to crown and country – and to be benefactors to the manor. The Digbys were as keen as anyone to see the Raleghs reinstated – but not at the expense of their possession which they had lawfully acquired by purchase. In this they had wide support. Any other course would have been adding injury to injustice.

Charles sought counsel from all quarters. When therefore a bill was again passed up by both Houses of Parliament for the Royal Assent he sent for Carew. He received him kindly and pointed out the position as he saw it. He promised to support the bill on condition that the current position in regard to the Sherborne land was confirmed in the same bill. Carew would also be granted the £400 annuity in remainder which under the arrangement the previous decade was payable to Bess and, on her death, Wat as the elder son. Failing this there could be endless years of fruitless and bitter legal contention. Carew consulted his friends. The vital concern was restoration of blood. Their advice was to accept. An Act of Parliament was enacted in 1628 accordingly.

Carew followed in his father's (earlier) footsteps. He was re-introduced to Court. He served a week in the Fleet Prison in 1639 for threatening a fellow courtier with his sword. He was elected Member of Parliament for Haslemere in 1648-1653 and was appointed Governor of Jersey from 1659-1660. He also wrote poetry but had not his father's literary skill. He found at the bottom of his father's cedar chest his *Art of War by Sea* which he had written for Prince Henry and sadly put away on his death, together with his draft notes.

The matter of Sherborne was not allowed to rest. Sir John Digby, made Lord Digby in November 1618, had four years later been created Earl of Bristol. He was a Privy Councillor. During the Civil War he fought for the King and had to flee abroad. Sherborne Castle, which put up a valiant resistance (as did Corfe Castle) was dismantled but (fortunately) not slighted. In the interregnum of the Commonwealth Carew renewed his attempts to regain the land. A reasoned summary of what he entitled, 'Sir Walter Ralegh's Troubles', including the dealings with the Sherborne estate, was set out in a petition submitted to and formally received by the House of Commons. It was drafted, as he put it, in such a manner as 'to avoid scandalizing particular and perchance noble families'. Restitution was his aim. But the same opposing arguments prevailed. He nevertheless joined those who at Cromwell's death enthusiastically supported General Moncke and all those engineering

Charles II's restoration to the throne in 1660 – and the Earl of Bristol's return.

The destination of the land remained unchanged. Carew was offered a knighthood, which he declined so that it could be conferred on his elder son, Walter. He and his brother Philip were the grandsons Ralegh never lived to see. Walter died in 1663 and Carew three years later. Philip married the wealthy widow of Sir Anthony Ashley. They had four sons – the two eldest named Walter and Carew – and three daughters.

A dazzling, tumbled hero of England's history had been reinstated. In the twilight, can he not still be seen parading the ramparts of The Tower – or sitting quietly in the garden at Sherborne having a final pipe, with his arm round Bess?

BIBLIOGRAPHY
(Books to which the author is greatly indebted)

All Saints Church East Budleigh Devon: *A Guide to the Church* Imprint (Print and Design) Ltd., Exeter, 1978

Churchill, Winston: *A History of the English Speaking Peoples of the New World* Volume II Cassell and Company Ltd., 1967

Department of the Environment: *List of Buildings of Special Architectural or Historic Interest*, 1973

D'Ewes, Sir Simonds: *Journals of all the Parliaments*, 1682

Dictionary of National Biography: Volume XVI: Founded by George Smith: Edited by Sir Leslie Stephen and Sir Sidney Lee, Oxford University Press, 1882, 1950

Edwards, E: *Life of Ralegh during the reign of Queen Elizabeth* (2 Volumes) Edited Paul Bowes. London, 1868, 1882

Fowler, Joseph. *Mediaeval Sherborne* Longmans (Dorchester) Ltd., 1951

Gibb, J.H.P: *Sherborne Abbey Guide*

Gibb, J.H.P: *The Book of Sherborne*, Barracuda Books Limited, 1981

Girouard, Mark: *Life in the English Country House* Yale University Press, 1978

Gosse, Edmund: *English Worthies: Life of Ralegh* Longmans, 1886

Gourlay, A.B: *The History of Sherborne School* printed by Sawtells of Sherborne Ltd., 1971

Hodges, C. Walter: *Shakespeare's Theatre* Oxford University Press, 1964

Johnson, Paul: *Elizabeth. A Study in Power and Intellect* Weidenfeld and Nicolson, 1974

Nye, Robert: *Choice of Sir Walter Raleigh's Verse* Faber and Faber, 1972

Oxford English Dictionary, Oxford University Press

Pitman, Gerald: *Sherborne Observed* L. Coldwell Ltd, 1983

Plumb, J.H. and Wheldon, Hugh: *Royal Heritage* British Broadcasting Corporation, 1977

Ralegh, Carew: *Humble Petition to Commons of England: Brief Relation of Sir Walter Ralegh's Troubles with the taking away of the lands and Castle of Sherborne*: Printed for W.T., 1669

Ralegh, Sir Walter: *Works* Oxford University Press, 1829

Rodd, Sir Rennell: *Sir Walter Raleigh* MacMillan, 1905

Rowse, A.L: *Raleigh and the Throckmortons* MacMillan, 1962

Royal Commission on Historical Monuments England. *An inventory of the Historical Monuments in Dorset* Volume I West. Her Majesty's Stationery Office, 1952

Shakespeare, William: *The Alexander* (Peter Alexander) *Text of William Shakespeare* Collins, 1951

Stebbing, William: *Sir Walter Ralegh* Frowde, 1899

St John, James Augustus: *Life of Sir Walter Raleigh* London, 1869

Stephens, Sir Edgar: *The Clerks of the Counties* 1360-1960. The Society of Clerks of the Peace of Counties and of Clerks of County Councils, 1961

Thompson, Edward: *Sir Walter Raleigh* MacMillan, 1935

The Times, The 'Rose Theatre' 3 March, 1989

Trevelyan, George Macaulay: *History of England* Longmans, Green and Co Ltd., 1937

Tytler, P. Fraser: *Life of Sir Walter Raleigh*, 1838

Walker, G. Goold: *Honourable Artillery Company* 1537-1987 The Honourable Artillery Company, 1986

Thanks too to my proof-reader Mrs Freddie Wells and to Dorset County Library.